"Steinberg's debut novel offers a ⸢...⸥ an informative exposition on Vedic philosophy and religious symbolism... A lively novel that teaches the precepts of meditation and the roots of religion."

—Kirkus Reviews

"*To Be Enlightened* by Alan J. Steinberg is one of the most compelling and in-depth introductions to meditation... It is not often that a great novel with interesting but flawed characters teaches you so much about reaching self-actualization but this superb story did just that."

—Readers' Favorite Book Review

"The spiritual and philosophical blend together beautifully in this compelling novel by Dr. Alan Steinberg. His deep knowledge of Yoga, meditation, and human nature make for a page-turning read that will enlighten all readers."

—Iris Krasnow,
New York Times bestselling author of
*Camp Girls: Fireside Lessons on Friendship,
Courage, and Loyalty*

"Dr. Alan J. Steinberg's debut novel in some ways echoes other works with similar themes, e.g., Nietzsche's *Thus Spoke Zarathustra*, or *Siddhartha* by Herman Hesse. But *To Be Enlightened* provides a distinctive, twenty-first-century take on setting and characters, giving it a uniquely California flavor.... *To Be Enlightened* is sure to illuminate the unenlightened readers, expanding their understanding of eastern philosophy and religion."

—Chanticleer Book Reviews

"Steinberg manages to bring together heady topics of Eastern and Western philosophy and spirituality, even science, in a breezy, easy-to-read novel. One couldn't make these extremely relevant topics—so urgent today given our dilemmas as a civilization—much more accessible. And as a bonus, we get to enjoy an entertaining and inspiring story."

–Bernardo Kastrup, Ph.D.,
author of *Decoding Schopenhauer's Metaphysics*
and *Rationalist Spirituality*

"If you're searching for a book that clearly distinguishes between teaching about enlightenment and living an enlightening life, congratulations. Your search has ended. I loved reading *to be Enlightened*."

–H. Ronald Hulnick, Ph.D,
co-author of, with Mary R. Hulnick, Ph.D.,
Loyalty To Your Soul: the Heart of Spiritual Psychology

"Dr. Steinberg's novel, *To Be Enlightened*, is a wonderful way to present the essence of meditation. Through everyday life experiences familiar to us all it tells the story of self-knowledge and enlightenment in a very comprehensible and fascinating way. I highly recommend it."

–Ivan Antic,
author of *Samadhi: Unity of Consciousness and Existence*

"*To Be Enlightened* introduces the reader to mind-bending concepts of quantum physics and teaches meditation through the medium of fantasy story-telling. It may be surprising that the two schools of thought, yet so different, come to similar conclusions about reality."

–Fred Alan Wolf, Ph.D.,
author of *Taking the Quantum Leap*,
and *Dr. Quantum's Little Book of Big Ideas*.

"*To Be Enlightened* by Alan Steinberg tracks the daily life of philosophy professor, Abe, as he navigates the demands of his marriage and career. Written from Abe's point of view, the reader vicariously experiences Abe's college course on Vedic philosophy, his life, and his meditations, which taken together, make his enlightenment an understandable and believable possibility. An intimate, highly intelligent, deeply thoughtful work, and an inspiring must-read for every spiritual seeker intending to fully awaken in this lifetime."

–Amanda Guggenheimer,
author of *The Twelve Hierarchies of Earth*

"From Patanjali to Plato to Planck, *To Be Enlightened* is a delightful romp through Eastern and Western thought, and a powerful rendering of how ancient wisdom has modern application. Entertaining and informative, this book will enlighten readers who are searching for meaning in a maddening world."

–Andrew Holecek,
author of *Dreams of Light: T
he Profound Daytime Practice of Lucid Dreaming*

TO BE ENLIGHTENED

To Be Enlightened

A novel
by

ALAN J. STEINBERG, MD

Adelaide Books
New York / Lisbon
2020

TO BE ENLIGHTENED
A novel
By Alan J. Steinberg, MD

Copyright © by Alan J. Steinberg, MD
Cover design © 2020 Adelaide Books

Published by Adelaide Books, New York / Lisbon
adelaidebooks.org

Editor-in-Chief
Stevan V. Nikolic

For any information, please address Adelaide Books
at info@adelaidebooks.org

or write to:

Adelaide Books
244 Fifth Ave. Suite D27
New York, NY, 10001

ISBN: 978-1-953510-60-0

Printed in the United States of America

I dedicate this book to my wife, Phyllis,
and my children—Noah, Leah, and Eliana.

Acknowledgments

I would like to thank Jack Forem and Kelly Magee for their expert editing, and my publisher, Stevan Nikolic, for helping make my dream a reality.

Contents

"He who knows others is wise.
He who knows himself is enlightened."

Lao Tzu

Chapter One

It's not that I hate everything about this world, I say to myself as I pick up a pillow from the carpet. *It's just that my life in heaven spoiled my life on earth.*

I carefully place the pillow flat with the long edge up against the headboard on my side of the bed, the right side. The other—thicker, firmer—pillow that I like is on the floor at the end of the bed. I swept all the pillows off this morning. This morning was…was…Wow. Retrieving it, I position it upright against the headboard. My arms feel heavy. It's been a long day, a long month, but the indecision I've wrestled with is gone. I've made my decision. I will do whatever it takes to get off this earth and back to heaven.

I sit on the thin pillow with my back up against the thick one and cross my left leg up and over my bent right knee, moving into half lotus. Doing so straightens my back and pushes my chest out, making me feel more alert.

My wife Sarah gathers three or four pillows of various sizes and consistencies up against her side of the headboard and sits directly on the mattress. She smiles gently at me, closes her eyes, and faces forward. I straighten my head, automatically taking in a deep breath, but my eyes are held open by the dripping of our bathroom faucet. I get up and tighten the hot knob. The dripping doesn't bother her.

Back in half lotus, I close my eyes. With a soft exhale, I settle in for meditation. Two moments later, my mantra wells up from deep inside. It's an old, wise friend. For the last few weeks, it has been taking me back down to where it comes from, closer than I have ever been to my real Self in over fifty years of twice daily meditations and my night technique. It has been a tantalizing journey, coming to the edge of my goal but stopping short, leaving me aching. The mantra comes from my Self, my consciousness—the kingdom of God within. It's my escape hatch from this deeply flawed, pain-filled earth. If I could just get to my Self, I'd escape and be back in heaven.

I begin my meditation, repeating my mantra silently, gently—easily returning to it after thoughts subside.

*Mantra, mantra, mantraaa, maaaa...*things soften, edges round; concrete into abstract...feeling at home. *Mantraa, maaantraaa, mmmm...*vague shimmering light ahead... stomach churns, tightens, *I'm hungry. We can watch the PBS documentary I recorded after dinner. Mantra, mannntraa, maaa...* sinking within, light grows, closer... *Mmmmaaa, mantra, mantraaaa...*light forward, back, in the middle, melting...ankle twinges; stretch, gone...glowing, melding onto the flat, endless mirror of light...so close. *Be brave, let go...Mantra, maaan...*

"Ahhhhh," Sarah sighs.

My heart warms, swells. *She is so dear, so alluring.* This morning, knocking pillows to the floor. Wanting her, needing her, having her...*Mantraa, mantra, mantra, mantra...*diffusing out into white, soft, illuminated fluffiness, feeling forever... thoughts of us fade into the background...stillness grows as I dissolve...Dull ache down below pulls me back, holds me back...*Sarah, Sarah...Mantra, mantra, mantra...*

Sarah lies down and stretches temptingly; she's finished meditating. I want to continue, but I lie down next to her, taking in her warm scent. *She is what keeps me in this world.* After a while, she tickles my left thigh.

"What would you like for dinner?" she asks.

"You."

"OK, I know just how to cook it."

It's early morning. I've slept deeply and well. The sunrise peeks through the open window and wakes me. I turn onto my side. Sarah rolls over to face me and gently rubs the inside arch of her foot up and down my right leg. I love her next to me. Very humid and warm this morning, though.

"How'd you sleep, honey?" I ask eagerly. Sarah finally learned the advanced night meditation technique yesterday afternoon. I've been trying to get her to learn it for years, hoping it would help. We did it for the first time together before going to sleep.

She stretches, flips onto her other side, and then scoots back to spoon me. She purrs purposefully but doesn't answer. Sarah likes to keep me waiting, likes my body heat even on warm days. "The night meditation technique felt like it stretched me. Us claustrophobics do better with more room," she says with her face to the wall. "Thanks for being so persistent."

Pleased by her answer, I follow the patterns of early morning sunlight playing on the wall, wondering if she's watching too.

"You know, I do feel real good right now," she says as she pushes back against me. "I think this new technique is going to help."

Music to my ears. Worrying about how to keep her anxiety and panic attacks at bay has been distracting me from my real goal. But it seems things are suddenly moving forward. My night meditation technique, like my daily meditations, has improved dramatically over the last few weeks. Something is changing. Doing the technique with Sarah for the first time last night was so blissful that I thought I might have fallen into It. Not so. I would have woken up enlightened.

We are drinking morning coffee on our cozy back deck over-looking Sarah's garden. The garden takes up most of our small back yard. Our kitchen's hand-painted tiles are visible through the open sliding aluminum door. Sarah's in her calico night robe. I'm in gym shorts and an old undershirt. Wind rustles the trees, tousling her thick dyed-blonde hair. I wouldn't mind if she went gray. Her pale green eyes are watching a bird peck at something in the small patch of green grass not taken up by her garden. She pulls her bare feet up onto the chair, tucking them under her, sitting taller to see better. The bird flitters away.

Turning toward me, head tilted in a way that draws me in, and with a tiny squint, she says, "I should have learned the night technique years ago. I don't know why I was afraid."

"Maybe you weren't ready?" I say.

"Yeah," she says. "I was always afraid you were trying to go somewhere without me." For years I'd sat up in bed doing the technique while she was trying to fall asleep.

"Never do that," she continues. "You're not allowed to leave me behind, buster. That would send me into one of my tizzies."

I smile softly at her. "Honey," I say, playfully swatting at her, "don't you worry. I don't think either of us can get very far without the other."

But my attraction to her, and my tiptoeing around her issues, are holding me back. She senses what's going on. The closer I get to escaping this world, the more afraid she becomes that I'll leave her behind, and the more she tries to lure me back. But I have made my decision. I have wrestled and won. If I can, I *will* let go. My chest rises and falls with an inaudible sigh.

"So," she says perkily, feet returning to the deck, "are you happy fall semester starts today so you can teach your favorite class again?"

Everything brightens. "I am. When I'm not teaching it, I'm thinking about how I'm going to teach it."

"You're so funny when you're doing that class." She thinks for a moment and then looks at me with conviction. "It's like your students are a mirror. You're such a narcissist. And so much more fun in the fall."

"Oh, I'm not fun enough for ya, huh?" I get up, walk behind her, and begin kissing the nape of her neck.

She speaks through the squirms. "Do you need to prepare for class today, or can we go out for breakfast? There's a—a great new French café in town I—I want to take you to."

I look up. It's a beautiful morning. The flowers and vegetables growing in her garden are vibrant, a reflection of her care. "Finished all my preparations yesterday. Let's meditate, then go for breakfast." Walking to our bedroom, I set my intention:, 'Given the chance, take it.'

As I trudge across the deep-green lawn, the white stones of old, stately Pearsons Hall grow larger and more distinct. I'm flooded with memories. I've taken this same path since I was a freshman here. I've always been on the same path. In a day or two the central mall will be filled with students lounging and playing, but today, as classes begin, everyone is preoccupied. I'm wearing my worn tweed blazer despite the heat because I think it makes me seem comfortable, approachable, and professorial. "Well begun is half done," as my guru has said.

I arrive at my third-floor office at 8:47; more than enough time before my 9:35 class. I could have stayed home a little longer. Sarah always wants me to. I rummage through my lecture notes, finding the short file for today's class. Ruffling the lecture notes stirs up some dust. *I'm going to sneeze.* I rush to find the nearest box of tissues, arriving just a little too late. Head down, I sneeze twice onto the floor, then wipe my nose and hands and the floor with tissues. My allergies, and my annoying sinus congestion, aren't getting any better despite having re-started Flonase a few weeks ago. I don't know why. It helped last time.

In my little office, it's already hot and stuffy. *It's gonna be a hot one; gotta love global warming.* I turn on the fan, careful not to let my stacks of papers go fluttering. I have an AC vent, but its weak airflow rarely gets the job done. I sit at my desk, feet up, fan on my face, feeling nostalgic. I close my eyes.

When I turned six, I was finally allowed to walk alone from home to first grade—an eleven-minute walk—like all the big kids in our neighborhood. The first time was a blustery day. I remember walking, hunched over, looking down to keep the blowing sand out of my eyes. Halfway there, the distinct, persistent, gnawing thought arose that there was something critically important I needed to begin working on right away. As I walked, the thought became clear. It was as if I had finally remembered an answer to a question stuck in my head. The answer was that somewhere hidden in this world was something I needed desperately. I would begin searching immediately, today, for what it was. The wind faded away. I walked to class with my head held high. I was on my quest.

I began my inquiry by working my way through the school library, religiously checking out books on UFOs, ancient mysteries, the Loch Ness monster, and—my favorite—Greek mythology, hunting for any clue as to what or where that hidden something was. I knew that finding it would be an arduous task and require great sacrifices. I continued to search for it over the years, knowing that if I was diligent, I would find it or it would find me. I was drawn to become a philosophy professor because doing so would allow me to work on my quest full-time.

The night I turned fifteen, my search was given focus. That night I was taken somewhere, perhaps in a dream. I'm not sure what it was. All I know is I'll do almost anything to get back.

I know that I went to bed after a typical school day and was woken by two unusual men. I wrote it all down the next morning. The men came to me as I slept and told me they were taking me to another world. I instinctively trusted them and happily went with them.

We arrived on a different planet that had different laws of physics. There was no sun or source of illumination in the sky, but everything was clearly visible based on its own intrinsic, enthralling luminescence. The people were male and female but had no sexual organs or sexual desire. Procreation wasn't needed. Like me, people just suddenly appeared.

In that heaven, desires were much more intense and refined. And desires were deeply satisfied in their proper time. Once satisfied, new, powerful desires would arise. Nature supported our desires. No one was ever bored, or rushed, or disappointed.

The men in that world were slightly more masculine-appearing and the women were a little more feminine, but the difference was small. Though we had beautifully shaped and proportioned mouths, they were for expressions only. We communicated mainly by some sort of empathic telepathy. It was explained to me that, there, we did not need to eat because we obtained our sustenance from the inner light with which everything shone. We did not have to urinate or defecate, as that was undignified, not to mention unnecessary, as our bodies produced no waste.

A couple took me under their wing. I had known both quite well during previous lives, which we all remembered in a vague way. It was so good to be with them again.

The man taught me about their world and its relationship to other higher and lower worlds. He told me that this world was our reward for the good we'd done during our last life on Earth. No spiritual progress could be attained on this planet because life there lacked adversity and temptation.

The woman taught me about relationships, which were profound and satisfyingly intimate in a platonic way. On Earth we all felt alone inside our heads. On this planet, we also felt alone, but much less so because the boundaries between each of us were softened and blurred.

We were in a mid-level world, not evolved enough to stay, but high enough that we lived joyful, spiritual lives. God was much nearer to us there than on Earth.

I lived a full, long life in that place. As the years rolled by, I was never sick, never unhappy, and did not miss my parents, siblings, or my previous fifteen years of life. There were enough ups and downs to keep things interesting, but it was always good. I had many sweet friends. When I was ready, I was reintroduced to my soulmate, whom I had loved and lost countless times during innumerable lives. She too was brought to that heaven while she slept. My soulmate was not Sarah, but they are quite similar.

My soulmate and I grew old together, which mainly meant that we became wiser and closer to each other and to our circle of friends. Getting older in that world did not entail a loss or diminishment in any of our physical or mental abilities. It meant becoming more complete.

Then, one day, the two unusual men showed up again. They told me it was time. They were taking me back to Earth. I should have been sad or mad to leave, but those emotions couldn't be felt there.

I woke up sobbing from my core. On Earth, sadness came easily. I was back in my room, in my fifteen-year-old body. The room was dark, something foreign to me, and I had to pee really bad. After breakfast, I found a notebook and wrote, "THE FOLLOWING REALLY DID HAPPEN. EVEN WHEN YOU GET OLD, DO NOT LET YOURSELF THINK IT WAS JUST A DREAM!" I wrote down seven pages of notes, convinced that I, and posterity, would be interested in my account someday. The pages are still hidden in a box in the attic.

Years ago, by mistake, I told Sarah about this heaven, but not about my soul mate. She's been suspicious of my meditations ever since.

The couple who had instructed me in heaven told me that if I was to be able to get back—or even to a higher heaven, and never have to fall back to Earth—I would have to reach enlightenment in this lifetime. Reaching enlightenment, they said, was the goal of the quest I found myself on at age six. After my experience at fifteen, I still wasn't sure what enlightenment was or where to go to get it, but I was determined to find out. Having tasted a heaven, I developed a distaste for life on Earth. Since then, I've never felt I belonged here.

I look at my iPhone. It's time to go down and put the lecture title on the blackboard. Feet come off my desk.

Walking to the first-floor classroom, I think about the ten students registered for my Tuesday-Thursday seminar: three juniors and seven seniors. I recall six names on the list from other classes I've taught. As meditation and enlightenment have gotten more publicity over the last few years, the students who enroll seem more serious and informed about the subject. This, in turn, has made teaching the class increasingly enjoyable. Thank God for my teaching. It's a welcome respite when Sarah is held captive by one of her episodes, which usually happens every few months.

The door to my classroom is open. A heavy wooden desk crafted from blonde oak commands the front of the room. Its battered surface is clear evidence of a long vigil, probably since before my student days here. To my left, arranged in three horizontal rows, are eighteen empty chairs—the kind with the awkward laminate desks attached—more than ample for this small class. An air-conditioning ventilator wafts cool, moist air from under a row of old latched windows that run the length of the room.

I stand behind the desk, gripping the standard gray, plastic chair and survey my dominion. Summer was fine, but now the real fun begins.

I turn to the large chalkboard behind me and write in exaggerated letters:

The Insider's Guide to Our Self

I underline "Self" once and then the capital "S" two more times. The feeling of the gritty chalk in my hand is familiar and reassuring. Rita, the department secretary, has asked a few times if I would prefer to teach in one of the renovated classrooms with a large whiteboard and erasable markers, but I like it this way. I teach old ideas and like getting my hands dirty doing so.

I walk back up the two flights of stairs to my small and cluttered office. It does seem a little silly that I walked all the way down just to write on the board, but having even a small presence in the classroom when the students arrive makes for a properly set table. I answer some emails and glance at administrative memos, waiting for my classroom below to fill up.

In my classroom at 9:38—three minutes late, according to plan—I set my papers and books on the desk. Leaning back against the front of the desk, I look out at my students, allowing my eyes to linger on each face one by one. Damn, Tom's here. I noticed his name but was hoping he wouldn't show up. I've heard he does that. Three times over the last few years philosophy professors have come to me as department chair wanting to kick him out of their classes due to his disruptive behavior and bad attitude. Each time I've counseled patience. I've also been told that he doesn't do the assigned work and is often close to failing. He will be a challenge, but the rest of the students seem attentive and receptive.

"I am Professor Abe Levy. This semester you will be learning about our Self with a capital 'S' as described in ancient Vedic literature. We will learn that your Self *is* our Self, according to this literature." I point at the capital "S" on the chalkboard behind me.

"We will be reading Vedic classics such as the Upanishads, the Bhagavad Gita, and two different translations of *Patanjali's Yoga Sutras*, one called *How to Know God* by Swami Prabhavananda, and the other is Dr. Egenes's *Maharishi Patanjali Yoga Sutras*. We will also read some more modern works in the Vedic tradition, including Maharishi Mahesh Yogi's *The Science of Being and Art of Living,* and parts of *Quantum Enigma: Physics Encounters Consciousness*, which was written by two physics professors from the University of California, Santa Cruz."

I take a breath. A shaft of sunlight slices across the back of the room as it always does at this hour on September mornings. The harsh light will be gone in about thirty minutes, but for now my students have moved their desks forward, away from the heat. We all eventually gravitate toward what is most pleasant.

"Maharishi, whose work will occupy most of our attention in this course, was the guru to the Beatles in the 1960s. He was a favored disciple of Guru Dev, who was Shankaracharya of the North in India until 1953." Feeling at home, I begin to pace in front of the desk, watching my students as they watch me. Most of them are dressed in Southern California summer casual: shorts, flip-flops, and some overly scooped, tight tops. "In Hinduism, the role of the Shankaracharya of the North is similar to that of the Pope in Catholicism. The knowledge of the Himalayan gurus and swamis is passed from one Shankaracharya of the North to the next in a tradition that is at least 2,500 years old. Maharishi died in 2008 at about 94 years of age. He founded the global Transcendental Meditation movement, or TM for short.

"Maharishi writes that his interpretation of the Vedic literature—which he says is a faithful conveyance of Guru Dev's teachings—has returned this knowledge to its foundations, from which Guru Dev believed it had strayed."

A petite blonde in the center of the front row, a first-time student dressed more formally than the rest, begins writing rapidly on a large legal pad. She's using some form of shorthand. Seeing her write so intently, other students begin taking notes.

"I call this class The Insider's Guide for a number of reasons, one of which is that this Vedic knowledge was, and is, meant to provide an explanation of one's inner, personal experiences during meditation as well as one's outer, spiritual journey."

Tom, sitting in the second row, his long arms dangling, yawns. He looks younger than I know he is.

"Meditation can be thought of as direct research into, or direct experience of, one's own consciousness. This is not, however, a class where you will learn how to meditate." I glance down at the girl's legal pad, curious about the symbols' correspondence to my lecture. "And, though we will be reading religious texts and teachings, this is not a class on any specific religion. Rather, it is an academic exploration of Vedic philosophy. God, and a belief in God, will come up in our readings and discussions, but you should know that atheists are quite welcome here and agnostic questioning is encouraged.

"You will notice as this class proceeds that it is my contention that Vedic philosophy offers a coherent, elegant solution to most, if not all, of the major problems and issues in Western philosophy. Some of the major problems we will discuss are: the problem of consciousness, the mind-body problem, the problem of evil, the problem of true knowledge, and the existential problem of meaning. And then there's what is probably the most important philosophical problem: making sure that one's philosophy fits in with, and is harmonious with, current science. Please note that just because I contend that Vedic philosophy offers a solution to these philosophical problems does not imply that I believe Vedic philosophy is true. I don't know if it is true or not. To rationally believe a theory or philosophy is true, it not only needs to make sense, it requires that predictions that spring from that theory or philosophy are scientifically verifiable."

I stop to let things soak in, scanning the room. Everyone except Tom makes eye contact.

I've been so close to my Self lately that I can taste it. But when I think I'm about to cross the goal line I'm suddenly yanked back by my collar. Last night was a prime example. It seemed I was about to let go of this world and dissolve into the glory of my Self, but my love of Sarah and my fear of stirring up her panic attacks held me back. If I had the courage of my convictions, I would cut those cords. I would devote myself to meditation—paring away everything else binding me to this broken world. But I love Sarah deeply. I don't want to hurt her. She needs me. She deserves better.

"During this class I will do my best not to influence you with my biases. Clearly, I have my own biases and my own beliefs. I will try to label my personal opinions as such."

"So, let's be clear," Tom says. "You're biased toward TM."

I look at Tom. Our eyes meet. He's not backing down. *All right, I can deal with that.*

"Yes, TM is one of many biases."

I pick up a stack of class syllabuses and hand them to the students in the front row. When everyone has a syllabus, I clear my throat.

"The first book we will read is the Upanishads. There are a number of different translations, so please make sure you get the one I have designated for this class. Its cover should look like this." I show the class my book.

"The Upanishads will set the stage for everything else in this course. After the Upanishads, we will read and discuss the Bhagavad Gita, which is often described as the essence of Vedic philosophy."

Chris, who has taken three other classes with me, raises his hand. He's an intense, edgy, but amiable guy.

"Yes, Chris."

"I have another translation of the Gita. Can I use it or should I buy the one on the syllabus?"

"Please buy the one on the syllabus, by Maharishi. The translation and commentary that you have is probably very different in perspective from Maharishi's." I hold up my copy. "And just so everyone knows, the version I had the bookstore order looks like this.

"Before I entertain questions about the course syllabus or any other course-related topics, I want to discuss the class participation component of the grading, which is a significant part of your overall grade, as you will see when you read the syllabus. In addition to wanting you to contribute to class discussions, I encourage and expect you to do the required readings prior to each class. You should formulate and ask questions or make comments in class that address those readings. Ideally, your questions and comments should also be important to your classmates. Ask a good question or make a good comment, get a better grade. And if you can catch me not thinking clearly, you'll get an even better grade. Better yet, prove me wrong, change my mind, or teach me something, and I'll be beholden to you. Any questions?"

I look around the room. The students avert their eyes. Then a sharp-jawed, handsome young man of apparent Asian descent looks up from his syllabus and tentatively raises his hand.

"Yes, I'm sorry. I don't know your name."

"Professor, I am Han. I was hoping to leave early for Thanksgiving. The class called 'paper work' on the Tuesday before Thanksgiving is a required class? Will I be marked absent?"

"Han, we *will* have class on the Tuesday before Thanksgiving, November 22, but no lecture. Because there's no lecture that day, I won't be marking students absent. I'll be there to answer questions and help you with your papers. The school's policy is that Thanksgiving recess officially begins on Wednesday the 23rd at 5:00 p.m.

"Are there any other questions?" I look around the room.

"All right, let's start by introducing ourselves to each other. Han, please start by giving us your first and last name, when you hope to graduate, what your major is, and why you decided to take this class." I motion with my upturned hand so that he stands.

"I am Han Song. I am from Korea. I will graduate this June. My major is physics. I decided to take this class because a friend said you are very good professor and the class will help me understand what physics does not yet know."

I motion to the next student.

Margaret, a rounded beauty with a strong, commanding presence, does not stand, gathers her thoughts, and then speaks clearly: "I'm Margaret Carona. I'm a philosophy major and will graduate in June. I was born here in Pomona. I took Professor Levy's Intro to Philosophy as a freshman, and his Socrates/Plato and Descartes/Spinoza classes last year. I love his teaching style, so here I am." She gives me a wide smile.

I nod at Chris, who sits next to Margaret.

Chris—tall, skinny, redheaded, with more pimples than most—stands and looks around. "Hi, y'all. I'm Chris Anderson from Atlanta. This is the fourth class I've taken from Dr. Levy. You all made a good choice. I'm a senior majoring in philosophy. I've been interested in meditation and enlightenment since high school."

An elegant black woman sits near Chris. She stands and says calmly, "I'm Tanisha Cooper from Los Angeles. I'm a junior majoring in psychology. I have always felt that there's much more to our world than meets the eye. Also, in one of my psychology classes, I was fascinated when we learned about what happens to people's bodies and minds when they meditate, so I'm hoping to learn more about it."

The next student, the energetic, blonde shorthand-er, glances around to make sure everyone is looking at her. She rises, steps forward, and faces the class. She's wearing a well-tailored sundress and is unusually short. "I'm Brittany Foster from

Sacramento. English is my major, and I will graduate next June. I'm taking this class because it got good reviews on the online student evaluation site. Thank you." She nods in both directions, as if taking a bow, and then sits as abruptly as she had stood.

I nod at the bearded, Jewish-looking, heavyset man next to Brittany. He makes no attempt to stand, looks up at me, and states, "I'm a senior majoring in biology, and I'm applying to medical school. During my studies, I've read about the health benefits of meditation and wanted to understand what meditation is from a deeper perspective. I took your Intro to Philosophy as a sophomore and wanted to take another class from you before graduating. Oh—my name is Asher Cohen, and I come from Los Angeles."

Sitting next to Asher is Tom, his thinning blond hair in a military cut. He's shaved his boyish face of whatever facial hair he possesses. He stands, towering over all of us. I think I can smell his aftershave. "I'm a philosophy senior. I'm here because Dr. Levy answered questions honestly when I took his Intro class." He sits down.

"Please tell us your name," I try to say soothingly.

"Tom Griffin."

"Thank you, Tom. Your turn, Ravi." I remember Ravi from my intro class two years ago. His paper on Plato's Form of the Good was almost brilliant, considering he was a freshman when he wrote it.

He stands: short, strong, dark, sincere. "My name is Ravi Bhutta, and I was born in Los Angeles, but my parents are from India. I'm a rising junior and a chemistry major, hoping to eventually get a degree in chemical engineering. My father saw this course online and thought I would like it," he says with a slight smile.

"Next."

The pale, thin, man with a scraggly beard and long limbs next to Ravi stands. "My name is Joseph Finestein," he says, his voice quavering. "I'm a senior majoring in chemistry. I've been involved in Kabbalah for a few years," he continues, building up a head of steam, "which is a Jewish mystical philosophy and practice, and I heard that this class discusses the foundations of mysticism. This is my second philosophy class but my first with Professor Levy."

The student to Joseph's right stands as Joseph sits. "My name is Obinna Ekezie. I am transferred from University of Lagos, in Nigeria, where I was born. I have two years more until I will finish a degree here. My degree will be in mathematics. I took philosophy classes in Nigeria and earned high marks, so I hope I will be able to stay in this class."

It seems like a good group. We will learn a lot from one another.

"Any other questions?" I wait, scanning everyone's faces. "OK, this concludes our introductions. Please start reading the Upanishads for our next class." I find the book on my desk and hold it up for emphasis. "I will stay awhile to answer individual questions. Otherwise, you're free to go."

All but three students file out. Two have not yet registered for the class and need my permission. I sign their forms and off they go, leaving Brittany in her seat, twirling her hair, writing in her notebook.

She looks up. "Professor, you said you had biases. What happens if you are biased against one of your pupils? Wouldn't that affect their class participation grade?"

"I don't believe I harbor, or will harbor, any biases for or against any of my students. I will do my best to make sure that the class participation grade, though subjective, is as objective as possible."

"Well, if it's subjective then it can't be objective. Right?"

"Ahh, as you will see in this class, that's a big question to ask a philosophy professor who teaches a class on Vedic philosophy. Suffice it to say, I'll try to be fair. OK?"

"Agreed. Thank you for your time." She stands and walks out.

I return to my office, busying myself with the tedious work of a professor and departmental chair. Tomorrow, Wednesday, is the first day of my Plato and Socrates class and the Intro to Philosophy class I'm co-teaching this semester. I have a lot to do between now and then. I'll just lower my head and bull my way through—that's my way.

I'm in my office late in the afternoon, having finished much of my work but with plenty more to be done. I get a text from Sarah: "Dinner with Sam and Shoshana tonight at 6:30. Come home zoom." She probably meant "soon," but maybe not. She rarely looks at her texts before sending them. I carefully read mine two or three times before hitting send. I'll finish my work later. She doesn't like me staying any longer than I need to, so I'm going home now before she gets anxious. I grab a few tissues from one of my many boxes, blow my nose unsatisfyingly, and tuck a few more into my pocket for my walk home.

It will be nice to see Sam and Shoshana and hear their watered-down Israeli accents after so many months. I met them during the late '70s at a week-long meditation retreat that was a preparatory course for the TM-Sidhi program, an ancient, advanced meditation technique. Back then we were young and on fire. We thought enlightenment was just a mantra or two away.

Sarah and I meditate, but this time instead of feeling as if she's holding me back, it feels like we expand out together.

She's not the problem—my attachment to her and my need to watch over her are the problems. Both began to grow early in our relationship. By our fourth date, I was already deeply in love with her and worried she was not so into me. Young ladies often found me too intense, too short, and apparently not too attractive. As I was driving her back to her mother's house, a little helmeted girl on a big bicycle appeared out of nowhere. I slammed on the brakes, swerved, and came to rest a foot from where she had fallen. After I checked to make sure she was OK, which she was, I returned to find Sarah hyperventilating, clutching her chest, and sweating profusely. She had told me how she had inherited panic attacks from her mother. I took her home and had her breathe into a paper bag. That helped some, but she couldn't calm down. Her mother was away visiting a friend. She kept saying, "Don't leave me. I can't be alone." I held her on the couch for hours. About 1 a.m. she fell asleep in my arms, so I covered her and slept on the floor. I believe I won her heart when she woke to find me sleeping against the couch. Since then, my job has been to guide her through a minefield of triggers. But she has given me just as much or more in return.

We make it to the vegetarian Indian restaurant a few minutes late, and there they are, sitting at a table, looking younger than I remember.

"So, how are the *kinderlach*? Where are the pictures? Important things first, you know," Sam says. "After the pictures, we can talk about you."

iPhones come out. We show pictures from this summer when our two girls, Rose and Rachel, were home. I'm surprised by the number of pictures that are of our eldest child, Amos, playing with his niece Becky, Rose's daughter, and our only grandchild. She's almost four and delighted with Uncle Amos's silly antics to get her to smile for the camera. Becky stayed with us for the first time this summer while her parents vacationed. If I could afford it, I would send her parents on vacations frequently so we could babysit more.

Amos has learning disabilities, which we think are related to a series of seizures he had right after birth. We bought him a condo with the college fund he never used—a gift from my well-to-do parents. He works at a movie theater in a neighborhood bordering UCLA. He has friends. He watches a lot of TV. He doesn't drive. A few times a week, he'll call to let me know he's just meditated, knowing that it makes me happy. Reading, writing, and math are very hard for him, but his verbal skills are just fine. As a child, he listened to the whole Harry Potter series on tape. Rose, the oldest of our two daughters and an English professor, says he understood and, during their heated discussions, remembered nuances about the books that even her obsessive, sharp mind had not grasped. He has a sweet soul—a warm, gregarious personality with big dimples. How my wife and I, short as we are, begat a six-foot, 210-pound son is beyond me.

We look at pictures of Sam and Shoshana's grandkids, who are getting big, and their two kids, Avi and Yael.

"All the kids are so beautiful. They are a deep blessing," Sarah says, reaching out across the table to touch Shoshana and Sam's hands, and then looking at the waiter hovering in front of our booth.

"Can I take drink orders?" he says.

"My husband and I will have mango lassis," says Shoshana.

Sarah says, "I'll have plain hot water, no tea. Abe?"

"A mango lassi sounds delicious."

"OK, three mango lassis and plain water, hot, no tea bag?" the waiter asks.

"Correct, *no* tea bag," Sarah says.

Alan J. Steinberg, MD

Shoshana's eyes follow the departing waiter. After he's gone, she lowers her head, glances at Sarah and me, and whispers loudly, "Have you heard what's been happening in Fairfield?" Without waiting for an answer, she goes on. "More and more people are starting to make enlightenment. They're saying that the world's atmosphere has purified enough so we are about to go into a phase transition. It's starting in Fairfield because it is so pure there from all the meditations over the years. The long-term meditators there, like us, are going like popcorn—you know, first a few, then many."

She turns to Sam and then back to us. "We're making plans to meditate full-time in Fairfield when it starts to warm up in April. It's too cold in Iowa in the winter. We don't want to miss the boat. One of our store managers will watch the restaurants for us. We'll be back next Thanksgiving."

Sarah and I should join them in Fairfield. It would be much easier to reach enlightenment there surrounded by thousands of other meditators. I could use the sabbatical I have coming and take next semester off. We could go in January and stay until mid-August. I'd have to skip teaching summer school, which would be a relief but also a financial pinch. Sarah won't go for it, though.

"Funny, Abe was telling me that something has changed recently," says Sarah. "He said it wasn't him that had changed, but that it was easier to settle down because the world's consciousness had settled down."

"Wow," I say to Sarah, "you really are listening when I pontificate. When I was explaining how at a deep level of an individual's consciousness we all are connected, I didn't think you heard." I realize as I'm saying it that I'm sounding a touch condescending, but I am happy she understood—which I then realize is very condescending.

"After all these years in the trenches," I go on, "doing our meditations twice a day, maybe we *have* cleaned things up, like Maharishi said we would. He said we were like washing machines—we meditate and practice the sidhis and we clean our consciousness and the world's." Shoshana nods.

I look over at Sam, who is staring at an attractive young Indian woman in tight jeans. He catches himself and nods.

"It's not just us," says Sam, uncharacteristically serious. "It's all those Vedic boys and young men, the pandits, in Fairfield and in India. Most of the money from teaching TM over the years was saved up to train and house them. They're Maharishi's army. They meditate and practice the sidhis for hours each day, and they do ancient Vedic rituals to purify the atmosphere. Maharishi really thought they would bring on an age of enlightenment, not us *pishers*, the regular old meditators."

Sarah's mouth is open in a little "o" as she digests Sam's statement. She asks, "Maharishi's army? Are they really…? Ah, I get it. Their battleground is the part of us that connects us all."

Sam smiles sweetly. "Yes. Your professor has done a good job."

"I agree," Sarah says. She turns toward me, gives me a hint of a wink, and says, "He *loves* to teach."

"Touché," I say.

The waiter brings our drinks. Sam stops him before he can leave and orders for Shoshana and himself. Sarah is happy with rice and dal and vegetable samosas as an appetizer. I order vegetable biryani, baingan bharta, okra, saag paneer, and a cauliflower dish. That should be enough so we don't run out of food. I like to prepare for tomorrow's battles today.

"The key to growth is the introduction of higher dimensions of consciousness into our awareness."

Lao Tzu

Chapter Two

Thursday morning, I arrive at my office at 8:03. I had to get in early because I didn't finish yesterday's work. Sarah refuses to understand why I can't work from my computer at home. I've told her that I still have paper files, and paper articles, and non-virtual stuff in my office. She is unconvinced and unimpressed. She wants me home more.

I finish a detailed email to my fellow Pomona philosophy professors summarizing how the five-college joint steering committee of the Claremont Colleges, on which I sit, plans to adjust each college's philosophy courses over the next few years to align with the unique educational goals of each college. All the while I'm fantasizing that Pomona might suddenly decide I have too much to do and give me my own full-time executive secretary who would do everything I dislike doing. A friend of mine at Yale has one.

I review my lecture notes. Time for class. As I walk into the classroom, the chatter subsides. I sit in the gray plastic chair behind my desk, more comfortable than I should be given the chair's inadequacies. I continue to sit nonchalantly, as if I'm a student, as tension and expectation builds. When it's just past comfortable I suddenly stand, turn, and read from the chalkboard what I had written this morning:

1. The I, the Knower, the Subject: Rishi
2. Process of perception: Devata
3. Objects of perception: Chhandas

"Vedic philosophy holds that at every moment of any perception there are three elements involved: a subject, an object, and, between the subject and object, a process of perception. Your mind and your five—or as the Vedic texts would say, six—senses are the process of perception. 'Devata' is the Sanskrit word for the process of perception." I point to the chalkboard.

"Then outside your head—and all internal thoughts, emotions, feelings, and experiences—are the objects of perception, or Chhandas." I wave, palm toward the class, in an arc, and then point to my head.

"Devata and Chhandas are important Vedic concepts, but right now we are going to focus on some deeper and more difficult questions concerning the Rishi: What, or who, is the 'I,' or the knower? What is he or she or it made of? How is it that each of us is able to perceive and be conscious of something?"

I walk to the front of my desk to get closer to the action. Once there, I say, "Any thoughts?"

Margaret raises her hand.

"I know that I experience the world, and feel my feelings, and hear and experience my thoughts, but I have no idea who or what is in the background doing the experiencing."

"Very few people do. That's what we're going to talk about now, and that will be one of the main topics for this class. OK, let me give you an analogy to help us understand the subject, or Rishi, and how we might get a look at It. Luckily this phone," I say, taking my own from the pocket of my pants and holding it up, "has a camera on both sides." They all look up at the familiar device. I touch the camera icon and show them the screen.

"Don't worry, I'm not filming. Here I can touch an icon, and instead of looking outward through my process of experience, or Devata, to experience objects of perception, or Chhandas, I can have the camera switch around and video myself with a lower case 's.' I guess this is called a video selfie. The phone is analogous to Devata." I stare at my face on the phone's screen, swiveling to each side so the class can also see. They're following me so far. I place my phone face up on my desk.

"Meditation, according to Vedic philosophy, is the easiest and most reliable way to turn the video camera of the mind and its senses from outward-facing to inward-facing, so that over time one can perceive the Rishi, or come to know one's Self, with an upper case 'S.' Wanting to know your Self seems like a simple, logical, and basic desire, and perhaps it is.

"You should know from your reading so far that the desire to know one's Self is an ancient concept in Indian Vedic literature, but the idea is also a very old one in Western civilization. We can trace the desire and the recommendation to know one's Self through the interlaced histories of Western philosophy and religion. We know that in Ancient Greece, for example, the oft quoted and somewhat cryptic recommendation 'Know Thyself' was inscribed on the front of the Temple of Apollo at Delphi, which housed the legendary oracle of Delphi, the most important oracle in the classical Greek world. Plato referred to this 'Know Thyself' inscription numerous times in his dialogues, suggesting it was an imperative, or command. Plato writes in his *Charmides* dialogue that '"Know Thyself!" was a piece of advice which the god gave.' Socrates, in Plato's *Phaedrus,* says, 'I am not yet able, as the Delphic inscription has it, to know myself; so it seems to me ridiculous, when I do not yet know that, to investigate irrelevant things.'

"The main ancient Egyptian temple at Luxor bore two inscriptions conveying the same type of message, each with a slightly different approach. The first inscription was on the outer part of the temple, which was as far as new initiates were allowed to go. The inscription read, 'The body is the house of God. That is why it is said, "Man know thyself."' The second inscription was on the inner part of the temple, where only seasoned practitioners went in search of higher knowledge. That inscription read, 'Man, know thyself…and thou shalt know the gods.'[1]

"In addition, this recommendation to know oneself is echoed in the Jewish and Islamic traditions. The Talmud, a sacred Jewish scripture, says, "The greatest wisdom is to know thyself,"[2] and a central Islamic text states, "He who knows himself, knows his Lord."[3]

Margaret raises her hand. "Professor, what is the difference between the Christian concept of the soul and the Vedic concept of the Self you're talking about?"

Looking at her, I'm reminded of how sweet it was to be young and curious. Her world is fresh and open. She's searching for her path. I'm locked into mine, rushing forward, head down, trying to get to the goal before the end of the game.

"Thanks for such an appropriate question. There's very little difference, in my mind. I think the main difference is Christian philosophers and mystics didn't have a systematic,

[1] Isha Schwaller de Lubicz, *Her-Bak: Egyptian Initiate* (New York: Inner Traditions International, 1978).

[2] The Talmud: selection from the content of that ancient book, 1876, E.S. Stuart, 252.

[3] Mizan al-Hikmah, hadith 12223 [Urdu trans.] quoting from *Ghurar al-Hikam Safinat al-Bihar*, vol 2, 603.

effective way to experience and explore the soul. There are many forms of Christian contemplative prayer and meditation. The ones I have studied, in my opinion, are not very effective methods of turning the video camera around so that it's inward-facing. In general, Christian meditation is the process of deliberately focusing on specific thoughts, like a Bible passage, and reflecting on that thought's meaning in the context of God. The crux of the problem with Christian meditation is its attempt to reflect on 'meaning.' 'Meaning' is in the field of Chhandas. The goal of meditation, according to Vedic philosophy, is to become aware of the field of Rishi. The Vedic gurus used mantra meditation to investigate the soul, which is the field of Rishi, systematically, and they found it to be pure consciousness and our Self.

"OK, where were we? Oh, yes. Here is a key tenet of Vedic thought: God created the inner and outer worlds in a symmetrical and analogous fashion so that as we come to know our Self inwardly, we also come to know God and our universe. We turn inward to know our internal Self, called the atman, or soul, when we meditate. Our internal Self, our consciousness, contains and is Brahman—the inner and outer Totality. This idea is reflected in one of the most famous passages from the Vedas:

> As is the human body, so is the cosmic body.
> As is the human mind, so is the cosmic mind.
> As is the microcosm, so is the macrocosm.
> As is the atom, so is the universe.

"In Western theology, a similarly famous line echoes the same concept. You might be more familiar with this verse: 'So God created man in his own image, in the image of God he created him.'[4] God does not have a physical image, so the image referred to here is an image of God's mind, or God's consciousness. So, because human consciousness was created in the image of God's consciousness, we can—and eventually will, according to Vedic philosophy—come to know God by coming to know our true, inner Self—our own consciousness. As is the human mind, so is the cosmic mind."

In the image of God.

I find the idea inspiring and captivating. Socrates was right: Everything else is irrelevant. Everything else is a distraction and a temptation. If I'm to be worthy of knowing my Lord, and my Self, I need to be completely devoted to that quest. Everything else needs to wait. Sam and Shoshana get it. I need to join them in Iowa. I pray Sarah will join me, but I don't think she can.

Brittany rouses me from my reflections. "Professor, I don't think we can know God in *this* world. We can know God only if we reach heaven. And Jesus said that the only way to heaven is through Him. 'I am the way, and the truth, and the life; no one comes to the Father, but through Me.'"[5] She interweaves her fingers, places them firmly on her desk, and looks around at her classmates, waiting for their reaction.

A hush falls over the room. Joseph pierces it. "Whoa, missy!" he says. "We're not all Christians here. Since you brought it up, do you *really* believe that? If I don't believe Jesus was the messiah, I cannot find my way to heaven? *Really?*"

Obinna raises his hand. I nod at him, figuring that Brittany hasn't yet gotten her due. He speaks to the class, not looking at Brittany.

[4] Genesis 1:27

[5] John 14:6

"I am not Christian. My faith, Islam, believes that Jesus was one of God's prophets, but not the only one. The Qur'an says that if we do enough good during our lives compared to the bad, we will go to heaven. That is all we need to do."

Tom has his hand raised. This should be interesting.

He turns and stares directly at Brittany with large, unblinking eyes and says, "I was raised with the idea that it was silly and weak to believe in God. First, we have to come to a good, logical reason to believe there is a God before we attempt to know It. Isn't that why we're here in this class, trying to find a valid reason to believe in something greater than our pathetic little lives?"

Brittany recoils.

"Tom, you are *so* weird!" she says to him, then looks the other way.

A few more hands go up. Deciding that Brittany has had enough, I put out my hand and wave down each of the raised arms with my fingers. When all of the hands are down, Brittany feels safe enough to speak again.

"Sorry I brought it up," she says with a huff. She doesn't look sorry.

Unable to resist, I weigh in. "We are all entitled to our opinions," I say in my professorial voice. "This class is meant to be about informing those opinions with logic and knowledge. Because Maharishi thought it so important, I'll add one more thing to our current discussion." I know this will upset her more, but that's OK. "Maharishi often quoted Jesus's proclamation, 'Behold, the kingdom of God is within you.'[6] We will talk about this idea in a few minutes, but first I need to explain a few things.

---

[6] Luke 17:21

45

"To begin with, I want to discuss my use of analogies in this class. It's a Vedic concept that analogies can be much more powerful, deep, and instructive than they may at first seem. For example, in the Western context consider the analogy implicit in calling God our Father in heaven. Because a father is someone who is supposed to take care of us, we all, hopefully, have a firm idea of various important attributes and qualities of our Creator. Vedic thought holds that our Creator put fathers and mothers in our world to help us understand important qualities of our Creator—in other words, that God wants us to know Him, and Her, and It. Vedic philosophy holds that whatever path we are on in our quest to know God, whether an inward path such as meditation or an outward path such as devotion to God, all paths to know God are also paths to know our Self."

I love talking and thinking about God. Thank God I'm a philosophy professor so I can do so without seeming too odd.

"Getting back to Rishi, Devata, and Chhandas. To extend our iPhone video analogy, we can say that we live our lives with the video camera of our mind and its senses directly in front of us, in outward-facing mode. We never put the video camera down, and everything we experience is heard on the camera's speaker, seen on the camera's screen, or experienced through Apple's super-secret, futuristic, next great thing: the iPhone 22 with a full-sensory-output camera. Our futuristic iPhone will be able to beam all five of our senses directly onto our screens of consciousness via Bluetooth brainwave technology. With this theoretical device, you can go to the beach completely bundled up, close your eyes, put your gloved fingers in your ears, clamp your nose shut, position your iPhone in your lap, and the phone will perfectly transmit the experience of the ocean, complete with the sound of the crashing waves, the seaweed smell of the beach, the coolness of the ocean breeze, and the taste of the salty ocean spray onto your screen of consciousness.

"The Vedic concept of Devata, or the processing of experience, says that we are all born experiencing the world through this kind of advanced device, which is an analogy for our brains, our minds, and our senses. In general, we are locked into an outward-facing camera. The ancient Vedic seers, based on their tradition of meditation, are saying, 'Hey, did you know that if you push this button, the camera will turn around and you might catch a glimpse of who and what you really are?' That button is the practice of using a mantra for meditation. Thousands of years ago, the gurus of the Himalayas found that button. They turned their cameras inward and began a systematic exploration of who and what was behind the camera. According to the Vedic texts, though, these so-called ancient Rishis did not discover meditation but rather were taught how to meditate by God, who they said was the original teacher.

"To help turn their cameras around and look inward during meditation, the Rishis say they were taught that they needed something to meditate on that originates from the subject, the Self, or the 'I.' The most accessible thing that comes from one's Self is one's own thoughts. Ask yourself this question: 'Where do my thoughts come from?'"

I pause to see if anyone is pondering the question. Most seem to be. I give it a moment, but no hands go up.

"The answer is as simple as it sounds: my thoughts come from me, from myself.

"In the tradition we are discussing, one meditates using a mantra, which is a special sound with no linguistic meaning but with specific beneficial qualities. The process of meditation requires thinking that sound or mantra repeatedly, easily, gently, without any effort, allowing the mantra to come by itself like any other spontaneous thought, while sitting up with the eyes closed.

"In meditation, the mind naturally tends to experience the mantra in subtler and finer ways as it experiences the mantra closer and closer to its source, which is the thinker, or Rishi. It is the nature of the mind, and its awareness, to be drawn to subtler and finer experiences of the mantra because subtler and finer states of thought are more charming and attractive. During meditation, the meditator's awareness is gently drawn toward the source of the mantra until it reaches the subtlest and finest possible perception of the mantra. Having been led back to the threshold of the source of the mantra, the awareness can then transcend the limits of perception. The awareness can go beyond experiencing the mantra as an object of perception via the process of experience by crossing the threshold and experiencing Itself *directly.* Then, one is aware only of one's awareness. Or, put in another way, one's consciousness is conscious of its own consciousness—a Self-referral experience."

Tanisha reaches down to get something out of her purse. Her blouse is low-cut; the resulting flash is way too revealing. A warm urge ripples up from below, stirring my mind, bringing thoughts I want to ignore but don't. This old body of mine is still an animal. Thankfully, she's sitting up now and has readjusted herself.

A perplexed, pensive look appears on Margaret's face. She raises her hand. I shift my head and look at her eyes, acknowledging her.

"I don't get it," she says. "Being conscious of your own consciousness seems like nothingness, like a cat chasing its tail."

"Or a serpent swallowing its tail, the ancient, mythical ouroboros," I say absent-mindedly, and then I decide this is a teachable moment. "Plato wrote, metaphorically, that the ouroboros was the first created living thing. From a Vedic philosophy standpoint, I think he was correct. As we will see during this course, turning back onto one's Self, or Self-referral, is what makes consciousness conscious, or in another word, alive."

Gathering my thoughts, I make a decision. "Let's approach this idea of Self-referral from a different direction. If you want to look at yourself, what do you need?"

"A mirror," Margaret says. "Or a cell phone in selfie mode. *Oh*—I get it."

"Exactly. For those of you who haven't gotten it, here is an example, and an analogy, that hopefully will make this clearer. First, the example is to think of the mantra as your cell phone in selfie mode." I pick up my phone from my desk, put it in selfie mode, hold it out as far as I can from my face, swivel it to each side to show the class, and then slowly bring it toward my nose. When the phone touches my nose, I close my eyes and go inward momentarily with a slight outward smile.

Eyes open, I continue. "The analogy that Margaret touched upon is to think of the mantra as a full-length mirror on wheels. The mirror is across a large room and you are standing in front of it, trying to look at yourself but barely able to make yourself out. As one meditates, the mantra—the mirror—moves closer and closer to you, the knower, or Rishi. As the mirror gets closer, you get a better and better look at your 'self,' with a little 's.' Eventually, the mirror is right up in front of you, and all you see is your 'self.' Then, to directly and fully experience your real Self, with a capital 'S,' the mantra/mirror moves up so close that it touches you, and as you continue to observe your 'self' in it, the mirror dissolves into you. The mirror has served its purpose to help your awareness, which is locked in an outward viewing mode, see and experience what is inward so you can come to know your true Self, your Rishi. We all need something like a mirror to see and experience our 'self,' with a little 's', and our Self with a capital 'S.'"

I scan my class. They look overwhelmed. It's time for a planned diversion. This one usually goes over well.

"Let's try something. Often the best way to understand something is to attempt to experience it, even a little."

I hop onto my desk and sit cross-legged facing the class—a bit awkwardly because of my brown loafers, which would make a half-lotus very awkward.

"OK, everyone, sit back and close your eyes. Don't worry, this won't get weird or last very long."

Most of the students sit back and close their eyes, but a few seem reluctant.

"If you don't want to close your eyes, that's OK. Now, those of you who have closed your eyes, look around inside. Notice that you can see inside even with your eyes closed. Ask yourself, 'Am *I* inside here somewhere, experiencing?' Look for yourself. Where are *you* in there? Take a few moments, and then slowly open your eyes."

All but two of my students are slumped back with their eyes closed. Tom is sitting up, craning his neck, looking to his left out the window, though from his vantage point there's nothing to see but sky. Asher appears to be staring at the ceiling.

When all eyes are open and looking at me again, I say, "Would anyone like to comment on their experience?"

Joseph and Tanisha raise their hands. I call on Joseph, feeling uncomfortable with Tanisha.

"My first thought, when I closed my eyes, was *cogito ergo sum*, 'I think, therefore I am.' My next thought was, 'If I am, then I must be in here somewhere.' But wherever I looked, I was always behind where I was looking. I see what you're getting at. I'm in there somewhere but being able to turn around to see myself seemed impossible. If I had a mirror, I wouldn't need to turn around."

Tanisha raises her hand again, this time with more urgency. I keep my eyes focused above her neck.

"As I was searching for myself inside, I noticed that if I relaxed and let go, I got closer. Was that part of the experience of meditation?"

"Yes, that was a part of it. Meditation utilizes that natural tendency of your mind to get closer to your Self when you relax and settle down. And it also works the other way around: the closer you get to experiencing your Self, the more relaxed and settled your mind and body become.

"But without a mantra, which is a thought and therefore an object of perception that originates at the source of your own thoughts, your awareness doesn't have a mirror to help it effectively turn around and find the inward path back to the thinker of that thought, to your Self. Without something like a mirror, one's awareness is left to wander on the surface. OK? All good?" I uncross my legs and hop back down to the floor.

"No, all is not good," Tom says. "I don't want to go inside. I want to go outside myself. Are there meditation techniques that take you away from yourself?"

The class gets quiet.

"Yes," I say. "There are such techniques, but we don't have time to discuss them now. You can come to my office during office hours and we can talk."

Tom doesn't reply. He appears to be studying Margaret's shoes. She is sitting in front and to the right of him. I give him a little more time to reply and then resume my lecture.

"Let's take our mirror analogy a little further. Imagine that you're staring at yourself in a mirror only a few inches from your face, then it comes closer, touches you, and your awareness observes as your reflection in the mirror melts into you, and you experience only your Self. Now let's suppose that your awareness can be split in two. While still experiencing only your Self, which is the unity of Rishi, Devata, and Chhandas, and also known as Samadhi, you are also able to step back out of the mirror and begin experiencing the diversity of Chhandas as presented to Rishi via Devata. Now you are experiencing two contradictory things at the same time: unity and diversity. This is the experience of Cosmic Consciousness, the first stage of enlightenment, which we will discuss during our next lecture."

Han raises his hand high, excited. "Professor, I have something to add."

"Yes, Han."

Han, sitting in the front row, turns his chair to address his classmates. "You may think two contradictory qualities cannot exist at same time in one thing, but current science has proved they can."

"Science has shown that contradictions are OK? That seems so unscientific," Asher says.

"I will explain, please," Han replies with a slight unconscious bow. Bowing is such a refined tradition.

"In classical computing," Han continues, "a bit of knowledge can only be *one* thing at a time: either it is one or it is zero, either is something or is nothing, but not both at same time. But in quantum computing, which I am very interested in, due to quantum principle of superposition, a quantum bit of knowledge can be *three* things at one time: it can be one or it can be zero or it can be both one and zero at same time.

Quantum principle of superposition shows that knowledge can be both something and nothing at same time. So, based on science, it seems no problem for consciousness to be contradictory. It can be both diversity and unity at same time."

"Thank you, Han. That was very appropriate. I completely agree that the concept of quantum superposition helps us understand why consciousness is inherently contradictory and paradoxical to our usual way of thinking. It also helps explain why descriptions of pure consciousness seem mystical."

I glance around the room. Margaret, with a determined look, raises her hand. "Professor Levy, in one of my other philosophy classes we spent a lot of time discussing consciousness and the problems philosophers have had trying to decide what consciousness is and how it's generated by our brains."

Pointing at her, I say, "That sounds like a very…important…class," emphasizing the last three words. "And what, may I ask, did you conclude?"

Her face softens. "In that class, we concluded there was no good answer as to what consciousness was. But most likely it was an overall feeling generated by our experiences in our memory. That's what gives people the sensation of identity. In other words, what we think of as the Self is really just one big feeling. Could it be that when the ancient gurus traced their mantras back to the source, they found nothingness because the only thing there was a feeling?"

"Ah," I say, stroking my chin. "It appears you have learned your lessons well from Professor Packer's excellent class, Epistemology and Phenomenology." I emphasize the 'p' sounds. Margaret smiles broadly, her serious look now gone.

"Dr. Packer and I have spent many a pleasant hour arguing about consciousness. I have a feeling, though, that for us to discuss whether consciousness is primary, as Vedic philosophy holds, or a secondary byproduct of our brain's functioning, which is currently the most widely held scientific theory, will be too much of a departure from my lecture today. Suffice it to say that modern neuroscience, psychology, and philosophy have yet to come up with a good model of how consciousness can be generated by our brains, yet the theory persists. I do think science will eventually 'discover' what consciousness is. I think science will end up concluding exactly what the Vedas have been saying all along. The Vedas say that consciousness is not created by our brains. It's not a feeling or a bunch of feelings related to memories. It's the only thing that exists. And as we will discuss later, modern physics appears to be barreling toward this same conclusion."

I pause to see if Margaret wants to respond. When she doesn't, I ask, "Are there any other questions, thoughts, or feelings that have bubbled up into your consciousness?" I scan the room, attempting to make eye contact with each student. Everyone is quiet. No one makes a move.

"Experiencing nothingness, *I* have a *feeling*, ipso facto *I* am *not* a feeling. We should move on." Margaret raises her eyebrows and nods. A few half-smiles appear.

"When the ancient Rishis followed their mantras back to their Self, what did they say they experienced? The authors of the Vedas, the Upanishads, and the Bhagavad Gita each offer a description that emphasizes the ineffable quality of consciousness, but they also go on to describe pure consciousness, or the Self, with a series of superlatives. They say that when they got to the Self it was pure Bliss. They found that the Self is Divine. They discovered that all Knowledge is found within the Self." I pause, trying to slow down but anticipating what comes next. "As they explored the Self, it became clear to them that your Self was my Self, that the Self was actually the only thing that existed in the universe, and that everything in this universe, and every other universe, was *nothing but the Self.*" I think I'm starting to shout. *Settle down,* I think; *your obsession with your Self can't intrude on your teaching.*

Composed, I continue. "They realized that the Self is transcendent—beyond time and space. It is unchanging and unbounded. They found that they were healed when they experienced their Self, literally as well as spiritually. If the ancient gurus are correct, then there are ample reasons to put a trip to your Self on your bucket list."

Tom leans way forward, his head almost on Margaret's shoulder. "So, if we're lost, all we need to do is turn around and go back inside, then we'll find our Self *and* our God? And that will also heal our pain? Isn't that too good to be true, Professor?" He looks sad, bewildered, like he's been scolded.

"We have all learned from experience," I say, "that things that seem to be too good to be true are usually not true. But the lucky ones who have experienced their Self all say that this is the ultimate exception to that too-good-to-be-true rule. In general, my understanding of Vedic philosophy is that a perfectly good and compassionate God created our universe in a perfectly good and perfectly compassionate way. If our understanding of it is different than that, it's because our perspective isn't large enough to see the whole picture."

Tom sits back, reflecting. He fades into a deeper melancholy. He's been abused somehow. Something that he needed in order to grow was never given to him—poor kid.

"In Maharishi's opinion, his tradition of ancient Vedic masters was not alone in recommending this inward trip to the Self. He claimed that Jesus, too, recommended it. As I mentioned before, Maharishi was fond of pointing out the moment in the Gospel according to Luke when the Pharisees asked

Jesus when the kingdom of God should come. Jesus answered, 'The kingdom of God cometh not with observation: Neither shall they say, "lo here!" or "lo there!" for, behold, the kingdom of God is within you.'[7] In the Gospel of Matthew, Jesus said that the inward search for the kingdom of God should be our first priority. 'But seek ye first the kingdom of God and His righteousness; and all these things shall be added unto you.'[8] Maharishi felt that Jesus wanted us to go inward so that we could come to know God and our Self. But either Jesus didn't provide us with an effective technique for how to do so, or that technique has been lost."

Brittany falls back into her chair, crosses her arms over her chest, and takes in a breath loud enough to hear. Something is brewing.

I continue. "I don't mean to step on anybody's toes by quoting Jesus or by bringing up Maharishi's views concerning the New Testament. My point is that the search for the Self and the exploration of the relationship between the Self, the soul, and God plays an important role in most religious and philosophical traditions, including Christianity.

"What I want to convey is the philosophical idea that Maharishi believed that all the world's great religions and their prophets were talking about the same thing from different perspectives, at different times, and to different audiences. And, he believed that what was missing was a practical, effective, simple technique to experience one's Self."

Asher is trying to hide his phone under his desktop as he reads something on it. Chris's eyes are glassy. Obinna just yawned a moment ago. This is a lot to digest. I'm trying to

[7] Luke 17:21

[8] Matthew 6:33

come up with some antic to wake them, but I find myself antic-less. I default to my standard. "Are there any questions?"

Brittany, who is wearing another bright floral sundress, raises her hand but not her arm.

"Professor, I don't understand why you think it's safe to assume that God wants us to know our inner selves."

"You're right. I haven't made the basis for that assumption completely clear. From a Judeo-Christian viewpoint, it's not that God wants us to know our Self, but rather that God wants us to know Her and Him. Consider this from the book of Jeremiah, 'Know the LORD: for they shall all know me, from the least of them unto the greatest of them, saith the LORD.'[9] And in the book of Proverbs it says, 'those who seek me shall find me.'[10] But Vedic philosophy holds that the easiest path to knowing God is also the easiest path to knowing our Self, namely, the inward path to the kingdom of God.

"Recall our discussion about this verse: 'So God created man in his own image, in the image of God he created him.'[11] If man's mind or consciousness is an image of God's, then coming to know our consciousness, or our Self, is one way to know God. Does that help?" Looking at Brittany, it's clear I've only made matters worse. Her jaw is clenched. She's sitting stiffly with her right palm flat against the desktop.

"I'm not happy with you quoting the Bible and Jesus the way you have," she says with now animated hands. "I don't think either the Bible or Jesus was talking about the Vedic Self or meditation. To use God's words to help you make your

---

[9] Jeremiah 31:34

[10] Proverbs 8:17

[11] Genesis 1:27

argument for inward meditation seems, well, inappropriate." Her jaw is now loose and her right hand is back on her desk, balled up in a fist.

"What you are describing doesn't sound like philosophy at all. It just sort of sounds like another religion." Her voice trails off, leaving an opening that I take to be a question. As I am about to reply, she adds, "Also, you said that…here, I wrote it down, 'Maharishi felt that Jesus wanted us to go inward so that we could come to know God and our Selves.' How would Maharishi know what Jesus wanted? Was the Maharishi some kind of a biblical scholar?"

Hands go up. I see them as red flags. I don't want the class to start after her again. I need to deal with her myself. I aim stern glances toward the raised hands and most are retracted. Redirection usually defuses this type of situation.

"Brittany, I understand your concerns," I say with a sincerity that surprises me given my rising internal heat. "They are appropriate and bring up important issues I want us as a class to discuss during this course. This is an excellent time to begin that discussion.

"First of all, this is a course about philosophy, not theology. I am teaching a philosophy that I understand to be coherent, internally consistent, and ancient but still current. I don't see any significant difference between my teaching Vedic philosophy and my teaching Plato's philosophy. As to whether what I am teaching is also a religion, I don't think so. All religions require that one accept the dogma basic to that religion. All religions involve taking a leap of faith, so to speak. Transcendental Meditation is a mental technique and does not require any beliefs or any leaps of faith to practice it. Skeptics can do TM just as well as believers do. Vedic philosophy explains how and why Transcendental Meditation works and how it fits into Vedic philosophy. Practicing Transcendental Meditation allows the practitioner, if she is so inclined, to do research into her own consciousness, potentially verifying, or not, Vedic philosophy.

"Millions of people in the West practice yoga stretches and postures every day for the health benefits without worrying whether it is a religion or not. As we will discuss later in this class, the yoga they practice is a part of Vedic philosophy just as much as Transcendental Meditation is." Brittany is leaning forward, elbows on her desk, eager to jump into the ring as soon as I stop talking. I'm not stopping. My tone harshens.

"This class is about understanding Vedic philosophy, its relationship to other philosophies, and its relationship to the philosophical foundations of various religions. After coming to an intellectual understanding of those relationships, we can make a more informed decision as to what is more likely true and what is more likely false. Doing your due diligence in your pursuit of the truth is what philosophy is all about. Socrates reputedly said, 'The unexamined life is *not* worth living.' I think that's overly harsh, but I applaud the sentiment."

"My type of life is *very much* worth living," Brittany angrily injects. "*I* do not need to *examine it* because God already has."

I look at Brittany. Her frown is now a scowl. My heart is pounding. I take a deep breath through my nostrils, trying to calm down. It would be a bad idea to fight her fire with my own.

With a calmer voice, but still hot inside, I resume. "I think that my bringing Jesus into the conversation was warranted because Maharishi's Vedic philosophy holds Jesus and his teachings in the highest esteem."

There is a palpable silence.

"Brittany, how does that sit with you?" Apparently, not well.

"I know about *your kind* of views. Jesus did *not* agree with you. You and this class are proselytizing, trying to convince us to learn to meditate. You are abusing your authority as a teacher."

The class is sitting to the side, not wanting to get bitten in this dogfight. If I escalate, I risk alienating many of them. But if I give in, I may lose some of their respect. "Brittany, I don't know if I'm right or not. If you don't agree with me because you aren't engaging with my argument, then you are missing the point of this class. I want you and your classmates to think logically and carefully about what I say. If you disagree with me or are not persuaded, then please attempt a well-reasoned, logical reply." I take a step back, looking at the class as a whole. Brittany's anger has taken her tongue. It's done.

"Anyone else have a question?" I hear a sigh of relief, the class knowing we've moved on. I answer a few mundane questions that come up every year. I could have handled her better. Sadly, it appears we are not that different. I'm just as zealously attached to my beliefs as she is. It's not good. I need to work harder at being objective and dispassionate, especially in this class.

I look around the room. It appears I have everyone's attention except Tom's. I see several weird but rather good doodles taking shape in his notebook. Still looking down, doodling, Tom says, "The TM people make a lot of bizarre claims. I did some research on the internet."

"Yes, they do," I reply. Tom doesn't look up. He continues to draw. We are running over. I need to finish.

"In summary, the desire to know one's Self, which is the observer, or Rishi, is an ancient one in Eastern and Western philosophies and religions alike. Meditation's goal is to know one's Self. Doing so one becomes conscious of one's own consciousness. Maharishi's Vedic philosophy takes the stance that using a mantra in a specific, gentle, and effortless way is the most effective technique for turning inward and experiencing, and thus coming to know, one's Self. According to Vedic philosophy, all of creation is the same consciousness and all of creation is the Self. Any final questions or comments?" None of the students make a move to speak.

"OK, then please finish reading the Upanishads for next class, and the first three chapters of the Bhagavad Gita." A rustle builds as the students pack up their notebooks. Brittany is one of the first out the door, almost knocking over Tanisha.

The Brittany exchange has me deflated. Despite that, I *do* think the class went well. I walk over to the window and look at the nearby mountain as my students file out.

In my first few years teaching this course, the students had a much harder time wrapping their minds around the concepts I was trying to convey. Their minds were more rooted in this world back then. They were not as interested in God, enlightenment, or meditation. Each year lately, there are more and more students who are seriously in search of spirituality and the Truth of life. Years ago, it was hard for most students to understand that the goal wasn't just a sculpted, healthy body and a happy mind. In this group, and in society at large, I sense a pang of hunger for higher consciousness and the experience of God. Deep within our society's zeitgeist, the desire for something more is waking up, and this class has been a good barometer of that change. Slowly, almost imperceptibly, the world's collective consciousness is evolving toward a higher state. It seems that we are now in the process of a phase transition, which is giving me and my spiritual comrades a leg up in our quest for enlightenment. That helping hand is strongest in Fairfield. That's where I need to be.

I turn from the window at the sound of footsteps. Tanisha walks back in, followed by Chris. I'm glad Chris is here. If she'd walked in alone, I'd feel uneasy.

"Dr. Levy," she says in a sympathetic tone, "I think Brittany was inappropriate today. And I think most of the class shares my opinion. We support how you dealt with her."

"Thank you. It's fine. It wasn't a big deal." I turn away from her eyes, toward Chris.

"Chris, did you have a question?"

"Oh, ah, I just wanted to hear what Tanisha had to say," Chris says.

"All righty, then. See you next class." I pick up my stack of books and papers from my desk and walk out briskly, leaving the two of them alone.

Walking up to my office, my legs feel shaky. It must be due to the Brittany conflict—funny how anger affects the body. I believe the shaky feeling is caused by catecholamines that are secreted during a fight-or-flight response. When I saw her balled-up fist, I was itching for a fight. A similar episode years ago, before I had tenure, taught me how dangerous it could be to fight with a student in class. A male student made a thinly veiled anti-Semitic comment in response to something I had said about the Pope. I got carried away and ended up regretting what I said and how I said it. Word got back to the chairman of the Philosophy Department. She called me into her office and let me know in no uncertain terms that if I wanted tenure, I'd have to learn how to control myself. Behind her overzealous admonishment, I always wondered if there was a hint of anti-Semitism. I was glad when she retired a few years later and I was asked to take over as department chair. The look on her face at the meeting when I was named her successor made me think that my suspicions were correct.

At the top of the stairs, I'm feeling spent. There's a lot I need to do, but nothing I feel like doing. In my office, I decide to call Sarah. No answer at home or on her cell or at her store—not unexpected. She's probably out with friends. Eleven years ago, when the last of our three children left home for college, she decided to open a gift shop called Goodness within walking distance of our house. We used money from a home equity line of credit to pay for the store's buildout and initial inventory. Two months ago, I was finally able to pay off that loan.

Sarah stocks things in her store that she would love to own, and she owns a lot of the stuff she has in her store. Her large circle of friends uses Goodness as a friendship hub. Many of her buddies will stop by the store knowing that either my wife or some of their friends will be there gabbing away and, occasionally, buying things. The store makes a small profit, but it would make more if she paid more attention to the business end of things. Because she doesn't want to be tied to it, we always have a college student or two working in the store, freeing Sarah to be Sarah, but that eats into our meager earnings.

I have a role in the business as well, which adds another dimension to our relationship. As the CFO of Goodness, I'm responsible for paying the bills, keeping the books, doing inventory, filing tax forms, and taking care of the payroll. I don't mind doing those mundane chores because they let me into another part of Sarah's world, giving me an additional way to help insulate her from her triggers. The store has been good for her. I've decided that even when I go into monk mode, I'll still help her with it.

By the time I finish the rest of my administrative work, it's after six. Sarah won't be happy. I'm tired, still upset over the

Brittany encounter, and need to go home. Eighteen minutes later, I turn onto our tree-lined street with well-tended California bungalows on both sides. I wave to our elderly neighbors sitting on their porch. On my right, Mount Baldy peeks between the trees, watching me walk up our five front steps onto the covered porch. The third step creaks loudly—that's new. As usual, walking home has softened my mood.

We remodeled the house when the kids were small, and since then we haven't done much work on it, mainly because we can't afford it. It needs to be repainted and a lot more. I enter the living room, passing the hallway that leads to the bedrooms on my right, and walk straight back through the living room to the kitchen. I'm looking for Sarah.

She's sitting at the round kitchen table, newspapers and this morning's breakfast still there, peeling an orange. I ease into the chair across from her and watch her gracefully peel and then eat. She's in a good mood and looks beautiful. Considering my awkwardness, how was I able to attract such a woman? I smile inwardly. It was because I was not doing the attracting. We were meant to be together.

"How's your new crop of students in your favorite class?" she says with orange wedge in hand.

"They're fine, maybe a bit dry. I'm hoping to water their roots to help them blossom. I had a run-in today with a closed-minded student." I reach for one of those wedges.

"Sorry to hear that," she says as she hands me more than half of the peeled orange. "Did it end OK?"

"I hope so. How's your store?"

"It's good. We just got some wild Italian crystal vases. I brought two home. I've decided to stock fine stuff, not just stuff that sells." She gestures toward the living room.

I finish the orange. Walking to the living room, Sarah asks, "Can you sign onto the store and adjust our QuickBooks to account for the vases I took?"

"Can't you do it?" I say. "I've shown you how many times?" Apparently, I'm still not over my day.

"No worries. I'll do it. Sounds like you had a tough day. Tell me about your student."

"It's not worth talking about," I mutter.

We sit on the sofa, facing the rarely-used fireplace, and admire the delicate glass objects. She says, "Let's go meditate. That always puts your day behind you. Then we can go out for a quick dinner, and there's a movie I think you'll like. The reviews say it's good—mystical and romantic. And maybe you'll get lucky after?"

"Let's do our asanas and pranayama, then meditate," I say, but I'm really thinking about getting lucky, and what happened in class with Tanisha and Brittany.

"If we do a full program, we won't make it in time for the movie," she says with an exaggerated sad pout. She gets up, stands in front of me, places her hands softly around the back of my neck, and leans over to kiss the top of my balding head. I stop thinking about what happened in class. Men are so simple.

We skip asanas. I follow her lead. Asanas, more commonly known as yoga poses, are done before meditation to relax the body. We do about thirty seconds of pranayama seated on the couch, instead of the five to ten minutes that I know I should do. Pranayama is an alternate nostril breathing technique done with closed eyes to calm the breath prior to meditation. While doing our abbreviated pranayama, I peek over at Sarah, who looks dignified even with her fingers at her nose.

"Let's go, don't want to be late," she says, getting to her feet and walking briskly toward our bedroom with a wave. I follow her. As I turn the corner into our bedroom, she's standing there, arms flung wide open. "Boo!" she says coyly.

"You're so scary." I reach around her with both arms, mouth going for her neck, which I nip and nuzzle as she sighs, head back. We embrace our way to the bed, where we snuggle until she pushes me away.

"Later, tiger," she says, sitting up, readying her pillows for meditation. I sit up, loving her game.

It's a pleasure to meditate with her. It always helps settle me down.

A few months after we met, before we were engaged, she said that she might want to learn my type of meditation. She was already practicing Buddhist mindfulness meditation because it helped decrease the frequency and severity of her panic attacks. She was curious, she said, "to see which would help more."

I took her to an introductory lecture at the Pasadena TM center, which was the closest one to her home. She liked the teacher but was not interested in hearing about the benefits of meditation or how it worked. She just wanted to learn so she could compare techniques. She set up a time for her instruction.

As I drove her to the TM center the day of her initiation, I tried hard to contain my excitement. She, on the other hand, was nonchalant. I paid her fee, and off she went with the teacher. Afterward, we went to the Huntington Library and Gardens near Pasadena. It was a fine spring day, warm and dry, with just a few clouds in the sky. As we strolled around the beautiful gardens, my twenty-three-year-old wife-to-be was walking on air. I kept looking down at her feet, expecting her to be skimming the ground somehow. She was not giddy or talkative, just happy in an easy way.

Later that night, after our first meditation together, she told me that the new technique was easier and seemed better at calming her down. She thanked me and said she would practice TM from then on. As she said it, tears welled up in my eyes, but not for the obvious reason. The way she looked at that moment, serene and at ease, brought back a memory from my other life in that heaven. I knew then that this heavenly creature, destined to be my wife, was somehow going to help me get back.

Now we settle on our pillows, backs to the headboard, and close our eyes...

Mantra, mantraaa, mantra, maaantra...relaxing, forehead itching—scratching. *Mantra, mmm*...distant, vague, shimmering point of light. *Mantra, mantra, mmmmmantra*...boundaries loosen, mind settles, breath slows, body follows. *Mantra, mantra, maaaaa, maa*...no thoughts, quiet stillness...nose itches, rubbing it. *Mantra, mantra, mantra, mantraaa...wonder if we'll like the movie...mystical, romantic...feeling lucky. Mantra, mantra, maannntraaa*...shimmering point where mantra emerges...*it's coming from my Self*...mantra about to begin...my face smiles broadly from an infusion of Bliss. *Mantra, maaa*...wafting down into source of mantra...losing small identity, blinding flashes of true Identity—universal, unbounded oneness...breath stops, moments stop, no need to breathe—just Being. *Mantra, maaa*... endless, mirrored, settled, silent luminescence...*let...go!...into... my Self. Mantra, maaantr*—

"Honey," Sarah says quietly. It hits me with the shock of a cold-water plunge. "We'll be late for the movie."

Back in the body with a thud, I lie down to warm back up into the world. To avoid shocking the mind and body, I was taught to rest lying down for several minutes after meditation, allowing for a smooth transition to activity.

As I rest, what just happened sinks in. That was the deepest, best meditation I've ever had. I actually stopped breathing, and my body didn't need to breathe—a very good sign. I *was* the flat, unbounded, timeless silence. If I hadn't been interrupted, I might have been able to let go and go beyond that self-luminous mirror and experience the fullness of my Self on the other side—just thinking about it sends a chill up my spine. Maybe that was my once-in-a-lifetime opportunity to grab the brass ring and I missed it because Sarah pulled me back. I cannot let that happen again.

A few minutes later, Sarah sits up and walks over to the closet. I get up, sit at the edge of the bed, and thank God for the gift of life and for the good health and happiness of my wife and three children. Don't want to be late for the movie. That might spoil the rest of the evening.

The movie involves time travel, the search for a long-lost love over the ages and incarnations, and an underlying goodness that guarantees all turns out well in the end—just my cup of tea. Afterward, Sarah says she didn't like the movie, though she did enjoy the romance and tenderness. She thought the whole thing was too far-fetched. I tell her I think the movie was more realistic than she knows.

Walking to the car, which is parked at the back of a poorly lit lot, the crescent moon is overwhelmed by the canopy of stars. Sarah notices, stops, her eyes to the heavens.

"When I was small," she says, "I was afraid to look up at the stars. I had a fear that if I gazed at them for too long, I would lose myself out there in that great expanse."

I look up and for an instant I *am* the mirrored flatness again. Coming back, I reply.

"Funny," I say. "I loved staring out at the stars as a kid. It felt like if I could just let go and disappear into that vastness, I would gain much more than I would lose."

"We're so different," she says. I glance at her; her eyes now cast downward in thought. "I'm rooted in this world and this life. You're in a hurry to see what else is out there."

"But you always know how to help me slow down and appreciate our life together." I take in what night gives off. "Thank you." The air is warm and pungent, reminding me of fertile soil. I reach over with my hand and hold hers. It's all so perfect. Why would I want to spoil this? It would be so selfish of me.

I look up again, not wanting to walk. The sky is dark, but the few clouds reflect the sliver of moonlight. Behind the darkness, the stars are there for the taking.

"Are we wasting our time?" she asks, letting go of my hand.

"What do you mean?"

"If there's really nothing out there—up there…"

"Yeah. I wish I knew for sure. I don't think we're just fooling ourselves."

Listening to the night together, we don't make a sound. When it's over, Sarah asks, "Will we find out?"

I'm not sure what to say. It would be too long an answer. I stay quiet.

When we get home, the house has not cooled off. I turn on the air conditioner.

"You're always so hot," she complains. "With the windows open, it's pleasant in here. Can we turn off the AC? It gives me a sore throat."

I turn it off.

Sarah puts her arms around my waist and hugs me tighter than I expect. She places her right ear firmly on the left side of my chest, as if she is listening to my heart. She says, "Abe, I'm afraid. That movie and your reaction to it scared me."

I caress her head. "I'm sorry, honey. I'm here for you. We're OK."

"You don't sound sorry," she says, looking up at me. "You sound like you're dying to move on from this earth, sure there's something better to come. Your dream of heaven was just a dream! We have a real life, a wonderful life, together here in this world. I need you to be here with me, *now*. You're not here." She steps back, raises her arm slowly, points accusingly at the heavens. "You're out there somewhere." Her hand collapses. Her eyes scald. "You're trying so hard to get out of here that you've forgotten about *us*."

I don't say anything. She knows me better than I know myself. She waits. I take a step towards her, arms reaching out. "Oh, honey…"

She steps back. She's breathing fast and shallow, her forehead moist. "I need to go to bed. I'm about to have an attack. I'm taking a Xanax or two." She walks toward our bedroom, leaving me alone and unlucky.

With Sarah in our bedroom needing to be alone, I decide to work at the kitchen table on an article for a philosophy journal. After fifteen tortured minutes, I've made no significant progress. I give up. I might as well try my night technique. I move to the couch, adjust my legs in half-lotus, and begin. After a few minutes, I calm down. A little while longer, I feel good, even blissful. What a relief. I hate fighting with Sarah, especially when it precipitates a panic attack. It makes me feel guilty, like I've failed in my responsibility. The attacks are painful for both of us and bad for our marriage. Once they're full-blown, they often last until she can fall asleep for the night. Daytime sleep doesn't help. The attacks can recur for days in a row. During a siege, Sarah goes to bed, taking a Xanax every few hours. I do the night technique for maybe another six minutes, and I'm finished. I lie on the couch feeling relaxed and resolute.

I've waited all my life to start this final push toward enlightenment, and down deep I believe I've waited much longer than that. It seems I'm getting close. I cannot, and will not, be distracted by the temptations of this world, even one as alluring as Sarah. And I refuse to feel responsible for protecting her from her genetically-induced panic attacks. I tried. I can't fix it for her. We've tried everything her physicians and I can think of. It's not my fault that her father abandoned her and her mother when Sarah was only five years old. What kind of man does that to his daughter? Sarah's told me that her mom's panic attacks were one of the main reasons her father left. They drove him crazy.

I can't wait any longer. I need to do everything in my power to reach enlightenment. Life on this earth is so hard and so complicated and, often, so very painful compared to the life I lived in heaven. Sarah's bogged down trying to deal with her life and its problems. She doesn't understand how high the stakes are. If meditators are becoming enlightened in the rarified atmosphere of Fairfield, Iowa, that's where I need to be. If she can come with me, that would be great. But if she can't, it'll be one less distraction. I get off the couch and quietly walk to our bedroom. Sarah's snoring in a Xanax-induced slumber. I'm relieved.

The next morning, I'm up early, as usual. I tidy up our messy kitchen, listening for her to get up so we can talk, but I'm afraid she'll get up and we'll have to talk. Maybe I should ask the administration if they'd grant me a sabbatical next semester before I talk to Sarah. It would be awkward to have a fight about going to Fairfield and then find out the administration won't let me.

I hear the toilet flush. She's up. Because she wasn't in a full-blown attack before she fell asleep, she should wake up OK. I'll wait until she's had her coffee to see where she's at. That's the humane thing to do, though after caffeine she'll be a more formidable opponent.

I walk to the bathroom and find her brushing her teeth.

"I have something I need to tell you," I say to her back, looking at her face in the mirror.

She raises her finger, signaling she needs a moment, bends over and spits out the toothpaste. She rinses her mouth and faces me.

"I'm listening."

"I need to meditate more. And I can't have my meditations interrupted. You know how important enlightenment is to me. I think I was close during my meditation before the movie."

"You're mad that I asked you to stop meditating? If I hadn't, we'd have missed the movie. You already meditate almost two hours a day. Isn't that enough?"

"Apparently not."

"What are you saying?"

"Basically, I'm going to spend time with you, teach my classes, and curtail everything else so I can devote more time and energy to my meditation practice. No one gets what they want without working hard. I need to work harder. And I want to take a sabbatical next semester. The college owes me one. I'll tell them I want to work on a new book. We could move to Fairfield and focus on meditation. People are becoming enlightened in Fairfield. It won't happen here."

"A semester? You want to leave for a semester. What about me?"

"I'll be with you. We'll be together."

"What happens if nothing happens? Do we stay for the summer? Do you give up teaching and our life altogether? What about my Mom? She needs me. What about my store? Our life is here, with each other."

She's sinking. Her face loses its color. She's going to cry.

"I can't talk about it anymore now." She walks out of the bathroom.

I watch her thin calico robe go through the door. She's the best part of my life. I'd be empty without her. How can I ask her to put up with my obsession? She would never drag me through something like this.

"When I let go of what I am,
I become what I might be."

Lao Tzu

Chapter Three

I'm chasing the large purple bee again. I *need* to catch her, now more than ever. She taunts me, allowing me to get close, allowing me to think this is it—and then *zip!*, she's just out of reach. I run faster, sweating, breathing hard, desperate, scheming how to outsmart her.

The alarm clock buzzes. I turn it off. I'm groggy and confused. I haven't had that damn bee dream in over a year. It leaves me angry and frustrated. I want more sleep.

Sarah gets up and goes to the bathroom. She doesn't say a word. When she's done and walks out of the bedroom, I get up. I'm a coward.

After brushing my teeth, I head to the kitchen and put the kettle on for my instant coffee. Sarah's stove-top espresso maker starts to boil. I turn it off.

"Is my coffee ready?" She's standing in the doorway between our family room and the kitchen. I glance at her, not wanting to make eye contact.

"Yes, it boiled. I turned it off."

"Thanks."

My water starts to boil. I pour it over the instant coffee, powdered creamer, and one packet of yellow sweetener. I take it to the kitchen table. She sits outside on the deck facing away.

I read the news and check our bank account, and Goodness's account, on my laptop. After I finish my coffee, I do my asanas slowly, mindfully, in our son's room and then alternate nostril pranayama breathing until my breath is calm. I'm ready to meditate. I walk to our bedroom, adjust my pillows, and meditate alone.

At the college, I teach my Friday Plato and Intro classes, distracted. Luckily, I've given these lectures so many times I can do them in my sleep. I know I'm doing the right thing, even if it's painful. I must go for the highest first. I have to be strong. So why do I feel like smacking myself? How can I allow myself to hurt her?

I arrive home in the evening and walk into each room looking for Sarah. I look everywhere. She's not here. She's home almost every Friday afternoon preparing the Sabbath meal for us and often guests, or she's getting ready because we're going out to a friend's home for the Sabbath. I am alone. The house becomes a vacuum, sucking everything from me. As soon as I think a thought, it's pulled away. I have nothing. I am nothing without her.

I need work. Work will make me feel better. I need to feel better. I wander around our house, ending up in our kitchen. It's filled with Sarah and her day. I begin to clean it like I'm taking care of her. Carefully, lovingly, I put things back together, making things right. The hand-painted Mexican counter tiles that Sarah chose when we remodeled years ago glisten. The dishwasher whooshes soothingly. The porcelain sink looks pure and simple.

She knows I'll make it up to her. There's nothing she needs as badly as I need enlightenment. I turn the AC on and wait, staring at our clean kitchen.

My phone says it's 6:47. She's still not home. She must really be mad. I decide to meditate even though the thought of meditating without her again weighs on my heart. I have no energy for asanas or pranayama.

Halfway through my agitated meditation, I hear her car pull into the driveway. It's cool in here, just the way I like it, but I get up and turn off the AC. I lie down to rest, waiting for her to come in, but I don't hear keys in the door long past the expected time. I start to sweat. I did hear her car pull in, didn't I?

Maybe ten minutes later, her keys fumble at the front door. She enters and walks toward the kitchen. Normally, she'd come in and give me a kiss. I'm getting hungry. I meet her in the kitchen.

"Have you had dinner?" she asks.

"I'm OK. I'll make some scrambled eggs and toast." She seems to have forgotten or doesn't care that it's the Sabbath. In all our married years, she has rarely forgotten to light the Sabbath candles on Friday night, even if we were traveling.

"I ate dinner with a friend, but I can make you some veggies and tofu. Thanks for cleaning the kitchen."

"Tofu and veggies would be great, thanks," I say, feeling helpless.

I watch as she cooks. When the food is ready, she serves me and sits across the table. Her eyes are puffy. I put a blob of seasoned white tofu in my mouth.

"Abe, I don't want us to ever be apart, but asking me to go to Fairfield in January to be away from my mother and my store and my friends just so you can withdraw into yourself is asking too much. It's freezing there in January." My spine feels cold. My feet tingle. "My mother needs me. Can't you just meditate more here, but not too much, so we can still have a life together?"

I stop chewing but can't swallow. It won't go down.

"I promise I won't interrupt your meditations," she says with a desperation that tears into my skin.

The backside of my right hand twinges. I just scratched myself. Everything slows down and is loud. I'm in a tunnel, with Sarah at the other end. We're connected. The thought of severing the connection feels like suffocation. I rally, pushing it aside, and swallow.

"I'm sorry. This is something I've needed to do for many, many years. Things are happening there *now*. Who knows what will happen later? Things could change. I could get sick, or worse, and miss my chance. It won't be so bad."

"I can't go. My mother is old. She couldn't bear it to be left again. I won't like it in Iowa. Don't make me choose." She's crying, but comforting her will make it worse.

"I never, *ever* want to hurt you." My voice is weak. I'm tearing up, but it's a poor ploy. I'm not sincere. "I only want to make you happy," falls from my mouth to the floor. She gets up, stands next to me, and draws me into her chest. We cry freely.

"I had always hoped," she says, seeing through me, "that I meant more to you than that."

We spend the weekend in an uneasy truce. We don't discuss Fairfield again, but I meditate a lot. She lets me. We go to dinner with friends Saturday night. Sarah is the life of the party, while I struggle to keep a good face on. I find the friction between us unbearable. Sarah acts as if nothing has changed, knowing that doing so will make me feel worse. I want to give her whatever she wants.

Sunday evening, halfway through my meditation, she joins me in bed. She quietly adjusts her pillows. I feel her starting to meditate. I don't think she's meditated all weekend, unless she did in one of the kids' rooms. Her strategy is working. Her cold shoulder is turning me into mush. It pisses me off that I'm so weak and she's so strong. I'm the strong one in this relationship. I take care of her, remember?

I'm a mess.

When I'm done with my meditation, she's still deep in hers. I lie down and look up at her and her calm, closed eyes. My youngest sister, Bracha, an OB/GYN, was the one who introduced me to Sarah. Bracha met Sarah at a month-long summer seminar for Jewish college graduates where Sarah agreed to lead Mindfulness meditations after the rabbi who had taught Jewish meditation left. A few days before the seminar ended, Bracha called me. She told me without hesitation, "Abe, I've met the perfect woman for you."

I had dated a few of Bracha's friends over the years, sometimes at her suggestion, but my sister is an understated, articulate woman, and she had never used anything like "perfect" to describe someone to me. I copied down the number Bracha gave me, and I called Sarah after the seminar ended to set up a date.

On our first date, we went to an old LA-area health food chain called The Good Earth, which was wholesome and quiet enough. By the time we sat down for dinner, I had the unmistakable, bizarre sensation of fate pulling at my strings. Never one to bow to fate, I spent the dinner monopolizing the conversation, barely asking her anything about herself, and basically making an ass of myself. I let her know, in various ways, and in no uncertain terms, all the difficult and obnoxious qualities I possessed. Figuring that if I had no choice but to marry her, maybe she could still decide against it.

After I dropped her off, I would much later learn, she ran to her mother's bedroom, jumped on her bed to wake her, and proclaimed that she had just met the man she would marry.

Sarah shifts on her pillow, bringing me back. We are *meant* to be together. I can't leave her, even for a semester. If I go to Fairfield without her and withdraw into myself, it would stir up her abandonment fears. When you're five and your father suddenly leaves you and your mother for a woman with a daughter your own age who happens to go to the same elementary school, you likely never recover. If I left her, she might feel a need to meet someone else. Men are always attracted to her.

I teach my Monday classes knowing that the deadline to put in for a sabbatical for next semester is tomorrow at 5:00 p.m. Once I've submitted the paperwork, it will be difficult to back out without losing face. Over the years, I've made a stink about this very issue: once we cancel classes for a professor's sabbatical or find a substitute, it's too difficult to go backward. I've always said that canceling a sabbatical should not be allowed.

As I'm walking home, my phone rings. Sarah tells me matter-of-factly that she has decided to drive out to see her mother in Orange County. She, or we, usually go a few times a month. She doesn't seem mad, distant, or upset. She's much better at this psychological warfare than I am. Her mom is free for dinner tonight. There's no lecture or concert scheduled on her busy Laguna Woods retirement community's social calendar. Sara invites me to join her. I decline, and then conclude the more strategic move would have been to accept.

Walking into the house, it now seems solidly silent—*strange*. I change and go for a long jog, happy to get out. After a shower and a full meditation program, I lie looking up at the ceiling. How did I get myself into this predicament? I don't want to have to choose. Distantly I begin hearing in my mind a sweet, simple song. At first, I don't place it. Then it comes to me. It's the song thanking the tradition of masters that my meditation teacher sang when I was seventeen, just before she taught me how to meditate. The song whispers to something deep in me, beckoning me onward. Momentarily, I'm seventeen again, gripping the wheel as I drive home after my first meditation, convinced that I had just found my way off this lowly speck of a planet and back to a heaven.

I have dinner at a less popular restaurant in town, not wanting to run into anyone I know. Back home, I work and then watch TV. Sarah calls. She's spending the night at her mom's. It's too late and she's too tired to drive home. Hanging up, I'm depressed. We haven't spent a night apart in years and never because of a fight.

The next morning, I wake long before the sun rises. I didn't sleep well. I boil some water for coffee. Sarah doesn't understand how I can drink instant coffee. She prefers the Alessi stove-top espresso maker we got for our wedding. I take my coffee and my laptop outside to read the news on our back porch and wait for the sun to rise. Even this early, it's still comfortably warm.

Vedic wisdom holds that during the forty-eight minutes prior to sunrise, which is called the Brahma Muhurta, a wave of purity and balance sweeps through the world, gently waking it up, along with the birds and other animals. I sip my coffee, enjoying the silence and morning calm. About fifteen minutes before sunrise, the birds start singing praises, enlivening and infusing the atmosphere with optimism for the approaching day. The transition rarely fails to uplift me.

A high-pitched fluttering followed by a distinctive buzzing draws my attention. I look up to see a large, shiny purple hummingbird hovering about a foot above the center of the table, looking at me as if wanting to speak. It flits its beak up, down, and sideways, and—*zip!* It's gone. I don't remember ever seeing a hummingbird so close. I sit for a moment. I *know* that hummingbird! I've seen her many times before in my dream. But she was always a bee.

I do asanas and pranayama and then walk toward our bedroom for my morning meditation. The hummingbird gets me thinking about omens. If there really are omens, does it mean that God communicates with us only at specific, special times? Or is it that at certain times we become still enough to precipitate an omen? Maybe there are always omens and we aren't aware enough to appreciate them? I bet it's even more complex than that. I adjust my pillows for meditation. In a half lotus, my eyes close.

Mantra, mantra, maaaantra, mmmannntraaaa, maaa… mantra emerges from shimmering pool, drop of water in reverse. *Mantra, mantra, mmmmaa…*the place on surface of pool where mantra will emerge begins to move, vibrate…*I am observing and hearing the mantra's emergence from my consciousness. It is separate from the real Me, the observer…The school's administrative board has asked me to head the search committee for a new chief of campus security. I don't know anything about security. I'm not going…*I observe that thought, and this thought, arise in the same way the Mantra emerges. *So interesting…Mantra,*

mantra, mantraaaaa, maaaantra…surface of pool, no ripples, no thoughts, no feelings coming from body or mind, endless… one side, silent awareness; other side, activity. *Mantra, maantraa, mmmmm*…mantra barely tickles my expansive surface… Bliss surges through body, mind. *Bliss is caused by awareness of subtle disturbance at junction between…Mantra, mantra, mantraaaaa, mmmmmmaaaaaaa*…flowing outward, all directions; I am a boundless, luminous mirror between my self and my Self… *Mmmaaaa…mmmm…maaaaa*…I am the surface of the ocean, impossibly still, deafeningly silent…needing to let go… ready to let go…fearing loss…*Mmmmmmmm*…decision made, *must go forward, will go forward*…surrendering all I thought I was for what I am…individuality dissolves: raindrop, ocean…

I am.

I am—the vast, unbounded ocean of consciousness. I am—unmoving wholeness. *I was never that body or that mind. I have been observing Abe Levy since the moment he was born, and much, much longer than that. I am—at peace. I am—now awake. I was sleeping before.* I can see the sun and the planets clearly. *They are so dear to have nurtured Mother Earth, allowing her to birth humanity.* I notice distantly that my body is glowing. Time is immaterial and has lost its grip on me…

Back in my body, I look over at my bedside alarm clock. More than an hour has gone by. I lie down to rest and a deep sleep envelops my body and mind, though I am awake, aware, and witnessing.

I get up and put on my robe. Something is very, very different. It's as if I am still meditating even though my body and I are active in the world. I am in two places at the same time—the unbounded ocean of consciousness and the bounded world of activity and senses. I have never, ever, felt so good and so focused. I walk to the kitchen, but I don't seem to be moving.

It happened. The thought comes that I should be jumping with joy, but I'm past that. A more pressing, evolving issue appears to be whether my body can contain my joy. I close my eyes and watch as thin, sparkling beams of Bliss increasingly poke their way through the shell that is my old body, shining out from my new one in a myriad of luminous, waving threads of various lengths and hues. The brightest and most numerous ones are congregated around my solar plexus and the top of my head. The weirdest part of all is that I'm not surprised or concerned by this in the least.

I make oatmeal with whole milk, dried cherries, roasted almond slivers, cinnamon, cardamom, and a hint of nutmeg. I notice something is gone. I am not, in general, an anxious or fearful man, but I now realize I had significant anxiety and fear all my life. I know this because, for the first time, I am completely without those constant companions. Along with my anxieties and fears, my worries about leaving Sarah to go to Fairfield have evaporated. I don't have to go anywhere now. I am where I have always wanted to be. I'm Here. The weight of responsibility that I had shouldered in guiding Sarah around her triggers has lifted. I think that I can now lovingly support her without feeling bogged down or burdened.

I shower, shave, dress for class, and it all seems to happen automatically, as if I'm uninvolved in the process. I was somewhat intellectually prepared for this, but even after over fifty years of meditation, I'm not prepared experientially. This will take some getting used to.

Walking to my office, the world is delicious. The singing birds are part of me, thrilling me thoroughly from the inside with our perfect twittering. My heart sings with them. My body hums with a hymn as my feet beat the rhythm into the sidewalk.

Arriving at the college, I glide across the central mall. The grass is the most vivid shade of tasty green, tingling my ear-lobes with its pungent texture. Smells waft all around. They are visual and auditory perfumes in various colorful shades and tones. My senses are enlivened and heightened with all sensory input melding into one exalted experience. I have stepped out of Kansas's shades of gray. All my senses have gone the Technicolor of Oz.

It reminds me of people's descriptions of LSD and other psychedelic drugs, all of which I have carefully avoided. The psychedelic literature is full of accounts of people having mystical and deeply religious experiences while high on hallucinogens. I bet what's happening to my brain chemistry now is similar to those changes, except, of course, that for me it's occurring naturally.

Maharishi strongly advised against using drugs. Many years ago, during a three-day Transcendental Meditation retreat, I watched a video that included a Q&A session with Maharishi, probably recorded in the late seventies. A long-haired, colorfully dressed young man asked Maharishi, "What's wrong with doing psychedelic drugs if they allow us to experience Reality, if only for a brief time?" Maharishi gently answered that psychedelic drugs can, at times, be a key that briefly opens the door to the experience of higher states of consciousness, but that key is flawed and will often break off in the lock, making it difficult, if not impossible, to open the door again.

As I'm getting close to Pearsons Hall, I notice a classic, beat-up VW van parked on the street. I've never seen it on campus before. On its backside are numerous bumper stickers that pique my curiosity. I approach and one sticker stands out: Heaven Is a State of Mind.

I am in the same world, but it's not the same because I'm not. I belong in this world.

I'm in my office opening snail mail, answering work-related emails, and preparing for class. My mind is sharp and clear. Today, these mundane tasks don't bother me. Throughout the ninety or so minutes of work, I experience none of the usual boredom or distractions.

Since my enlightenment this morning, I've had a clear and abiding sense that nature is supporting me and all my desires. I am gently floating on the lazy river of my life, being taken where I need to go. My emotions are so refined now, and I'm feeling so fulfilled that I could not possibly desire anything that's not in my best interest or, indeed, the world's.

We all have had moments a little like this. The psychological literature calls them peak experiences. We have them spontaneously. We have them when we are feeling peaceful while gazing at a beautiful sunset. We have them when we are feeling deeply in love holding hands during a stroll through a park on a perfect day. We have them when we are playing sports and everything we do is effortless and better than we thought it could be. Over the years, as my meditation experiences have deepened and grown, I've had many more—and longer lasting—peak experiences than I'd had in the past. But those were a fraction of what I feel now.

I walk down to the classroom—or more accurately, my body walks down to the classroom. I seem basically uninvolved with what Abe Levy is doing. It feels liberating but too new. I probably should not be teaching today. But I love teaching. I hope I will be able to pull this off. I write on the chalkboard:

THE BIG BANG:

Consciousness Knowing ItSelf

Walking back upstairs, I decide that since all the work I needed to do before class is done, I have time for brief emails to my kids. I'm tempted to tell them that I have been Enlightened for about four hours now, but it's still too soon. Three short emails later, it's time for class.

I reenter the classroom about two minutes late—perfect. The students are seated and seem unusually quiet today—or is it me? Brittany's not here. Intuitively, I know she won't be back. That sixth sense now seems to be as active, and as accurate, as my other five senses.

I pace leisurely in front of my desk as if I am deep in thought. I can feel their eyes as I walk back and forth with my forehead furrowed, staring at the floor. I stop, look out the window into the distance, and say clearly and slowly, "Why is there *something* rather than *nothing*?" I pause for effect, and then address my class.

"An obvious but incorrect answer is that if there were only nothingness, we wouldn't be here to try and answer this question. There are several competing answers to this 'why something' question. Modern physics has an accepted theory of *how* the universe was created—the Big Bang theory—and an accepted theory as to *what caused* the Big Bang. But physics does not have an accepted answer as to *why* the Big Bang occurred, which rightfully may be said to be outside the realm of physics and into metaphysics.

"According to contemporary theories in physics, before the Big Bang there was no universe, no space, no time—nothing—only potentialities and probabilities. Then, when time was about to begin, a 'singularity' occurred that would become our universe. It was infinitesimally small, infinitely hot, and infinitely dense. Where did it come from? There are many contested scientific theories, but no accepted answer. Why did it appear? Again, we are uncertain. Western philosophy has several answers as to why the universe came into being. Vedic philosophy has its own answer, which we will discuss today.

"According to the Vedic tradition, ancient Yogis in very deep meditation were able to cognize, or perceive, a particular part of their own consciousness. This specific, non-manifest structure in their consciousness was the Vedas, the holy scriptures of Hinduism. Historians believe that the Vedas are among the oldest of the world's holy scriptures, but exactly how old is difficult to determine. The Vedas say there is only one thing in the universe, consciousness, and that everything in the universe is made of consciousness. They declare that what appear to us to be objects separate from ourselves and beings separate from ourselves are actually, ultimately, illusions based on our ignorance of the True Reality.

"The Vedas state that in the beginning there was only pure, homogeneous consciousness. Based on its inherent creativity, its inherent curiosity, and its inherent playfulness, pure consciousness desired to know itself—a desire that continues today. The only way that non-manifest pure consciousness could know itself was to divide itself in two. But in reality, it was still one thing: pure consciousness. Consciousness divided itself so that it became both a subject and an object of perception. When the one part tried to observe the other—when it tried to understand and know itself—it became a process of perception. This is how the three values of Rishi, Devata, and Chhandas, which we discussed in the previous lecture, came into being— and how they are still being formed at every moment.

"Notice that this division of consciousness into three values, which happens when consciousness turns back onto its Self to know its Self, can also be thought of as a circle or a loop that, in a sense, is attempting to 'digest or swallow' itself. Plato said that the first living thing was the ancient, mythical ouroboros, symbolized by a serpent swallowing its tail. When consciousness turns back onto its Self, this process of knowing, or digesting, its Self can be thought of as the fundamental first step in being alive. My bet is that physics will end up concluding that superstrings, which according to physics are the fundamental building blocks of this universe, are circular, and self-referral, like the ouroboros.

"Consciousness initiated the singularity, which is Chhandas, so that the singularity would expand and consciousness, or Rishi, could thereby observe and experience what happened during the expansion of the universe. By observing and experiencing what happened in the universe, consciousness could know itself, because in a universe made of consciousness, everything that happened—good, bad, beautiful, or ugly—was a quality of consciousness. This is Vedic philosophy's answer to the 'why something' question."

I look at my students. They are, as every sentient being is, unique qualities of consciousness—unique personalities which existed virtually before the beginning and will continue virtually after the end. They are, we are, Platonic Forms. Chris, with his standard issue tattered blue jeans and sloppy, vintage

Grateful Dead T-shirt is so sincere he makes people uncomfortable. Margaret, front and center, plainly dressed, is solid to the core. I could depend on her for something important and she'd come through. Ravi wants so badly to be good it almost hurts. And Tanisha—Tanisha bears the heavy gift of attractiveness with aplomb. Knowing them is knowing facets of my Self.

"Quantum mechanics, the bedrock of modern physics and cosmology, has an answer to the question, 'What caused the Big Bang?' Its answer is the same as Vedic Philosophy's answer—the Big Bang was caused by consciousness observing and becoming aware of the pre-universe, the universe before the singularity occurred. To help you understand this, I will give you a little lesson on quantum mechanics.

"OK. When a bit of knowledge is in a superposition state, being one, and being zero, and being zero *and* one all at the same time, as Han has explained to us, we can describe that state mathematically as a wavefunction. According to quantum mechanics everything in the universe, even the whole universe, can be put in a superposition state, often *is* in a superposition state, and when in that superposition state, *is* only that specific, mathematical wavefunction, nothing more, nothing less—it *is* that virtual, non-material, wavefunction—yes, bizarre and counterintuitive.

"Here is where it gets interesting: If a conscious observer observes that bit of *potential* knowledge while it is in the superposition state, the observation instantaneously collapses the wavefunction to either zero *or* one. Now it's not just *potential* knowledge, it's *actual* knowledge because it has been observed and known by consciousness.

"According to quantum mechanics, the conscious observation of anything in a superposition state immediately, instantaneously, collapses its wavefunction to one of the possible outcomes of that wavefunction. Then it can be known by the observer's consciousness. Quantum mechanics says that the consciousness of the observer somehow interacts with a mathematical, virtual, wavefunction to cause its collapse.

"How can something as ethereal as consciousness interact with something so abstract as a wavefunction? Both seem different, no? I think the answer is that they can and do interact because both are the same thing, consciousness—and they are not two different consciousnesses but the same consciousness. The question then arises in quantum theory…On second thought, it turns out that our book, *Quantum Enigma: Physics Encounters Consciousness*, asks the question quite well. In fact, this question summarizes one of the book's main points."

I reach for the book on my desk and read.
"…in principle quantum theory requires a conscious observation, consciousness, in order to collapse a superposition state…Is a conscious observer *needed* to collapse a wavefunction? One can defend either a "yes" or a "no" answer to this question.[12]

"I believe that the reason both a 'yes' and a 'no' answer to this question can be defended is the same as why a bit of knowledge can be zero and one at the same time.

"Martin Rees, an author and renowned Cambridge University professor and England's Astronomer Royal, sums up quantum mechanics' answer to the question, 'What caused the Big Bang?'"

---

[12] *Quantum Enigma: Physics Encounters Consciousness* – second edition (Oxford University Press, 2011), 238-239.

I find the bookmarked quote and read.

In the beginning there were only probabilities. The universe could only come into existence if someone observed it. It does not matter that the observers turned up several billion years later. The universe exists because we are aware of it.[13]

"Vedic Philosophy holds that the universe came into existence when pure, homogeneous consciousness split into an observer and an observed. Quantum mechanics says that when the consciousness of the observer became aware of the observed, that caused the pre-universe's wavefunction to collapse, which caused the Big Bang and the universe began. Remember, Vedic Philosophy says that the consciousness of everyone, of every sentient being that has existed or will exist, is the same consciousness that collapsed the pre-universe's wavefunction in the beginning.

"Quantum mechanics' answer to the question, 'What caused the Big Bang?' in my mind, is only a small metaphysical step away from Vedic philosophy's answer to the question, 'Why does the universe exist?' Vedic philosophy's answer is viewpoint dependent. From our viewpoint as humans, the answer is that the universe exists so that we can come to know it and thereby know our Self and God. From God's perspective, the universe exists so that from every possible point of view— through the senses of every sentient being and from every other possible perspective—God can come to know His Self and Her Self. And, God has always known Itself. God is inside and outside of time.

---

[13] As quoted in *Quantum Enigma: Physics Encounters Consciousness* – second edition (Oxford University Press, 2011), 257.

"I know this is a lot to digest. Does anyone have a question or comment?" I ask.

"I do," Tom says. "You said there's only one consciousness. That each of our individual consciousnesses are the same as God's. Does that mean we ultimately are God? And if we're God, how can we suffer? God can't suffer. Or is our suffering somehow related to Jesus's suffering?"

"Excellent, difficult questions, Tom. You've raised important issues." I nod and grin at him. His face beams with satisfaction. "Vedic philosophy holds that we are not God. I think the best way to think about it comes from the biblical verse, 'God created man in his own image.' In that analogy, we humans are as insubstantial, virtual, and dependent as an image in a mirror. God, standing in front of the mirror, is substantial, real, and independent. We will discuss possible answers to your questions as this class proceeds, but for now we need to move on.

"According to Vedic philosophy, the universe was created in a symmetrical and analogous fashion so that humankind could more easily come to know and understand the universe and itself. In so doing, pure consciousness furthers its original and ongoing desire to know itself. This desire is echoed throughout creation in many ways and forms. The quotation we discussed from the Vedas concerning the symmetry inherent in our universe is so important to this discussion that I will read it to you again:

"As is the human body, so is the cosmic body.

As is the human mind, so is the cosmic mind.

As is the microcosm, so is the macrocosm.

As is the atom, so is the universe.

"Just as the cosmic mind, in the beginning, desired to know itself, which is also an ongoing desire, the human mind, during its many lives and incarnations, desires to know itself. Desire, as we will see in this class, is a fundamental driving force in the universe. Desire finds its fulfillment in Self-knowledge, according to the Vedas.

"In addition, a growing number of physicists believe there are many separate universes, possibly an infinite number of universes, governed by many different laws of physics—the multiverse. This is exactly what the Vedic tradition says. To know itself fully, consciousness must manifest itself in every possible permutation and combination from the smallest of the small to the largest of the large. Maharishi has said that consciousness is the lively field of all possibilities.

"Was the universe created solely for pure consciousness to know itself? Or did God, the Supreme Being, create the universe for our benefit? Or was it God's desire to know Herself and Himself that caused this universe's creation? Was the universe ever created? Are we just characters in an infinite virtual novel on God's expansive bookshelves?"

Tanisha's mouth is open in rapt attention.

"The answers to each of these questions is 'yes' from one perspective, 'no' from another perspective, and 'yes *and* no' from a third perspective. Quantum mechanics tells us that questions can and do have contradictory but correct answers.

"And there are questions that can be answered only from a higher level of consciousness, which is analogous to having a higher perspective. Maharishi was fond of saying that 'knowledge is different in different states of consciousness.' For example, if you ask me whether I experience the passage of time, I will answer correctly and truthfully, yes."

Yes, I experience time now, though it has lost its hold on me. Now, I'm not caught in the moment. I am both inside and outside each moment. I feel like I have been freed from jail.

"But when I reach Unity Consciousness, God willing, which is the subject of a later lecture, I will answer correctly and truthfully, no, I do not experience time and its passage, but it is real for you. Einstein said the following about time: 'the separation between past, present, and future is only an illusion, although a convincing one,' and 'the only reason for time is so that everything doesn't happen at once.'"

I walk around my desk and hold on to the back of my plastic chair too tightly. I need some space between me and my students. Gazing into their eyes as they attempted to fathom eternity, I saw a reflection of my Self. I looked away, concerned I'd be overjoyed and overwhelmed. The chair and desk between me and them serves as a boundary between me and the boundless.

Han raises his hand. "Professor, if consciousness created the universes to know itself, then consciousness is Creator. Consciousness as Creator is different concept than Judeo-Christian concept of God as Creator. Also, my understanding is that Hindu religion has many gods that are very different than the Western concept of God. How do these many gods relate to consciousness as Creator?"

"A perfect question. Vedic philosophy holds the following: there is a Supreme Being, or God, who is outside, and inside, of time. The Supreme Being is the Creator of this universe. The Creator has many attributes, some are feminine, some are masculine, some are a mixture of both, and some are neither. All true teachings emanate from God. God is the sustainer of our universe and is the source of goodness, compassion, truth, dharma, justice, and all other absolutes. The Hindu religion has a pantheon of lesser gods, each with his or her or its own personality and qualities. The Hindu gods are personal, approachable, and understandable for the average Hindu believer.

Maharishi explains that each God in the Hindu religion represents various qualities of a single unitary Divine Being. It's very difficult for us three-dimensional creatures of limited intellect to get our minds around a concept as large as God. We understand God through analogies and personalized, anthropomorphized concepts.

"Here is the analogy Maharishi has used in his commentary on the Bhagavad Gita, chapter 3, verse 11, to help us understand the relationship between the Supreme Being and the Vedic gods. He says we should think of each cell in our bodies as having a discrete consciousness, personality, and set of qualities, like each of the Hindu gods, but as a whole, the cells compose units that are our bodies. Each of us—as consciousness dwelling in a body—is like a Supreme Being or God to each of those cells. All of the Vedic gods are like cells in the body of the Supreme Being who dwells in a body composed of the Vedic Gods and the various Gods of other traditions. 'As is the human body, so is the cosmic body.'"

Chris has something to say but isn't sure how to say it. I glance at him. He tries so hard because things are hard for him. His face tightens perceptibly and forces out his question. "Ah, are you saying…does that mean that, like, the Greek gods, the Norse gods, et cetera, might be real?"

"Could be. Vedic philosophy suggests something like that. This concept of one supreme God and a multitude of lesser gods may at first seem foreign to those of us brought up in a Western, monotheistic tradition. There are, however, many instances in the Old Testament that seem to imply the same understanding. The verse I find most telling is Deuteronomy 10:17."

I pick up my well-worn Bible from the desk, find the bookmarked quote, and point my index finger upward. Channeling my inner southern preacher, which today seems surprisingly natural, I read in a flamboyant, deep voice, "'For the LORD your God is God of gods, and Lord of lords.'"

I half expect the heavens to answer in a resounding amen. When no affirmation comes, I retract my finger. "To get back to Han's question about whether pure consciousness or God created our universe, the answer, from the perspective of our common, unenlightened state of consciousness is that they both did. This is because from our limited perspectives they are both different aspects of the same thing.

"Maharishi has said that consciousness, which is all there is, is by its nature contradictory. Among other things, consciousness is the paradoxical coexistence of two contradictory qualities: unity and diversity. Our universe is a paradox that can be understood only by rising to a higher level of consciousness. Many other traditions have understood this. Consider the Zen Buddhist koan: What is the sound of one hand clapping? This koan has no answer in the material world, but according to an old tradition of Buddhist monks, it does have a perfect answer in another higher level of consciousness. Han, have I answered your questions to your satisfaction?"

"Thank you, yes, Professor."

"Any further questions or comments, or shall I proceed?" My arms, and legs, and neck, and every part of me feels lubricated and alive. They move, and I do nothing. I'm in the background, taking it all in, huge, attentive, and still—activity is separate from Me and does not overshadow my silence. Professor Abe, stunned by the contrast, takes in a deep breath, breathing in what the universe breathes out.

Observing Abe melodramatically revel in his enlightenment, Abe's amused. He chuckles audibly. Margaret looks at him askew. She asks, "Did I miss something, Professor?"

"I'm sorry. I had a funny thought." Not good—I need to be more careful. I need to learn how to control this, integrate this. If my students tell people they think their professor attained enlightenment, those people will think I'm mentally ill. The administration would hear about it, they always do, which would put this class in jeopardy. The administration already feels this class is controversial.

Tanisha raises her hand delicately. I nod at her. "I'm not sure how to put this, Professor, but this all seems so depressing. What is our place in the universe? Are we just passive conduits for our knowledge and experiences to flow into pure consciousness? Were we created just to feed a voracious pure consciousness our experiences, painful and horrible as they may be? It all seems sterile, heartless, and scary."

Everything stops. I am unbounded, and I am also standing in front of my class listening to Tanisha. I feel my body, in a visceral way, connect to Tanisha's pain and despair, which come from a place much deeper and older than today. As I would do for my own children, I am soothing it. The silence within me pulls in her sadness, then calms and uplifts her spirit. The moment passes. I speak.

"It's all OK. We really have nothing to fear. Even though this universe can seem cold, heartless, predatory, and impersonal, it is actually filled with love, compassion, and joy. From one point of view, we were created to feed a voracious pure consciousness our experiences. From a higher viewpoint, we *are* pure consciousness and we created the universe to know our Self. Vedic philosophy's view is that our Heavenly Father and our Heavenly Mother have an amazing future planned for us, better than we can imagine—the best it can be. We just need to be patient and learn the lessons they are trying to teach us. Eventually we all will graduate to better and better places."

Tanisha blinks and a bewildered grin spreads across her face. She mouths silently, "Thank you."

Tom, who has been watching her intently, sits up straight, his eyes growing large. He looks over at me, suspicious. He saw that something happened between me and Tanisha. It appears only he noticed.

In an instant, my perspective shatters into multiple fragments. I'm looking out through many eyes—those eyes belong to my students, and Abe, all at once. I am our underlying super consciousness being fed through multiple channels. I am aware of each of my students' experiences, what they see, hear, feel, think, want, all filtered and colored by their different minds, just as clearly as I am aware of Abe's. I am them just as much as I am Abe. We are all the same—gender, race, age, social class are insignificant compared to our oneness. As one, we feed our experiences into our identical, shared, pure consciousness—God's consciousness. Just as quickly, my lesson evaporates.

Margaret is staring at me. I'm still not back. I'm stuck between here and There. I struggle, trying to look at my students. Through a haze I see worried faces.

"Professor—*Professor*, are you OK?" Margaret asks. "Can I get you a glass of water or something?"

I blink a few times. The room starts to come into focus. "I'm fine," I hear myself say.

Margaret studies me carefully, deliberating, not sure what to do. I step back and lean against my desk.

"Don't worry," I say. "I got a little dizzy. I was in a rush this morning and didn't eat breakfast. This would be a good time for a question."

Margaret raises her eyebrows, clearly with question. She looks down at her notebook to review her notes. She then swivels to address the class. "Throughout the Upanishads, much is made of the syllable 'Om.' The Upanishads recommend meditating on Om as a mantra. They say that Om is a symbol for the Self. They also say that Om is not just a symbol, but Om *is* Brahman, the Totality." She turns back around, looking at me. "What is Om?"

"Well," I say, dwelling on the *L* sound as I think. "Om is a mantra and much more. Every mantra has specific qualities associated with it. When one meditates using a specific mantra for many years, the meditator begins to take on the qualities associated with that mantra. The qualities associated with Om can be appropriate for a reclusive monk whose focus is solely on enlightenment, but Om is not an appropriate mantra for people who are engaged in the world of activity, who are spoken of as householders. The mantras given by Transcendental Meditation teachers have qualities that are appropriate and beneficial for householders.

"So, you ask, 'what is Om?'" As I finish saying the word, I continue to hear it. I check to see if I'm still saying it, but my vocal cords are not vibrating.

"My understanding of Vedic philosophy is that in the beginning, when pure consciousness divided itself in three—Rishi, Devata, and Chhandas—that division was caused by the Om vibration, and the sound that resulted from the division was Om. Again, a paradox—but we have come to expect them when we discuss such things. Om *caused* pure consciousness to manifest as the singularity of the Big Bang theory, and the singularity *is* Om. Om is the sound of the Big Bang." Everything and everyone in the room are now quietly humming with *Om*.

"I usually talk about Om during another lecture, but let's do it now. Some experts believe that the concept of Om is fundamental not only to Vedic philosophy, but also to Christian theology, though of course in different terms. I'll read you two quotes, the first from the book of John and the second from the Rig Veda, one of the earliest Hindu scriptures, written at least a thousand years before Christ."

I grab my New Testament, easily finding the quote, though I know it by heart.

"From the book of John: 'In the beginning was the Word, and the Word was with God, and the Word was God.'[14] Compare that to a verse in the Rig Veda, 'In the beginning was Brahman, with whom was the Word, and the Word was truly the supreme Brahman.' The sound of the word being referred to in this quote from the Rig Veda is 'Om.'"

I am still hearing Om, but now I'm feeling it, seeing it, smelling it; I'm beginning to taste it. It's getting louder and stronger. I am Om, inside and out. Time stops. The classroom lights from within and all is celestial. Everything is Om. Everything glows and hums from its core with golden regal light. I am in awe. I am humbled. While Abe and his class are frozen in a moment, I look at my students. Each is not only emanating the golden light, but also surrounded by a vibrating, singing aura. Each aura is a different shimmering mix of colors, songs, and smells. Each aura perfectly represents its source, its person. It is holy.

I look over at Tom. His aura is muted, it sounds confused, and it smells off. He needs help. I would love to help him. Could I connect with him and uplift him as I did with Tanisha? My stomach sours at the thought, but it actually doesn't feel like my stomach. I look at my other students. I'm surprised by how much fuller all the other auras are.

"Abe," something from the pit of my stomach says to me through some new intuitive pathway, "you're losing it. Call it a day. Tomorrow will be better."

[14] John 1:1

Whoa! Great—did that really just happen? Am I hearing voices, and from my own stomach no less? I need to get out of here, quick. Time resumes. Abe picks up his iPhone from his desk and looks at it. The phone recognizes him and unlocks. Eleven minutes until the end of this class period. I press the text icon conspicuously and pretend to read, then announce, "We need to end class early today—sorry. Everything is OK but something just came up. For class on Thursday, finish reading the Bhagavad Gita. Also, on Thursday I'll give you three prompts, one of which you will choose to use as the basis for your first paper. Enjoy. See you then."

I leave before the students can stop me with further questions or comments. When I get up to my office, I close the door. By the time I'm seated, things have settled down. The celestial celebration has subsided. I don't think most of the students found my demeanor too suspicious or out of place, though Tom apparently saw something happen between me and Tanisha, and I'm sure a few of the students, especially Margaret, are worried about me. This is all so wonderful but so strange. Maybe I need a few days off from teaching to let me get used to it? Nah, tomorrow will be better.

As I'm sitting in my office trying to digest how amazing and startling my life has become, I notice one of the additional benefits. I have been feeling increasingly clear-headed the last few hours—not just in my mind, but also in my sinuses. My chronic sinus congestion has opened up. My head and sinuses feel better than I can ever remember. I'm not sure which I am enjoying more, enlightenment or cosmic sinuses.

Keeping my door closed, which I rarely do when I'm in my office, I get to work. I have to finish coordinating the hiring of a new chief of campus security, among other dreary tasks.

The administration asked me to do it because many years ago I headed the campus security committee. Abe stays, working rapidly and tirelessly. I, on the other hand, go out to play in my new cosmic playground of consciousness. When I get back, Abe's ready to leave.

As I lock my office door to go home, something is missing, but I'm not missing it. It's the feeling that I've forgotten something or left something undone. For decades I've locked this door and had that same feeling as I locked it. Now, I trust myself and trust that all the myriad pieces of my life will be coordinated without me having to worry about them. I feel like I finally have that cosmic executive secretary watching over me, anticipating any and all issues. He's ready to alert and inform me when needed, but slick enough to stay in the background. I can relax and go about my day, confident he'll steer me in the right direction. He's a vague, guiding compass completely different from the independent, intuitive thing that spoke to me from the pit of my stomach. I can't even begin to think about that.

My executive secretary has informed me of one pressing problem on my agenda—Sarah's panic attacks. We are both concerned my enlightenment is going to set her off because she will feel I no longer need or want her. If that happens, it won't be pretty. Once they get going, they're hard to control. For about two years, when she was in her forties, they got so bad, and so incapacitating that she had to curtail much of her life. During that time she started intensive, and expensive, talk therapy. That helped, but not a lot.

Those two years were a very rocky time for our marriage. She was so needy that it drove me crazy and caused me to emotionally withdraw, which only amplified her neediness. If I had to stay late at work or go in early, she was sure I was doing it to get away from her. Once, during those dark days, she even accused me of having an affair, stringing together paranoid, circumstantial things and events to prove her case. She was so overbearing that my eye and my thoughts did wander, but I would never do that to her, or to us. During those difficult two years, she clung to her meditation practice because it helped calm her attacks. I think her excessive meditations during that time were a main factor in bringing her attacks under control. It was such a relief. My executive secretary is convinced that the only thing that will cure Sarah's panic attacks is to be up here in the clouds with me, sharing this same wonder-filled world, together. I agree. That's my new quest.

I stroll home, trying not to get too caught up in how beautiful and profound everything is, but I don't succeed. As I saunter on, a bounce in my step, I think of Gene Kelly in the rain. I sing part of a Psalm in self-amusing variations: "This is the day that the Lord has made; let us rejoice and be glad in it." I check my surroundings, making sure no one will see, before doing a few poorly executed dance steps. "Abe, you're out of control," my solar plexus intuitive voice tells me. "Get some exercise. No more dancing." Good advice, I think.

Home, I change and go for my jog—about four miles in a little less than one hour. Not much better than my usual time, but I feel a lot less tired today. After a shower, I'm feeling more in control. I do asanas and pranayama, adjust my pillows on the bed, close my eyes, and I'm back to where it all began.

Mantra, mantra, mantraaaaa...Without effort, hesitation, or fear of losing my identity, I dissolve into my consciousness, luxuriating in the invigorating ocean of my Self.

This time, though, things are much clearer. I'm not as overwhelmed by the Bliss and silence. A fog has thinned out and I'm able to perceive and understand what is happening with greater clarity. *I am back home. I am where I have wanted to be. Mantra, mantra…*Something has changed. I have a new ability. Now, as I'm meditating, the mantra can bubble up from my consciousness while I might also perceive another separate thought bubbling up. Neither the thought nor the mantra capture my awareness, which is continuously aware of my Self in the background. It's like watching two TV screens at the same time while also being aware that you are watching the TVs. I just sit back and take it all in, a silent witness. *Pretty groovy. Mantra, mantra, maaaa, mmm…I have been meditating for a long time.* My body hasn't moved or itched, and only rarely takes a breath. *I can see how gurus and swamis have been known to meditate for days at a time without moving.* The body feels like a mountain, deeply centered. *I should stop meditating. Enough already.* I lie down to ease my transition into the other world.

After a few minutes, a tidal wave of gratitude washes over me, and I begin to weep. I feel so very good and so very grateful. I know that everything is exactly as it should be. I have struggled deeply to find my way here for who knows how long. I notice I have spontaneously raised my hands and placed them together, fingertips to forehead, in a position of prayer. I begin praying part of the prayer my guru has suggested for people who are not sure how to pray: "In Thy fullness, my Lord, filled with thy grace, for the purpose of union with Thee, we accept in all gratitude thy gift as it has come to us." I then say the Shema out loud in English: "Hear, O Israel, the Lord is our God, the Lord is One." I watch as my body and mind fall back into an easy sleep.

Abe wakes to the sound of the front door opening and the unmistakable tingling of Sarah's keys. She comes into our bedroom, gives me a wet kiss, and says, "I *thought* you'd still be in bed when I got home. I ordered extra Indian veggie food for you. It's in the kitchen."

Great news. I'm quite hungry and hadn't even thought about what I was going to do for dinner—very unusual for me not to plan ahead. Abe used to worry that he'd somehow run out of food. Nature is clearly supporting my desires. I go to the kitchen, ready for dinner. I unpack the Indian food, grab a bowl and a fork, and we sit at the kitchen table.

Between bites, I ask, "How's your mom?"

"She's OK. Her arthritis is really bothering her. The new arthritis pills she was prescribed made her stomach ache, so she stopped them. But her walking was much better when she... was..."

Her voice trails off. That solar plexus thing seems to have opened some type of channel to her. It pulls me and her together. We meet. Without our physical bodies constraining us, we mingle and merge—subject/object; object/subject. It's deeply satisfying and sexual. She shakes her head; her body quivers. The connection breaks.

"Abe—Abe what was that? What just happened? Did you feel that? Did you just do something to me? Something's happening. I was furious at you before I opened the door and walked in. I thought it was just coming home—being in our house. It's not. It's you. What is going on?"

"Honey," I say, "something did happen. This morning during meditation I went into pure consciousness and achieved Samadhi. I'm still in It."

"What—what are you saying?"

"It seems I am enlightened."

Her face is incredulous and intrigued. Her eyes widen.

"You're…you're not kidding? You look serious and different. My God…"

She reflects for a moment, and then another, looks at me carefully, moves her chair closer, tentatively taking my hand, looking deep into my eyes. "You, you *are* serious. You're not kidding. In your eyes, I—you—you are really, *really* there. Amazing. What's it like?"

"It's perfect." I tell her what it's been like, how I've been feeling, how my meditations have gone, but skip the part about Tanisha and the Om incident.

Then it hits her, hard. She drops my hand. Stung by our difference and our separation, her old wound reopens. From that deep, sickening place of her abandonment, her demon reaches out, taking hold. She is being dragged back down to where he lives. It's a childish place from long ago, a place she can't understand. I can smell his fetid breath.

With fear and trembling in her voice, she asks, "Now that you've reached It, how do the kids and I fit into your life? Do you still need us? You've left us behind, haven't you?" She's breathing fast and shallow, her face tight and white. She's let her demon take her into a panic.

I scoot my chair closer to hers. With both hands I grip her right arm, its inner surface cold and clammy. Her pulse is pounding. The thing from the pit of my stomach stirs, attaching to her again. It begins to pull her back.

"Don't worry, Sarah," I tell her. "I'm still me, just who I was before, but now I am what I was and more. I need you and want you. Nothing will change in our lives except for the better."

Her shoulders settle. Her breath softens. But she holds onto my forearm firmly, needing my strength to extricate herself.

"I didn't turn in the paperwork for a sabbatical," I say. "We don't have to go to Iowa now."

"Oh," she replies. Her grip softens, but she doesn't let go. After a few minutes, the color returns to her face and her eyes begin to twinkle.

"Shoshana told me," she says, her voice coy, "she heard that some of the men in Fairfield who reached enlightenment had lost interest in sex. Wives talk, you know. Did that happen to you, my dear?" She's tickling my fancy, testing me, needing reassurance.

"Sarah, please. I want you in every way, now more than ever."

"Good to hear because I'll have you know I find enlightenment to be a *big* turn on." She stands in front of me, taking my head in her hands, bending down to run her tongue around my lips. After a few circles, we both forget everything except each other. We take a leisurely bath, talking sweetly, and then make love. I do my best to reassure her I'm still with her in her world. A while later I get up, hungry again. I look for what's left of the Indian food.

After my second dinner, we watch a documentary I recorded called *Herb & Dorothy*. It's about two Manhattan civil servants of meager means who amassed a hugely important collection of modern art by buying what touched their hearts. Watching two people in love doggedly follow their lifelong quest with the result being a great treasure seems appropriate for this special night. After the documentary, we go to bed.

Before lying down, I suggest we do our night program. She agrees and we begin. As I practice it for the first time while enlightened, it's clear that the technique stretches the part of me that's aware, making it bigger, and helps my awareness dissolve the boundaries between it and objects of perception, or Chhandas. I shake my head, realizing how deeply I'm a philosopher.

As I sit, I feel Sarah's sadness rise again. I look over at her. In the darkness, whatever light there is glints off her moist eyes. Slowly, painfully, she turns toward me and whispers, "You ran off ahead of me. You've left me behind."

"When nothing is done, nothing is left undone."

Lao Tzu

Chapter Four

I wake up Wednesday morning feeling extraordinary. Both my body and mind are deeply rested. They slept beautifully while I remained completely aware, blissfully witnessing my sleep. Witnessing sleep is wonderful and comforting. Now, at every moment, even in the deepest part of sleep, the real Me is lively in the background. In retrospect, the loss of consciousness I used to experience during sleep always came with a sliver of fear. Would I wake up? Would I regain what I was about to let go of? My youngest daughter, Rachel, who had significant problems sleeping as a child, asked me those same questions the many nights I lulled her to sleep.

I put on my robe in the dark, trying not to wake my snoring wife. How such a delicate creature can snore is beyond me, though I guess I've heard all three of my children snore during my early morning wanderings over the years. When I would peek in to check on my little ones as they slept, I often felt I was seeing them at their purest. It's good to look back, but now I feel exhilarated thinking about the future.

I brush my teeth in the Jack and Jill bathroom between the kids' bedrooms. Much of their old stuff is still here. As I go about my routine, the Bliss and glorious heightened sensory smorgasbord that I experienced yesterday is much less distracting. It's still there, as strong and wonderful as it was, but I'm getting used to it.

Finished with the bathroom, I decide I need to work on an article I've been asked to write: a summary of my views on personality theory from a Vedic point of view. Over the last few years, I've published various articles about this theory in philosophy journals, and four months ago, a paper of mine was published in a psychology journal for the first time. The new article is to be included in a psychology textbook a colleague at Brown is compiling. Due to my enlightenment, I feel responsible for sharing my enhanced knowledge with my colleagues and even the public at large. They need to know that enlightenment is a real possibility, how it happens, and how it fits in with current academic thought and modern science. I will be careful, though, not to make this about me.

After drinking half of my morning coffee, the caffeine starts to kick in, and it doesn't feel good. I'm already so awake I'm afraid I might get jittery if I drink more. I pour the remaining coffee into the sink and place the mug in the dishwasher. There are lots of cups, plates, and utensils in the sink and on the counter that have been there since yesterday. I rinse them and put them into the dishwasher as well. I then quietly tidy up the kitchen, the family room, and the rest of the house. Maybe I now have the energy to clean my office at work? Cleanliness feels like it *is* next to godliness.

Sitting at the kitchen table, I write quickly and concisely. Words and ideas flow from my mind to the screen almost by themselves. In about ninety minutes of nonstop work, most of the article comes together. Even without my usual quota of caffeine, I'm able to stay focused without fatigue. I had been planning on spending a week or two writing and rewriting the article, but now I'm likely to finish as soon as tomorrow.

Done with my morning fun, it's time for my real work. Walking to Amos's bedroom, which we've turned into an asana room and an additional place for meditation, I'm almost skipping. I'll meditate here because Sarah is still sleeping. Doing my asanas, I notice my body is much more limber now than pre-enlightenment. I wonder how that physically works? I do alternate nostril pranayama, which also is now much more effective than before. Everything is better. *I am so lucky! Thank you, my Lord.*

I sit on Amos's bed and cross my legs into full lotus. I haven't been able to meditate in full lotus since I was in my thirties. My eyes close and I settle into my consciousness, my awareness silent and without activity. It's as if I'm meditating at the bottom of a perfectly warm, crystal clear swimming pool. I notice above the still water's surface, out in activity, my mind and intellect are excitedly working away on the Plato lecture I will give in a few hours. Enlightenment-related insights have come to them and they are busy incorporating those insights into my lecture. I'm unaffected and uninvolved.

I walk briskly to the college, having left Sarah sleeping. She'll find my love note on the kitchen table. I've left early so I can make significant changes to today's Plato lecture based on the work my mind and intellect did during my meditation. Normally, I'd feel guilty if I left before she woke up. Today, that feeling did not arise. I recognize now that there are lots of ways to adjust things at work so that I can work more from home. Once they're implemented, I don't think I'll have to stay late or go in early as often. Sarah will like that.

I've spent decades studying and contemplating Plato's philosophy. Though my years of meditation have given me insight into his philosophy, this morning it all finally came together. I realized the key to understanding Plato is to view his philosophy from both a transcendental (unity) perspective and a cosmic (diversity) perspective—at the same time. That's because Plato wrote from those perspectives. But more importantly, I'm already planning a paper that should help my colleagues understand Plato better.

In my office, happy with the changes I made, I gather the improved lecture notes and walk down to my Plato class. Because of quirks of scheduling, I teach this small class in an amphitheater that could seat sixty students. As I walk to the podium I nod to most of my twenty-two students who are spread out and comfortable. I like this. The extra space promotes a relaxed but formal environment conducive to the learning process. I place my lecture notes on the lectern.

In the front row, to my right, sits Steve, a math major in his senior year who serves as student body president. He's medium height, muscular in a non-weightlifter way, blond and blue-eyed. He has a wry smile that makes me think he's clever. I remember him well from my Intro class last year. One of his papers for that class compared two very different but fundamental mathematical theories to Plato's theory of true wisdom. After researching his ideas more thoroughly, I incorporated a few into an article that was published in a philosophy journal. I shouldn't have done it. Now that I'm enlightened, I wouldn't do it again. I write on the large whiteboard behind me with a blue erasable marker:

The Allegory of the Cave & the Theory of Forms

Standing behind the lectern, I feel cut off from my students. I can give this lecture without my notes. I walk around the podium and begin, note-less.

"Today we will be discussing Plato's Allegory of the Cave as it relates to his Theory of Forms. As you know from your readings and from Intro to Philosophy, the Allegory of the Cave is about certain prisoners who have been chained facing a wall in a cave all their lives. They have never seen the light of day. Behind them burns a large fire, and all they can see are the shadows cast on the wall they are chained to, as people and things come between the fire and themselves. They believe the shadows are the extent and reality of life. One of the prisoners somehow escapes his chains and makes it out of the cave. After being dazzled by the sun's brilliance, he begins to see things as they really are. The 'enlightened' and liberated ex-prisoner feels bad for his former cave-mates, who are still chained to their false perceptions and beliefs. He cannot fully enjoy the sunshine of the Truth knowing his friends are in the dark."

That hits home.

There's a subtle shift. I'm observing Abe from the unitary silence of my Self, a transcendental perspective that was in the background, but now is foregrounded. The experience of being Here, in unity, in the foreground, and being there, in activity, in the background, at the same time is a much higher truth than just being there or being Here. It's living 200% of life, 100% in activity and 100% in unity. I've known that intellectually for years, but now that I'm experiencing it, I truly Know it. Plato Knew This. Plato felt compelled to teach This.

Abe is lecturing: "The Allegory of the Cave is an example of a concept: knowledge clarifies and deepens experience, and experience deepens and clarifies knowledge. For example, if you know almost nothing about Picasso and see an exhibit of his work, you won't get very much from it. But if you've studied Picasso's art and the history and artistic milieu he worked in, then experiencing the exhibit will be much more transformative. The point I'm hoping to make is there's an important synergy between knowledge and experience.

"Applying this concept to The Allegory of the Cave, no matter how much the chained prisoners could have learned about what it would be like to be in the light, only an experience of the light could transform them and allow them to realize true knowledge. And the prisoner who escaped his chains and experienced the light does possess some true knowledge because of his experience of the light, but that knowledge would be deeper, more profound, and more transformative if he were given an intellectual understanding of what has happened to him. Much of Plato's teachings were meant to do just that.

"Plato's Theory of Forms states that every object of perception and every quality or property found in our world represents an ideal Form. The Form is the essence of the object or quality. What we perceive with our senses is an unreal shadow of the Form in its various manifestations, much as the prisoners mistook the shadows they saw as being real. For example, for every kind of table in the world there is a Form of table-ness that is the essence of those tables. And for every round object in the world there is a Form of roundness that exists independently of those round objects and is the essence from which they derive and copy their round quality.

"The Forms are transcendent to our world of the senses, but they are the foundation of what we experience via our senses. The Forms are also transcendent to space and time. They are not eternal because eternity implies existing within time. The Forms exist outside of time. They are perfect and unchanging. They are the true reality of life, according to Plato. In *Phaedrus*, Plato says the Forms exist in 'a place beyond heaven.'"[15]

I've been to a heaven. Beyond heaven is my Self. I'll take my Self every time.

"The ex-prisoner who escaped his chains and the world of shadows, and who now lives in the sunshine, is a man possessed of wisdom, according to Plato. Such a man experiences the world as it truly is. He perceives it as a world of transcendental Forms and, at the same time, as a world of diversity that he perceives with his senses. His world of Forms is unchanging, transcendent to space, time, and the discrimination of his senses, and therefore unitary. Simultaneously, he perceives our shared world of change and diversity via his senses. Plato writes that 'in that state of life above all others…a man finds it truly worthwhile to live.'"[16]

Steve raises his hand. "Professor, was Plato, as you said, a man possessed of wisdom? If so, how'd he get there? My understanding is that the Socratic method of learning would have given him a deep intellectual understanding of philosophy, but Plato says that won't bring him to a state of wisdom. I know from a friend who took one of your other classes last year that you said you believe Plato was enlightened."

"Yes, in my course The Insider's Guide to Our Self and in some of the articles I've written, I discuss the reasons why I think it's highly unlikely that Plato could have conceived his ideas and descriptions without personal experience. I argue

---

[15] Selected Dialogues of Plato: The Benjamin Jowett Translation (Modern Library Classics), 2001, section 247c

[16] Selected Dialogues of Plato: The Benjamin Jowett Translation (Modern Library Classics), 2001, section 211d

that the pictures he paints as to what it's like to experience wisdom are so detailed and so personal as to make it difficult to believe that Plato was not at least temporarily enlightened. For example, if you have been to Machu Picchu numerous times and have studied it carefully, there's a good chance you'd be able to tell whether someone else's description of Machu Picchu comes from personal experience or just from some travel book they read.

"How he might have reached enlightenment is a subject of speculation among a small group of academics. There are several scholars who believe Plato went to India during his travels after the death of Socrates and before he founded the Academy. Some of these scholars also write that while there, he appears to have studied Vedic philosophy and possibly Vedic meditation. Also, many scholars think he traveled to Persia and Babylonia, where he was initiated into the Chaldean Mysteries, which seem to have involved various contemplative methods for purification of the mind and body. We will never know for sure."

"I have a follow-up question," Steve says. "Why do you think the state of wisdom Plato spoke of is the same state of enlightenment that Vedic philosophy speaks of?"

"I don't want to go too far afield from our topic today, but your question is compelling and related to Plato's Allegory of the Cave. Mystics down through the ages write that reaching enlightenment is often experienced as going from darkness into the light, just as Plato described in his Allegory of the Cave. In my mind, it makes more sense to think the mystics and Plato are all describing the same state of mind, just from different times and different perspectives. That state of wisdom happens to be what I was planning to discuss next. Here is a quote from Plato's *Phaedrus* I'd like to read to you."

I read with a lilting, theatrical voice.

"Of the heaven which is above the heavens, what earthly poet ever did or ever will sing worthily? It is such as I will describe; for I must dare to speak the truth, when truth is my theme. There abides the very being itself with which true knowledge is concerned; the colorless, formless, intangible essence, visible only to mind, the pilot of the soul. The divine intelligence, being nurtured upon mind and pure knowledge, and the intelligence of every soul which is capable of receiving the food proper to it, rejoices at beholding reality, and once more gazing upon truth, is replenished and made glad...[17]

"Let's pick apart what Plato is saying to make it clearer. He describes a state which is 'above the heavens' or, in other words, beyond or transcendent to any world we could experience with our senses. He seems to have experienced that state 'above the heavens' himself because he writes 'as I will describe; for I must dare to speak the truth.' Beyond the heavens 'abides the very being itself,' which he says is a 'colorless, formless, intangible essence,' which would mean that 'being itself' was beyond the world of the senses, which is our world of activity. That state of being is 'visible only to mind, the pilot of the soul' which suggests that the mind is active in its role as the soul's pilot, while the soul is outside of activity, experiencing what the mind

---

[17] Selected Dialogues of Plato: The Benjamin Jowett Translation (Modern Library Classics), 2001, section 246a–248c.

'pilots' it to or shows it. The mind is 'replenished and made glad' when it experiences 'the very being itself' which seems to be a report of something Plato personally experienced."

As Abe is professing his newly realized Platonic knowledge, I notice distantly that I have another body that isn't breathing. It's sitting on the bed in Amos's room in full-lotus doing this morning's meditation. I observe on that earlier body's screen of awareness its mind and intellect excitedly revise the Plato lecture Abe is now delivering. The other body I'm currently aware of is the one I came in with. That body is now about a third of the way through Abe's lecture. A lesson, and an intuition, comes to me. The lesson: I could contact the Abe from this morning and let him know how our lecture is going, or I could stay with the lecturing Abe—time has lost its grip on me. The intuition: I shouldn't time travel now, but I will when it would be of service to our world. One day, when the need arises, I will contact an earlier version of myself to convey important information.

I'm going to make it home before four o'clock, the earliest I've been home on a regular workday in years. Sarah will be pleased and relieved. I've been getting so much done so well and so efficiently that as I walk home the thought comes that maybe I'm experiencing a form of mania. I have no history of bipolar illness and have not felt a hint of depression in years, but my understanding is that some people can be in a manic state without ever having had any corresponding depression. Even a single episode of mania qualifies for the diagnosis of bipolar disease if memory serves. I remember reading a bipolar man's account of mania in my college Psych 101 textbook. He said there was nothing better than being manic. He had tried cocaine, amphetamines, heroin, and sex with two women at the same time, but being manic was better than all of it. Mania has interested me ever since.

Is enlightenment an unusual form of mania? People in a manic state have delusions of grandeur, hallucinations in which they talk to God, excessive energy, and believe they are finally healthy compared to their previous non-manic frame of mind. Since enlightenment, I have gone from a consistent six hours of sleep to about four and a half—but I haven't had trouble sleeping, which usually happens with mania. I don't have racing thoughts. If anything, my thoughts are fewer and my mind is much calmer. I'm not manic.

Sarah gets home at about four-thirty. I'm so happy to see her. And so happy that I beat her home. Even though I was feeling complete and whole before, I immediately feel a thrill when she walks into the living room.

"What a treat," she says. "Did you come home early looking for something?"

"Yeah, you."

"I'm here, dear. So, you're still enlightened? Give me the whole truth and nothing but the truth, so help you God," she says with a sly grin. She plops herself on the sofa, pushing me over a bit, and pivots to rub my cheek with the back of her right hand. It feels nice. Maybe I am looking for something?

"Yes, I am still enlightened. The whole truth is that enlightenment has brought me closer to the Truth, with the help of God. I think I've made real progress in my understanding of Plato."

"That's wonderful, honey. Has your enlightenment made you feel disconnected from the world?"

"It did, but it's getting better each day. Every day my love and appreciation for this perfect world deepens and matures." I rub my hand up and down her thigh and kiss her temple. She turns to me, kisses me, but holds back.

"How was *your* day?" I ask. I look at her and see something dark run across her eyes. "How are you feeling?"

"I'm feeling *so* much better now that you're not going to leave me."

"Sarah, dear, I'm not your dad. I'm not going to leave you."

"What do you mean? You *were* planning on leaving me. If you hadn't reached enlightenment, you would have taken off for God knows how long."

"I wanted you to come. If you hadn't, I would have come back."

"What, like my father came back?"

She was so buoyant a moment ago.

"How could he do that to us? My mom told me even yesterday that not a day goes by that she doesn't get sick to her stomach thinking about him with her." She sighs. "Sorry, I'm not sure why this has hit me so hard."

She looks down at her hands, which are resting on her knees, then turns them palms up. "My mother told me," she says to her palms, "that my father left us because he got tired of her, of her anxieties, her panic attacks. She said he stopped needing us, wanting us." She's looking at her palms as if she's never seen them before. She turns them over again and faces me. "I'm terrified you're tired of me and don't need me anymore. You've been tired of this world since you were fifteen."

I put my left arm over her bowed shoulders. She collapses into my lap, hugging my legs. She's sinking.

"*Sarah*, we will always be together. Nothing can separate us. I do need you. I want to be with you." She's not hearing me. She's distant.

She starts sobbing. Her heart pounds on my legs as she grips them tighter. Her breath comes fast and shallow. I move close, lips to the back of her neck—kissing her back to me, back to where she belongs. After a long while, when her sobbing softens, her breath begins to ease.

I say in an upbeat tone, "Let's see if Javier and Ann are free for dinner tonight."

"I can't go out like this," she mumbles from my legs, which are damp from her tears.

"We should get out. It'll be good, I promise. Text Ann and ask, or I can do it." Getting out of the house usually helps her.

"I can't go." She sits up. "Please don't make me."

I turn toward her. Bending over, I whisper in her ear, "You're OK. It's passed. I love you, honey. We both have our issues. That's who we are. I love you exactly as you are. We help each other. That's how it's been. That's how it'll be. Let's go out. It will do us both some good." I sit back.

After a few more deep breaths, she says, "Maybe. Give me a few more minutes. Let me see how I feel." She slouches on the sofa, staring at the fireplace. I give her space.

"It's passing," she says after a time. "I'll try. Just a quick dinner. It would be good to get out. We'll tell them you have work to do after, OK?"

"It's a deal."

She texts Ann. Minutes later a reply comes. They're free.

Javier is a beautiful man. The attention he pays to Sarah tends to perk her up. Ann's a physics professor. She's dry but crackling smart and extremely well-read. She seems oblivious to Javier's flirtations. I enjoy talking with Ann. We've had several fascinating discussions over the last few years about theoretical physics and its views on consciousness.

Sarah's looking better. She asks if I have any food preference. I surprise myself, answering, "Anything but Indian—too much Indian lately." Sarah texts Ann, "sushi k 7?" The immediate reply: "sushi @7 is."

"All set," Sarah says, sounding more like herself. "Let's go meditate. Can we meditate with our shoulders touching?"

Thursday morning, I'm ready for class. Still enlightened—fifty-two hours and counting. I walk into the classroom with photocopies on top of my usual stack of books. I stayed late with Sarah and didn't get here early enough to write today's lecture title on the chalkboard. When I left her, she was holding it together.

"Here are the three prompts for your first paper," I say as I pass them out. I return to the front of the room and read the prompts aloud.

"Number one, the ever popular and often maligned, 'Why and why not?—from a Vedic perspective.'

"Number two, the beguiling, 'I am! Are you?'

"And last, but certainly not least, 'What's it all about?'

"I'm passing around a sign-up sheet for half-hour one-on-one appointments with me to discuss your papers. The appointments start one week from today. Everyone should sign up for two appointments at least one week apart. You should have a four-page rough draft to bring to the first meeting. The second meeting is to review the progress you've made. Your papers should be based on ideas brought up in lecture and focus on the course readings. If you want to read ahead and discuss texts that haven't come up yet, that's great. Email me your rough draft by noon on the day before our appointment is scheduled. That way when we meet to discuss your essays, I'll have had a chance to read what you've written and will be able to give you feedback and discuss further avenues down which you might want to proceed."

After passing the sign-up sheet to Chris, I walk around my desk to sit down. As I'm walking, I get the strong, intuitive feeling that Chris passed the sheet to Tom, who passed it on without signing up. Knowing that Tom's paper is going to be an issue, my first thought is to tell him he needs to make an appointment. I don't—got to keep this enlightenment thing under wraps.

I wait for the shuffling of papers and scribbling of pens to subside. "Today we will discuss Maharishi's theories about Cosmic Consciousness and higher stages of enlightenment as found in his translation of the Bhagavad Gita." I begin to erase another philosophy professor's chalkboard notes—something about Nietzsche and the death of God, God forbid. I enjoy erasing it; that was all so 1960s. I pick up a piece of gritty chalk and write:

Enlightenment: Cosmic Consciousness,
God Consciousness, and Unity Consciousness

Now *that* is a much more appropriate, timely topic for young minds.

I rub my hands together to get rid of some lingering chalk and begin. "Scholars of the Hindu religious tradition often call the Bhagavad Gita the essence of the Vedas. In the Gita, Lord Krishna describes to Arjuna a technique for meditation that will permanently liberate him from our world of sorrow, sickness, decay, and rebirth. Maharishi writes in his Gita translation and commentary that the meditation technique given to Arjuna was the precursor to Transcendental Meditation.

"One way of thinking about Transcendental Meditation is as a method of refining and purifying the nervous system so that it can experience subtle thoughts as they arise from our consciousness. This refinement and purification occurs spontaneously the longer one meditates. Meditators, practicing TM or otherwise, have long been subjects of scientific study, and these studies tend to show that the process of meditation over time produces a nervous system that is less stressed, more relaxed, and more capable of making fine discriminations. The research that has been done to date shows that Transcendental Meditation produces these effects more quickly and with less effort than other studied forms of meditation."

Tanisha raises her lovely, long arm gracefully. She asks a question I've been asked many times. I answer it, but I'm thinking about her—and not in an animal, sexual way. The animal part of me is still there, but it's subdued and satiated. A higher part of me is firmly in control and merely notices the animal's urges. Tanisha is lovely as a sunrise is lovely. *Thank you, my Lord, for creating such beauty in our world.*

"The refinement and purification of the nervous system grows over the years as one meditates, reducing the noise in that system and allowing the meditator's awareness to settle down and become capable of experiencing the finest qualities of pure consciousness—one of which is infinite correlation. The concept of infinite correlation is useful when thinking about Vedic philosophy. We will discuss it now.

"We can start from the idea that came up in our last lecture, that there is only one thing in our universe: pure consciousness. So, if we begin with the assumption that everything is made of the same pure consciousness, then we get something we might call infinite correlation, whereby every point in the universe is correlated or in synchrony with every other point. This is because, according to Vedic philosophy, each point in the universe is ultimately the *same* point as well as a different point. Think back to our discussions concerning unity and diversity.

"As one meditates over time, one's body and—"

"Professor," Margaret interrupts, and then raises her hand. "Wait a minute. I'm not buying this. It's too convenient. Han, does quantum mechanics say that every point in the universe is both different and the same at the *same time?*"

Han looks to me.

"Go ahead, Han, if you want to and have something to say."

Han says, "Yes, different and same. One-way physics has proven this is because of quantum entanglement. Any object theoretically can be entangled with any other object, but now is easy to entangle photons and electrons. Once photons or electrons entangle, they could be at opposite sides of universe and if we affect one of the entangled pair by measuring, same as observing, the other entangled partner instantaneously is affected—distance, not a problem for entanglement. Two hugely separated objects are really one correlated system—only seem different. Because everything is entangled with everything else, at root, everything ultimately is one correlated system—yes, same *and* different."

"Ah, yes," I remark. "That bothered Einstein very much. He called it 'spooky action at a distance.' According to Einstein's theories, which, to my understanding, are only applicable to space-time and things within space-time, nothing, including information, can travel faster than the speed of light. But experiments with quantum entanglement have demonstrated *instantaneous* transmission of information and causally linked effects at increasingly great distances—in other words, infinitely faster than the speed of light. In my mind, this problem is solved by Vedic philosophy's stance that there is a state transcendent to space-time, a state from which space-time originates, a state where all points within our space-time *are* the same point. That state is pure-consciousness, the singularity, or the Samhita of Rishi, Devata, and Chhandas. It's the ouroboros, the serpent, having completely swallowed its tail until it becomes a point.

"Because this is such a bizarre idea that is contrary to our everyday experiences, and contrary to Einstein's law that nothing can move faster than the speed of light, I'd like to read you a passage from the *Quantum Enigma* so some of you don't think I'm just making this up." I glance at Margaret playfully.

> "Separability" has been our shorthand term for the ability to separate objects so that what happens to one in *no way* affects what happens to others. Without separability, what happens at one place *can* instantaneously affect what happens far away—even though no physical force connects the objects...
>
> That our actual world does not have separability is now generally accepted, though admitted to be a mystery...Quantum theory has this connectedness extending over the entire universe...a universal connectedness whose meaning we have yet to understand.[18]

"Dr. Levy," Joseph says, raising his hand. "May I add something?"

---

[18] *Quantum Enigma: Physics Encounters Consciousness*, second edition (Oxford University Press, 2011), 188–189.

"Please," I respond, and then nod toward Han. "Thank you, Han. That was an excellent summary."

"There are rabbis who teach Kabbalah who say that our universe is essentially just a dream in the mind of God. You said a little while ago that Vedic philosophy says that everything in every universe is made of the same pure consciousness. Is that pure consciousness God's consciousness or God's mind, according to Vedic philosophy?"

"Yes and no," I say.

"Awesome," Tom interjects. "So, nothing has ever happened. We're living in God's mind." He speaks slowly, wheels clicking for all to see. I also detect a faint smirk. *Out of the mouths of babes*, I say to myself.

Tom's remark elicits eye-rolling from the class but nods from Han and Joseph who apparently are having mini-epiphanies of their own. It's time to move on.

"Picking up the point where I left off." I pick up something unseen in the air with my finger and thumb, and then cast what I pinched toward my class. Chris's abdomen spasms, forcing air out of his nostrils. No one else responds. That's too bad. That joke has gotten me a few snickers in the past.

"As one meditates over time, one's body and mind gain access to this undercurrent of pure consciousness and take on some of the qualities of pure consciousness, one of which is infinite correlation. Applying this idea of infinite correlation to the brain functioning of meditators, we can see if this concept manifests in some measurable way during their meditations. It turns out it does.

"If a subject was having an experience as powerful and overwhelming as the experience of pure consciousness has been described to be, we would expect to find something dramatic on the subject's EEG tracings to corroborate such an experience. We might expect that a meditator experiencing a state of infinite correlation would have an EEG coherence pattern that would somehow reflect this infinite correlation by showing that every part of her brain was in synchrony with every other part of her brain. This is exactly what cognitive researchers at the Maharishi International University, or MIU, have demonstrated. MIU was formerly called Maharishi University of Management and was founded by Maharishi in 1973. Its campus is in Fairfield, Iowa.

"Professors at MIU have published a number of articles detailing increasing EEG brain wave coherence that occurs the longer one meditates. When some of these same long-term meditators reported that they had reached what they thought was Cosmic Consciousness, the investigators repeated an EEG and found much higher EEG coherence in the enlightened subjects compared to their coherence pre-enlightenment. Such extremely high EEG coherence had never been reported before. According to MIU researchers, they have at least some objective evidence that Cosmic Consciousness isn't just a mythological dream."

Asher raises his hand and waits to be called upon.

"Yes, Asher."

"I think they're making this up. They find what they want to find. How can you prove someone's enlightened? You can't get inside their head, even if you measure stuff about them. People fool themselves all the time."

"Those are excellent points. Science is ultimately objective. Enlightenment is ultimately subjective. Should we believe the researchers at MIU? Is there proof of modern-day enlightenment? We need to be aware of the potential for bias in MIU researchers' publications. At the least, this is an avenue for future research that might, or might not, provide significant evidence that Cosmic Consciousness is attainable."

Could I be fooling myself? I don't think so, but the psychological literature is filled with case studies of people with conversion reactions who, among many other things, think they have become blind even though they're not because deep in their psyches they don't want to see. And mass hysteria is a well-known phenomenon where groups of people develop collective illusions. Maybe all of us TM-ers are so desperate for enlightenment that we have come down with a case of mass hysteria? People in the grip of mass hysteria are sure their illusions are real. What's happened to me does seem too good to be true.

I look around the room. Everything is perfect and divine. That's just how someone in cosmic consciousness would see their world. If how I see the world is part of a mass hysteria-based illusion, it's a pretty convincing one.

"Having broached Cosmic Consciousness from the objective perspective of neurological functioning, we might want to ask, from a subjective perspective, what happens experientially when someone actually and fully experiences the Experiencer, or the Self? When an individual's awareness becomes fully immersed in pure consciousness, the state of samadhi, it's like a raindrop coming in contact with the ocean. The raindrop touches the ocean and is no longer just an individual raindrop. Its individuality merges with the ocean. Did it actually have individuality as a raindrop, or was it a part of the ocean that was only temporarily separated from itself? The answer to each question is yes *and* no, and, as I have said repeatedly, the answer depends on one's perspective.

"Returning to the world of activity, the newly enlightened meditator's awareness now experiences two things at once. One aspect stays dissolved in the ocean of their Self, experiencing the Self and silently witnessing the world, while another aspect experiences and interacts with the world. This state of mind where one's awareness is in unitary pure consciousness continuously yet at the same time aware and active in the world of activity and diversity is called Cosmic Consciousness.

"Maharishi has used several analogies to help us understand the process of attaining Cosmic Consciousness. I will only discuss one of those analogies for now: that gaining Cosmic Consciousness is similar to how the women of India traditionally dye cloth to make it colorfast. They dip the cloth in dye, take the cloth out, and set it in the sun until the color fades. They then repeat the process over and over until the color no longer fades, even in the harshest sunlight. Following this analogy, a meditator dips her awareness into a little bit of pure consciousness during each meditation and comes out with some of the color or qualities of pure consciousness infused into her awareness, her mind, and her body. The pure consciousness fades as it is exposed to the stresses of her daily life, only to be re-dipped during the next meditation. Reaching Cosmic Consciousness is like becoming colorfast: the meditator's mind and body become so imbued with pure consciousness that even under the harshest sunlight of her daily existence the color does not fade.

"This analogy helps explain why some people have reported that they thought they were in true Cosmic Consciousness for a few hours, a few weeks, or even for months, only to lose it. They had achieved by far the brightest color they had ever experienced, but when exposed to the stresses of life, the color eventually faded. True Cosmic Consciousness is the state of being colorfast. It doesn't fade.

"Eastern mysticism is full of accounts of people who experienced the Self or who reached enlightenment, at least temporarily. Western literature also has its share of authors who have written about the experience of pure consciousness or of enlightenment. What I find fascinating is that, as a whole, the descriptions are similar, regardless of whether the author is from the East or the West, and regardless of the author's religion, philosophical leanings, or time period. It seems they all describe the same experience from different perspectives. If anyone is interested, there's an excellent book by the MIU professor Dr. Craig Pearson describing many such experiences. It's called *The Supreme Awakening: Experiences of Enlightenment Throughout Time.* In addition to detailing experiences of our Self by many notable historical figures, it also contains an extended interview with a modern-day meditator who claims he's reached Cosmic Consciousness.[19] I'd be happy to loan out as many copies as I have.

"Moving forward, I'll read you a few quotes to give you an idea of the kinds of experiences that have been written about. Hearing about these experiences should help us flesh out the intellectual theory of meditation and enlightenment that we have been discussing."

Obinna raises his hand. I'm glad to see it. He's been fairly quiet. I bow toward him and take a half step back, giving him the floor.

"Professor, what is the relationship between love and enlightenment?"

"*That* is an interesting question," I say slowly, trying to buy time to formulate my thoughts. "Love is a difficult concept to

[19] Craig Pearson, Ph.D, *The Supreme Awakening: Experiences of Enlightenment Throughout Time—And How You Can Cultivate Them*, second edition (Maharishi University of Management Press, 2016), 497–515.

pin down. I am not an expert on the philosophical exploration of love and still have much to learn about it. I've heard it said that all love flows to the Self. I think, from a Vedic viewpoint, that's correct. I think love is, among many things, a force that breaks down boundaries. It's a force that desires to unify the lover with the loved. The biblical injunctions to 'love the Lord your God… and love your neighbor as yourself,[20]' I believe, find their fulfillment in Unity Consciousness, which is the highest state of enlightenment. After the lecture, if you like, we can discuss this further."

Ravi, sitting behind Margaret and to her right, is staring at her long, thick brown hair as it cascades over the back of her chair, his eyes dreamy. Sharp, clear sunlight mixes with the bluish fluorescent lights humming above, swirling and tumbling together. *I am in love with this life, my Lord. Thank you for allowing me to live it.*

"Plato was born around 424 BC to an aristocratic family. At the age of nineteen, he became a devout student of Socrates. He continued to study with Socrates until Socrates's death ten years later. After traveling extensively, Plato returned to Greece at the age of forty and founded the Academy, which was the first Western university. The Academy continued for nine hundred years and educated such noted figures as Aristotle and Heraclides.

"Plato has been called the father of Western philosophy. In addition to having a profound influence on Western philosophy, his ideas have helped some physicists conceptualize what modern physics says about our universe. Werner Heisenberg of Uncertainty Principle fame wrote that 'modern physics has definitely decided in favor of Plato. In fact the smallest units of

---

[20] Luke 10:27.

matter are not physical objects in the ordinary sense; they are forms...'[21]

"It seems to me that Plato was, at least for a while, in Cosmic Consciousness and possibly had some experiences of God Consciousness, or even Unity Consciousness, both of which we will talk about today. I will discuss my reasons for thinking Plato experienced some form of enlightenment during our lecture entitled 'Plato and Enlightenment.' This is one of many passages from Plato's works that suggests Plato had direct knowledge of enlightenment:

> "But when returning into herself... [the soul] passes into the other world, the region of purity, and eternity, and immortality, and unchangeableness, which are her kindred, and with them she ever lives, when she is by herself and is not let or hindered; then she ceases from her erring ways, and being in communion with the unchanging is unchanging. And this state of the soul is called wisdom...[22]

"Plato uses different words to describe what we have been talking about. Based on this and many of his other writings, the state of the soul called wisdom is, I think, the same state of the soul we have discussed as Cosmic Consciousness, or possibly an even higher stage of enlightenment.

---

[21] Werner Heisenberg, *Das Naturgesetz und die Struktur der Materie* (1967), as translated in *Natural Law and the Structure of Matter* (Warm Wind Books, new edition, 1981), 34

[22] Plato, *The Dialogues of Plato*, trans. Benjamin Jowett (Oxford, England: The Clarendon Press, 1892), 222.

"Moving forward about eight hundred years, we come to St. Augustine, who lived AD 354–430, a towering figure in Christianity and Western philosophical thought. His auto-biographical *Confessions* influenced many philosophers who came after him. In *Confessions*, Augustine writes:

> "I entered into the innermost part of myself...I entered and I saw with my soul's eye (such as it was) an unchangeable light shining above this eye of my soul and above my mind...He who knows truth knows that light, and he who knows that light knows eternity.[23]

"Anyone care to venture an explanation of how the 'unchangeable light shining above this eye of my soul' and the rest of this passage would correspond to the Vedic concepts of Rishi, Devata, and Chhandas? I'll give you a hint: think back to my mantra as a mirror analogy. I'll read it to you one more time." I read the quote again slowly. Most of the students write down as much of it as they can.

There's a pause as everyone thinks about the question. After a short while, Margaret raises her hand. I smile at her.

"As we discussed before," she begins tentatively, "we all need a mirror to see ourselves." She sits up straight and barrels forward. "The 'eye of my soul' has to be his Rishi, the observer. And the 'unchangeable light shining above' the eye of his soul has to be a reflection of his Rishi as it sees its Self in a 'mirror,' which is his equivalent of a mantra. The 'unchangeable light' is a reflection of his Rishi, or his Self, because only the Self is unchangeable and, according to our readings of the Upanishads,

---

[23] *The Confessions of St. Augustine*, trans. Rex Warner (New York: New American Library, Mentor Books, 1963), 247–248.

only the Self is self-luminescent. Because he perceives the light 'above his eye,' the light is Chhandas, an object of perception. Between the unchanging light, Chhandas, and the eye of his soul, Rishi, is Devata, the process of perception. If his physiology was more settled, he might have been able to quiet his Devata enough so that the unchangeable light/mirror was, metaphorically speaking, right in front of the eye of his soul. Then, if he settled Devata even further and it became still, he might have experienced the light directly, merging Rishi, Devata, and Chhandas. Then he would have fully, directly known the Truth and the eternity he spoke of." She relaxes back into her chair, sure that she nailed it.

"Couldn't have said it any better myself," I say, waiting for her grin, which appears on cue. She's a valuable ally in creating a classroom conducive to learning. It's been three years since a student was able to give such a perfect explanation of that passage.

"Coming from a very different direction, there's a body of literature describing the experiences of people under the influence of hallucinogenic or psychedelic drugs, such as LSD, peyote, mescaline, and psychedelic mushrooms. The experiences described in the psychedelic literature are very much like those described by people in higher states of consciousness without drugs. My feeling is that they are somewhat akin to what happens during high-energy physics experiments when researchers smash atomic particles together to see what's inside of them. Psychedelic drugs probably offer a means of discovering what's inside our minds and psyches, but those who choose this route take a huge risk. In cracking their minds open with these powerful drugs, they face the possibility—the probability—that damage will be done.

"Along this path, we come to Aldous Huxley, who was a prominent English writer, known for his dystopian novel *Brave New World,* and for *The Doors of Perception,* a book that was the darling of the 1960s, when Timothy Leary led the psychedelic movement. The book describes Huxley's personal experiment taking mescaline. Huxley takes care to relate his experience to both Eastern and Western philosophic traditions and details a number of incidents in the course of his mescaline trip that he recognizes as experiences of pure Being, or as we have called it, pure consciousness. Early in his experience he describes the simple act of looking at a chair as a moment of divine transcendence.

"[I was] in a world where everything shone with the Inner Light, and was infinite in its significance. The legs, for example, of that chair—how miraculous their tubularity, how supernatural their polished smoothness! I spent several minutes—or was it several centuries?—not merely gazing at those bamboo legs, but actually *being* them—or rather being myself in them...[24]

"The mescaline has settled his Devata enough that his Rishi is able to more directly know the Chhandas that are the bamboo chair legs. He experiences this more direct knowledge of the bamboo legs as 'being myself in them.' Of note, the 'Inner Light' he writes about is commonly experienced during God Consciousness, which we will discuss in a moment.

"Moving from the relatively recent past to the present, we also have modern-day descriptions of higher states of consciousness. The following quote is taken from a book of

[24] Aldous Huxley, *The Doors of Perception* (HarperCollins Publishers, Adobe Digital Edition, August 2009), 22.

experiences of participants in an intensive ongoing meditation course at MIU in Fairfield, Iowa. The book I have taken this from purports to show that the ancient experiences of our Self documented thousands of years ago by Himalayan sages are again being experienced by meditators today.

> "My experience of 'experience experiencing itself' is growing, expanding, and overtaking my small-self awareness...The experience of 'I' is growing into 'That which always was, has been, and will be.' I am becoming a silent witness and humble servant to the process of Being in its ever-expanding state of bliss...All silence and diversity coexist simultaneously, as do all pairs of opposites. Time seems to be an illusion; there is only the wholeness of infinity...I experience an ongoing expansion of my small-self awareness...I become the universe...[25]

"Cosmic Consciousness and enlightenment sound kind of cool, no? Well, if the only benefit of reaching Cosmic Consciousness was to enjoy your current life more, that alone might be worth the significant effort needed to achieve it. But there's at least one additional benefit to achieving enlightenment that, according to my understanding of Vedic philosophy, makes reaching it the most important goal in everyone's lives. Vedic philosophy says that when we die, our awareness and sense of identity transition to another realm where we experience the rewards and punishments our karma

---

[25] *Invincible America Assembly: Experiences of Higher States of Consciousness of Course Participants* (Fairfield, Iowa: Maharishi University of Management Press, 2012), 25.

merits. Good karma will get you a good afterlife; bad karma will get you your just desserts. If you don't reach Cosmic Consciousness in this lifetime, then once your karma from this life is expended in the afterlife, you temporarily lose all memory and sense of identity from this lifetime and its afterlife and are reborn. You are essentially sent back to school to continue your lessons. You are not allowed to graduate to the next level until you have learned them well enough. And this school is like elementary school. You are required to attend and to repeat until you've graduated. Eventually, even the slowest learners, over many, many lifetimes, mature and learn enough to..."

"Sir," Tom interrupts, "what happens if you hate school?" His voice has an insistent, whiny edge. "Can that be fixed?"

Fixed? He wants to be fixed? Hoping to disarm him with some humor, I say, "Those people will have to stay after class and write on the chalkboard 'I love school' until they do love it." That didn't work. He looks worse. He takes in a deep breath—and holds it. He sits taller, inching toward the edge of his chair, shoulders moving back, pushing his chest out. I think he wants me to fix him? I think he wants me to do to him what he saw me do to Tanisha? It's a sad sight. He's sitting there, puffed out, exposed. I would if I could. But I have no idea how to control that thing that happened between me and Tanisha, and Sarah. I'll try a different approach.

"Tom, I understand that life can be very hard." He deflates. His shoulders sag, his chest retracts. He *was* hoping I would fix or heal him in some magical way. "We all are engaged," I say to him softly, "in a fearsome fight with a powerful, equally matched opponent, our lower selves." Tom nods. "Vedic philosophy says the fight goes on and on, life after tiring life, until our higher Self is victorious. No matter how many times we get knocked down, our will kicked out of us, we always get back up, dust ourselves off, and resume the fight. Eventually, our higher Self wins. That's how our universe is constructed."

"It's too hard." He looks up at me, then down, examining his large shoes which stick out in front of his desk. He's embarrassed.

"OK," I say, wanting to divert the class's attention from Tom, "are there any other questions, thoughts, concerns, or conundrums I, or your fellow classmates, can address?" I take two steps backward and hop up on my desk from my tippy toes without using my hands—plop. *Ow!* I won't do that again, but it worked. Everyone's attention is now on me and my tender tushy. As I look at my students, love starts to flow. They are a part of me and I, of them. I am much more than the sum of my internal experiences and memories. I am part of everything out there: all people, relationships, emotions, beauty, and pain. I am an actor in and the audience of a Divine play that teaches me who I am. Coming to know my Self is not just inward knowledge.

"The second stage of enlightenment is God Consciousness, according to Maharishi. What is it that moves someone in Cosmic Consciousness to evolve toward God Consciousness? The answer is an expansion and purification of the heart.

"In Cosmic Consciousness, as the enlightened yogi continues to more fully know and thereby take on qualities of his Self during increasingly deep meditations, this further refines his senses. His senses, due to the purifying effects of deeper meditations, naturally and progressively become subtler and more capable of experiencing the celestial value within objects of perception, which is the 'Inner Light' of which Huxley wrote. The outward world is experienced as more beautiful, charming, and attractive. Its sounds become angelic, its smells become heavenly, its tastes become divine, and its touches become, well, quite touching.

"Just as the awareness is attracted inwardly to the charming, settled states of the mantra during meditation, the awareness is now attracted outwardly to the charming, settled states of the external world. Every perception of the world becomes so amazingly near and dear to one's heart that the heart expands outwardly, overflowing with appreciation, gratitude, and love for God and God's perfect universe. As Cosmic Consciousness matures and ripens, the heart fully expands and becomes so purified that God Consciousness dawns. Then the world is experienced in terms of its divine qualities. Consider Mathew 5:8: 'Blessed are the pure in heart: for they shall see God.' We can think of achieving God Consciousness as getting a master's degree, with the PhD yet to come.

"There are a number of Western writers and religious figures who appear to have had celestial experiences that are the hallmark of God Consciousness. For instance, William Blake, a nineteenth-century English poet and artist, claimed to have had numerous experiences of the celestial and the Divine. He writes in *Auguries of Innocence*:

"'To See a World in a Grain of Sand
And a Heaven in a Wild Flower,
Hold Infinity in the palm of your hand
And Eternity in an hour.'

"And in *The Marriage of Heaven and Hell*, he writes the famous lines that gave the title to Huxley's work, 'If the doors of perception were cleansed everything would appear to man as it is, Infinite. For man has closed himself up, till he sees all things thro' narrow chinks of his cavern.'

"Blake is describing the type of celestial experiences that bring on God Consciousness. God Consciousness develops due to a cleansing, refinement, and settling of Devata, through which we perceive and experience the world. As Devata, or the doors of perception, are cleansed, we will perceive the celestial value, or heaven, in a wildflower, and everything will appear as it is, infinite, and as a heartfelt gift from God.

"Another noted historical figure I believe achieved God Consciousness was the Baal Shem Tov, who lived from 1698 to 1760. The Baal Shem Tov, which means Master of the Good Name, was the founder of the Jewish Hasidic movement and a mystical Jewish rabbi. The Baal Shem Tov often claimed that he truly experienced God in all things and said that was because God is all things. Though he left us no books, it's clear from historical accounts that he taught that everything in the universe—spiritual, mental, and material—is a manifestation of God and His Divine Being. His followers claim that he performed many miracles. Here is a quote attributed to the Baal Shem Tov: 'The world is full of wonders and miracles but man takes his little hand and covers his eyes and sees nothing.'

"The third phase of enlightenment, the PhD so to speak, is Unity Consciousness. As God Consciousness naturally evolves, the outside world of activity increasingly becomes even more attractive and appealing to one's awareness. The awareness rises up in waves of love and begins to batter down the perceived boundaries between Rishi, the observer, and objects of experience, or Chhandas. Even as they are broken down, these boundaries are revealed to be illusory to the increasingly enlightened vision of the Self. Achieving Unity Consciousness completes the symmetry of life—inner life becomes outer life.

"The Upanishads succinctly sum up Unity Consciousness in one of the *Mahavakyas*, or great expressions: '*Aham Brahmasmi*—I am Totality.'[26] According to Maharishi, Unity Consciousness is the fulfillment of life's ultimate goal, complete Self-knowledge. And with that, I am feeling fulfilled. Why don't we take a three-minute break, then I'll attempt to answer whatever questions arise?"

I can almost hear a collective sigh of relief. About half of the students stand and some stretch. I sit back in my chair and check my email on my phone.

The academic dean of Pomona College has sent an email to each of the members of the five-college joint steering committee with her suggestions for "streamlining and coordinating our course offerings in accord with the shared vision of specialization for each of the five colleges." She is relentless, as she should be. Truth be told, her ideas are not bad, but I can't let this class become a course at Scripps College or incorporated into an existing course at one of the other colleges. As I plot my strategy, I overhear Margaret asking Ravi about his religious beliefs. More interested in their conversation, I suspend my machinations and listen in.

Margaret asks Ravi, "You meditate as part of your religion? Have you ever had religious experiences like we heard about from the professor today?"

"I have had some, a little bit, a few times," Ravi says. "Our religion requires us to meditate every day. Over the years, we get better. We also pray to God. Sometimes the Lord smiles on me when I pray and I feel Him."

"I would love to feel that, just once."

[26] Brihadaranyak Upanishad, 1.4.10, translated in William F. Sands, and Mahesh Yogi, *Maharishi's Yoga: The Royal Path to Enlightenment* (Fairfield, Iowa: Maharishi University of Management Press, 2013), 96.

"If you are sincere and diligent, He will come to you. Be patient."

It's time to resume. I clear my throat, stand, walk to the front of my class, and begin again. Abe answers two good questions and one not so good, but my awareness has shifted to the Transcendent. From Here, everything is the same. It's not that Abe doesn't care. He cares deeply. It's that he is now deeply content. The part of his brain that kept pushing him, wanting more, wanting it quicker, never content, always on guard, has been silenced. He has escaped from a harsh taskmaster. His peace has softened.

I look around the room and see a few more hands in the air, but then I check the time. Almost eleven. "We are running over. Sorry, we don't have time for more questions today. Not everyone has signed up for one-on-one meetings to discuss their first paper. If you haven't signed up, please look at the sheet on my desk on your way out and find a time to meet. OK, see you next class." Only Tom and Asher haven't signed up.

"Dr. Levy, sorry to interrupt, but can I ask a pressing question before you go?" Chris asks as he fidgets in his seat, waving his hand in the air.

"Chris, I'm happy to answer your question now, but I don't want to hold your classmates over any longer. Everyone, please feel free to leave or you are welcome to stay and hear our discussion." Tom brusquely walks out, but the others remain.

"You mentioned during your lecture that there are people at the TM university who claim to have reached Cosmic Consciousness, and they have documented EEG evidence that something dramatic did happen to them. That seems too convenient and self-serving. Do you believe them?" Chris asks.

"You're right to be skeptical. Do I believe their research? Not all of it. But I don't think they are deliberately falsifying their data. I think their bias toward what they want and expect to happen based on what Vedic philosophy predicts colors what they see and how they see it. I do think there are some real, fundamental truths behind what they are publishing.

"The papers did create a bit of a tempest in a teapot among neuroscience circles for a short time, but I don't think most neuroscientists believe Cosmic Consciousness is real. It will take something more dramatic to change their opinions. If you want to discuss this more, you can come to my office during my office hours. I know many of you wanted to speak earlier, and I'm sorry I can't stay longer. I just realized there's something I must attend to."

Everyone files out except Asher, who signs up for an appointment. I don't know why I decided not to take more questions. I usually stay longer. I have nothing in particular I need to do now—do I?

I walk up to my office and find Sarah in front of my door, waiting for me. I knew it.

"You hate to be late, yet the day I decide to surprise you, your class runs over," Sarah says with feigned indignation. She's cute with her hair back in a ponytail, the way I like it. "I was excited to see if your new enlightenment would magically cause your office to be more organized."

I unlock the door and let her in, hoping we'll experience a miracle and my office will be clean. We glance around and share grimaces. No miracle. Two stacks of papers in the far corner have gone unchanged since her last visit.

"Believe it or not, I'm planning on cleaning it up. I'm so glad you came," I say, giving her a kiss. "This must be the first time you've been here in years. To what do I owe this honor?"

"Nothing in particular. It's a beautiful fall day. Some of the leaves are turning. Let's take a walk."

We stroll around our compact college town for an hour, trying not to walk on the same street twice, catching up with each other and talking about the kids. We walk past Goodness and stop in to say hello. I haven't been there in months.

Back on our stroll, she asks, "What did you discuss in class today?"

"The three stages of enlightenment."

"Sounds like an appropriate topic, given your situation. Have your students or colleagues said anything about your new frame of mind?"

"No, I'm trying to keep it a secret," I say, head lowered, with an exaggerated, hushed voice, while glancing furtively side to side.

She stops, steps back, and looks at all of me with faraway eyes. "Maybe only I can see it because I know you so intimately, but you definitely have a glow of calmness. It's faint but real. I can feel it even when I'm not looking at you. You are at peace. Nothing is pushing you now. Is it as good as we have been led to believe?"

I place my arm around her shoulders and whisper in her ear, "It's better than I thought. As each day goes by, it's less overwhelming, so I can appreciate it more. I pray you will join me here soon."

She kisses my cheek softly like she's done thousands of times and then rubs her cheek against mine. She whispers in my ear, "Abraham, I've been trying to find the right time to tell you—I guess this seems good."

She takes hold of my hands with a firm grip, a serious look on her face. "I'm not sure how to say this, so I'll just say it. I reached Cosmic Consciousness about a month ago. I'm so thrilled you finally caught up to me." She gives my hands a tighter squeeze.

I watch my body tense into a competitive mode and my previously placid mind snaps to attention, ready to meet the challenge. *She's not enlightened. Relax!*, my intellect tells them both. *Can't you guys take a joke?* They immediately settle down.

She drops my hands, and her fingers go up, right foot moving behind left in a dainty curtsy. "Just kidding!" she says, sweeping her hands behind her with a bow, a broad, triumphant, smile crossing her face. Her heel returns to the leaf-covered ground, parallel to its mate.

"Abe," she says, beginning to flush, "I'm not holding it together. My attacks are getting worse. I have one, or fight one off, a few times each day now. I carry Xanax with me wherever I go. I needed one before I left the house today. I'm running out. I'll need more soon. You must be getting sick of having to take care of me. I'm tired of all this, my weird thoughts, my damn anxieties. You must be exhausted by them. I'm having obsessive thoughts again, about you leaving me and other things. I think I need stronger meds like my mother used to take. I keep thinking you're having an affair. I know you're not, but I keep thinking you are. And you're always cleaning our house and picking up after me. Stop it! I can't take it! I'm not your child. I'm your wife, your partner. Why are you feeling so guilty?"

She breathes deeply, hyperventilating. I try to wrap my arms around her, but she pushes me away. She sits on the ground, her head heavy. Her back heaves up and down, each breath a fight. I stand by her as the minutes tick by, unable to help. The sun comes out from behind a cloud, warming my back. The brightly colored leaves on their branches shimmy to a song the breeze is singing. There must be a way to ease her pain.

After another Xanax and a rollercoaster lunch, Sarah leaves me in front of Pearsons Hall and walks home. I return to my office and knock down tasks like I'm at a shooting arcade. My aim is flawless. *Bang!*—I review the six resumes for the new chief of campus security position, decide on the best candidate, summarize my thoughts in an email to the other committee members. *Bang!*—I send out my counterproposal to the academic dean's email to the members of the five-college joint steering committee outlining a different realignment of all philosophy classes at the Claremont Colleges under a unified theme, while still preserving a good reason for Pomona to continue offering my Self-guided course. *Bang!*—I revise my lecture for the intro class next week to account for changes my co-instructor and I have agreed on.

As I'm working, I get an odd sensation in my abdomen and a feeling that I'm about to continue my lecture from this morning's Self class. It's almost 2:30—time for my office hours. A few minutes later, Margaret, Ravi, and Chris arrive together.

I look up at the three of them standing in my doorway. "What a pleasant surprise. I'd invite you all in, but the laws of classical physics preclude that. What's on your collective mind?"

Margaret immediately takes charge. "We had a few more questions that didn't get answered today and were wondering if you had time to discuss them."

"Sounds like fun. Shall we go down to a classroom? I know one that's empty."

"Yes. A different classroom," Margaret says.

The three start walking. I grab a folder of articles from a pile opposite my desk and catch up with Margaret.

Walking down the stairs, I say to her, "You said you were born in Pomona. Are your parents still living here?"

"My whole big Catholic family is a few miles from the college. We were all raised looking up to Pomona College. My parents still can't believe I got enough of a scholarship so we could afford tuition."

"Does your Catholic upbringing create any issues with what we're discussing in class?"

"No, not at all. Growing up my mother would read us children's books about the saints. She's *very* Catholic. Even as a teenager, I read tales of the saints from books my mom would buy me. Your class makes those tales come alive." She looks down at the steps with a shy smile.

"I've read many of those tales. They *are* beautiful, and inspiring."

We arrive at the empty classroom. Ravi seats himself to Margaret's left. Chris sits on the other side of the table to my right.

Margaret looks at her classmates and asks, "If you Google 'Devata,' it doesn't talk about perception. It just says that the Devatas are Hindu deities. You never told us that. Why not? What do deities have to do with the process of perception?"

"There's more to that question than meets the eye. Another way of thinking about Rishi, Devata, and Chhandas is to think of them as a simple sentence: subject, verb, and object. The verb, Devata, describes and governs how the subject, Rishi, interacts with the object, Chhandas. Devata *are* Hindu deities when viewed from one perspective, but from another perspective they are like verbs. Devata govern and preside over the innumerable laws of nature that determine how Rishi interacts with and experiences Chhandas."

"OK, I see, but I still think you should've mentioned that Devata are commonly thought of as Hindu gods, so we wouldn't get surprised later," she says.

"Fair enough," I say. Ravi stares at her as she looks at me. Her solid strength, even disposition, and motherly sweetness attract him. I glance at Chris. He's noticed Ravi's stare.

Margaret ignores them both. "Another question I have is that I have been doing Buddhist mindfulness meditation with the meditation club here on campus since I was a freshman. I was instructed to sit with my back straight and watch my breath and my thoughts. I was told to take a passive attitude toward my breath and thoughts and try to be in the moment. During my meditations, I have felt some relaxation and a few moments of calmness, but in general I find the process difficult and tedious. It's nothing like the glowing, blissful descriptions you talk about."

"The various forms of Buddhist meditation," I reply, "as currently practiced, can be effective given sufficient time and effort, but Maharishi wrote that all are fundamentally flawed. Here, I'll read you what Maharishi has to say about the Buddha's teachings." I pick up my Gita, knowing exactly where the bookmarked quote is, and read.

> "'[Lord Buddha] advocated meditation in order to purify the field of thought through direct contact with Being...but because his followers failed to correlate these different fields of life...the whole structure of Lord Buddha's teaching not only became distorted but was also turned upside down. The effect was mistaken for the cause.'[27]

"There's a professor at MIU, Evan Finkelstein, who has written and spoken about how mindfulness meditation, as it

[27] Maharishi Mahesh Yogi, *Maharishi Mahesh Yogi on the Bhagavad-Gita: A New Translation and Commentary, Chapters 1–6* (London: Arkana, 1990), 4.

is practiced today, is most likely a misinterpretation of, and straying from, original Buddhist meditation because it encourages practitioners to keep their attention on their breath, or other aspects of the body, instead of encouraging total transcendence to the state of pure consciousness, which corresponds with the Buddhist state of nirvana. He says that over time, the Buddha's instructions concerning correct meditation and his descriptions of the effect of correct meditation were reversed. The *effect* of proper meditation—settled breathing and few thoughts—was mistaken for the *cause*, or method, of proper meditation.

"Dr. Finkelstein writes that the Buddha originally taught his disciples mantra meditation, with the addition of a few other types of meditations as they progressed. I think I can find a passage from Buddhist scripture to that effect." I open the folder I brought downstairs. An article written by Dr. Finkelstein is in it. I read.

"'There's no need for you to give up,' said the Buddha. 'You should not abandon your search for liberation just because you seem to yourself to be thick-witted. You can drop all philosophy you've been given and repeat a mantra instead—one that I will now give you.'[28]

"Professor Finkelstein believes that the original disciples of the Buddha attained enlightenment fairly quickly and easily, probably because they were utilizing the mantras the Buddha had taught them in an effective manner. History shows that

[28] Majjhima Nikaya, qtd. in Evan Finkelstein, "The Buddha's Meditation," *Elephant Journal*, July 1, 2011.

as we got farther away from the time of Buddha, fewer of his disciples reported attaining enlightenment.

"You look like you might have a follow-up question?" I ask.

Margaret grits her teeth and asks, "If God is good, kind, and merciful, and Vedic philosophy is the Truth, and all other religions and philosophies are incorrect, then why did such a God allow the vast majority of humanity to be deceived?"

"That's a difficult and important question. According to Vedic philosophy, pure consciousness wants to know itself in all the infinite permutations, combinations, exaltations, and tribulations possible. The world's major religions are not untrue. Each major religion is a branch of the tree that grew from the seed of pure knowledge. The tree takes its sustenance from the soil that is our collective Self. The fruit from each of those branches is different, but each is sweet and each belongs to us all, equally.

"My religion, Judaism, was grounded in the truth that there is one God who created the universe and who has set certain laws that govern human behavior. I believe the Ten Commandments given to Moses were exactly what the world needed at the time. Judaism is concerned with doing good deeds and putting work, rest, and worship in perspective. Instituting the Sabbath as a day of rest and worship every week was a novel and brilliant way, at that time, to add meaning and spirituality to Jewish life. Personally, as a Jew who believes there is much truth to be found in Vedic philosophy and meditation, I don't feel deceived in recognizing that my Judaism is not the whole truth. Judaism is a great, enriching way of life for me. There's no conflict, in my mind, for a Jewish person to continue to be observant of Jewish laws and religious practices while also practicing meditation as a simple mental technique to improve his health and augment the spiritual practices of his religion. I don't think Vedic philosophy is the whole truth either. The whole truth is the whole tree. It's a fruit salad harvested from all the branches. Does that make sense?"

Margaret looks at me, inspired by my sermon. "I like that a lot. No religion is wrong. Each is a piece of a bigger puzzle. It is our ego and self-righteousness that get in the way of putting the puzzle together."

"I like your puzzle more than my fruit salad," I reply. "Ravi, Chris, do either of you have any questions?"

Ravi and Chris look at each other, then shake their heads.

"OK, if you don't have a question, then I have one. Do you have any suggestions as to how we can make our class better?"

Chris thinks for a moment, looking over my head, and then regards me cautiously. "I doubt you would do this, but I think it would be instructive if you told us some of your personal experiences. You know, add some spice to the philosophy. Just a thought." He turns to Ravi and Margaret, pleased with his directness.

I should have expected that. I have assumed that some in my class have noticed at least something about my transformation. And I'm sure they all talk among themselves. He is right about adding some spice. More descriptions of experiences of higher states of consciousness would add depth to the knowledge, but this class can't be about me. "Thank you for the suggestion, Chris. Maybe I'll start reading you short tales of the enlightened from different cultures. I have a few fun ones in mind. Anything else?" I look at each of them. Realizing we're done, we all start to stand.

Ravi raises an eyebrow at Chris, who suddenly remembers.

"Oh, ah, one more thing, Professor," Chris says.

"Yes," I say, standing with my stack in hand.

"Are we allowed to help each other with our papers?"

"What do you mean?"

"As long as each of us writes our own paper, can our class-mates help, ah, you know, edit them or things like that?"

"Everyone needs to write their paper themselves. Helping each other with editing and revising is OK, but you can't cross the line where it's no longer your paper," I say, looking at Chris, then Ravi, then Margaret. Ravi lowers his eyes. Margaret has a blank look on her face, which makes me especially suspicious.

"Good," Chris says. "It's OK to help each other. I'll be helping Tom."

"Helping Tom?" I ask. "Is he paying you to help him?"

"In a way," Chris answers.

"Chris, we should go," Margaret says, pointing her chin toward the door. "We've already taken up enough of Professor's time."

Margaret leads the way. The other two follow her out the door.

"From wonder into wonder existence opens."

Lao Tzu

Chapter Five

Sarah and I sit in bed doing our night techniques. *Darn, I forgot to turn my phone off—it could start to buzz and disturb us.* It's plugged in on the table at the other side of the bedroom. I should wait to finish my technique, rest, and then turn it off, but I might fall asleep. Up I go, as quietly as possible. Halfway to the phone, something's wrong. I look back at Sarah, and I'm still sitting next to her. *OK, stay calm*—it appears I'm having an out-of-body experience. I look over at the phone. *I won't be able to turn it off without physical hands, will I? It is kind of cool, though. Should I walk around and explore the possibilities? No, not going there!* We've been warned not to go down that path.

Flash! I'm back in bed, in my body, behind my usual eyes, bewildered and amazed that I can go from there to here in an instant. The philosopher in me is more intrigued by the instantaneous movement of my awareness than the out-of-body experience. Were my two bodies somehow quantumly entangled?

I remember seeing a tape of Maharishi many years ago. A pretty young woman went up to the microphone and told Maharishi she'd had an out-of-body experience, wondering if it was a good thing. Maharishi was uncharacteristically stern in his reply. He said that our bodies are extremely precious. We should not encourage out-of-body experiences because being out of the body is equivalent to leaving something very valuable unattended. Being outside of the body puts it at risk.

As I resume my night meditation technique, my physical body starts to feel sleepy, but I also sense that the other ethereal body is still separate. It's energized and itching to go elsewhere. Curious, I shift my attention to the other body and observe as I move my right hand. Sure enough, I see two of them; one that hasn't moved at all and a shimmering one that I'm clenching and unclenching. *Oh, my.* My ethereal body is loose. I bring the shimmering hand back to where it was, attempting to superimpose it on its mate and hold still.

Abe's physical body wants to lie down. Fine, both bodies will lie down together. We do so without too much slippage. Sarah joins us a minute or two later.

I need to figure out how to put myself back together. Part of the problem is that my ethereal body is agitated and hyper. I'll have to calm it down. I could meditate, but my physical body and its associated mind are almost asleep. The ethereal body that I'm in now is vibrating so fast I'm sure I couldn't begin to meditate in it. All I can think to do is lie still and try to keep my ethereal body within the boundaries of my physical body. I've never heard of, or read about, someone becoming permanently split.

While Abe's corporeal body and mind sleep deeply over the next hour, my ethereal body and its associated mind has insomnia. I sit up and observe my physical body. Looking down at it, I'm struck by how dear it is to me. It feels like a reflection of who I have been and what I have done during my last few lives. My face has a sweet, kind, easy smile and soft, inviting cheeks because I have been sweet, kind, and inviting for a long, long time. My body is relatively short, which for many years was a source of disappointment to me, especially during adolescence and when I was dating. It comes to me that in my case, my lack of physical stature is retribution for my outsized ego during too many of my more recent incarnations.

Concerned about being outside of my physical body too long, I lie down again. Lying in bed, trying to keep both bodies together, I stare at the ceiling even though my ethereal eyelids are closed. Minute after minute goes by. My ethereal body refuses to be lulled. The ceiling becomes hazy, then dissolves. I see the full moon above as if I were in an open field. I find myself attracted to the moon's beauty and allure. My interest seems to stir her. She smiles maternally, amused at my predicament. Entranced by her gaze, I relax. Feeling sleepy, I notice a milky-white, honey-like fluid coalescing in the air of my bedroom. How strange. Intuition tells me it's soma, the favored drink of the Gods, an expression of the moon's love.

The soma flows down to my sleeping corporeal body and my ethereal body. My physical body sighs as soma melts into it. My ethereal body wants to latch on before it's let down. I can feel the soma soothing and purifying both bodies.

Things get hazy as my ethereal body becomes intoxicated with the moon's ministering. I hear it whisper, "So, *so* nice; hope it happens every night." Drunk from the moon's milk, I watch as both bodies slowly dissolve into the other. They sleep as one in the embrace of lovers' dreams.

It's very early and dark Tuesday morning, but I'm ready to get up. Was the soma just a vivid, enlightened dream? My body feels different—better now than ever. It feels as if it's been cleansed inside and out. And the two separate bodies seems like a distant memory, one that I now barely believe. I'll try not to analyze the experience too much. I don't want its aftereffects to fade under that hot light.

I visit the kids' bathroom and tiptoe back to bed, wanting a long meditation before class but not wanting to go to Amos's room. Sarah will probably wake up during my meditation and rub my leg. She knows she shouldn't disturb me, but I hope she does. I adjust the pillows, do my pranayama breathing, and then begin. I don't feel like doing asanas this morning. It's too early.

*Mantra, mantraaaa, maaaantraaa, maaaa…*I am everywhere and nowhere. There is profound, deep silence and a hum of activity deeper in the silence, as if something is bursting to get out. My intellect now accepts contradictory, paradoxical experiences, yawning instead of perking up as it did in the past. The silence deepens, giving way. I am watching the majestic, stern sun hold on to his children, the planets, with an iron grip, swinging them around with perfect precision. The sun is the planets' guru and father. They revolve around him, held by their love and respect. Each planet has its own unique consciousness and personality. They are not just inert, floating orbs.

I want more. I expand out. As I journey past the limits of our solar system, the depth of the silence deepens dramatically. Inside our solar system there had been a buzz and liveliness; outside, I am almost painfully deaf.

Soon I see that our solar system is just a small part of a much larger, spinning galaxy of stars. It's insignificant and far away, yet I know I'm connected to the distant Earth by some thread of affection that will help me find my way back. Now there are many galaxies, and the Milky Way is like one star in a sky filled with stars. Nothing has ever happened. I have always been this big, this unchanging. I feel some fear mixed with the sublime. If I continue to expand, I would leave this universe and begin to experience other universes and dimensions. There's much more than just this one, but an experience of the Totality would be too much for me now. I know that I am Brahman, the Totality, but I am not ready to Know It. I am not that strong yet.

I lie down to rest. Minutes later, Sarah wakes my body as she kisses my left shoulder. "Can you meditate some more?" She purrs and stretches. "That way I won't have to. I felt like I was meditating lying down, even though I was half asleep. I was feeling good, but then you stopped. Do it again."

"Have you felt anything like that in the past?"

"Not much; maybe a little. Today, though, your meditation drew me in and then sent me out somewhere. I *love it* when you overpower me." Sarah reaches over with her left hand, turning onto her side, and begins to play with the gray hair on my chest, which tickles. I flinch.

"Sorry, I couldn't resist." She stops. "We have time for a jog before you escape to your favorite class. We both could use it. Let's go. I'll meditate when you leave. We can jog up the hill so we can see the sunrise together."

She always gets me going. I tend to be a stick-in-the-mud, focused on my intellectual pursuits, meditation, and family. She likes getting out, doing things, socializing, having fun, and teasing me. Balance and perspective are important. We dress for a jog. She's so much fun when her mood is good.

Jogging uphill, I have a hard time keeping up. She runs ahead, then circles back, jogging with me for a while, then off again. I seem to be more out of shape today? I haven't been jogging as much as I used to. I stop, head lowered, panting for breath. She jogs back, a jaunty smirk on her lips.

"I thought enlightenment was supposed to improve everything? What happened to you?"

"Go on," I say between gasps. "I'm getting too old for this." I start walking home.

She catches up to me. "Abe, we don't have to jog. We can walk up to the vantage point together. Even if we walk, we'll still get there in time."

"I'm going home. Finish your jog."

"You're not mad? I'll come home with you."

"Go on, I'm OK. You can tell me about it," I say, still panting.

"Are you sure? I'd love to see the sunrise. It makes me feel optimistic."

She looks toward our house, turns, and runs toward the sun. I go home, fuming—mad at myself for becoming mad for no good reason. Enlightened people shouldn't be so petty.

I walk to my office, looking forward to my Self class. The last few days have been hard for Sarah. She needs me near, constantly. Not as bad as it was years ago, but the storm isn't blowing over as it usually does.

Despite thinking about Sarah's issues, today's walk is especially sweet. Today it's a stroll down memory lane. I'm feeling as connected to my student days here as I am to the present. I have watched these trees get bigger and fuller. I have watched that gardener get grayer, wider, and less sure-footed. I have watched each season blend into the next in a faster and faster turning of the wheel. And today is my best walk ever, a magical mystery tour dying to take me away. I stay on course, careful not to get sidetracked by each bug or flower that pulls at my attention with its captivating beauty.

Just as I am about to ascend the steps at Pearsons Hall, a weird, prickly feeling unfolds in the pit of my stomach. As it fades, I'm left with a sense—a gut feeling—that someone is waiting for me in front of my office, somewhat distressed. It's someone I know, but I can't quite place the name or face.

When I get up to my office, a less-pimpled Chris is there, though my office hours aren't until this afternoon. He must be taking a medication for his skin. It has gotten progressively better over the last week or so.

"Hi Chris," I say cheerily. "How can I help you? Would you like to come in?"

"Thanks, Professor. Do you have some time to talk?"

I look at my phone—more than twenty minutes until class starts. "Sure, what's on your mind?" I unlock the door, hold it open, and wave him in. Chris steps in and looks around, but every surface is papered over with folders, articles, and drafts. I've been so focused on getting home early to Sarah that I haven't found the time yet to clean. I pick up a folder of resumes from the chair next to my desk and gesture for Chris to sit.

"Professor, I don't think you know, but after I took your Intro to Philosophy course as a freshman I learned your meditation. It's been good." He tries to sound upbeat, but his slumped shoulders reveal a sadness he's tried hard to hide. I settle back in my chair, letting him know I'm listening.

"Overall, my anxiety and stress are better since I've been meditating, but my lifelong struggle with depression is getting worse. It runs in my family. My mom and older brother are both on antidepressants. My doctor has tried me on a bunch of drugs over the last few years. They help, but then I feel insulated from the world, like the Michelin tire man." He puffs out his cheeks and raises his elbows, letting out a nervous laugh. Despite his thin frame, I imagine him white and round.

"I hope this isn't out of line, but do you have any suggestions? I don't want to take any more numbing drugs, but I'll have to if that's all I can do."

I can feel his despair. I then feel that thing stir in the pit of my stomach. It wants to reach out and envelop Chris, to sop up his anxiety and sadness. Without his consent, it's not right. I try to hold it back, not knowing how. Nothing happens.

"I'm glad you feel comfortable enough with me to share this. There's an old Ayurvedic technique that might help. It's not talked about much, but it's not any kind of secret. I'll tell you a quick story." I look over at him. He's ready for a story.

"My youngest daughter, from the moment she was born, was never a good sleeper. By the time she was seven, we had discussed this with her pediatrician numerous times. The pediatrician had her try a few mild sleep aids. When they didn't help, he referred her to a child psychiatrist who gave her stronger drugs, which messed her up. Nothing worked. In the middle of most nights she would wake me up and tell me she couldn't sleep. I'd take her back to bed and kiss her forehead till she fell asleep, but she would come back an hour or two later."

I'm relaxing him, but not in any mystical way. He wants time with me and wants to know that I'm willing to give him my attention.

"Back then, I heard about a new TM treatment called Vedic Vibration Therapy. It's actually an ancient technique, but Maharishi revived and standardized it, so it could be useful and verifiable in Western cultures. At the time, Indian couples toured the country with the treatment, going to most of the TM centers in every state. We took my daughter for a treatment when she was eight. After the first of three sessions, she walked out, crawled into my lap, and whispered in my ear, "I can sleep now, Daddy."

"That night, she didn't wake up for the first time in weeks. In the morning, my wife and I asked her how she slept, and she told us, 'I'm all better. The Indian lady cured me.' She's still not a great sleeper, but she's been much better ever since her treatments."

"Whoa, that's interesting," Chris says, clearly intrigued. He sits up, shoulders straight. "I think I'll call the center where I learned to meditate and ask them about it. Never heard about it before—thanks. I'll even tell Tom about it."

I extend my right hand. He shakes it heartily and stands. "I knew you'd be able to help me," he says.

"Chris, I'm curious about you wanting to help Tom. Is there something else I should know?"

"I don't think so. No. Everything's cool. Tom's failing one of his other classes. We don't want him to fail."

"Who is 'we'?"

My directness catches Chris off guard. "You know, his friends, our senior class."

He fumbles with the doorknob and waves over his shoulder as he leaves.

I answer some emails, and it's time to write today's lecture title on the blackboard. I walk down to my classroom. I've been concerned that the frequent cosmic flashes and space outs that have been happening might become noticeable to my students and impair my teaching. It seems to me that over the next few weeks this will all settle down. Until it does, I've come up with a strategy. If something starts to look or sound too beautiful, or strikes me as heavenly, I will consciously focus my attention on something sad. The best I've come up with so far is the image of my father, may he rest in peace, sobbing as he was shoveling dirt onto his mother's grave. It hurts to think about it, but it has been effective the few times I've tried it.

I write on the chalkboard:

Consciousness and Physics

Walking back up to my office, I think about my little one, my Rachel. According to Sarah, she's been worried about a midterm exam she took yesterday. She never talks to me for long, but I always feel better afterward. I manage to reach her.

"Hi, Daddy."

"Hello, my honey. How are you?"

"Things are going wonderfully. I think I've finally figured out how to study for my exams. Instead of *me* trying to decide what's most important, I'm figuring out what the professor thinks is most important and spending my time studying that. I took a midterm yesterday and just got my score a few minutes ago. I got one of the highest grades in the class. First time that's happened," she says, slightly out of breath. "I gotta go. I'm on my way to meet some friends. How are you and Mom?"

"Thank God. We're well. Have fun with your friends."

She sounds so strong.

Rachel meditates a few times a week—too busy to do more, she says, because of the intense nurse practitioner training course she's enrolled in at NYU. She lives not far from her sister. Once a month or so, they have Shabbat dinner together. Her long-term boyfriend is very nice, treats her beautifully, and is officially Jewish—his mother is Jewish, but not his father.

I look at my phone in my hand. I find the contact for the Claremont TM center and call. A gentleman answers. It turns out the Vedic Vibration couple will be doing treatments at the Orange County center in three weeks. That's a fifty-minute drive from us—doable. I go online and apply for Sarah. She's done it twice before. Each time it helped, but the effect only lasted a few months. Something is better than nothing.

It's time for class. I bounce to my feet and grab my stack, which I had gathered up when I first got to my office. I descend the stairs two at a time.

I walk into class a minute or two late, ebullient. *Watch yourself, Abe.* Standing in front of my desk, I begin.

"To recap our previous lectures, we first discussed that one's awareness during meditation could effectively be turned around from its fixed, outward-looking perspective by using a mantra as a metaphorical mirror. The awareness could, by experiencing finer states of a mantra, follow the mantra back to its origin, which is the thinker of the mantra, the I, or the Rishi, and then go beyond that and transcend the world of activity and diversity and directly experience one's own consciousness, or one's Self. We discussed that our Self is pure consciousness and that Vedic philosophy believes that pure consciousness pervades and comprises everything in our universe. There's only one thing in our universe: pure consciousness.

"It might seem odd that the Vedic gurus thousands of years ago taught such a counterintuitive philosophy. Yet this ancient Vedic philosophy bears striking similarities to that which has emerged from modern physics—similarities that were not lost on the early pioneers in the field. As old ideas and theories about reality and the universe crumbled in the early 1920s and '30s and a new understanding of quantum mechanics and physics emerged, a number of the physicists at the forefront of this revolution began writing books and essays that can be described as mystically inclined.

"One quote that, in my mind, epitomizes this new understanding is from Erwin Schrödinger, who was a pioneer of quantum mechanics and won the 1933 Nobel Prize in Physics. In his 1944 book, *What is Life? and Mind and Matter,* he wrote,

"'Subject and object are only one. The barrier between them cannot be said to have broken down as a result of recent experience in the physical sciences, for this barrier does not exist.'[29]

"At the time Schrödinger published his book, many physicists were in a state of disbelief because theoretical physics, based on experimental evidence, was moving toward the unacceptable conclusion that subject, object, and the process of perception were all made of the same stuff, not independent from one another. Here, Schrödinger basically says to his fellow theoretical physicist, 'get over it.' There *is* no real barrier or difference between subject and object.

"Another noted physicist, Max Planck, winner of the 1918 Nobel Prize in Physics, and considered by many to be the founder of quantum mechanics, also espoused what can be described as a mystical point of view as new experimental evidence and evolving quantum mechanical theory increasingly pointed in that direction. In 1931 he was quoted as saying, 'I regard consciousness as fundamental. I regard matter as derivative from consciousness.'[30]

Han raises his hand. I nod at him.

"Dr. Levy," Han says, "there is well-accepted idea in physics and mathematics, that more intuitive, elegant, and beautiful a theory, more likely it is true. Is that because God designed it that way?"

"I think so," I say. "And I think Vedic philosophy would agree. According to Vedic philosophy, the closer we get to the

[29] Erwin Schrödinger, *What is Life? and Mind and Matter*, (London: Cambridge University Press, 1969), 137.

[30] Planck, qtd. in *The Observer*, Interviews With Great Scientists. VI. - Max Planck, January 25, 1931, p.17.

Truth, the closer we are to God. When we discover a Truth, it resonates at our core, letting us know we are on the right path. Thank you for pointing that out." This class, my students, repeated year after year, are like a mantra, a mirror, helping me to see and know my Self. Dear God, thank you for allowing me to teach your children.

"Moving on," I say, "physicists, neuroscientists, neurologists, psychologists, and academics in other fields have struggled to develop a theory that explains how our physical brains can generate something so unique, and by definition, alive, as consciousness. According to Vedic philosophy, any academic search to explain how consciousness is generated must be fruitless because our brains do not create consciousness; consciousness is primary, or 'fundamental' as Max Planck put it back in 1931. It existed before there were any brains, and it can exist without a brain.

Obinna raises his hand, and I call on him, but I'm being pulled away by the expansion that has been tugging at me since this morning's meditation. The cosmos beckons. It would be the easiest thing to give in, but I'm concerned that doing so will interfere with my lecture. I try thinking about my father with the shovel, but it only fills me with overwhelming love and respect for him and the most tender of feelings for his strong, altruistic mother. With nothing to constrain me, I am taken away.

I expand out. Space and time are not barriers. They have no grip on me. I am, and I am witnessing, the universe. From the outside, I watch in utter, rapturous awe the glittering, vividly colored, spinning galaxies infinitely more glorious than any puny fireworks on the Fourth of July. From the inside, I reveal to my audience how grand I am.

I answer another student's question and move on with my lecture. I have no problem lecturing and being lectured to by the cosmos at the same time. There, I am engaged with my students, watching them, their faces, and their movements. I tailor my actions and words trying to foster a milieu conducive to learning, always looking for a crack into which to inject some humor. I am there, and *I am Here*.

Here, time reverses. I observe as the universe contracts, going backwards in time. Everything comes together. All collapses into a single, pure pinpoint of light. The light goes out. I am alone. From an empty, timeless desire, the soundless Word, Is. The sound of the Word begins—Om. Om is the pinpoint of light. Om explodes. Time moves forward again. I bow in reverence to the Supreme Teacher's perfect lesson.

Back "there," as I observe, everything proceeds as usual. I get to the part of my lecture that holds a special interest for me, given my current state. I'm about to discuss the Meissner effect, which is a phenomenon of physics that helps explain why being enlightened is more than an experience—it physically changes how that person interacts with his or her surroundings.

"Under normal conditions an ordinary conductor of electricity, such as a piece of metal, contains incoherent, disordered electrons that allow penetration by an external magnetic field. When that same piece of metal is cooled to a very low temperature, it suddenly takes on a whole different set of properties called superconductivity."

I draw two rectangles on the chalkboard, one disorderly and one with orderly electrons. I describe how becoming a superconductor is similar to calming the mind during meditation to the point that it suddenly undergoes a phase transition and merges with pure consciousness. Pure consciousness is a perfectly orderly state. I compare its properties to that of a superconductor. I like this part of the lecture. I look serious but serene.

"When a conducting piece of metal is cooled enough for it to transition to a superconductor, then outside magnetic fields no longer affect it. This is called the Meissner effect. In a similar way, enlightenment, according to Vedic philosophy, creates a physical barrier to negative outside influences." I see and hear myself drawing rapidly on the chalkboard. As I write facing the chalkboard, Tom attempts to pass a note to Chris who does not want to take it, but Tom scowls at him until he does. I can sense that Chris likes Tom but is afraid of his volatility.

I continue to explain how the Meissner effect applies to physical and environmental changes that occur as a result of enlightenment. I discuss the body of research on large groups meditating together and how this is also analogous to the Meissner effect. As soon as I am satiated from my cosmic extravaganza, my focus changes. I'm back in my classroom, in my corporeal, bounded body, standing in front of my desk. But I'm content to be there. The silent witness, watching two screens of consciousness at the same time, is now attending more to the "Abe in the classroom" screen than the "cosmic extravaganza" screen. I have not lost my cosmic perspective.

The class seems fatigued by all my science talk. We need a diversion before we move on. What I have in mind usually wakes everyone up.

"Everyone, please stand," I say in a firm voice and walk over to the window. They look at me, wondering what I'm up to. Most of the students scramble to their feet. "Tom, Asher, Margaret, I want everyone up." They get up reluctantly.

"OK," I say. "We are going to change our perspectives. I'm hoping that with a new perspective, the rest of the lecture will seem fresh. I want each of you to change seats. Move to a seat you feel would give you a new perspective. Trust your feelings—don't think about it. There is no wrong choice. If someone gets there first, sit in another seat. Ready, set...go!"

Some eyes get wide, some heads shake side to side, then a few start to move, followed by the rest. Tanisha moves up front into Margaret's seat, whispering to Margaret who is still deciding, "I've always liked your perspective on things." Chris walks on his toes to the back row and murmurs, "I like musical chairs." He sits in a chair no one was sitting in. Tom walks forward decisively and plops himself down into my seat behind the desk. That happens every few years. Taking his cue, I sit in his empty seat in the second row. Everyone sits quietly. I resume my lecture from Tom's seat.

I take in a deep breath, and with that breath say, "Now that everyone has a new perspective—and we all completely understand the intricacies of Rishi, Devata, and Chhandas, and their relationship to consciousness and the Meissner effect and its correlation with individual and collective consciousness—what about time?" I inhale in an exaggerated manner and let it out similarly. "Do we have the time to discuss time?"

I take my phone out of my pocket and look at it. "Ah, yes. I see we do have time, but time is of the essence. But more importantly, *what is the essence of time?*" Didn't smile—I played it well. I see a few half-grins around the room. I'll take that. I walk to the window, creating a triangle with Tom and the class.

"Space and time, based on our everyday experiences, seem like separate, unrelated concepts. Physicists say, however, that our everyday experiences are misleading with regard to space and time. They say that space and time, which seem very different, are actually part of the same, inseparable thing called space-time.

"This unification of seemingly disparate things and concepts follows a long history of unification in physics, envisioned as ultimately leading up to what is the Holy Grail of physics, the theory of everything, which Einstein sought unsuccessfully during his last years. This elusive theory has been crystallizing slowly in the minds of current theoretical physicists, and most feel confident it will eventually be spelled out. One of the current frontrunners for the theory of everything is superstring theory.

"If and when the theory of everything is discovered, it will unite all other theories of physics into one. The theory of everything will explain the illusionary boundaries between objects, time, space, and all the forces in our universe. In case you have not noticed by now, the dissolution of boundaries as we move forward individually and collectively on our evolutionary paths is and will be a major theme of this class just as it has been in the history of theoretical physics.

"According to physics, time is an inextricable part of space-time. Einstein theorized, and physics proved, that space-time can be curved or warped by gravity. Depending on your perspective and relative motion, space-time can become longer or shorter, time within it can speed up or slow down, or time can stop altogether. Time and space are not absolutes. They are malleable, changeable, and relative.

"Within the unified field or ground state, from which physics says all matter springs, physicists say there is no time. Sound familiar? The Vedas and Upanishads state that within pure consciousness, from which they say all matter springs, there is no time. Vedic philosophers hold that time is experienced as a function of our Devata, our physical brains and the software our brains run.

"We have time for a few questions and hopefully, we will have time for my time-consuming answers. Anyone want to score some points with a question?"

Han raises his hand.

"Professor, if passage of time is created and generated by brains, does time stop existing if brain stops functioning? Also, how are we able to agree we experience time in similar fashion when brains function differently?"

"Ding-ding-ding!—I can hear the grade points ringing up," I say with a flourish, but no one laughs. "It's a difficult question, and the answer can be hard to understand because our minds are firmly embedded within space-time.

I grab my tattered copy of *How to Know God* and hold it up for the class to see. "This is one of the two translations of Patanjali's Yoga sutras that you should finish reading before our next lecture. *Patanjali's Yoga Sutras* was written at least 1,700 years ago and is one of the definitive texts on yoga and Vedic philosophy." I leaf through the book. "I think I can find quotes that address Han's questions.

"Ah, here's one. Patanjali writes, 'There is a form and expression we call "past," and the form and expression we call "future"; both exist within the object, at all times…' So Patanjali is saying that past and future exist independently of brains. An object's past and future exist within the object, simultaneously, like an infinite spool of old super 8 movie film. And then farther down, addressing the substance of Han's question, Patanjali says, 'The object cannot be said to be dependent on the perception of a single mind. For, if this were the case, the object could be said to be non-existent when that single mind was not perceiving it.'

"So, to head you all off at the pass, the next logical question is, can we know the past and the future? Incredibly, Patanjali says yes. Here, I'll find it for you." Again, I flip through the book, finding the right sutra. "OK, I got it, 'By making samyama on the three kinds of changes, one obtains knowledge of the past and the future.'

"Not to worry, samyama will be one of the subjects of our next lecture—or have I already given you that one? Or maybe that future lecture is already here with us now, in the present? I know I have the lecture notes in my files. Maybe if we could just adjust our processing of perception, or Devatas, then we could know the lecture before I give it, thereby saving some time. But can we save time like money in a bank? And if so, what is it exactly that we save? We have established that space-time can be warped so it can get longer or shorter. But what is it that gets longer and shorter? It's all so confusing." I put my palms on my temples and move my head and upper body from side to side as if I was a metronome, ticking each time I change direction. This time I do hear a few real laughs and unstifled giggles. The ice has cracked.

"Getting back to Han's question: How is it that we all agree we experience time similarly when our brains function differently? In general, we agree we experience time similarly because, on the whole, the similarities in how our brains function overwhelm the differences. We have time for a few more questions."

Chris motions subtly but effectively with his finger.

"Yes, Chris."

"Professor, you said our brains are just extremely complex computers that store our memories, but there are many stories and books of people who experience what they believe is an afterlife while their brains, from a medical standpoint, have flat-lined. These people say they retained their sense of identity and their memories during their afterlife experiences. How can that happen if the medical records showed no significant brain activity when they were experiencing what they felt was the afterlife?"

"This gets into a somewhat esoteric and vague area of Vedic philosophy that says one's memories and sense of identity, as developed in this life, are stored in the computer that is one's brain but are also 'backed up' on a metaphorical cloud server, and even downloaded and synchronized to a number of other metaphorical devices—one's phone, tablet, laptop, desktop, etc. for safe keeping. The Vedic literature describes one of these storage places as a subtle or ethereal body that is superimposed physically on our corporeal bodies, although it can and does exist independently from them. Vedic philosophy explains afterlife experiences, and out-of-body experiences, by pointing to this ethereal body as the source of continuity of identity and memory when the corporeal brain is not working. Our ethereal bodies do not need our physical brains; they have their own ethereal brains."

I stand in front of my desk, my backside to Tom, partly obscuring him from his classmates. He'll think I can't see him. I bet he'll begin clowning. Extra humor is always welcome. Right on cue, Tom makes a show of peeking into my desk's middle drawer, raising his eyebrows theatrically, pretending he's amazed then frightened by the contents. Tom can be pretty funny.

"We have time for another question or two. Anyone have any questions? Or even any answers?" I survey my class. It looks like they sense that if no one asks another question, I might let them out early. Perfect. I can almost hear some of them thinking, *No questions. No questions!* I cross my arms over my chest and pout, like I'm willing to wait them out.

"OK, I'm getting desperate here, so help me out. Ask me anything that will kill some time," I say, still pouting, arms still crossed. "Come on, you can ask me…what is the meaning of life or does life have meaning—or, better yet, what is the meaning of meaning? I have an ulterior motive for not wanting to let you out early."

I survey my students again. Most of them look out the window or at the floor, carefully avoiding my gaze. They're onto the joke. I re-cross my arms the opposite way, which is visibly awkward, and then cross my feet in third position, bending my knees in a poor plié, which I learned in a dance class I dropped in college. I took the class thinking I'd meet girls. The ballet move gets most of them to look at me and even produces a few smiles. A moment or two later, I uncross my legs and look over at my phone on my desk. "My lecture on physics and space-time seems to have shrunk. It usually lasts longer than this. At this rate, without any time-lengthening questions, I won't be able to deliver my favorite line from this lecture, which is only appropriate for today's material—and only when we are running late, which is the norm. Still no questions? OK, I'll deliver the line anyway. Please attempt to shift your Devatas forward in time so we're running late."

I pick up my phone in an exaggerated fashion and say, "Oh my gosh! We have run out of time, which seems odd because *we have nothing but time.* Please ponder 'we have nothing but time' from a Vedic perspective for our next class. I will ask someone to provide us with the results of his or her ponder for extra credit. Class disss-misss-ed! See you on Thursday. Please read the two translations of *Patanjali's Yoga Sutras* assigned in your syllabus prior to the class: one is *How to Know God* by Swami Prabhavananda, and the other is Dr. Egenes's *Maharishi Patanjali Yoga Sutras.* They are both short books."

The students pack up their books and such, happy to get out a few minutes early. They do seem more lighthearted after my gags and Tom's drawer peeking. I like that. Tom leaves. I return to my seat, finding it warm.

Tanisha, Obinna, Chris, and Ravi end up in the front row after everyone else filters out. Tanisha has Obinna on her right, Chris on her left, and Ravi to Chris's left. Tanisha moves her left four fingers off the desk into the air, signaling a question.

"Does Vedic philosophy say it's possible to travel to other dimensions?"

I answer, "I think Vedic philosophy would have no problem with such a concept."

"Growing up," Tanisha says hesitantly, "my father was into Eckankar. Do you know about Eckankar?"

"A little."

"He would tell me stories about how he could go into his ethereal body, then soul travel, as he called it, to other dimensions. What do you think about that?"

"Could be."

Obinna turns toward her. "Did you enjoy your father's stories?"

"I love my father and his wild stories," she says, looking into his large brown eyes. Time slows. I speak to prod it along.

"Any other thoughts or questions?"

I answer a few more questions, then Chris says, "Professor, did you hear the news today about Tom's father?"

"No," I say.

"I saw on my phone this morning that the artificial intelligence company he started was merging with its main rival, and Tom's father would become the CEO of the merged company. I asked Tom about it. He said his dad wouldn't agree to the merger without remaining in charge."

"I see. Good for Tom's father. I hope it ends up being good for Tom."

"Tom sure thinks it will," says Obinna, causing Tanisha to roll her eyes.

"Then good for Tom. Now the question is, will that also be good for Tom's friends?" I put each one under the spotlight going down the line, staring at them with large, unblinking eyes. Each cringes as I focus on them. Done, my faces cracks into a grin, letting them know I was kidding.

"I know Tom's up to something. I *bet* it's good," I say.

"You know Tom," Chris says. "He does have a flair for the dramatic."

After class, I eat an early lunch in my office. Sarah packs my lunchbox most workdays to save money, help me eat better, and let me know she cares. For many years Sarah and I were ovo-pescatarians; I wouldn't give up eggs or sushi despite knowing that the branch of Vedic philosophy concerned with a healthy diet, Ayurveda, does not recommend eating either. Two and a half years ago I began eating some chicken, and even, God forbid, beef under unusual circumstances. My family was surprised when I began including those meats sparingly in my diet. No pork products, though, the thought of which nauseates me. Since enlightenment, I have only had a taste for all things vegetarian. I ate sushi with Javier and Ann the other night but didn't enjoy it. I don't think I'll eat it again. I am less interested in eggs, but dairy products seem good and don't cause me the gas and stomach upset they used to.

Today I have a sandwich with avocado, Swiss cheese, alfalfa sprouts, pine nuts, cucumber, a few roasted sunflower seeds thrown in for texture, a touch of mayonnaise, and Dijon mustard on thick, fresh multigrain bread—delicious. A nice-sized piece of cherry cheesecake for dessert; I know my wife really loves me. My appetite has not decreased with enlightenment, but now I don't worry about running out of food.

Sarah texts: 'Not doing well. Picked up last xanax. When will you be home?' She's been meditating three to four times a day, trying to keep her attacks under control. I bet picking up her Rx was the only time she's been out of the house all day. We can't wait until her Vedic Vibe. She needs something sooner. I text: 'Honey, I'll be home soon.'

I search online for a psychiatrist, choose one, and call. He can see her next Thursday, nine days from now. The secretary agrees to call me if he has a cancellation.

That done, I turn my attention to grading papers. I have lots of them from my Intro to Philosophy class. I'll take them home and try to grade some of them there, but given Sarah's state, she may not let me. I better do some now. Even though it's early in the semester, I assigned a three-pager to help the students learn what I expect from the two major papers required later in the class.

I finish reading a poorly written and argued paper about Plato's Theory of Forms, which was the topic of my first lecture. The student attempted to say the idea of Forms was too silly to be taken seriously. Before enlightenment, I would have written some sarcastic remark about how a student taking his first philosophy class should take care before dismissing the ideas of a philosopher that has stood the test of time. Now, given my enlightened perspective, I write encouraging remarks about the few aspects of the paper that have some merit, correct as many of his grammatical errors and illogical arguments as space permits, but still give him the C- the paper deserves. After finishing twice as many papers as I planned, it's not even three o'clock. I'm going to beat my previous record at getting home early. Good—I need to check on Sarah. Optimistically, I put all the papers in my briefcase, which has recently begun to get a lot of use, and lock my office door.

"To the mind that is still, the whole universe surrenders."

Lao Tzu

Chapter Six

Thursday morning, lying in bed after meditation, I feel an itch spreading just below where my ribs meet my sternum but deeper inside. I have the strange sensation that something is beginning to open there. I look down. The skin is fine. No redness or rash and no obvious opening, but I still sense a new orifice about the size of a plum. With a form of sight I have never used before, I can see a lively, warm, yellow light deep in the center of the orifice.

I put my head back on the pillow. As I lie in quiet observation, the light rises and expands outward. It reaches out of me and explores our bedroom, embracing things of interest to it. It lets me know its interests are like mine, but it is separate and independent. It appears to be showing itself to me. *So that's what it looks like.*

I hold still and stay quiet, afraid it will close if I move or do much else. When the light engulfs something in the room, I get a gut feeling about the history and qualities of the object. After watching it grope around the room for three or four minutes, I decide to will it to connect with Sarah, who is resting next to me. Try as I might, I'm unable to affect it. But the intuition comes that as time goes on, we will learn to work together. *'We're partners,'* it conveys.

Learning about this new, intuitive part of my body reminds me of an experiment in predicting the future that I performed months ago at the racetrack. Comparing the two, I think knowing the future is different from intuition, which is a sixth sense. I shouldn't have done the experiment, but it was so interesting and profitable I'm tempted to try again—still, I know where temptation leads.

In the *Yoga Sutras*, Patanjali says special abilities can and should be cultivated over time during one's meditations. The process of cultivating these special abilities is called samyama, which the Transcendental Meditation movement has incorporated into the TM-Sidhi program. The TM movement continues to teach thousands of students this TM-Sidhi program every year as an advanced form of meditation. One of the special abilities is knowledge of the future.

Last May, seeking proof of Vedic philosophy, I picked up Amos on my way home from dropping Sarah off at LAX. She was on her way to visit our daughters in Manhattan. I brought Amos home to Claremont for the weekend. My Sunday plan was for Amos and me to go to the Santa Anita racetrack, which is only a twenty-five minute drive from the college. I would practice the samyama for seeing the future while Amos watched over me when my eyes were closed. If Sarah were there, she would not have let me do it.

During the TM-Sidhi course we were instructed to practice all of the sidhis equally and not to do one samyama by itself because that would imbalance us. They also told us not to practice samyama for any material benefit, only for the spiritual benefits. I convinced myself before going to the track that little harm could come of breaking the rules this once.

The day we went to the track was dreary and overcast. In between each race, as discretely as I could, I practiced just the samyama to know the future. Amos played on his iPhone while checking on me. We bet five or ten bucks between the two of us on each race, losing most of the bets. Before the seventh race, doing samyama as I had all afternoon without any results, I found myself watching the end of the seventh race with my mind's eye. It was not very clear, but I could tell that horse number 4 had won, finishing just ahead of horse number 7. I told Amos something had finally happened. I rushed to the betting window and wagered $400 on the exacta with 4 in first and 7 in second.

It worked. The end of the race looked different from our vantage point, but the outcome was the same. While in line to collect my winnings, I watched the replay on the TV monitors and was blown away to see it was just a clearer version of what I had seen in my mind. I was shaking from head to toe when I got to the window and picked up my winnings of $11,018. We quickly left the track, watching behind us to make sure we weren't being followed. I knew using samyama for material gain was bad karma, but it was a one-time experiment. In the car, Amos and I agreed not to discuss this with Sarah. I squirreled the money away, afraid to spend it.

"What are you thinking about?" Sarah says, rolling onto her side, bringing me back to the present. The intuition light is gone. How does she always know when I'm thinking about something that would interest her? I won't tell her about my new appendage and orifice for now, if only to spare me the jokes. Thankfully, she seems in a good place this morning, so far.

"I'm thinking about the lecture I'm giving today and how it will be received by the kids. Today is Patanjali day, which can be something of a shock to their nervous systems."

Sarah gazes at me, cradling her chin in her hands. I look up at her as she speaks. "Don't worry about them. I'm sure they've heard from friends or read online how far out the stuff you teach is. Kids nowadays are jaded from all their media anyway. Not much gets through their thick hides, is my guess. Tell me, what was really on your mind?" She reaches down and momentarily touches my third eye area and, instantly, as if shocked by static electricity, I'm zapped with a flash of deep all-knowingness.

I try to respond to her question, but I'm in a fog of profound revelations, my intellect overwhelmed by the smorgasbord. As it clears, my intuition appendage, in its small, distinct voice, says to me, "Oh, what a tangled web we weave when first we practice to deceive." I shake my head, still not back. *Did Sarah do something to me with her finger or was that some spontaneous enlightened thing? She couldn't have done it, right?* Intimidated by the shock and shamed by my appendage, I decide on the truth. "Honey, did I ever tell you what happened last May when you went to visit the girls?"

"No?" she says. "Tell me."

"I went to the racetrack with Amos. While he watched over me, I did the samyama to see the future. It seemed to work. I won over eleven thousand dollars. I know it was the wrong thing to do, but it was an experiment."

Her eyes rise, looking upward. She returns to me, serious. "Abe, you've hidden it from me all this time? That made it worse. You know we were taught that using the Sidhis for material gain would end badly. Have you spent the money?"

"No, it's in the online money market account we set up last year to get the promotional two hundred dollars."

"Good, leave it there. It should only be used for something that uplifts us."

We shower away the stickiness of the hot, humid September night and spend the morning cooking a fun breakfast together. I make Indian chapatis stuffed with freshly made mango chutney from a recipe I found online. Sarah makes Cream of Wheat with spices, whole milk, and golden raisins, which she's never used before. The kitchen morphs into a major mess as we bounce off each other, cooking away. My dish is not very good, but her Cream of Wheat is just what I wanted. We laugh and joke as if her attacks were decades away. After breakfast at the front door, she kisses me without holding on. "That was fun. Thanks for staying late. I'll do the dishes and clean the kitchen, scout's honor."

Walking to my office, my mind is fixated on what "something that uplifts us" would be. I'm not thinking about what else I could do to help Sarah. I'm thinking about enticing ideas which I'm surprisingly excited by, even though I know we really can't afford any of them. *A new plug-in Prius gets four times the electric range that my old, worn-out Prius gets. A new one would be good for the environment.*

Something's wrong. I should be immune to the lures of the material world, but I don't seem to be. A few days ago, this wouldn't have happened. I'm worried my brightly dyed color is starting to fade—Dear God, help me!

As I walk, my thoughts settle, and I become entranced by the beauty around me. Part of me has expanded past my body, surrounding it in a large, glistening, sticky-sweet bubble about ten or twelve feet high and at least as wide. I could stay down here inside my head or go up there and enjoy the view. Instantly, I'm looking down at my body bouncing along, cute and endearing. I can see much farther from these heights. In fact, I can see forever. I perceive my surroundings in all 360 delicious degrees, all at once, and the rush of sensory input feels like a breath of fresh air in an old, musty passageway, long closed but now open and airing out.

I pass under a stately oak that was here long before my body was, and *I am* that tree. It knows me well and I it. I often passed under it as a student many years ago, and it lets me know it remembers. Most days I walk under its protecting arms on my way to my office. Now, I am its slow, heavy aware-ness, its giving and nurturing nature, and its delight in the sun and the sky. It's a noble creature. I'm proud to share this earth with it.

As I approach Pearsons Hall, I shrink, collapsing into my skull. It's tiny and confining in here, and lonely. I get up to my office with just a few minutes to spare before class. Standing in front of my disheveled bookshelves, I rub my solar plexus, where that intuition thing resides, and say to it, *sotto voce*, "Oh, great intuition light, tell me what I'll need to answer all my students' questions today." When no reply or intuition comes, I grab the books I think I might need and walk down to my classroom.

Before walking in, I assess my mental preparedness. Bliss under control, check; remembering to divert my attention from anything celestial that might pop up, check; holding myself in, check; giddy patrol, in place. All set. I've got this covered. With books and lecture notes in hand, I walk in. All but two students are seated. I set my books down, and then write on the chalkboard:

PATANJALI'S YOGA SUTRAS

The two stragglers find their seats, and the spotlight shifts to me. I'm on.

"Before we discuss Patanjali, I'm interested in the results of your pondering of my statement, 'We have nothing but time.' Anyone have some thoughts to share?"

Ravi raises his hand confidently, which discourages two other more tentative hands. He wears a plaid, short-sleeved shirt that's tight on him. He opens his notebook, glances seriously around at his classmates, and begins to read. "Professor, if I close my eyes and ask God, 'take back what is not mine,' I can imagine that God could take my body, my memories, even my sense of identity, and I would still be alive and left with what I truly possess, which is my consciousness and its experience of time. If God took either of those, my consciousness or my experience of time, then I would cease to exist as an individual. The only things *I really have* are my consciousness and experience of time. Everything else is extraneous, on loan from God, can and will be taken back. As Lord Krishna said to Arjuna in chapter 2 of the Gita, 'There never was a time when I was not, nor you…Nor will there ever be a time when all of us shall cease to exist.' God promises us time and consciousness, nothing more. We have nothing, we possess nothing, but time. We witness time's passage. What we witness is not ours."

"Thank you, Ravi—*very* impressive," I say sincerely. Ravi lowers his eyes and chin but seems pleased with himself. "Your answer was so good that I have nothing to add. Would anyone else like to share an answer with the class?" No hands go up. "How many of you have taken a yoga class?" Seven students raise their hands.

"Does anyone know what the word 'yoga' means?" Three students—and Ravi, of course—keep their hands raised. I call on the person most likely to know as a reward for his powerful ponder.

"Ravi, what does the Sanskrit word 'yoga' mean?"

"It means union," he replies.

"Exactly. The union we are talking about occurs when one's consciousness becomes conscious of its own consciousness, or its Self. Doing so, our self with a little 's' merges, unites, or becomes one with our Self with a capital 'S.'

"Patanjali's *Yoga Sutras*," I continue, "were written at least 1,700 years ago. The collection of sutras is widely acknowledged as the definitive text on yoga. Patanjali's *Yoga Sutras*, in general, describe all the methods, techniques, and tools that are available to each of us in making progress toward the state of yoga. They also describe things *not* to do because they are detrimental to the quest. The book, as you have noticed, is terse and to the point, which is why this is a book of sutras. The Sanskrit word 'sutra' means thread or rule.

"Yoga is not what most people think it is. Yoga is not just postures or stretches, which seems to be the most common misconception. Those are called asanas. Asanas are a part of yoga, but yoga is much more than that. Yoga includes breathing exercises, which are called pranayama, and meditation. Patanjali classifies any activity that promotes spiritual growth leading to union with our Self as part of the process or path of yoga, and, in addition, defines 'Yoga' as experiencing or knowing one's Self. Dr. Sands makes this distinction clear in his book, *Maharishi's Yoga*." I pick up the book and read:

"'Yoga is a state of consciousness—the experience of pure Being—as well as a path, or technique used to attain this experience. Thus there is a distinction between the *state of Yoga* and the so-called *path of Yoga*.'[31]

"According to Patanjali, even if you have never been to a yoga class at your local mall, when you are praying at your church or temple or mosque, you are technically on the path of Yoga. He also says that doing good deeds and avoiding doing bad is part of the path, or technique, of Yoga. The path of Yoga, according to Patanjali, encompasses many complex human activities and endeavors, but his theory of the state of Yoga is quite simple, and in my mind, elegant. I'll read you the first three sutras, and we will see if you agree."

I pick up a thin, blue book and hop up on my desk, using my hands to ensure a soft landing. Feet dangling, I face my students. "This is Dr. Egenes's translation, which you should have read for today," I say, waving the book in front of me. "It's a more exacting translation than the *How to Know God* translation."

I find the right bookmark and read. "'Now is the teaching on Yoga. Yoga is the complete settling of the activity of the mind. Then the observer is established in the Self.' These three sentences are so important to our discussion today that I will read them again slowly. Please think about what Patanjali is saying: 'Now is the teaching on Yoga. Yoga is the complete settling of the activity of the mind. Then the observer is established in the Self.'

"How does the path of Yoga—which includes asanas, pranayama, prayer, meditation, devotion to God, doing good, and

[31] William F. Sands, *Maharishi's Yoga: The Royal Path to Enlightenment* (Fairfield, Iowa: Maharishi University of Management Press, 2013), 19.

not doing bad—lead to the state of Yoga, the 'complete settling of the activity of the mind'? The answer is that things done on the path of Yoga tend to settle the mind's activity. Are there longer and shorter paths to the state of Yoga? Is there a quickest path to the state of Yoga? According to Maharishi and Patanjali, the answer to those questions is yes.

"Both Maharishi and Patanjali, who are from the same ancient Yogic tradition, say that the quickest path to the state of Yoga always includes mantra meditation, because it's the easiest and most efficient way to settle the mind's activities completely. In addition, both say that doing asanas and pranayama prior to meditation makes the path even shorter because they help settle the body and the breath respectively, which then helps the mind settle during meditation. Starting meditation with a relaxed body and breath allows one to get a head start on settling the mind, and thus helps meditation proceed more efficiently.

"Patanjali, in addition, says that if we want to help the mind settle as part of the path or technique of Yoga, we should perform proper action. Proper action promotes a settled mind; improper action unsettles the mind. To this end, Patanjali lists, or *prescribes*, various activities that promote a settled mind, and he *proscribes* those that produce the opposite effect." I shift on my desk, my rear uncomfortable from its hard perch, causing my shoes to each hit the front—thump, thump.

It's all so simple. Because I am established in the Self, I have a responsibility to show others the way. We are walking together in the desert, on the same long path of time; some ahead, some behind. Those ahead must lead the way and circle back to help those behind. Our collective journey isn't over until we are all home, in the promised land.

"My point in describing the various ways Patanjali says spiritual progress can be made is that Patanjali's definition of what constitutes the path of Yoga is broad enough for yoga to encompass all religious activity and all proper action. Patanjali thus defines 'yoga' in a way that allows us to make theoretical sense of how multiple religions have been able to cultivate enlightenment in some of their devotees.

"Although Patanjali says that mantra meditation is the most effective and rapid way to settle the mind, it's not the only way to do so. Think back to our discussion about St. Augustine. This saint appears to have experienced or achieved some form of enlightenment. Patanjali would say that his prayer, spiritual exercises, devotion to God, the attunement of his mind to Jesus, and the good deeds he performed are all part of the path of Yoga, and each helped settle his mind enough for him to experience the state of Yoga, which leads to enlightenment.

"Patanjali does say, however, that enlightenment can occur seemingly spontaneously in rare individuals based on the progress they've made during previous lives. We pick up the path where we left off. Progress toward enlightenment is never lost from lifetime to lifetime. If a spiritual aspirant is close to reaching Cosmic Consciousness in one life, then a little meditation or some good deeds in the next life may be enough to allow her to achieve enlightenment with apparent ease." I'm about to hop off my desk, having been here too long, but I see Margaret's face light up. She raises her hand. I see clarity in her eyes.

"Are you saying that our quest to know God, like St. Augustine's quest to know God, is ultimately fulfilled simply by settling the mind's activities?"

"That's what Patanjali is saying. This recalls Psalm 46:10, which I think also says it quite clearly and simply: 'Be still, and know that I am God.'

"Patanjali would say that when we are walking on the beach at sunset, overwhelmed by the beauty and feeling of God's presence, the process of walking on the beautiful beach settles our mind and allows us to feel what is always there. I would take this concept a few steps further. The history of humanity can be described as a history of our desire to know and experience God. In addition, the history of humanity can be seen as a very different, seemingly opposite quest: our desire for pleasure. Can those two seemingly contrary desires be the same desire seen from a greater perspective?

"Briefly, it's my contention that the experience of God is the ultimate pleasure, but there are obviously many other pleasures that we have sought. What causes pleasure? If we can come to understand what pleasure is and how it comes about, we will gain great insight into what motivates us. In a nutshell, I have written that pleasure is caused by a diminishment of boundaries, which is really the same thing as settling Devata, or the mind. We will begin our discussion concerning these ideas next week during our lecture about my Vedic personality theory.

"Any further questions?"

"Actually, I do have another question," Margaret says. She opens her notebook, finds what she was looking for, and begins.

"Professor, the Buddha taught four noble truths that were the essence of his teaching: life is not ultimately satisfying, dissatisfaction with life comes from cravings and desire, cravings and desire can be overcome by enlightenment, and enlightenment is attainable by anyone if they behave correctly, are disciplined, and practice meditation. Is there a difference between the Buddha's four truths and the Vedic philosophy we are discussing in this class?"

"In my opinion, there's no real difference, only apparent differences. Maharishi said that the Buddha's teaching was perfect but that over time his followers misinterpreted and strayed from the Buddha's instruction on proper meditation techniques. Are there any other questions?"

No one else raises their hand. Thinking about the Buddha, I decide that I need to be more careful to avoid preaching. Doing so is my natural tendency. I am a professor, not a preacher. My students are in this class to learn philosophy, not to hear me sermonize. I slip over that line too easily.

I hop off my desk, and as I land, a shiver rises from the base of my spine. As it enters my head, everything drops away, leaving me alone, looking down a long, long corridor. My intuition appendage, which is now out and lively, tells me that below the corridor are my innumerable lives, hanging like folders on a file. Ahead of me is Abe's future, directly behind me are my last few lives. Afraid of the future, I cautiously turn and begin sensing, via my trusty new appendage, whom I have been recently. It reaches down, touches a life, and I'm flooded with memories and longing. My appendage and I experience a number of lives until I'm exhausted. My appendage then points out the file for my life in heaven, letting me know it would have been a mistake to do that one.

It's so odd. I knew it. I *have* been a preacher and a rabbi, black and white and brown and yellow, and a preacher's wife, in the not-too-distant past. We are all the same. Each of my lives, each of our lives, demands the same dignity. Our differences are inconsequential and transitory.

Distantly, I hear someone calling me. It comes into focus. "Dr. Levy, Professor, are you OK?" *Who is that?*

Someone nudges my right shoulder. I sway backwards, my head hitting the front of something. *I'm in my classroom.*

"Should we call 911?" someone asks.

"Wait, I think he's coming back?"

I open my eyes and look up. A few of my students stand in front of me. I'm sitting in front of my desk. I shake my head. I ask, "What happened?"

Margaret, to my left, says, "You jumped down from your desk, then you got a big smile on your face like you were looking at something beautiful in the distance, then you sat down, crossed your legs in a half-lotus, and closed your eyes. You sat there, not moving, barely breathing, for many minutes. At first, we all thought it was one of your stunts, then we realized you were really gone and got worried. Are you OK? Do you need to go to the hospital?"

"I'm fine. I'm sorry. I must have gotten dizzy getting up so fast." I get to my feet. "You can all sit back down." They look at me and I stare hard back at them. They file back to their chairs.

When most are seated, I say with a sonorous voice, "Neither snow nor rain nor heat nor gloom of night shall keep me from my appointed rounds." That gets some grins. Damn it, my control is getting worse, not better. Worse yet, someone will tell someone, who will tell someone else, who happens to know someone in the college's administration. It always happens. It won't go over well. They'd love an excuse to stop me from teaching this controversial class.

I stand as tall as my short body will let me, squinting at each of my students as if I'm spraying them with water, and ask in a serious voice, "Is the experience of God different for the enlightened Catholic saint compared to the enlightened Jewish Hasid compared to the enlightened Muslim Sufi master compared to the enlightened Buddhist monk?" My voice normalizes. "Patanjali thinks so. Does this mean there's more than one God, or that one enlightened soul's vision of God is more correct than the others? No, says Patanjali. According to him, there is one God with many, many attributes and qualities. One tends to experience the God that one worships. He says: 'As a result of study, one obtains the vision of God which one has chosen to worship.'[32] By 'study,' Patanjali is referring to the study and practice of one's religion and its teachings."

Asher raises his hand. "Dr. Levy, in the reading that we did for today, Patanjali says that by doing certain types of samyama, a Yogi could walk on water, levitate, become invisible, see the future, and do all sorts of superhuman feats. That's just too weird for me."

"Thank you, Asher. I was going to discuss samyama soon, but let's do it now." I chuckle inwardly, thinking about my inappropriate samyama experiment betting on the ponies. It will end up costing me much more than I gained, but it was valuable because it helped dispel my doubts.

"Patanjali says that practicing samyama in addition to meditation results in more rapid progress toward enlightenment than meditation alone. Also, as a side benefit—and a serious temptation—practicing samyama can result in the special abilities, or sidhis, you referred to.

"Most commentators on Patanjali's *Yoga Sutras*—and there have been many over the last few centuries—write that Patanjali never meant for spiritual aspirants to practice samyama. The general opinion is that Patanjali included the sidhis only to be comprehensive in his description of what can be accomplished by practicing yoga. Many commentators say he included them in his Yoga sutras as a warning of

---

[32] Chapter 2, Sutra 44

the danger inherent in the sidhis, and that they are a distraction from the proper path to enlightenment. Maharishi, on the other hand, says this is a misinterpretation of the *Yoga Sutras*. He believes that practicing samyama was Patanjali's prescription for even more rapid spiritual growth than can be had by practicing meditation, asanas, pranayama, prayer, and good deeds.

"Maharishi's teacher, Guru Dev, and his tradition of Himalayan Masters—which includes Patanjali—have been teaching samyama to their disciples for many centuries. In my mind, if Patanjali did not want samyama practiced, he would have made it clear in his Yoga sutras. Not only is there no proscription against practicing samyama, but Patanjali extolls its virtues."

I pick up my copy of *How to Know God*, which is sitting in its usual place on my desk. I find the quote I'm looking for and read aloud. "Chapter 3, Sutra 5. 'Through mastery of samyama, the splendor of complete wakefulness dawns.' Patanjali is clearly recommending the practice of samyama. 'The splendor of complete wakefulness' does not seem like something Patanjali would want a spiritual seeker to miss during his or her lifetime.

"Per Maharishi's instructions, his movement has taught— and continues to teach—the technique of samyama to thousands of dedicated meditators each year. When pupils are taught the technique of samyama, they are instructed that although these are techniques meant to speed up the process of enlightenment, they do carry a risk. The pupils are warned that they should not be tempted to utilize any of the powers and abilities, the so-called sidhis, which might manifest except during meditation. Giving in to the temptation to use them otherwise can lead them astray. Patanjali writes:

"'By giving up even these powers, the seed of evil is destroyed and liberation follows. When tempted by the invisible beings in high places, let the yogi feel neither allured nor flattered; for he is in danger of being caught once more by ignorance.'[33]

"According to Patanjali, even when you are enlightened, the world still can be an excitingly dangerous, tempting place. Watch out for those invisible beings in high places—they are out to *get us!*

"The so-called 'invisible beings in high places' and the power inherent in the sidhis are only two of the many causes of temptation. Temptation is sewn into the very fabric of our world. Eve succumbed to the snake's temptation in the Garden of Eden. Adam succumbed to Eve's temptation and ate the forbidden fruit. Temptation has been an incessant, corrosive part of our world from the beginning. That won't change. We will discuss Eve, Adam, and temptation more during an upcoming lecture.

"Temptation to stray from the proper path constantly beckons. Doubt and negativity, scourges of many a spiritual aspirant, may also have the same origin as temptation. Making progress toward enlightenment requires extreme dedication and single-minded perseverance. Patanjali implies that any success practicing the sidhis would result not only in more rapid growth of enlightenment, but also in the side benefit of strengthening an aspirant's resolve. Patanjali writes, 'Those forms of concentration which result in extraordinary perceptions encourage perseverance of the mind.'[34] Along that same

[33] Chapter 3, Sutra 51–52.

[34] Chapter 1, Sutra 35

line of reasoning, I think one of Jesus's statements from the Gospel of John 4:48, is apropos: 'Then said Jesus unto him, "Except ye see signs and wonders, ye will not believe."'

"*Professor*, that is *exactly* the problem!" Tom throws up his hands. His classmates flinch as his long arms suddenly fly over their heads. "I haven't seen any signs and wonders. Where did all the miracles go? I need to see people walk on water and the sea split in two. And people can say they're enlightened all they want, but that's just more talk. I need proof before I change how I live my life. Without a miracle to give us a reason to believe in something more, all we can aspire to is power." His face is flushed and resolute.

"Tom, you've hit the nail on the head, now just be careful not to hit the heads of your neighbors," I say. "Seeing miracles would help us believe and persevere, but even then, we would be subject to temptation. The sidhis, extremely helpful for rapid spiritual progress, are also about resisting the temptation of power. It has been said, rightly so, that 'power tends to corrupt, and absolute power corrupts absolutely.' Not succumbing to the temptation of power that the sidhis represent is one of the greatest challenges in the pursuit of complete enlightenment.

"I'm told that the most advanced, dedicated meditators from the TM movement have been in an ashram in the Himalayas for many years, meditating and practicing samyama full-time in an attempt to gain Unity Consciousness. If they achieve mastery over some of the sidhis, I've heard they might demonstrate the abilities to the public. Keep in mind that we glean the physical limitations of our universe from experimentation and observation, and we therefore have adjusted doctrinal physics hundreds or maybe thousands of times in the course of our history. If a group of meditators could demonstrate abilities not currently thought possible, in controlled and replicable circumstances, scientists would adjust their understanding of physics accordingly.

"I think this is a good time to stop."

Tanisha, looking down at her notes, raises her hand high and says, "I did some research about the so-called lost years of Jesus, and there is considerable speculation that Jesus went to India during that time. Could Jesus have been practicing meditation and samyama during those lost years?"

"I'll try to rephrase your question—let me know if I've gotten it right," I say, but I've already decided it would be a bad idea to answer her question, my run-in with Brittany in the back of my mind. Jesus can be a third rail in our society. If I tell my class there are some scholars who think it's possible Jesus could have learned the sidhis in India, I could end up touching that rail. "Could Jesus have learned how to meditate and how to perform samyama during his so-called lost years? Is that right?"

"Yes, that's it."

"I prefer not to answer that question. I have researched this topic, but almost all of what I found was speculation. I try, though not always successfully, to avoid speculation in this class."

"*Come on*, Professor!" Tom blurts out in a startlingly loud, indignant tone. "Answer her question!" He sits bolt upright. "What are you afraid of? Jesus should be fair game. We've been talking about him all along. I think you know exactly what you want to say but are afraid to say it."

There's a hushed silence. Everyone except Tanisha looks at Tom again. He's fuming. Tanisha sits back in her chair looking vindicated, pleased that she has a defender, even if it's Tom. Chris, sitting next to Tom, whispers loud enough for all to hear, "Tom, cool it."

"Tom," I say clearly and slowly, "we are *not* going there. If you like, we can discuss this in private after class." I look him in the eyes and see that my intuition appendage has already connected with his awareness through his right eye. I feel his anger dissipate, being drained away by the soft yellow light. I'm sorry about that. Tom has a legitimate beef. I think we should be able to discuss Jesus's miracles in this class with the same impunity as I could in discussing the Buddha's miracles, or Krishna's miracles, or the Baal Shem Tov's miracles. But a few years ago, the academic dean took me aside and privately warned me to be careful this class doesn't bring up anything that might be construed as attacking Christian dogma. As a side issue, my appendage, having just snooped around inside Tom's head, informs me with a serious tone that Tom will greatly help Sarah and I in the future. Great, now it's dabbling in prophecy.

Tom sits quietly, his face glazed, breathing shallowly through his mouth. A few of the students stare at him, wondering what happened. That's not good. We need to move on. "Are there any other questions I can refuse to answer?" I hear a few stifled, defusing snickers. I look at the time—we've gone over by a few minutes.

"For Tuesday, please finish reading the chapters I've assigned in Maharishi's *Science of Being and Art of Living*. You will see that Maharishi applies the ancient Vedic concepts we have been discussing to many different fields of academic study as well as to common problems that beset us all. The next class is all questions, answers, and discussion. Please review your lecture notes and readings to date and formulate at least one hopefully profound or insightful question. I will call first on students whose class participation grade needs attending, but everyone is fair game. Have a good weekend. Class dismissed.

See you Tuesday. Oh, and, uh, may the Force be with you." I raise both hands, palms toward the class, third and fourth fingers split in a *V* shape, thumb to thumb. This gets me rolled eyes from most of the class and blank stares from a few.

Tom, looking like a spooked jackrabbit, is the first one out the door.

Given Tom's outburst, I find it interesting that I didn't have the physical reaction I would have had before Cosmic Consciousness. I would expect a rapid heartbeat, sweaty palms, and some anger, but I'm feeling quite tranquil. I'm reassured.

A few students stay after class, and we have a lively and entertaining what-if discussion about gurus as superheroes. After our discussion winds down, I walk up to my office knowing I'm being followed. I clear off the chair next to my desk for Tom. He arrives three minutes later, knocking harder than necessary on the open door.

"Come in, Tom."

From my seat, he looks imposingly tall and broad. He clasps his hands in front of him. His hands look older than he is.

"Professor, do you want me to apologize?" It's not much of a question.

"No, there's no need for an apology."

"Good." He steps inside my office, closes the door firmly, but doesn't sit down. He towers over me. I catch a whiff of body odor; his breath is heavy.

"What the *hell* did you do to me in class?" he says, hands by his side, showing me his twitching palms. "One minute I'm like a rubber band ready to snap, then you look into me and everything went away." He leans forward. "I saw you do it to Tanisha too. I asked around in class. Even Tanisha wasn't sure something happened, but *I* saw it. I didn't give you permission. Why do you think...?"

My intuition appendage grabs him, settling him. Damn that thing. *Stop it!* I think as forcefully as I can. *I need to be in charge!*

Tom sighs, staggers, and sits. I want to apologize to him.

Gathering himself, he whimpers. "Professor, I came to your class to find my own answers. I need to form my own opinions, not be overpowered into believing yours."

Feeling shamed, the intuition thing retreats. The color returns to Tom's face. *At least it has a sense of decency.*

Untethered, he leaps back to his feet. "You're *just* like my dad!"

Surprised to be standing but pleased to be at an advantage again, he resumes his tirade. "My dad is into money because it can buy power; you're into yourself because of the power you get. Is that what it's all about? Is power all there is? There has to be more than just perpetual war between the power hungry. Why aren't we hungry for something better, something higher than power? Isn't that what your class is about?" He's aiming his fingers down at my chest as he glowers at me. His words cut. I need this; my appendage needs this.

"My dad laughs at God; you talk all holy about God's glory. Either way, it's still about power. Who's right? Have you really found God or is it the dark lord? Maybe you've gone over to the other side and don't know it?"

Spent, he sits down again, looking at the floor. He's not going to cry. When he's ready, he looks up. His eyes are empty.

"I need answers. My dad has nothing for me," he pleads. "You have good arguments and lots of big ideas, but I can't get a grip on them. They're just smoke and mirrors. My dad says I'm a wimp, but he's an idiot." His eyes get red, but that quickly fades. He's not a wimp; he's a baby.

"You're right, Tom. Ideas and arguments can rarely change you without experience. You need the experience of your—"

"I don't need more lectures!" he hisses.

"Tom," I say in an even voice. "We all deserve—"

"You don't know *what* I deserve!" he snaps. "Do you know I was arrested when I was seventeen for shoplifting? And that's not all, I promise you. My dad expunged my record so I could get into Pomona. And why do you hide behind that Jedi mind trick you keep doing to me, and did to Tanisha? Stop it! It's an abuse of power. Deal with me straight."

"I'm sorry," I say, looking him in the eyes.

"Thank you," Tom says, surprised. The heat drains from his face.

"Why," he asks, "were you afraid to answer Tanisha's question about Jesus? Are you afraid of college politics? Politics, you know, are about power."

"Yes, it's about power and politics," I say flatly. "That's why I don't want to talk about it."

"I figured. I understand the politics at this school. My father went here too. He knows you."

"Your father knows me?"

"Yeah, he was a year behind you," he says almost absentmindedly. Tom's tired from his fight. But the fight is not with me, it's with a much more formidable opponent: his self. "He says he remembers you mainly from a philosophy class, but you also took Intro to Calculus together. Ben Griffin. He's very tall. Even taller than me."

I remember a tall student named Ben in at least one of my philosophy classes. I remember him being smart and cunning, though I don't remember why. "Actually, I think I do remember your dad. He was wiry with blond, almost white, thinning hair?"

"That's him; been bald for years."

"How is he?" I ask earnestly.

"He's rich and powerful."

Tom shifts his chair toward me. Then he glances at my stacks of papers as he speaks. "My dad gives a lot of money to the college and loves to be in on school politics."

"I'm happy he's successful, and happy he donates to my favorite college."

Tom looks at the door. Studying the doorknob, he says, "I wanted to ask you one more thing. Do you think that Vedic Vibe thing you told Chris about would help me?"

"Maybe—you can talk to Chris about how to get one if you like."

Entranced, he walks over to the doorknob and touches it with the fingers of his right hand.

"Tom, before you go, is there anything I can do to help you with your first paper? You never scheduled the required one-on-one appointments. I don't want you to fail this class."

The trance breaks. He looks over at me, face flushed. "My dad always tells me that us Griffins cannot fail. *I will not fail!*" He turns the knob and opens the door. "My paper will be fine. Chris is working with me," he mumbles with one foot out the door. He pulls the door shut soundly behind him.

Tom knows how to draw blood, but a little bloodletting can be curative and strengthening. I open the door. Sitting again, I put my feet up on my desk and ponder Tom's question about the dark lord. The Devil should never be underestimated. His main objective is to obscure the Truth and the path to the Truth, and he's very clever in doing so.

A few minutes later Margaret and Chris arrive in my doorway. I raise my eyebrows at them and smile, feet still up. Their open mouths are just what I was looking for. I put my feet back on the floor.

"Ah, hi, Professor," Margaret says from the doorway. "Did we catch you at a bad time? Should we come back later?"

"Your timing is perfect."

"We," she motions toward Chris, "were discussing your lecture and have some questions."

"Shall we reconvene downstairs?"

"Sure," Chris says.

"Follow me." As we walk, my intuition appendage checks out Chris and Margaret's relationship. It's a nosy little bugger. *Shame on you!* I tell it. By the time we're seated in my go-to classroom, it's telling me that though they aren't dating now, they may be soon.

We sit as before, but with Margaret on Chris's right. Chris sits on my right, and I sit at the end of the large conference table, looking out at the open door. Margaret asks, "What did you mean when you said that pleasure is caused by a diminishment of boundaries? What boundaries are diminished when I'm enjoying the pleasure of an ice cream cone or the pleasure of beating my tennis partner?"

"To help you understand my theory of pleasure, I'll need to reacquaint you with Plato's Theory of Forms. As you'll remember, Plato held that every object or quality of perception, or Chhandas from a Vedic perspective, is a representation of—" Steve, from my Plato class, peeks his head in the doorway, making eye contact with Chris and Margaret.

"Hi, Dr. Levy. Sorry to interrupt. I was walking by and heard your voices. I was looking for Chris."

"Hi, Steve. Do you and Chris need a word together? We were just about to begin discussing pleasure."

"Pleasure," Steve says, taking a seat to my left, opposite Chris. "That's one of my favorite topics."

"You're welcome to sit in."

"Thank you." Steve turns toward Chris and says under his breath, "Chris, I texted you? Can we talk afterward?"

Chris looks surprised. "Sorry, phone's dead. Sure, is everything OK?"

Steve, exasperated, says, "It's about Tom."

"Oh, OK, we'll talk after."

"I assume you and Margaret know each other?" I ask.

"We're all seniors," Steve says. "Pomona's pretty cozy. After four years, all us seniors basically know each other. Tom Griffin was my roommate freshman year."

"I see. Margaret had just asked me to explain my theory of pleasure." I explain my thoughts on pleasure from a Vedic perspective, and how we are all attracted to the path of increasing pleasure over our innumerable lives, eventually leading to Self-knowledge and the experience of God, the two ultimate pleasures, each being opposite sides of the same coin. Steve's and Margaret's sharp, inquisitive minds closely analyze my ideas, making for a lively discussion. Chris follows along but doesn't add much. As our discussion progresses, I begin thinking about Tom. This is a good time to get some information about what he's up to. I say, "Is that all clear?"

The three glance at one another and decide we're done.

"Thanks for your time," Margaret says. She gathers her things.

"Before you leave," I say, fishing, "I wanted to talk about the thing Tom's doing."

A startled look appears on their faces. Steve recovers first, saying, "Tom's not bullying us, if that's what you think. We all freely chose to participate, and the few who aren't participating are under no pressure."

I decide to see if I can catch some more. "I wanted to make sure that if the administration finds out no one will get into serious trouble. What do you all think?"

"Professor," Margaret says, "I think the administration might suspend Tom or something, but the rest of our senior class would be OK. We've discussed it. It doesn't violate our honor code or anything. Please don't tell the administration. They would stop the program. Many people, including me, depend on it."

Chris and Steve nod. Chris says, "It's a good thing for our senior class, even though it gives Tom way too much power."

"Good to know," I say. I'm satisfied whatever it is isn't too bad. Margaret and I walk out together, leaving Steve and Chris alone to talk.

I walk up to my office and gather a few things. I lock the door on my way out. It's a beautiful day, cooler than it has been. I look at my phone: 4:18, still early. Let's see how Sarah's holding up.

I find Sarah in bed meditating. The kitchen is just as we left it this morning. She opens her eyes, turning to look at me. Her face and eyes look calm, but behind them is a dark storm.

"Yeah," she says, "I'm becoming the recluse you wanted to be. If I don't meditate a lot, my anxiety and panic attacks get worse. But even with all of my meditation, I'm not getting better. One of the college kids who works at my store texted me asking if I'm sick. I haven't been at the store much. I'm sorry I've become such a mess again."

"It's OK. I meant to tell you. I hope you don't mind but I was able to get you an appointment with a psychiatrist next week."

"I'm that bad? I guess I am. I'll go. I need to go. I need something stronger."

"Good. Let's go for a jog. It will be good for both of us. I'll be right by your side. I won't run off ahead of you, like someone else I know."

"You better not!"

"No worries, honey."

She lies down to rest after her meditation, then we go for a jog. When we tire and start to walk, she fills me in on our plans for the weekend. Her mood, improved by the exercise and my attention, is good and strong. She enjoys thinking about and working on our social plans and then experiencing their fruition.

For tomorrow evening, her plan—our plan—is to drive into LA to have Shabbat dinner with two couples who are some of our dearest friends. We'll pick up Amos on our way. Both couples have children who grew up with Amos and are coming for dinner. It will be just like old times. We'll return home late Friday night, and then Saturday morning Sarah wants us to go to our temple. This Saturday, it's not only our Sabbath, but also the holiday of Sukkot, which Sarah enjoys. I go to temple only a few times a year, but she goes more frequently, meeting friends and enjoying the spirituality she finds there. I have found some spirituality over the years praying in a temple, but my usual excuse is that given all the time and effort of getting dressed up, driving to the temple, and sitting there for hours, I could have stayed home and done asanas, pranayama, and a long meditation and gotten more from the time spent.

That evening, after our jog, we are lying down, resting after meditating together. I'm thinking about my next book. I've been slowly fleshing out a philosophical theory of personality in the academic literature that straddles the fields of psychology, philosophy, quantum mechanics, and comparative theology. I take a leap and decide the new book should be a novel that illustrates Vedic philosophy, even though I have no idea how to write fiction. A novel would have wider appeal than nonfiction and make Vedic philosophy easier to understand. Just as I was during the weeks and months prior to my enlightenment, our world seems to be in the beginning stages of a phase transition to a higher level. I'm hoping my novel, by being at the right place at the right time, will help make what will be a rocky transition smoother and less traumatic. We fear what we don't understand.

As I rest, thoughts and emotions well up. With the dawning of my Cosmic Consciousness, the plight of humanity has taken on a greater poignancy. Many good people have worked so hard and so long for just a taste of what I am now living at every moment—not that I didn't work hard to get here, but not *that* hard compared to the many monks, priests, nuns, and rabbis who dedicated their lives to God and religion. I pray that they will come to know the God they love, just as I am beginning to.

The next day, after my classes, Sarah and I leave for the city in the late afternoon. Given the usual rush hour traffic on a Friday evening, it will take ninety minutes or more to pick up Amos and get to our friends' house. The plan is to arrive forty-five minutes early for dinner. We'll find a quiet area to park and then meditate in the car before we go in. It will be dark by then, not too cold, and hopefully we won't be bothered.

I enjoy longer drives with Sarah. We have a chance to catch up, and after that, we have real conversation. After exchanging this week's stories, my wife says, "Have you noticed a difference in the kids the last week or so?"

"Maybe," I say. I'm often not in the inner circle of shared emotions that my wife enjoys with our daughters.

"Both girls are definitely on a roll. They're in especially good moods, and good things are coming their way. Same thing with Amos, it seems, but you would know better. Do you think it has something to do with your enlightenment?"

"Could be." I reflect on what I have heard from my daughters and son over the last week. The idea that the sins and the blessings of the parents are visited upon the children is both a Vedic and biblical idea. Things do seem to be going well for my kids since I've reached Cosmic Consciousness. *Please God, this should extend to Sarah.*

We pick up Amos and arrive near our friends' house in good time. We find a secluded place to park in their neighborhood and then adjust our seats for meditation. Although I like my well-worn, plug-in Prius, its tight quarters make it difficult for me to sit in a half-lotus. Legs on the floor will have to do. My son has done a lot of meditating with us in our cars over the years and knows the drill. He has the whole back seat to himself, but lying down to rest after meditation is difficult given the small car and his large body. Sarah does two minutes of pranayama, and not to be outdone, I follow suit. Then we begin.

*Mantra, mantraaaaa, maaaaa…maaantraaaa…*I am shimmering consciousness, luminous, large. Sarah, next to me…a cloud, tingling femininity, spilling over to my side, mixing—*ahhh. Mantra, mantra, mannnn…*Going inward; following mantra down to source; deeper, finer, smaller; so, so small, atoms large; smaller, smaller than smallest…snug, swaddled…*I am point, within me is whole.* Remembering, in car, curious about surroundings, scanning area. Someone getting in car, houses up. Old, bony man walking hairless Chihuahua opposite side street, under streetlight. Seeing clearly, *fascinating…Mantra, mantra, mantra…*Unbounded…*this I am, this I was, this I will always*—a voice comes. Actually, it's a deep chorus of voices in unison, speaking slowly and distinctly, with a slight echo.

"You-will-lose-what-you-think-is-enlightenment, which-is-all-you-have-of-value. Our-way-will-always-be-here-for-you. You-will-never-lose-it."

I'm back in my body, frightened. What was that? That was *not* my intuition appendage. Am I getting ahead of myself? I'm not so advanced a meditator as to be "tempted by the invisible beings in high places"—or am I? Why would they bother with me? I thought only fully enlightened figures like Jesus and the Buddha experienced serious temptation, not enlightenment newbies like myself who are in just the first stage. My stomach knots and a wave of nausea rolls over me, then it's gone—*that was weird; that shouldn't happen?*

I recline my seat, careful not to squish Amos. Sarah, hearing me, says, "We have time. Can I meditate more? I need to settle down before I socialize. Are you OK?"

"I'm fine. Just a little sleepy."

Amos lies down, relaxed from meditation, but happy I'm done so he can stop and take a nap.

After an adequate rest we adjust ourselves and drive the two blocks to our friends' house. We're on time and the other couple and their kids have not arrived yet. Austin, our host, is in a good mood. It seems he's already had a few drinks. His wife, Lillian, has put on a few pounds, which looks good on her, softening her angular features. I'm not jealous of their large, modern, neat home, but I think Sarah is. Our house is what a professor can afford. Lawyers with their own firms can afford much more.

"Abe, so good to see you!" Austin offers a firm handshake and a quick hug. He's a charismatic guy, tallish (at least by my standards), butt-chinned, and intentionally scruffy. His firm specializes in health care law, especially for Southern California biotech companies. I give Lillian a kiss and hug, and we sit on their couch with glasses of wine.

"Abe, you have—have you lost weight? Have you been working out or running more?" Lillian asks. "You look younger and, ah, well, good."

Sarah answers for me. "We've been jogging more lately, enjoying the warm fall weather." I nod. Sarah underestimates me at times.

Sarah met Lillian at a Mommy and Me class when our sons were infants. Their son, Max, has always been very nice to Amos. His wife isn't coming tonight. It's a shame because she is also very friendly with Amos.

For many years, especially when we first met, Austin was very much into EST, or Erhard Seminars Training, which later morphed into The Forum. EST was founded by Werner Erhard, a former salesman and executive in the encyclopedia business, who explored numerous Eastern mystical practices but was mainly influenced by his study of Zen. During the original EST training, two hundred fifty participants or so would be sequestered for fifteen to eighteen hours per day for two consecutive weekends in a hotel ballroom, agreeing not to talk, eat, or go to the bathroom except during rare scheduled breaks. It was popular in the late seventies and early eighties. The goal of EST was to "get *it*." Getting *it* meant coming to an epiphany about personal integrity, letting go of the past and its influences on your present state of mind, and living in the moment—all noble goals that an enlightened person lives and experiences without having to strain his bladder.

Austin wanted me to take EST, or later, a beginners' class in The Forum. I always politely refused. My problem with EST was that it seemed to work on the surface—the psychological part of the mind—but there was no corresponding physiological change in the body or the nervous system that would allow the epiphany to continue. It had always been clear to me that if there was such a thing as permanent enlightenment it would require a purification and refinement of the body and nervous system to support getting *it* in the long term.

Aaron, Barbara, their two kids, and their spouses, arrive in separate cars. Aaron's a law professor at UCLA, specializing in intellectual property. She's a yoga teacher focused on therapeutic yoga. Hearing her stories about how she's helped clients by having them do specific yoga asanas and different forms of pranayama has been food for thought. She's told me that the school of therapeutic yoga to which she belongs believes that meditation is just a small part of the Yogic healing process. I've learned the hard way not to challenge that belief.

We're ushered into the dining room for the Shabbat prayers and dinner. The young adults are seated on one side of the long, beautifully set table and are excited to catch up with one another. They're old friends. As I get up from the couch to take my place at the dinner table, I find myself tipsy for the first time in many years. I've had almost three glasses of wine, which have quieted the fear brought on by the chorus of voices I heard in meditation. I haven't had a fear since my enlightenment, and though it's partially suppressed by the alcohol, I'm still uneasy. Will I lose my enlightenment, as they predicted? It does seem that my brightly dyed cloth could be fading. Frighteningly, I find myself intrigued by the voices' haunting promise, 'Our way will always be here for you. You will never lose it.' I need to be vigilant. The Devil is extremely cunning and knows our weaknesses.

Dinner is delicious. We all take in and give out as much information about our lives as efficiently as we can. It's been too long since we've seen each other.

After dessert, which is varied and scrumptious, Austin asks, "Abe, still writing about Plato and Indian philosophy, or have you moved on to something new?"

"I tend to get stuck on certain topics until I feel I've conquered them. Plato's relationship to Vedic philosophy will still be a significant part of my writing, but I think I've finally figured out what I want to say about it. I'm ready to conquer something entirely new. How's your practice going?"

"Almost too well. Our biotech niche is booming right along with the myriad of newly sprouting biotech companies. The hardest part is keeping all the lawyers and staff from killing each other." I turn toward Aaron, sitting on the other side of me. "Do the professors in your department get along well?" I ask.

Aaron is short and struggles to keep his dense beard shaved. He has put on weight over the last ten years, most of it going to his belly. What's left of his salt-and-pepper hair is in full retreat. When he smiles, which is often, there's a gap between his front teeth. I was told a few years ago that I could be his brother.

"There's always a lot of infighting and political maneuvering among the law professors," Aaron says. "There's not much to be gained, but what little there is, is pursued with great skill and cunning. Are philosophers any better?"

"I'm sorry to report we're just like everyone else. We all want something. As for me, I just want the status quo in my department, and it's hard enough to protect and maintain it."

Austin turns to Aaron and raises his eyebrows. Aaron nods. Austin turns to me and says, "We'd like to talk about something we think you'll be interested in. Care to join us in my den?"

"Sure," I say, intrigued.

The den is sumptuous but not overdone—rich, warm woods and a lush beige carpet. Austin closes the door. It's remarkably quiet. I sit in a brown, tufted leather recliner I've always liked. Austin and Aaron sit on opposite edges of a matching leather couch, looking at me. My stomach knots up again.

Austin begins, "I spend a lot of time at biotech companies, reviewing their contracts and such. Two weeks ago, I was at a small company in La Jolla that's growing rapidly. The secretary brought in a stack of folders containing documents I needed to review, and I noticed an envelope marked 'Highly Confidential' in the center of the stack. I was alone. I decided to open it."

I think to myself: *We are never really alone. Our Self is always observing.*

"The envelope contained a draft of the results of a large, scientific study concerning the company's new bio-engineered cancer immunotherapy treatment. Word on the street was that it might work, but not well, and that it had significant side effects. What I saw contradicted that. The results looked very promising. I called the secretary and showed her the envelope.

I told her that since it was marked 'Highly Confidential,' I figured it was given to me by mistake. She became agitated. She asked if I had looked inside and was relieved when I said no. She said she must have misfiled the folder and asked me not to mention the mishap to anyone. I agreed.

"In three weeks, the company is scheduled to present the data at a national cancer conference. The stock has already gone up thirty percent since I saw the draft—there are always leaks and insider buying. Because of my work inside the company I had to sign an agreement not to invest, but Aaron and I have discussed it. He bought highly leveraged, out-of-the-money call options on the stock. Do you know what those are? It gives you the right to buy stock at a specific price for a fixed amount of time. Depending on which call option you buy, if the stock goes up, say, fifty percent, the call options could go up ten or twenty times, or more."

"I've already doubled the money I've put in," Aaron says. "I'm going to buy more on Monday."

"I believe what we are talking about is called insider trading—that's not legal," I say.

"Technically, you're correct," says Austin. "But no one will ever know that I saw the contents of that envelope. The secretary would be fired if someone found out she gave it to me. We've had to listen to you complain for years about wanting to remodel your house. Here's an easy way. I think if you put in ten thousand dollars or so, when the results are presented at the conference, the call options should be worth a hundred thousand, maybe a lot more. The results I saw were that good."

Aaron says, "You'll have to act soon. The stock is rising. An opportunity this good won't *always be here for you.*"

Those words reverberate in my head, making me shudder. It's their words. I push that aside. I could do a very nice remodel with a hundred thousand dollars or more.

"I don't have an options account and I've never bought options before," I say.

Aaron says, "I'm happy to show you how."

I could invest the eleven thousand dollars I've stashed away without telling Sarah. She never checks any of our accounts. *Don't do it!* It would be a step down the slippery slope to the dark side.

Not wanting to, I force myself to say, "Thank you for trying to help. I appreciate it. I'll have to pass, though."

"We understand," Austin says, glancing at Aaron. "You won't mention this to anyone? I just thought we could help you afford to remodel your house."

"No worries," I say. "It is tempting."

The next morning, we dress for synagogue. Sukkot is a curious holiday. Religious Jews build huts, or tabernacles, on their properties during Sukkot, and eat and sleep in them for the week—which can be quite cold back East. The hut, a Sukkah, is built and taken down each year. It cannot be a permanent structure. I've been taught that the Sukkah symbolizes the human body, impermanent and frail. In my mind, the practice of building the Sukkah anew each year is suggestive of reincarnation, but rabbis have told me that while Jewish thought does not rule out such a phenomenon, Judaism, in general, is concerned with this life and the afterlife, and does not have much to say about what, if anything, happens after the afterlife.

The rabbi's sermon is about the Sukkah itself. He tells us that the Jewish people built Sukkot during our forty years of wandering in the desert after leaving slavery in Egypt. He says the process of living in the Sukkah represents a journey away from the slave mentality and toward freedom. I love learning new things. Given that I'm currently enjoying a taste of true freedom while living within my corporeal Sukkah, the sermon hits home. Sarah likes the sermon, too, and asks me about it as we walk out the back of the synagogue toward the large Sukkah that has been erected there. I start to share my thoughts but stop myself. We've already heard one sermon today.

As we mingle, I'm surprised to run into the new philosophy professor, Steve Lavin, whom I helped recruit and hire, and his wife, Sari. We sit with them to eat the light lunch set out for us.

"Steve, how long have you been coming to this temple?" I ask.

"This is the fourth time for Sari and me. I love the rabbi. He really knows Jewish law. We've also been interested in their preschool. It's gotten rave reviews."

Sarah says, "Oh! Is there some good news you'd like to share?"

Sari blushes, "It's so early, we weren't telling anyone." She glances at Steve with a sweet, excited reproach. "Yes, I'm ten weeks pregnant."

"Mazel tov!" Sarah and I say almost simultaneously.

"Our kids all went to preschool here," says Sarah. "We think highly of the school."

"That's good to hear," Sari says. "Abe, were you brought up religious?"

"Not that religious. When Sarah and I were growing up, Conservative Judaism was being watered down. Now, more and more people are looking for spirituality within Judaism. I find that refreshing."

"Steve says you meditate. You seem so completely at ease. Do you practice Jewish meditation?" Sari asks.

"I like to think so."

It was such a delight praying today. Going to temple enlightened was a whole new experience. In general, I've found it boring over the years. Singing the prayers in Hebrew (which I only vaguely understand) and doing the rituals have been mostly empty exercises. What was missing was my own deep sense of spirituality and connection to my God. Maharishi said that spirituality begins after Cosmic Consciousness. Now that statement makes perfect sense.

"At the center of your being you have the answer."

Lao Tzu

Chapter Seven

As I sit in my office responding to emails, waiting for my Tuesday Self class to start, my phone buzzes. It's Rose. How nice.

"Daddy, I got the job!" she says. "I didn't think I would, so many people were applying. I got it!"

"Oh, my Lord. The one at Pomona? For next fall?"

"Exactly."

"My sweet Lord. My Lord. I'm so happy for us."

"I'm beside myself with joy," she says. "I'll be teaching senior seminars on my two favorite writers, Walt Whitman and Ralph Waldo Emerson. Can Becky, Isaac, and I all fit in our old house?"

"Not a problem. It'll be wonderful."

"Gotta go. Gotta call Mom."

Language is often so descriptive of experience and can tell us quite a bit about reality. Rose said she was "beside herself with joy." There's a school of philosophy called the philosophy of language. One of its goals is to determine what we actually mean when we say things like that. Lately, being "beside myself with joy" has become my new baseline. From the part of me that is beside myself, I now can, and often do, rise to heights of exultation, or dive deep into reverence of the Holiness, or expand out to embrace the bounty of Beatitude, or just bask in sunny silliness. A variety of emotions and entertainments help pass the time, and we have nothing but time.

On a higher high, I stroll down to my classroom, picturing child-Becky's feet swinging back and forth as she waits for the French toast I'm cooking. I'll have to figure out how to work less when they're here. Maybe I'll even meditate less. I'm already enlightened. But maybe I shouldn't slack off, just in case?

Glancing through the classroom door, I see everyone seated except Obinna and Tom, who are both standing close to Tanisha. Obinna is above average in height, but Tom still towers over him. I stop for a moment to observe, sensing I won't be seen. Based on Tom's gesticulations and facial expressions, he's telling Tanisha a story. Obinna is trying to get into the conversation, without much success. Tanisha appears uncomfortable with Tom's attention, but she's listening politely. I walk into the classroom, breaking up the triangle. They seat themselves. Tom sits behind Tanisha. On the chalkboard is my prompt for today, which I wrote when I first arrived this morning:

Questions?

"I hope you all enjoyed our fine Southern California weekend. I'm assuming you came prepared with at least one question. As I mentioned last time, I'm going to start with students who need more class participation grades, and then I'll open the floor. I'm sorry to put anyone on the spot, but not *that* sorry."

I look through my grade book, which I keep in a notebook with a pencil. Not everything is better on a computer. There are four students who have not yet participated significantly enough. I'll start with them. I look for Asher, who changes his seat every class. He seemed shy even when I met with him one-on-one. There he is in the back, my first victim.

"Asher, do you have a question we can discuss today?"

"I do." He seems apprehensive. He strokes his beard and looks up at me. "Professor, there's a rumor going around that you've recently reached Cosmic Consciousness. Is it true?" Everyone stops. They lean forward, waiting for my answer. Even Tom is attentive.

I expected as much sometime during this class. Though I've been trying hard to downplay it, there's a noticeable difference in me since my enlightenment. I respect Asher for having the courage to broach the subject. It's fair game for my students to want to know if they have an enlightened teacher in a philosophy class about enlightenment.

"This course is not about me, though it is ultimately personal. This course is about your Self and my Self. One of the reasons I feel I'm qualified to teach this class is that I have practiced and studied meditation for many years. This has given me insight into what Maharishi and the Vedic literature are talking about. Other than those qualifications, we will not discuss my state of consciousness because it isn't relevant. What is relevant is using your question as a learning opportunity." The disappointment is palpable. They were hoping for something juicy.

"Asher, in the Bhagavad Gita there's a discussion about whether an enlightened person has any external distinguishing signs or qualities. Here, I think I can find it." I pick my Gita up and flip to my bookmark. "Chapter two, verse fifty-four. 'Arjuna said: What are the signs of a man whose intellect is steady, who is absorbed in the Self, O Keshava? How does the man of steady intellect speak, how does he sit, how does he walk?'

"Asher, do you remember the answer to those questions posed by Arjuna? Does a man absorbed in the Self, a man of steady intellect, have external signs that can be attributed to Cosmic Consciousness?" Asher seems shaken that the question has been turned back to him, but then he relaxes. He knows the answer.

"Maharishi, in his commentary, says there aren't any clearly distinguishing features. It's impossible to tell for sure."

"Correct. Very good."

I glance down at my list for the next student: Joseph.

This is Joseph's first class with me. He took Intro to Philosophy two years ago, during one of the few semesters I didn't co-teach it. When he showed up last class, he had shaved off his scraggly, failed attempt at a beard—a smart move. I found him intelligent and well-spoken during our one-on-one. His rough draft incorporated fascinating aspects of the Kabbalah, some of which I hadn't previously encountered. Of course, after I read it, I researched those aspects so I could help Joseph correlate those ideas with Vedic concepts. I'm looking forward to reading the final version.

"Joseph, what question of yours can I attempt to answer?"

He gives me a half-smile. "Patanjali says that it's possible to gain mastery over nature by practicing the sidhis. Doesn't that turn man into a god? And if man can become a god, then won't the power corrupt him, putting our universe at risk? You've said temptation is a basic fact of life at every level. It seems like science fiction. I think we all want power, and Patanjali is just giving us false hope."

"Excellent questions. These are the kinds of questions that reading and digesting Patanjali should bring to mind. If I may, I will extrapolate. First, how is it possible for us puny humans to gain mastery over nature? As we have discussed, Vedic philosophy holds that we are pure consciousness, that everything in our universe is made of the same pure consciousness, and that the laws of physics spring from pure consciousness. If this is true—and if we are completely absorbed in our Self and can learn to act while absorbed in our Self—then it follows that we can control the universe and nature because we can control our Self. In Unity Consciousness, there is no boundary between one's inner Self and one's outer Self, or Chhandas, since all objects of experience are experienced as Self. In the same way we can control our bodies, in Unity Consciousness we can control the universe, according to Patanjali.

"But don't worry: God, in Her and His infinite wisdom, has created absolute safeguards to protect against some enlightened Yogi in Unity Consciousness running amok. It's impossible to be in Unity Consciousness—or Cosmic Consciousness for that matter—and not act in accord with God's wishes and plans. It's not that free will has been lost but that being in such an exalted state necessitates being in harmony with God's will. There is evil in the world. This is in harmony with God's plan. According to Vedic philosophy, a Yogi in Cosmic Consciousness or higher will not do evil because the desire to do so would not arise."

As I've been walking back and forth lecturing, I've watched Tom doodle on his yellow legal pad. He draws well. There are no notes on the pad. Noticing I'm looking at his doodles, Tom raises his fingers and continues to add finishing touches.

"I have a comment," Tom says.

"Yes, Tom."

He stops drawing.

"You said that evil is in harmony with God's plan. If there is a God, then that has to be true because God can do anything *It* wants to do. It could get rid of evil with a snap of Its fingers. Those invisible beings in high places reached one of the lower stages of enlightenment, right, then gave in to temptation to get power? They didn't keep playing the game until its end. They lost and they knew it. They then tried to lure weaklings into the same temptation they fell for. But temptation is just God's way of separating the weak from the strong, isn't it? God's just trying to keep our universe fun and interesting. Isn't it like a video game? Once we get good enough and do the things the game teaches us to do, we can get to the next level, and the next, until we win."

"Thank you, Tom. You did a great job of explaining some difficult concepts. Your analogy between game design and life on Earth is very appropriate."

Tom looks down. He's pleased with himself.

"Joseph, getting back to your comment—that this all seems like science fiction—brings up a concept that I have written about. I believe that most of the major works in the arts, theater, and literature are considered major because they strike a harmonious chord within our collective consciousness. The works help us remember something important we need in order to continue our collective growth. Remember, Plato said we are born possessing all knowledge, and our goal is to remember it. Also, one of my favorite quotes from the Baal Shem Tov, Jewish mystic and founder of Hasidic Judaism, is 'Forgetfulness leads to exile while remembrance is the secret of redemption.' I believe the Baal Shem Tov is saying that if we forget who and what we are, which is part of God, then we lose our connection to God. Reconnecting to God and thereby remembering and knowing our divine Self is God's plan to save us from our limited selves."

Ravi raises his hand. He's dressed more conservatively today: a gray, plaid button-up, hair slicked back. His new look is quite dapper.

"Professor, may I ask a question I've prepared?"

I'll take it as it comes. Ravi is the first Indian student I've had in this class in two or three years. Given his excellent answer to the 'we have nothing but time' question, he already has the highest mark for class participation.

Ravi opens his notebook and carefully reads, "Professor, you have not discussed the role of desire as it relates to enlightenment. Maharishi discusses desire in his commentary on the Gita, but his ideas are contrary to the views of my guru, Guru Parkash Ram. My guru and his movement, Siddha Fellowship, say that even within a marriage, after sufficient procreation has taken place, the husband and wife should strive for celibacy in order for their marriage to rise to a higher spiritual level. My guru said that if a spiritual aspirant were truly focused on enlightenment, he would become a reclusive monk, removing himself from the world of desires and ridding himself of desire through austerities, yoga, and meditation. The monk needs to give up all earthly possessions and renounce and defeat his desires. Doing so is the first step in attaining liberation." He turns the page.

"I will read you a quote from the Gita: 'Arjuna said: What is it that impels a man to commit sin, even involuntarily, as if driven by force, O Varshneya? The Blessed Lord said: It is desire…all-consuming and most evil. Know this to be the enemy here on earth.' And here is another: 'When a man acts without longing, having relinquished all desires, free from the sense of "I" and "mine," he attains to peace.'"

I feel warm inside. I didn't know how serious Ravi and his family were in their search for enlightenment. A feeling of kinship surges through me. It's as if we have bumped into each other in an exotic, remote land and discovered that we both come from the same rural city in California. I hold myself in, thinking about my father and the shovel.

"Ravi, I have deep respect for your enlightened guru and the Siddha Fellowship. Maharishi's movement and the Siddha Fellowship have different focuses. My understanding is that your guru wanted his fellowship to be a religious organization. I have been to prayer services at your temple in Malibu a few times. The temple and the services were beautiful.

"Transcendental Meditation was never meant to be a religion, nor was it meant to be a religious organization; it was meant to be a mental technique that could be done by anyone, regardless of the practitioner's religious or philosophical beliefs. It's my understanding that Maharishi did not give many recommendations as to sexual conduct, deferring to the precepts of one's own religion. Maharishi, though, did discuss the general problem of desire.

"There are many great traditions that feel desire must be conquered or extinguished for spiritual growth to occur. That can work, but it's difficult—and not much fun. Maharishi's tradition of Vedic masters believes that an easier and more pleasant way to deal with the problem of desire is to satiate it, not fight or kill it. During Transcendental Meditation, the awareness is naturally drawn toward the charm, peacefulness, and Bliss of pure consciousness. The closer the awareness gets to experiencing its Self, which is pure consciousness, the more it and its desires are satiated. When the awareness comes out of meditation, it's like the cloth dipped in dye. The awareness retains some of the satisfaction of desire it experienced during meditation. This grows over time.

"As a spiritual aspirant continues to meditate, over the years she will find herself acting in accordance with God's will. The more she acts from that level, the more she experiences God's support in the fulfillment of desires. Taking the satiation of desire to the extreme, a meditator might practice samyama and thereby achieve the special abilities, or sidhis, that Patanjali writes about. To use the sidhis in an improper manner to satisfy one's desires, or in other words, in a way contrary to God's will, is an alluring temptation that can lead the yogi astray. Not succumbing to the temptation to use the sidhis for improper desires and only practicing samyama for the spiritual growth it provides, the yogi then gets much, much more than he gives up. By renouncing the fruit of samyama, the special abilities, the yogi's desires are satisfied to an even greater degree. Eventually, God willing, the yogi will achieve the fulfillment of our greatest desire, that of liberation and true freedom. Desire *is* the enemy, but it can be defeated in a much easier and more pleasurable way than by trying to suppress it or kill it."

Thank you, my Lord, for allowing me to attain enlightenment without having had to suppress my desires. I was about to fully devote myself to my quest for enlightenment, detaching myself from the world and from my dear Sarah. You took pity on me, and I never had to make that painful sacrifice.

"Ravi, does that answer your question?"

I look at Ravi. He's not buying into Maharishi's theory of satiation of desire. I can see, even upside down, that his notebook is filled with neatly written questions. He chooses another from his list, and reads aloud in a monotone, "In my tradition, a Yogi is required to be brahmacharya, or a celibate. Patanjali's *Yoga Sutras* lists brahmacharya specifically as one of the yamas, or great universal laws for yogis to follow. You have not discussed celibacy as a spiritual prerequisite in this class yet. What are Maharishi's views concerning celibacy?"

"I have wondered about that. To my knowledge, Maharishi did not discuss celibacy much, at least not to meditators like me who were not teachers of TM. In Maharishi's translation and commentary on the Bhagavad Gita, he speaks of two different but equal types of spiritual aspirants: the monks who retire from society to dedicate themselves to rapid spiritual progress, and the householders who continue to live in society while on the path toward enlightenment. I assume Maharishi felt monks would be well-served in their quest by being celibate, whereas householders, I think he would say, should practice moderation in all things." I want to move on. I look at my grade book again.

There are two students left whom I was planning to call on today; one of them is Tom. I'm interested to see if Tom has prepared a question. He still has not scheduled a one-on-one meeting. I was planning to ask him about it again after class, even though that could spark an explosion, until I reviewed the course syllabus this morning. Though I mention the one-on-one meetings, there's nothing in the syllabus that specifically says they are a requirement. I have a feeling Tom knows this all too well.

"Tom, do you have a question we can discuss today?"

Tom glances at his fellow classmates and leans back in his chair. "Why does *shit* happen to people who don't deserve it?" He then studies the ceiling as if something interesting is there.

"A good, classic question—though usually phrased differently. Thank you, Tom. When I answer this question, there are three scenarios I give that, taken together, will help you understand my reasoning.

"First, when a good, well-meaning parent punishes a seriously misbehaving child, that child may believe he did not deserve it. The parent knows better and administers the punishment, hoping it will help the child resume the proper path. Years later, when the child is wiser and perhaps also a parent, he concludes that the punishment, though seemingly harsh at the time, was necessary. Now having greater maturity, a higher perspective, and possibly even the experience of parenthood, he forgives the parent. Lesson learned.

"Second, when a judge sentences a criminal to incarceration as punishment for a crime, she is not necessarily attempting to teach the criminal a lesson, as was the point in our first scenario. It's possible that the judge, like the parent, hopes the criminal will see the error of his ways and correct his future behavior—what the law calls specific deterrence. But first and foremost, the judge must mete out justice for reasons of fairness and to deter others, so she adjusts the punishment to fit the crime. The criminal, under this second scenario, may not understand and does not need to understand why he is being punished.

"Third, a more theoretical approach, and one that I think Han will appreciate: Any finite number divided by infinity, which is the same as comparing that finite number to infinity, almost equals, or approaches, zero—the infinitesimal. Also, consider the passage Ravi read to us in our last class." I reach for my Gita. I find the right page, having read this passage at least once each year to students in this class. "Lord Krishna, in the Bhagavad Gita, says, 'There never was a time when I was not, nor you...Nor will there ever be a time when all of us shall cease to be. As the dweller in this body passes into childhood, youth, and age, so also does he pass into another body.' If all of us will never cease to be, then *this* life, however painful or wonderful, when compared to our eternity approaches zero, or insignificance."

A memory of that long, long corridor with all my endless lives envelops me. This life, Abe's life, is everything and almost nothing.

"As we mature and grow in wisdom, lifetime to lifetime, Vedic philosophy says we will gain a higher perspective where we will be able to remember our multitude of lives and see that the pain and indignities we endured were beneficial and fitting. Coming to that realization, we will forgive God for inflicting such pain upon us just as the parent forgives his parents. Also, given the infinite nature of our souls, when we compare on the one hand our increasing Bliss and knowledge over the vast expanse of time and the infinite grace bestowed on us by God, and on the other hand the pain we felt as metaphorical children, the pain approaches insignificance. We must endure, buoyed up by the knowledge of better times to come. As one old adage has it, 'all things come to those who wait.'

"When all things have come and the individual soul has reached Unity Consciousness, as all souls will according to Vedic philosophy, then past pain, past loss, past horror fades toward the infinitesimal in comparison to the magnificence of the realized Self. In Unity Consciousness, the dualities of life, the agony and the ecstasy, are found to be just different sides of the same thing. In Unity Consciousness the realization comes that it was all your Self. To know your Self, it had to be this way.

"Tom, how does that sit with you?"

Tom glances around. His jaw quivers. He's holding his breath. He explodes. "I can't wait until forever! You're talking about the end. I'm talking about now. If the God you talk about is so good and almighty, why does he make us suffer? You said we're just children who need to be punished. Why can't your God teach us without hurting us? You say He has the power." Tom stands. He's shaking.

He looks around, trying to make eye contact with any of his classmates. Their eyes are averted.

"You're all sheep!" he yells at them. "Baa, baa, baa—you question your all-knowing professor. Cut the crap! We're here for answers that will help us *now*. If we can't get help now, then—then, what's the use?

"I, for one, will *not* be placated. I'm out of here!" He grabs his notebook and backpack and starts to walk.

My heart pounds. I'm furious. I'm being disrespected in front of my class. *I am going to fail that son of a bastard!*

"Tom, if you walk out now, you may fail this class."

He stops and looks at me, his eyes burning with rage. "Sir, we have already talked about failure." He walks out.

Maybe I won't be able to fail him. If his father is as big a donor as Tom suggested, I should ask the administration before failing him. Damn these school politics! Then it hits me: I'm enlightened. Why am I so angry and petty? What's the big deal if Tom walks out of my class, dissing me? I settle down, but not completely. Something is wrong.

Abe, resorting to his standard go-to, asks if there are any more questions. He takes a few, pontificates loquaciously, but I've escaped. I was taken by my Self. It snuck up and snatched me as silently as an expert thief, whisking me away from my worry and anger. I was taken gently, without a struggle. I was happy to go.

Abe walks over to his desk, where my phone is resting. He looks at it. Five minutes until the end of class. He gazes at his students—so attentive and young. They're waiting to hear his decision. Should he answer another question, or expound upon another Vedic concept, or let them leave early?

"On Thursday the twenty-ninth, we will discuss my theory of personality from a Vedic perspective. I'm passing out a sheet of paper with directions for downloading a copy of a soon-to-be published chapter I wrote, detailing this theory. Please download and read it prior to Thursday's class. I look forward to seeing you then."

As the rest of the students vacate their seats, Obinna, Tanisha, and Chris switch so they occupy every other seat in the front row. I sense growing heat between Tanisha and Obinna. They'll be good for each other.

As we talk, it's clear Obinna wants to discuss political philosophy, especially Marxist theory concerning the evolution of the world toward communism, but Abe hijacks the conversation, adding some of Maharishi's age of enlightenment theory to Obinna's Marxist ideas. They spend a productive half hour solving the world's problems.

When I get home, I find Sarah in our backyard, harvesting her garden. She texted me a few hours ago that Shoshana and Sam were on their way home from Las Vegas—the route back runs through Claremont—and timed their drive to pass us at dinnertime. Much of what we will eat tonight will come from Sarah's garden: fresh herbs, lettuces, squash, zucchini, heirloom tomatoes, corn, and cantaloupe for dessert. Sarah gives me my marching orders, and we prepare a fall feast, skip asanas and pranayama due to time constraints, and meditate.

*Mantra, mantra, mantra, maaaaa...*Abe's world fades out; my Self fades in. Abe is a distant, small part of who I am. *I am so much more than Abe and his little life. Mantra, mantra, mantraaaaa...*Deep in the center of my ocean of consciousness, I sense something is looking for me, something I, in return, have been searching for—something fundamental and foundational. Though I am already still and silent, I let go of everything Abe holds near and dear, and settle down further. The less Abe is, the closer It is. It is the pinpoint of Holy Light. I know that It is what allows me to Be. I bow before It in complete supplication. It Is. I am not. It commands me, *"Be still!"* And I am so, so still that Abe and I are gone. It reaches out and gathers us in…We lose consciousness momentarily, overcome by Its majesty. *It is simple. We are full. We are loved.*

I lie down, content. A short time later I begin to feel an odd, radiant warmth coming from Sarah, who finished meditating a little while before I did. She's usually colder than me and likes to snuggle for my heat. Now, she's warming me up as if I was in front of a winter fireplace. *What's up with that?* I turn toward her, unfocus my gaze, and with my second sight I see she is glowing from her center. *What…? How odd?* I don't want to disturb her. I look at the clock. We have a little bit of time before our guests arrive. I'll let her rest. I need to rest after that meditation.

My mind/body wakes up after nine minutes, feeling special. I look at the clock again. Sam and Shoshana should be here soon. I get up and get dressed. There are lots of things I need to get done.

The Israelis arrive eighteen minutes later, tired from their drive but excited to see us. I usher them in with happy hugs and kisses. Seating them on the couch, I serve them the mint iced tea Sarah knew they would like after their drive, proud that the mint is fresh from her garden. I put out the fresh-cut veggies with dip as an appetizer, as Sarah planned.

"Abe, what's new?" Sam says cheerfully. "You look real good, very good, like you have been meditating a lot. Where's your better half?"

"We just finished meditating before you arrived, and she fell asleep. If she doesn't get up soon, I'll wake her."

Shoshana raises her finger to her lips. "Shhh, let her sleep! We should talk quietly out back." She motions for us to follow her. We pick up our drinks and appetizers and pad to the back of the house. Shoshana opens the screen door; we seat ourselves at the table on the porch.

Sam says, "Vegas was good to us again; won enough to pay for the vacation and a little extra."

"How's Sarah's store?" Shoshana asks. "Is it still making—" She freezes midsentence. I look at her and then at Sam. Both are transfixed by something behind me. I turn. Sarah is there, her hair down. She closes the screen door and walks toward us. I was right—something is very different. She walks the walk of a saint.

She sits next to me. "My store is doing very well, thank God."

None of us can talk. We all see it. A halo surrounds Sarah's head and shoulders. I have a strange urge to kiss her feet.

Shoshana stammers for possibly the first time ever. "It, it, wow, it—oh my God, it happened, do you see it too?"

I look over at Sam. He's speechless. Sarah lowers her chin and eyes toward me briefly. I need to say something.

"Shall we have dinner?" I ask.

"Most of it is freshly harvested from our garden. Abe helped," Sarah says sweetly. She stands, and we follow her magnetically.

We sit at our dining room table. Sarah moves but seems to be standing still. The individually prepared salads we put in the refrigerator appear before us magically.

"We should say a prayer," Sarah says. "If I may?" She closes her eyes. "Dear holy Father, we thank you for your blessings. It is with your grace that we enjoy your bounty. *Baruch atah Adonai, Eloheinu melech ha-olam, ha-motzi lechem min ha-aretz.*" Her eyes open. She breaks off a piece of bread from the braided loaf, places it in her mouth, and then tears off a small piece for each of us, tossing them to us one at a time. Sam and Shoshana catch theirs. I drop mine, still in shock.

"Please, let's not talk about me," she says with a disarming smile. "I want to hear about you. How was your trip to Sin City?"

We have a pleasant dinner and evening. We honor Sarah's request, though her radiance is impossible to ignore. Our friends don't want to stay long. They must be at work early to check on what has happened while they were away.

At the door saying goodbye, Shoshana kisses Sarah on the cheek and says, "When you're ready to talk, call me. I need to know how it is. No hurry. When it's time."

Sarah kisses both of her cheeks and does the same to Sam. "We missed you both. I'm so glad you stopped by. We'll try to visit soon. We'll talk." We finish our goodbyes. I'm alone with my Sarah. She takes my hand and leads me to the couch facing the fireplace.

She rests her hands in her lap, and her visage, shadowed by the floor lamp, reminds me of a blonde Mona Lisa. She raises her eyebrows, looks at all of me, and says, "We are much closer now."

"What happened? Do you want to talk about it?"

"Our Father found me and brought me home. I was lost. Let's clean up and do our night program together. It will work wonderfully. We can talk tomorrow when things are clearer."

We do the dishes and clean the counters, tables, and floor. I want to know everything, but I'll wait. When all is clean, we get ready for bed, prop ourselves up, and start our night techniques. She's right. It's a work of wonder. *Thank you, my Lord, for taking care of Sarah.*

"The world is won by those who let it go.
But when you try and try, the world is beyond the winning."

Lao Tzu

Chapter Eight

My alarm chirps, jolting me awake. It's 7:04. I'm running late. I'll have to cut corners this morning to make it to my first class on time. I sit at the edge of the bed, stretch—my body and joints are stiff and sore. *Haven't felt that in a while?* Everything in our bedroom is flat and dull and stagnant. I go inside. I don't find my Self—only my constricted little self. Things are close in on me. I feel so small. I don't feel God. Where did God go? My eyes moisten. *Such a baby.* Something grips me by the scruff of my neck. I lash out, thrash around, trying to free myself. Nothing happens. I'm caught. I'm dangling. I'm being pulled by an icy, hard hand. It's Time. Time has imprisoned me in each moment—each moment—each moment. I am back in the grays of Kansas. Technicolor Oz is a dream. *Damn! Damn it! I won't! I will not! I can fix this.*

I need to meditate. That's *got* to do it. I brush my teeth and visit the bathroom, then prop myself up against the headboard in our bed. What if it doesn't work and I stay this way? *No! I dedicated my life to enlightenment; I deserve to be enlightened!*

*Mantra, mantra, mantra…*feeling antsy, can't settle down… *Mantra, mantra, mantra…can't get those voices out of my head. To Hell with them! Did they just predict this or did they do it* *to me? Mantra, mantra, mantra…*breath not slowing; anxious, angry…*Mantra, mantra, maant…*

This isn't working. I need Sarah. She got up hours ago, when it was still dark. I give up and lie down. I'll try again later.

I showered last evening. I'll skip morning coffee, won't read the news. There's time to do asanas and pranayama and meditate again. I'm going to call in sick.

I find Sarah on our back deck, sitting at the table, facing the house. She's sipping coffee and reading on her iPad.

"I made extra coffee for you. You'll enjoy it more than your instant."

"Running late, slept in—gonna do asanas, pranayama, and a full meditation before class. No time for coffee."

"Drink some coffee. You have time. You'll get a headache without it."

"I don't want coffee. It can't be good for us."

I go to our son's room with the yoga mat on the floor and do my asanas and pranayama exactly as they should be done. Then I go to our bedroom and meditate for longer than I should, using all the time I have before class. My meditation is OK, but not enlightening. I feel queasy.

I dress for the day and find Sarah, still out back. "How are you feeling, honey?" I ask. "You look, ah…enlightened."

"I feel good. I'm so sorry you have to rush off for class. It's such a delightful, warm morning." She wraps her arms around my waist. I bury my head in her neck and hold on. I am weighed down, heavy inside. *All that I have done is undone.* My knees buckle. She supports me. Futility fills me like water in a plastic sack. Sarah rubs my neck and back. I am punctured. I sob as it streams out in slow, tiny trickles. She waits until I've been emptied.

"It will come back. We can't know our Father's ways, but it's always for the best. I am here for you. I love you deeply."

Of course she sees it. We'll talk about it later; the wound is too fresh. I try to pull myself together—stiff upper lip and all that. "Gotta go. I'll be home around five. Let's meditate and go to our Indian restaurant."

"Sounds nice. I'll be here when you get home."

On my way out, I look in on the girls' and Amos's rooms. We haven't changed them since the kids left, other than moving Amos's bed to the side so we could have two asana mats. When they come home, they sleep as they did as children. I wish they were all here now.

My walk to work is fine. I just need to calm down. I'm acting like a spoiled child. I've heard about this happening to people who thought they had reached Cosmic Consciousness. Paul, a good friend of mine who teaches philosophy in Fairfield, recently told me about a math professor who said she was enlightened for a week, only to lose it while playing tennis.

I felt predestined to achieve enlightenment in this lifetime, not to finally get to the top of the mountain only to tumble back down. Sarah's enlightenment feels like a cruel joke—God rubbing salt into my wound. I need to be bigger than that. I need to look at things from that higher perspective I keep preaching about. Only yesterday I knew and experienced the world as a divine gift from God. I witnessed it and reveled in its grandeur. I need to accept what's happened graciously, humbly. None of us deserve anything. We are not entitled to anything, except our experience of time. Focusing on that will bring me closer to where I need to be.

In my office, I find my laptop turned off—strange, as I don't remember turning it off. It feels like forever waiting for the old thing to boot up.

Ever since I got my new home laptop with a solid state drive, my work computer feels so slow.

I chuckle at my own impatience. When it's finally on, I sign in to my campus email. A few students have sent me questions and some have sent papers to read prior to our appointments. There are the usual administrative memos, the morning spam, and an email from the academic dean. She wants to meet with me later in the week and has suggested a few dates and times. I check my calendar and send her a short response. I wonder what she wants. It's probably something to do with the five-college joint steering committee.

I need to relax and come up with a plan before class or I'll be too distracted to teach. What do I need to do to get it back? I could try Ayurvedic Panchakarma purification. Yogis have used it for thousands of years to help their spiritual progress. The two times I've done it, I found it quite helpful, but it's expensive. If I go to the Raj Spa in Fairfield for Panchakarma, I can also get a Vedic Vibe treatment to remove obstacles to enlightenment, but that's pricey too. I do have my racetrack winnings. Sarah will let me use them for a good cause. I'll need to be vigilant with my diet. From now on I'll eat only what is appropriate for my Ayurvedic body type. And I'll take those Ayurvedic supplements I was prescribed last time I was at the Raj.

Ravi's question about chastity comes to mind. Now that Sarah's enlightened, maybe she'll understand.

I open my phone's calendar. If I go to Fairfield, it'll have to be over Thanksgiving. I'll have to miss Thanksgiving in New York with the family. I should call Sarah and discuss this with her, but I just don't have the emotional energy right now. I'd also have to cancel classes on the Tuesday and Wednesday before Thanksgiving, which won't make the administration happy, but this is an emergency. I'll call the Raj after class and schedule my treatments.

Shit! I'm getting a caffeine-withdrawal headache, and it's gonna be bad. I take my stack of class stuff and head down to Rita's office. She should be in by now, and she always has a pot of coffee ready. I just hope she's busy; the thought of small talk is too much to bear. Maybe the coffee will clear my head. My cosmic sinuses went with my Cosmic Consciousness.

I teach my two classes for the day, my head throbbing the whole time. It's torture. The students don't care. I don't want to teach.

In my office, I bull my way through the work I shouldn't take home. I want to get home. I keep envisioning Sarah as a life raft. I'm swimming toward her in the open ocean. Maybe she can save me. Maybe Sarah will somehow get rid of this blasted headache.

I call the Raj and schedule my Thanksgiving Panchakarma treatment. Luckily, they happened to have the afternoon treatment time I like available. At least something is going my way.

When I get home a little after five-thirty, the house smells wonderful. Everything has been cleaned and rearranged; not just maid-day clean, but reorganized and placed just so. I do some exploring. New items have appeared, some from our attic, some from Goodness, and some are just a surprise. A few old things have disappeared, but everything seems to be within a clear, new decorating scheme. I never would have thought

Sarah had it in her to redo our house. Her store always looks great and she keeps her garden in perfect order, but our home has been eclectically chaotic from the beginning.

I find Sarah in our polished kitchen, apron on, dressed as if she's going out. She's been busy cooking. I survey the bounty, finding a few of my favorites as well as some new things.

"Indian tonight sounded boring and too spicy for you," she says matter-of-factly. "I cooked Pitta-pacifying veggie dishes to soothe your fire and anger. Your Pitta is aggravated given your new state of affairs."

I sample a vegetable stir-fry with seasoned tofu—very tasty—and examine the other dishes.

"Honey," I say, "you've been working hard. The house looks amazing and the dinner even better. Come, sit."

It's too hot in the backyard, so we sit on the couch. I think about turning the AC on but opt to just take my shirt and pants off. Sarah positions herself at the end of the couch, bare feet in my lap. I massage her feet.

She looks at me from her end of the couch. I'm almost naked and sweating from the heat. She smiles, not at my comical frustration, but from her center. It's infectious, uplifting. My breath softens. I relax.

After a few seconds of silence, she says, "Yes, I'm still in Cosmic Consciousness. It has been a great, eventful day. I spent the morning getting used to all of the changes. I was so fascinated by what I was feeling and seeing and everything that I forgot to meditate this morning. By about midmorning, I had adjusted enough to start doing things and I haven't stopped since. It's amazing what I can do when I can focus and have boundless energy.

"We needed a new atmosphere in here, so I moved things around. I stopped by Goodness and took a few things. I already adjusted our QuickBooks to account for it. In retrospect, I wasn't ready to leave the house."

She's right. The atmosphere needed a change. The house feels harmonious now. She is so content and centered; I think she's ready for questions. I'm dying to know every detail.

"I don't know if you want to talk about it," I say, "but I'm curious. What happened when you reached enlightenment? Was it just out of the blue or was there a lead up to it?"

"So," she says, raising her finger, waggling it in the air back and forth and then pointing it at me, "you want me to be your second case study for your new book, huh?" She circles the finger, accusingly. I watch it go around and around. I want to laugh but don't need to. I feel happy. That dainty, sweet finger must be a magic wand.

"Well, I'm more than happy to be one of your subjects," she says, placing both hands on her thighs, leaning back. I glance at that finger, wanting more.

Looking above my head, she goes on. "I think what tipped the scales for me, allowing me to settle down and let go, was the terrifying realization that I was no longer needed. You were enlightened. You didn't need me to take care of you, or really need me at all. Our kids are grown. I felt alone and abandoned, without a purpose.

"The only person I could take care of was me. That was the only purpose I could find for my life. Without that, there was no reason to go on. And I had to take care of someone who didn't want to be taken care of—someone who had given up. The world outside was not going to bring my father back. I was exhausted from searching outside for something or someone to replace what he tore from me. I had been treading water, but I was spent. I had no energy, no will to keep going. I sunk under the waves. Under the water, in its quietness, I was able to hear our Father's still voice, calling to me from within."

"I'm sorry I wasn't able to support you more. I didn't realize how down you were. I thought it was mainly anxiety... Had your meditations gotten better before it happened?"

"Not really. But the pain outside had become so unbearable that the only refuge I had was to transcend this world. Now I forgive my dad and wish him well."

"Would you want to see him?"

"I'm not that enlightened. It would hurt my mom. I do think I'm over my panic attacks. And I have no anxiety or sadness now—it's so weird. It's like I was asleep in a dark cave, having recurrent nightmares. I'm now outside in the sunshine, knowing that I've woken up."

"I see—that's a classic description."

"Enough about me. Tell me about your day." Her voice is as smooth as maple syrup on warm pancakes.

Thinking about what to tell her, my happiness evaporates. I'm surprised at how shrill my thoughts are and how bad my head hurts. "I'm OK, but I've got a caffeine-withdrawal headache that's resisting both coffee and Tylenol. Maybe I'll take some ibuprofen?"

She readjusts her position so she's sitting against the back of the couch and directs me to lie with my head in her lap. I feel silly, but right now I'll try anything. I lie face up, head in her lap, feet stretched out on the sofa. She strokes my forehead and sings "Here Comes the Sun" in a soothing, swaying voice.

I haven't heard her sing in years. I've always thought of her voice as flat and fair, but now it's positively angelic. It hits me. Our anniversary is tomorrow. How could I forget?

She massages my forehead and sings the song again. I wake up, never realizing I had fallen asleep. I feel much better. "How long did I sleep?"

"Oh, maybe eleven minutes. Let's meditate."

"Fine." I get up. We move to the bed, adjust our pillows, close our eyes, and off we go.

Mantra, mantra, mantraaa…my headache is gone. *Gotta love her!* Sinuses still irritatingly congested, though—*this is life, back in the real world. Mantra, mantra, mantraaa…*

My meditation is fair. Sarah's radiating next to me, filling the room with sparks of Bliss, as I sit there like a lump of coal hoping I'll ignite. I feel so petty; I wish she'd turn down her intensity. Most likely, though, she's working hard to downplay how good she's feeling. Maybe I should retire at the end of this school year and move to Fairfield with Sarah? I have to get back to enlightenment.

After meditating, we eat the dinner she cooked. It's truly amazing. I can taste the love and care she put into it. Eating her food is the closest I've been to enlightenment since it abandoned me this morning. *'The Lord giveth and the Lord taketh away.'* After cleaning up, we sit on the back deck. It seems like it's going to cool off, but over the course of a few minutes, the wind shifts. It blows from the east, off the desert, instead of the west, off the ocean.

As Sarah looks things up on the internet on her tablet, I guzzle a large pitcher of sweet, iced Ayurvedic Pitta tea she made for me and my anger. I'm trying to cool down, barely tolerating the hot, dry Santa Ana wind. It's called the devil wind, and they say it can drive you crazy, which is absolutely true. Sarah looks immune to it.

We don't talk for a while. I'm ready to go inside when Sarah says, "Abe, I've been thinking. I know we've planned to see the girls for Thanksgiving, but maybe you should go to Fairfield for Panchakarma and a Vedic Vibe treatment. We could put those racetrack winnings to good use. Last time you went there, you said it was quite helpful."

I won't be able to keep anything from her now. I need to get out of this heat, but Sarah's given me an opening to smooth over my trip to Fairfield, probably just as she's planned. I say, "That's a great idea. I'll call the Raj tomorrow and see if they can accommodate me." I push my chair out to stand.

"I don't think it will be a problem," she says. I sit on the edge of my chair. "Also, I'm not sure how to say this, so I'll just say it. I know how much enlightenment means to you. I am now even more in love with you and want you more than ever, both emotionally and physically—but maybe we should put our lovemaking on ice for a while. It seems to me that if you build up some extra energy you could use that for spiritual advancement. When you want or need me, in whatever way is good for you, I'm there. It's up to you."

Apparently, living with the enlightened Sarah is going to be an exercise in humility—not my strong suit. Sweat runs from my armpits. I have nowhere to hide. She's run ahead of me and has to keep circling back. *I am the professor. I do the teaching.*

"Are you sure?" I ask curtly. But my peevishness is sucked away like lint in a vacuum. I can't be cross with her. "I'll take all the help I can get," I say. "Also, we should do something special for our anniversary tomorrow. Can we go inside and turn on the AC? I can't think with this furnace in my face."

"We should have gone in when the wind shifted," she says to my back. I open the screen door and glance behind me. She's standing. "Go sit down," she points inside with that finger of hers. "I've got something else up my sleeve to help cool you down."

I collapse onto our sofa, thinking about what's up her sleeve. She comes in, turns on the AC, and gracefully moves to each window, shutting them. Then she disappears into the kitchen, reappearing with a pint of rocky road ice cream from the Ben & Jerry's a few blocks away.

"After I stopped at Goodness, I picked this up," she says, posing like a gameshow model with the alluring container. "I thought you'd like it."

As I luxuriate in the chocolaty cool creaminess, I offer her a scoop, but she turns it down. I smile, thinking she would've bought a quart if she wanted any. When I've cooled down, she asks, "Do you think it would help you back toward enlightenment if we lived in a Sthapatya Veda home?"

"According to Vedic theory, it would help. I think I've told you that there are quite a number of academics, myself included, who think that, historically, Sthapatya Veda philosophy was the source of Feng Shui. But we're not even *close* to being able to afford a Sthapatya Veda home. Our home faces north, which is OK, but we couldn't remodel it to be an east-facing Sthapatya Veda home. We'd have to build a new one. Ain't gonna happen; that's quite a dream." The thought of Austin's biotech company flits through my mind. I'll have to check its stock price.

"What's wrong with dreaming, mister? Didn't you tell me once that Freud wrote in *The Interpretation of Dreams* that dreams are really our attempts to fulfill wishes and desires? And don't you always say that an enlightened life is getting more and more? More of what we want and wish and dream until our desires are fulfilled? May it please the court, I petition Your Honor to think big, and I move to rescind your pragmatism.

Consciousness is a field of all possibilities, and we are pure consciousness, or so I have been told. I rest my case."

She picks up the empty ice cream carton and its clean spoon, inspects the inside in an exaggerated manner, and then nods at me as though I'm a child who just finished his medicine.

I look up at her and laugh heartily. She is delightful. Her comic timing is perfect. "Very impressive, Counselor," I get out. "I find in favor of living our dreams! You can defend me anytime."

"Let's just hope my little thief doesn't end up needing my skills," she says, wrinkling her adorable nose. "Let's go to bed early and do our night technique. I really enjoyed it last night. Remember, 'Early to bed and early to rise makes a man healthy, wealthy, and enlightened.'" Her joy is irrepressible. She knows exactly what she wants and is so strong now she'll get it. With her on my side, I'm starting to feel optimistic.

Walking toward our bedroom, it comes to me. If she wants us to live in a new Sthapatya Veda home to help me get back up there with her, it could happen.

It's Thursday morning. I slept OK—could have been better—but at least I'm not feeling as angry and overwhelmed as I did the last few days. It's early enough that I can go for a jog, shower, meditate, and still get to my office in plenty of time. Of course, Sarah has been up for who knows how long. She probably has run and cooked breakfast and done our laundry and mowed the lawn. I get dressed for exercise.

I find Sarah sitting at the child-sized green desk between the twin beds in our daughters' room, her laptop in front of her, papers and notes scattered all around. There are handwritten notes on the desk, some on each bed, and four or five sheets of paper behind her on the carpet. She glows at me as I enter, then turns back to her work.

"Our girls won't be coming home until their Christmas breaks," she says, as she types something into her iPad, "so I'm going to use their room for my office. I'll be done with it by the time either of them comes home."

I sit on Rose's bed, careful not to disturb Sarah's filing system. I peek at one of her notes.

Without turning, she chirps, "Curious as to what I'm doing, are ya? Well, I've decided to change the focus of my store."

"What's the new focus?"

"Do you remember that documentary we watched, *Herb & Dorothy*?" She shuffles some papers around.

"Oh, yes. Absolutely. That was a special night," I say as my heart sags.

Her face, when she looks at me, is broad and smooth, expansive like a cloudless spring sky. "Herb and Dorothy collected art because they loved it. They bought what moved them and what they could afford from struggling young artists. I want to go a step further."

I lose my focus, lost in the fine lines at the sides of her eyes.

"I want to change the business plan," she says, almost blushing, noticing my swoon. "I want my store to support undiscovered artists who have a special gift. I want to give them an annual contract, pay them decently for their art, then sell a lot of it at a small markup."

"I'd love to work with you on a new business plan," my heart says to hers.

"I wouldn't have it any other way, my dear. If the artists know they'll have a steady income, they can relax and create better stuff. Even in conflicted, agitated artists, art that will move us ultimately comes from their quiet, still core. And I want as many ordinary people to own original art as possible. It shouldn't just be for the well-off. Of course, we'll need to make a profit to stay afloat, so we can continue our mission. If our business plan is successful, I'd like to spread the idea to other communities."

I knew it! My mind races ahead. If it's successful, and it should be, we could hire more staff, open other stores, and eventually franchise the idea. She may not completely see the connection, but I do. This is her way of doing good, having fun, *and* getting us a new house. Buying call options on that biotech company was a bad idea anyway.

"Sounds exciting," I say. "Where are you going to find these artists?" I downplay my enthusiasm.

"I've already found a few online. Everything is online, if you're persistent. And I'm nothing but persistent at the moment."

"Let me know if there's anything I can do to help you," I say in earnest. "I'm going for a run. Wanna come?"

"Sounds good. Give me nine more minutes?" she says with unusual precision.

Nine minutes later, we're out the door. She keeps running ahead and circling back. After a mile, I slow to a brisk walk to catch my breath. I don't think she had such energy even in her forties. With all of her circling, she'll end up running at least twice as far as me. To her credit, she doesn't leave me behind.

As I walk to the college, I feel stronger. I *am* going to be OK. If I almost reached Cosmic Consciousness once, even briefly, I should be able to do it again, this time for good. My dazzling color has faded, but I have to hope I'll be able to dip myself into my Self again, and become colorfast. The air has a hint of crispness. Summer can't hold on to us much longer.

Approaching the college, I notice an elderly man in his yard wearing a buttoned-up gray cardigan. He's struggling with the latch on his white picket gate, trying to get out. I haven't seen his wife in maybe a year. I suspect she's passed.

"Can I help?" I ask.

"This damn gate is getting worse. It won't open." The man jiggles it.

The hinge is coming loose from its frame. I pull the gate up and inward, which re-aligns the latch so it can be opened. "There you go."

He looks at my face. "You're a professor at the college. My wife used to point you out to me."

"I remember your wife," I say gingerly.

"Yeah…She used to market for us. I've run out of food. I'll call my son. He'll come and fix the gate."

He steps through the gate, carefully holding on to it as it swings shut, making sure its strong spring doesn't force it back into the latch. It doesn't close. He'll be able to get back in. He totters off in the direction of the market. I walk the other way.

Now that I'm thinking more clearly, I need to figure out what went wrong. Why did I lose my enlightenment? Karma must have had a lot to do with it, and hubris for sure. Though I attempted to fight it, it has been my nature to act like I was intellectually and morally superior—just the poor shmuck the universe loves to knock off their high horse. I always was afraid that Proverbs 16:18 was somehow speaking to me, "Pride goeth before destruction, and a haughty spirit before a fall." When I was enlightened I knew that none of us was better than anyone else. We were all the same. And my experiment betting on the ponies probably was the final straw. A crow caws from high on a branch across the street. It sounds like it's laughing at me.

"Blessed are the meek: for they shall inherit the earth" pops into my head. True, it's not my nature to be meek. That's why I was humbled. Sarah, however, has always been much more meek, humble, and patient than me. I bet she won't lose her enlightenment. The crow caws again sharply and jumps off the branch. It falls much farther than I think it can, making me afraid it will hit the ground, and then it spreads its wings, rising as it beats the air. Two other crows perched nearby also take flight, rushing to join the one who laughed.

It comes to me. I think Jesus was ultimately referring to the enlightened when he spoke of the meek. The enlightened shall inherit the earth. That makes sense from a Vedic perspective. But there is something more to this. *What is it?* Something about Psalm 37 comes to mind. *What does Psalm 37 say?* Lost in thought, I almost trip on a broken, raised part of the sidewalk, the offending old tree oblivious to its spreading, swelling roots.

Oh yes. I mouth the part to myself: "*Be still before the Lord and wait patiently for him…the meek will inherit the land and enjoy peace and prosperity.*" The enlightened are truly still before the Lord and are perfectly patient as they wait to know Him. That was my experience. And what about Sarah? She is already enjoying the peace her enlightenment brings. I'm looking forward to sharing the next part, prosperity, with her. I'm in front of Pearsons Hall. It's a shame. If I had more time, I'd keep walking.

I go up to my office. There, I put in the necessary time and energy, and I manage to get a good deal of work done. An email pops up. The dean can meet with me tomorrow at three.

I review my notes for today's lecture, which I will give in, let's see, nineteen minutes. I would have preferred to give this lecture enlightened. Discussing how our personalities, individually and collectively, are shaped and directed by an unseen force of cosmic evolution makes perfect sense from an enlightened perspective, but now it seems so far away. I usually especially enjoy giving this lecture—professors love talking about their work—but today I'll have to pretend. I think about going downstairs to write the lecture title on the chalkboard, but I don't want to.

A few minutes before class, I walk downstairs. Most of the students are seated. They greet me courteously, as usual, but somehow they seem disingenuous today. It must be my imagination. I write on the chalkboard:

The Pleasure Principle: A Theory of Personality

I underline "pleasure" twice, which oddly gives me some enjoyment. It's time to begin. I stand up from my chair and speak from behind my desk.

"People are motivated by pleasure. We all take our pleasures in different ways. We all have different likes, dislikes, desires, and aspirations. Is there a common thread, a way of understanding what pleasure is, that will help us understand why we do what we do? Can we come to a simple theory of pleasure that can help us understand what we know about ourselves, our relationships, our civilizations, our history, and our place in the universe? I believe Vedic philosophy can be the foundation of just such a theory of personality, one that unifies what we know to be true according to scientific thought and experimentation and according to basic principles that various academic disciplines hold to be true. Much of what I will discuss today is covered in the article I authored, which I asked you to read for today's class..." I drone on and on. I'm barely listening to myself. I sit in my chair.

"...The urge to merge, so to speak, that Freud writes about and which is so pervasive in our world and societies..." Sex always gets our attention. We are part animal, after all.

"...This concept of pleasure, or happiness, being caused by the dissolution or diminishment of boundaries, allowing us to experience pleasurable qualities of our Self more fully, is hinted at a number of times in the Vedas and the Upanishads. One of my favorite quotes is from the Chandogya Upanishad: 'That which is unbounded is happy. There is no happiness in the small.'[35] Vedic philosophy holds that our universe was created with purposeful, symmetrical, and scalable incentives that lead us over the eons toward Unity Consciousness..."

I finish the lecture, I think. I'm not really paying attention. Most of the students leave but four stay to discuss Freud, Jung, and some newer psychologists—a few of whom I have never heard of—and their theories for over twenty minutes. That should be a sign that the lecture was successful, but my heart wasn't in it. I was born to be enlightened. I *will* get there again! I'm going home to meditate with Sarah. Isn't that what partners are for? To help each other get what they want and need? Sarah's my helpmate, and I'm hers. *Damn, almost forgot! Today's our anniversary.*

[35] Chandogya Upanishad 7:23

On my way home, I make dinner reservations at the most romantic restaurant in Claremont. Then I go to the flower shop and buy a bouquet she'll like. Eleven minutes later, I round the corner onto our block.

"Honey, I'm home," I say softly. Our home feels so quiet—Sarah will hear me wherever she is. She appears from the kitchen.

"Flowers! They are lovely. You're delicious." She takes the bouquet, places it on the coffee table, and kisses me back to an earlier time.

Reeling, I look at her, dazed. The air around her shoulders and head seems to shimmer.

"Happy anniversary!" stumbles out of my mouth. "I made reservations at Michelle's at eight. If you don't think you should go, I can order in. It *would* be fun though, watching people's reactions if they catch a glimpse of your glow."

"We'll be fine; the restaurant's dark and we won't see anyone we know. I love Michelle's. I'm sorry I didn't get you anything. I didn't want to leave the house today. I'm still getting used to this enlightenment thing, though it is getting easier. I think in a few days I'll be able to go out without being noticed. Thank you again for the flowers." She picks them up as we walk toward the kitchen.

I sit at the table. She cuts the stems with cooking shears and places the flowers in a large vase. Normally, Sarah would have made me a card or something. She's so solid, allowing me this little victory. Strength starts from our core.

"It's hot in here. Want some iced Pitta tea with mint?" she asks.

"That would be great."

"I'll turn on the AC," she says.

When the tea is ready, we sit on opposite ends of the couch, facing each other. I'm sweating; she's not.

"How'd your class go today?"

"Not too bad. Could have been worse, but I'm trying to stay optimistic."

"I can see that."

I take a sip of my ice-cold tea, revel in the AC breeze blowing directly on me, and remind myself that September is the hottest month in Southern California. At least I can look forward to cooler temperatures in October.

"The academic dean wants to meet with me. We're scheduled for tomorrow afternoon. I'm not sure what she wants." I'm thinking now it has more to do with Brittany than the five-college joint steering committee, but it could also be about the time I passed out in class.

Sarah searches inside and says, "I don't have a good feeling about the meeting."

"I'm sure it'll be something bad. That's how things are going lately. I'm getting used to it."

"You're right. This way when the wind shifts again and your luck turns, you'll appreciate it more. Gratitude is one of the driving forces of spiritual evolution. Didn't you tell me that?"

"Apparently I've told you more than I want to hear. Karma is relentless."

We shower, meditate, and walk to the restaurant for our anniversary dinner. The food is good. The restaurant is dark. We don't run into anyone we know.

The next day, Friday, as I walk over to the academic dean's office, I try to convince myself that I'm feeling good. My negativity is diminishing, a least a little. I'm not that much different now than I was before I was enlightened. I was fine before. It's just that enlightenment spoiled me. It will be so nice to be alone with Sarah this weekend.

The academic dean's office is in Alexander Hall, a large, quasi-Mediterranean building that hasn't changed since I was a student here. Entering her office, it still has the same musty smell, like a cathedral. It's decorated with 1930s and 1940s California-craftsman restored furniture. I give my name to the secretary and she ushers me in. The dean and a male associate dean whose name I've forgotten are seated behind her desk. They rise to shake my hand as I enter.

"Hi, Meg. Good to see you again," I say as I shake the dean's well-worn hand.

"Abe, it has been too long. This is Alex, one of my associate deans," she says, still shaking with her right and gesturing with her left. The associate dean is a tall man with a round, pink face. He gives me a nervous smile.

"Alex, good to see you again." I reach over to shake his hand with my recently liberated one. He mumbles something.

"Shall we?" Meg motions for me to sit in a chair in front of her imposing desk. She and Alex walk opposite ways around to find their seats.

"How are Sarah and your children?" she asks. "It seems like yesterday when Sarah was pregnant with them."

"Everyone is doing just fine, thank you. I trust all is well with you and yours?"

"Can't complain. Well, I could, but no one likes to hear complaints."

"You're always welcome to complain to me if you like," I say, amused at the prospect. That remark elicits more of a pause than I expected, followed by an embarrassed smile.

She composes herself and says, "I was so happy to hear that Rose will be visiting us to teach some classes next fall. They love her at NYU."

"Yes, it appears that dreams can come true. She and her husband will live with Sarah and me, but most importantly, my granddaughter will be coming, too. Becky is almost four, and we're crazy about her."

"Sounds like it'll be cozy and fun. Abe, we have a problem with one of the classes you teach. Can I speak frankly, off the record?"

"Sure. I'd rather know exactly what's going on. Don't worry about me."

"A student who started your Insider's Guide to Our Self course this semester has filed a formal complaint. Normally, we would address the complaint, placate the student, and it would fade away. These things are fairly common. Unfortunately, her father is a big contributor to the college and he's well-connected. This one's not going to fade away. Unless we make a show of canceling your class, he won't stop until they make everyone at the college miserable."

"Cancelling my class because of one complaint? There has to be more than that," I say, struggling to contain my rising heat.

"There is—ah, the class, I'm sorry to say, isn't a good fit here at Pomona. Maybe at Scripps? We discussed it at a meeting of the five-college joint steering committee."

"I would have remembered that." My ears are sizzling. My breath is hot.

"It was at a meeting you missed," she says cautiously.

I did miss one meeting toward the end of the last school year. I knew Meg had an issue with that class. "What is the substance of the student's complaint?"

"The student says you are proselytizing for a religion, Transcendental Meditation, in your class. I know you are teaching a class on Vedic philosophy, but apparently a number of students have been convinced to start doing Transcendental Meditation based on your class. We have two similar complaints on file, one from two years ago and the other from a year before that. This time, though, the student claims you made a personal threat, that their life would not be worth living if the student didn't learn to do Transcendental Meditation."

I give the dean a sad smile. "Actually, I quoted Socrates to her: 'The unexamined life is not worth living.'"

"I figured it was something like that. I'm sure the student made more of it than was there. Normally in these situations I could just make a report and put it in your file but, unfortunately, this time it's different. The bottom line is—well—the administration has decided that you can finish teaching the class this semester, but after that the class will no longer be offered here. When this blows over, we can discuss incorporating parts of it into an existing class at one of the other four colleges, maybe at Scripps?

"I'm sorry it's come to this, Abe. We'll tell her father that you've been disciplined and have agreed not to proselytize in any of your other classes. We investigated your Insider's Guide class thoroughly before coming to this decision. In general, our students have loved that class. The student evaluations are more positive than for almost any other Philosophy Department class we offer. Three complaints against a class that has been taught for so many years is on the low side, but this time, there's just nothing we can do. I really am sorry. I've heard how much you enjoy teaching that class."

Bam! My nightmare whacks me in the head. The room's spinning. I hold on to the arms of my chair, afraid I might fall over. I *am* that class. Teaching it gives me hope and the strength to persevere. I try to reply, but my tongue is numb. What happens if I can't talk? *I will not embarrass myself here.* I grip the chair tighter. I feel something on my tongue.

"It appears you've made your decision," I spit out. *Keep going. If you stop, you won't be able to go on.* "I'm not happy about it, but I accept it." The room is coming back into focus. I've been vanquished. "I will not do anything to circumvent it. You may have my head for your platter." I lean my neck forward, head down, eyes looking up at her. Her soft, heavy features tighten.

"Abe, are you OK? You seemed out of it for a moment. We've heard rumors," she glances at Alex, who nods, "that you've spaced out, or passed out, in your class recently."

"No, I'm fine, Meg. My doctor says I'm fine."

"You've been eligible for full retirement for many years now. Let's hope you don't have any more episodes while teaching, shall we?"

"I love teaching. I'm fine."

"OK. Let's see what happens. We do appreciate you and the many years of service you've given to Pomona. Give my best to Sarah."

She stands, wanting to get this over. She walks briskly around her desk to shake my hand again. Alex, realizing he should do the same, pushes his chair back but can't get out of it on the first try. Using his arms as levers, he finally extricates himself from its depths. I finish shaking Meg's hand and almost tap my foot as I wait for Alex. Meg grins weakly as he approaches. He makes his way around the desk, reaching out to me. I meet him halfway and shake his moist hand.

I make it home somehow and climb my front steps. I've lost my class and my enlightenment. Even Sarah is out of reach. What else am I going to lose? From deep in my dark side comes a chorus: *Our-way-will-always-be-here-for-you. You-will-never-lose-it.* "Fuck you! Leave me alone!" I say too loudly. Damn, the neighbors may have heard that.

"All streams flow to the sea because it is lower than they are.
Humility gives it its power."

Lao Tzu

Chapter Nine

As I walk through the front door, Sarah meets me in the foyer.

"How'd your meeting go?"

"Just as we feared," I say, feeling my knees get warm and weak. "Meg says hello. She tried her best to be nice about it."

"I'm so sorry. Things will turn around. It's not over yet." She takes my left hand in both of hers and kneads it in an unusual way. It feels nice.

"They won't let me teach my Guide to Our Self class after this year. The young lady with whom I had a run-in at the beginning of the class has a powerful father. She dropped the class, then filed a formal complaint that I've been proselytizing for TM."

Sarah tugs at my doughy hand, and I let her pull me along. We end up in our bedroom. She puts me in bed and takes off my shoes and socks. She kneels on the carpet at the edge of the bed and massages my right ear and earlobe, which seems to help.

"Do you think you were proselytizing for TM?" she asks tentatively.

"Probably. I tried not to. Is teaching the Truth proselytizing?"

"It can only become their truth when they are ready to hear it," she says tenderly as she moves on to my right neck and shoulder. "It's Shabbat tonight. I've prepared a Shabbat meal and invited Steve and Sari for seven-thirty. I enjoyed meeting them at temple when we went for Sukkot. I know I should have asked you first, but you've been in such a difficult mood recently that I was afraid you'd say no. It will be good for you to socialize on your own turf."

I almost start counting to ten, as my mother told me to do to control my anger. I don't want to say something I will regret. I don't feel like socializing, and she knows that all too well. She should've asked me before inviting guests. That's been our rule for years. Having had my favorite class ripped from me today, on top of the threat of forced retirement, makes the thought of having to interact with anyone painful. I want to be alone to wallow. Sarah is smart, though. Having them over will stop me from spiraling into self-pity, at least temporarily—can't go there and still play my part of department chair and esteemed senior colleague. And I bet Sarah wants to use them as her guinea pigs. They will be the first outsiders to interact with her for any significant amount of time since her enlightenment. Steve knows that if he wants tenure, he'll need my support. If either of them sees Sarah's halo, they won't spread it around. It will be good practice for her. I succumb to her better judgment: "Honey, I'm not happy you invited them, but it was a good idea."

"That's my boy! Everything is already done. The table is set. The food is ready. I'll just need to heat it up. I'll even clean up afterward. You won't have to do a thing, except be nice and socialize. Let's go do a full program." She walks toward Amos's room, beckoning me with a wave. I'm so down even her beckon is not enticing.

Steve and Sari arrive at 7:38. Steve hands me a very nice bottle of Pinot Noir. It looks delicious. Sari, it turns out, is a

headhunter for high-tech companies that are relocating or expanding in Southern California. She's older than I remember,
and after a few minutes of conversation and guacamole with
hard cheeses and crackers, I find her witty and breezy. I can
see why Sarah likes her.

I open the wine. With Sari's pregnancy in mind, I pour
everyone half a glass except her. It's as tasty as I was hoping.
We chat and eat, and I pour myself a full glass, feeling a lot less
sad. I already know all about Steve, having interviewed him
twice and researched his publications. Sari grew up in West Los
Angeles in a Kosher home and went to Jewish day schools. She
received a degree in psychology from UC Berkeley, tried a few
different jobs, and has been a headhunter for nine months now.

The table is set beautifully. Sari and Sarah light the
Shabbat candles. When they close their eyes and begin saying
the candle-lighting blessing together, it's as if the room fills
with God's light.

I say the prayer over the wine and make the blessing over
the challah. I tear off three pieces of challah and throw one to
each of our guests and Sarah, all of whom make good catches.
The ritual is working. I feel better. I pour myself another glass
and open another bottle of wine.

After a scrumptious dinner and some left-leaning discussion of environmental issues, we move to our living room. It's
quite comfortable with the AC on.

Sari turns to Sarah. "Steve says that you and Abe have been
meditating for many years. Is that why you're both so calm?"

Sari is trying not to stare at Sarah. She's not succeeding.

Sarah says matter-of-factly, "The meditation helps. But
we've always been pretty easygoing."

"As a—" Sari stops. The three of us look at her. She
realizes she'll need to finish. "As a child, my grandfather used

to tell me stories of the Baal Shem Tov. Being with you now somehow reminds me of those stories. I hope I'm not making you feel uncomfortable."

Sarah smiles sweetly, picks up her glass of wine, tips it toward Sari and Steve, and takes a sip. "Hashem has blessed Abe and me with a good life. We meditate and pray together regularly. Things come and things go. Maybe this is a good night for all of us."

"That's fine. I shouldn't have brought it up," Sari says self-consciously.

I've just finished my fourth glass of wine, I think, and I refill my glass. The room is unsteady. My tongue feels loose and wants to talk. "Sarah recently reached an important meditation milestone. I have been teaching a class about the philosophy of meditation for many years. She is my best student," the wine slurs.

Sarah reaches over and takes away my glass. "Abe rarely drinks," she says with a stern undercurrent.

We schmooze for another forty or fifty minutes. Steve says he wants to keep up with departmental and college politics. I fill him in on the current state of affairs, but I say more than I should. I don't tell him about my rebuke today; word will get around soon enough. Steve doesn't seem to have noticed Sarah's deep grace, or maybe he doesn't care. Sari clearly is in awe. I've always thought pregnant women had enhanced intuition. Steve is focused on the world, his new job, and social climbing. I don't hold that against him. He's a good-hearted man.

By the time we say our good-byes, I'm starting to sober up. As the wine leaves me, my despair returns. We hug and kiss at the door, promising to get together soon. They're pleasant people who clearly love each other. I like that.

When the door is closed, Sarah takes my hand, as she's been doing lately, and leads me to our backyard deck. It's too warm and humid outside, but the open air and crickets are calming. She arranges the chairs so I'm facing outward, facing her. Sitting, she leans forward, taking my fingers in hers, looking into me. "Abraham, I'm sorry you are so down. It will pass, honey. You need to be patient. The battle is not over, it's just beginning."

"I want to be patient. And I know things are OK, and, yes, it will get better. Intellectually, I know I should be optimistic. I think it's chemical. I think my brain's serotonin and other neurotransmitters must be at an all-time low. I want my class back and I want to teach it enlightened! Hopefully, by Monday my mood will be better. Right now, I just want to curl up in a ball and sleep forever."

I feel like Sisyphus. I rolled my boulder to the top of the mountain. I was happy and proud. Now it's flattened me on its way down. All my lives, all my efforts, have amounted to almost nothing, the infinitesimal. There's no light at the end of my tunnel. A memory of that long corridor and its many lives comes back to me. In each life I struggled to get somewhere, get something. Sometimes I succeeded, sometimes I failed. But in the end, it didn't matter. The only thing I kept from life to life was my goodness, and that has grown so slowly, so fitfully, it's excruciating. I can't take it anymore. I've been flattened for the last time. I refuse to push my boulder again.

I pull my fingers from Sarah's. I don't want to be touched. She sits in front of me, unperturbed. I look down at our deck. It needs to be re-stained. I wait for Sarah to sooth me.

My breath gets heavy. I breathe in pain from this life, from other lives, from lives I can't bear to remember. I get heavier with each breath. The weight is too great. I can't exhale.

With each inhale, the pain fills my lungs, my abdomen, my body, weighing me down from within. It won't go out. I try to stop breathing, but I can't. The air I breathe makes me short of breath. I want to die; I'm terrified I can't die.

I sob. It's pitiful. I expect Sarah to comfort me in the way only she can. She can make me feel better if she wants to. But she sits there with that wisp of a smile on her pretty face. Why is she letting me suffer and embarrass myself? I cry uncontrollably and she observes, unaffected.

After too long a time, she stands up—abruptly, forcefully. Her chair scoots back a few inches on the rough wooden deck. I stop crying and look up at her. The hair on the back of my neck stands on end. She crackles with static electricity. Her eyes are not here, not hers, and she says distinctly, "Stop your whining." She leans toward me, her right hand stretched open, coming at me slowly like a freight train. She plants her palm firmly on my forehead.

As she touches me, I know that she is a conduit. I am now connected to pure knowledge, and the download is beginning. For the first few seconds, I'm in philosopher's heaven. I know everything, profoundly, completely, intimately. That knowledge satiates me in a way I didn't think possible. Then it speeds up. It's out of control. I already know everything, but I'm being force-fed more and more—more than I want to know, more than I can know, more than I can contain. I try to scream to Sarah, 'Stop!' but my mouth is frozen. It won't help me. I am overfilled. I shatter.

I wake up in bed. It's dark, but I can see Sarah's outline sitting next to me. She's placed a cold compress on my forehead and is softly singing the same song again and again as I come in and out of consciousness. "Day after day, alone on a hill, the man with the foolish grin is keeping perfectly still…But the fool on the hill sees the sun going down, and the eyes in his head see the world spinning 'round…" And now it's morning. Was last night a dream? I'm not sad, not depressed, and not enlightened. Feeling happy to be back in one piece and happy that Sarah may have cured me, I roll up in a ball and sleep some more.

Later, Sarah checks on me, waking me as she sits on the edge of the bed.

"How are you feeling? You scared me." She places the soft back of her hand on my forehead, then her palm on my cheek. It feels good. "No fever," she reports.

"I'm better. What did you do to me?"

"Not sure." She sways her head side to side, watching me. "After I touched your forehead, you became catatonic. You wouldn't speak. You just sat there, staring."

I sit up against the headboard in a comfortable half-lotus, interested to hear what happened. "Was I drooling or twitching or anything like that?"

"I didn't think you had a stroke or a seizure or anything like that, but I was afraid. I'm so glad you're better. I waited for five minutes, hoping it would go away. It didn't. You wouldn't follow commands, but I was able to push and prod you, and you stood up and shuffled to the bed. I was finally able to get you to lie down. I was afraid you'd stand there all night."

"How bizarre. Did I moan or make any sounds?"

She pivots her feet up onto the bed, reaching for my hands as she starts to fall backwards. I catch her, helping her sit upright. She crosses her legs.

"I almost called 911." Using my hands, she pulls herself closer. "But I was afraid they'd arrest me for witchcraft." She gives my hands a squeeze as the corners of her mouth twitch up. "Do you know what happened? Do you remember anything?"

"I remember crying out of control. You stood up, placed your palm over my third eye area, and then I knew everything. But the knowledge wouldn't stop. It kept coming until it felt like I exploded."

"I remember being yanked upright and feeling a force take over. I watched as I placed my palm on your forehead. Then I came to and you were blank and immobilized in the chair. How did I do that? What came over me?"

I search my memory. "There's a spiritual phenomenon called shaktipat. Usually it occurs from guru to disciple. Maybe that's what happened in our case." I think some more. "It could have been spontaneous shaktipat. Actually, it had to be something like that or else I have no explanation."

"What is shaktipat?"

"It's an act of grace where the Self of an enlightened person connects to the consciousness of another. Spiritual energy or knowledge is transferred from the enlightened person to the unenlightened person. It's something like a lightning strike but with a higher purpose.

"Do you think it will happen again? I'm not going to start doing that to people on the street, am I?" she asks.

"I've never heard of that. The enlightened do what is in harmony with God's will. Little old ladies out for a stroll should be safe."

"Glad to hear it. This enlightenment thing is a bit over-whelming. All sorts of things keep happening. But I can handle it." She lets go of my hands, falls backward gracefully, and then wriggles around until she is on her side, head in my lap, snuggling.

I want to lean forward to kiss her temple, but don't be-cause I'm not that flexible. "Shaktipat," I say quieter, speaking into her upturned right ear, "has been said to occur spontaneously, where the guru does it without intending to or understanding how he or she did it. Anyway, whatever happened, I lived, barely, and I feel much, much better. I have a strong feeling that my ennui will not come back anytime soon."

She twists around, legs out straight, and looks up at me. "Do you think I could learn to control it, so I could go into the academic dean's office, go postal, and stupefy all of them into submission? Now that sounds like fun."

"I wish you would." We both chuckle. "Let's meditate, eat, and go for a hike on Mount Baldy. We can bring a picnic. We haven't done that since the kids were teenagers. It should be cool and beautiful up there today."

"Said and done," she says.

"It will give us time to work on plans for your new store," I say.

It's a hot, dry Monday morning. Walking to the college, I feel OK. I'm happy to teach my Monday classes but sad about my Tuesday Guide to our Self class. The sadness feels more like an exaggerated nostalgia than the low neurotransmitters of depression. I bet what Sarah did to me was the mystical equivalent of electroconvulsive therapy.

My two classes go well. Feeling relieved that my teaching duties are done for the day, I decide I deserve to relax. I manage to get some satisfactory work done on my novel. Based on what I've written so far, I think I'll have to find the time to take a fiction writing class. My novel seems less like a novel and more like one of my academic journal articles.

Enough fun, I need to grade papers from my Self-guided class, which were due last night. If I read and grade two or three per day, I should finish by the end of the week. I sort through my emails, download each paper, and put them in a folder on my computer's desktop. There are ten. Everyone finished on time, even Tom. I'm pleased. Very curious about Tom's paper, I decide to read it first. I print, staple, and place it flat on my desk. He chose the prompt, "Why and why not?" His title, at first glance, is thought provoking:

Boredom: The cause of Good and Evil:
In answer to the prompt: Why and why not?

by Tom Griffin

Before there was a beginning, there was consciousness, only consciousness: no time, no space, nothing to see, nothing to do. "Now" hasn't happened yet. "Now" requires time; there is no time. Boredom, only, only, boredom. Something has to happen! Consciousness, by its very nature, desired. It desired to end the boredom. It desired to know itself because that was the only thing it could do. There was nothing else to know or to do. To be able to do something, consciousness split itself into a subject, an object, and a process of experience. To split itself, to start something, the vibration, Om, out of boredom, began within the silence of homogeneous consciousness. Om was the beginning of the end of boredom; the big bore ended with a big bang. Om was the singularity that got the show started. Now, *that* was exciting! *That's* entertainment...

Tom's paper goes on to discuss other qualities of pure consciousness that lead to creation, including curiosity, creativity, playfulness, and desire for Self-knowledge, but he argues that the main cause of the big bang was boredom. Once creation had occurred, he says, the battle between the forces of good and evil became the dominant theme of creation. He says that this battle is not a fundamental battle that has to be waged for an outcome; this endless war occurs only because it is the ultimate cure for boredom. Consciousness is watching, seeing itself unfold. As with any good action movie, he writes, an exciting plot is the best way to pass the time. Consciousness has nothing but time and refuses to be bored again.

He attempts to make the point that in the biblical creation story, when God surveyed all that He had made on the sixth day and said that it was very good, He meant that evil itself, and the battle between good and evil, are also very good. Tom writes that God, by saying creation is very good, is really reviewing his own theatrical creation, giving it two thumbs up. In his conclusion, he finds the good within evil based on the idea that God needed to write evil into the story to make His universal play exciting enough to banish boredom.

The writing, the logic, and the flow of the paper are much better than I expected, and, as I did expect, it was often quite quirky. His conclusion was not as well written as the rest. And his excessive use of *Star Wars* analogies, though not wholly inappropriate, was distracting. (I always liked Yoda.) I find myself smiling and shaking my head in disbelief as I write, "Good job! You surprised me. B+" on the front of the paper in red pencil.

I read Margaret's paper next. She wrote about the prompt "I am! Are you?" Her idea, which we explored during our one-on-one sessions, is that all individual souls are qualities of the Self, based on Plato's Theory of Forms. Each individual soul is a specific quality of personality and, when taken together, are all the infinite permutations of personality that are possible. When each soul attains Unity Consciousness, that soul comes to know all of those permutations of consciousness equally as its Self—not just the personalities it has lived in on its way to Unity Consciousness. The idea had much promise, but the execution is disappointing. The actual paper is not much better than the second draft. She didn't spend the time to incorporate the concepts we discussed, nor did she expend much effort in cleaning up her grammar and sentence structure. I write "C+. I suggest you rewrite this for a better grade—lots of potential here. Meet with me to discuss."

After the letdown from Margaret's paper, I'm too tired to concentrate on reading a third. I want to go home.

I find Sarah sitting on the green wicker chair in her new office in the girls' room. I stretch out on Rose's bed, fingers laced behind my head. Sarah turns in the chair, knees up against the bed in the tight quarters. She circles my knee with her index finger. It tickles.

"I went to the grocery store today, so you don't have to worry that you'll run out of food," she says, tapping my kneecap once for emphasis, "but I went to one far enough away, so I wouldn't run into anyone I know. I need things to settle down more. Stuff keeps happening."

"Such as?"

"I don't know exactly what things were like for you, we didn't speak of it too much, but I have attacks of such Bliss and encounters with God's glory that at times they're almost overwhelming. I had a delightful episode today while I was driving, and I'm proud to say I was able to continue driving safely as it unfolded."

"Strong work—yeah, those type of things happened to me too. It got easier." I think about asking her if she's noticed that her intuition comes through her solar plexus from her gut but I'm afraid she then might ask me about my enlightened intuition. I'd be embarrassed to discuss my intuition appendage. I've concluded that my appendage was a hubris related, macho idiosyncrasy. I researched the subject and could find no reference to anything like it.

"Did you see and feel God around every corner? Was He that close for you?" she asks.

"At times. A few times. I think you're more into the God thing than I was because of your father. I'm more of a pure Knowledge kinda guy."

"True—I still haven't gotten over my need for a father, heavenly or otherwise. It's so much better than it was, though. Oh, tomorrow I've set up two meetings with promising artists at their studios, and Wednesday I have two more. If their stuff is as good as it seems online, I'll sign them to exclusive contracts. I found some boilerplate contracts on the internet."

"Be careful. I'm afraid if they don't do as you ask, you might palm-to-the-forehead them and turn them into your disciples."

"Don't you worry. I have no interest in disciples. I don't want to get into that business, even though it has been a lucrative one for too many."

Sarah stands and twists her chair around, its back away from me. It's sideways between the beds. She sits on the chair, facing me, and easily assumes a full-lotus. I haven't seen her do that before. She asks, "As my CFO, do you think my new plan is worth the risk? According to my calculations, after the fire sale at Goodness, using up the reserve we have in the store's bank account, putting most of the art purchases on the store's credit cards, and paying the contractor, I figure we'll be about $90,000 in the hole on opening day."

I gulp. "That's a deep, deep hole. What's your intuition? Will the art sell well enough to get us out of the hole?"

"My intuition is that the store will be successful enough. And I can see myself loving the journey—searching for artists whose work can move us, then nurturing them so they can produce even better stuff. That would be a fulfilling use of my time."

She sits up tall, and it's as if she's become an impossibly high-powered light bulb turned all the way up. Her overwhelming brightness penetrates me, shining through recesses that have been dark since my light went out. For an exquisite moment, we are one. It is so sweet. The taste lingers; my heart aches.

She says authoritatively, "We will hire more staff for the store. I will train them to run it and to take care of our artists. We can then spend summers in Fairfield meditating with the large groups there. It will be easier for you to regain your enlightenment if you meditate in a group. If that isn't enough, we'll do whatever it takes. We will figure out a way to sneak past death, so we can continue our journey together. I am *not* ready to concede to 'till death do us part.' You're not going anywhere without me, buster. Do we have a deal?"

Still not back to my senses, I try to speak. "It—it—it's a deal made in heaven. *Yes*, I accept your proposal." Full of her and her light, I wander toward the kitchen, not knowing or caring where I'm going. As I walk, she fades out of me. I'm left in awe of her power and her will.

During my walk to work Tuesday morning, it's cool, breezy, and misty. My phone says it'll rain later, which will be a nice break from the months-long dry spell. I'm ready to hydrate up and cool down. October is clearly establishing herself.

It's strange that none of my colleagues have dropped by my office or stopped me around campus to ask what happened between me and the administration. It's been my experience that everything that's gossip-worthy immediately leaks out.

Today's lecture is about pragya aparadh—mistake of the intellect. It's important that the students understand the concept because it underlies the whole field of Ayurveda and Ayurvedic medicine. Based on students' in-class questions over the past two years, there was plenty of room for improvement in the lecture, so I've revised it to make it clearer. I've also incorporated some ideas I'll use in my novel. I'm eager for feedback. Young, sharp intellects can, at times, see flaws or make connections I might miss.

Feeling more like my pre-enlightenment, good-enough self, I walk down to the classroom to write on the chalkboard:

Pragya Aparadh—Mistake of the Intellect

I walk back up and print out Ravi's and Tanisha's papers. I'll read them after class. I answer a few emails but get distracted reading an article in *The Stone* on the *New York Times* website. It's so cool that *The New York Times* has a column devoted to philosophy. The moderator is a colleague and friend of mine. Last week he emailed, asking if I'd be interested in writing an article for *The Stone* about Vedic concepts and how they correspond with quantum theory. I've been researching old articles on and off since then. I've decided to do it, if only to generate some buzz for my novel, which is coming along nicely.

I return to the classroom early and sit at my desk feeling nostalgic, watching the students filter in. Teaching this class each year has given me insight into a microcosm of our society's collective consciousness as it evolves. The evolution is not steady. It has ups and downs, progressions and regressions, but on the whole, over the years, it's clear that things are moving in a good direction.

Twenty years ago, Vedic and Buddhist philosophies were popular but not commonly considered worthy of serious academic study. Now, many colleges and universities have a course on Buddhist philosophy and a number have courses on Vedic philosophy. Increasingly, I've been contacted by colleagues at other schools who are teaching courses on, or giving lectures about, the problem of consciousness. And many of those young professors, as well as their students, now practice yoga or some form of meditation.

Outside, there's a flash of light, and a few seconds later, thunder. It rains. Fall is here. Class has not officially commenced—some of the students go to the window to see the rain and lightning. Everything old is new again.

I walk to the front of my desk, and the students scurry back to their seats.

"Today we will be discussing pragya aparadh." I point to the title of today's lecture.

"The first part of the lecture draws on a book I'm currently writing. This part is more theological than philosophical, but I include it in today's lecture because I want to make the point that Vedic philosophy can help us make sense of a lot of what is unclear in the scriptures of the world's major religions. If Vedic philosophy can clarify and unite theological issues in various religious traditions, then it adds credibility to the philosophy. Ultimately, it is my contention that each major religion describes parts of the same thing from different perspectives, to different people and cultures, based on the needs of their time. I especially invite you to share your thoughts and reactions to this first part of the lecture, though as always, I encourage you to share your thoughts on anything I say.

"In the Garden of Eden, the snake tempted Eve into making a mistake. Adam made a mistake in eating the fruit Eve gave him. According to the standard interpretation, they were then forced to leave their perfect place and live in our imperfect world. Were they expelled because of the mistake, the sin of disobeying God's command, or did they automatically find themselves out of the Garden because of what the mistake did to them? Did eating the forbidden fruit change something within Eve and Adam so that their perception of the Garden changed?

"My understanding of the scripture is that it was mainly the change that occurred in Eve and Adam due to eating the fruit, not the sin itself, that forced God's hand. What did God say was the result of their mistake? Adam and Eve ate the fruit from the tree of knowledge, and in Genesis 3:22, God speaks about what changed: 'And the Lord God said, "Behold, the man has now become like one of Us, knowing good and evil."'

"Was there something about knowing good and evil that caused Eve and Adam's experience of the Garden to suddenly devolve into an experience of our messy world? In my mind, the answer hinges on the idea that the Garden of Eden is a metaphor for pure consciousness. Within pure consciousness, there is no good and evil—there's only the virtual fruit from which good and evil springs. Within pure consciousness, all dualities are merged, all dualities are one. Good and evil, subject and object, are dualities.

"After eating the forbidden fruit, Eve and Adam's perception changed. The Bible says, 'The eyes of them both were opened, and they knew that they were naked.'[36] Once Adam and Eve's eyes were open, they saw duality. They saw their world as good and evil, subject and object. Their Rishis, their opened eyes, saw their naked bodies as Chhandas. You cannot know you are naked without experiencing your world as subject and object. Within the Garden, subject and object—Rishi, Devata, and Chhandas—all merge into the singularity of the Samhita, the fruit from which knowledge of good and evil springs. Once their eyes were open, they were no longer in the Garden of Eden."

"Professor," Margaret says. "Your interpretation is very different than what I and probably everyone else here was taught about Adam and Eve, except maybe Ravi?" She turns to Ravi, and all eyes follow.

Ravi slumps back, looking sheepish. "I do not know much about the Garden of Eden story," he says, as if it's a major character flaw.

Margaret smirks, amused, and then brings the focus back to herself. "I was taught that Adam and Eve disobeyed God's command and ate from the tree. They gave in to temptation, following the snake's advice, instead of obeying God. Disobeying God's command was the original sin. Adam and Eve, and all of us, were punished for this sin by being expelled from Paradise."

"That's basically what I was taught," I say. "I'm not saying that's not a correct interpretation. I'm saying that according to my interpretation of Vedic philosophy there's an additional, deeper meaning that's appropriate for our time. In my writings, I argue that the world's scriptures have many levels of meaning. As time goes on and our collective consciousness

[36] Genesis 3:7

matures, those scriptures can be understood as saying many of the same things. If there is a God, we should assume She and He have the same teachings but needed to convey them in different forms, at different times, and in an appropriate way to each of their different children."

"So, are you saying that eating the fruit was like Om for them?" Margaret says. "They ate, causing their personal Om to begin, and that caused them to experience the world as subject and object, good and evil, which was, in addition to their sins, the cause of a change within them which was incompatible with being in Eden or pure consciousness? Once they saw the world as subject and object through a process of perception, they were already outside of Eden, correct?"

"Yes," I say.

"And," Margaret resumes, "we know that once there is an object, things begin to happen to it, some good, some bad, or even evil. Oh, ah, couldn't it be that only good things happen to the object and no evil?"

"Not in our world. Only in a heaven," I reply wistfully, a vision of my heaven hanging heavy in my head. "I think things will become clearer as I go along." *Focus forward! Do not dwell on the past.*

"Woman and man made a choice," I resume. "Eve chose to listen to the snake. Here is what the snake told her:

> "'Then the serpent said to the woman, 'You will not surely die. For God knows that in the day you eat of it your eyes will be opened, and you will be like God, knowing good and evil.'[37]

---

[37] Genesis 3:4–5.

"Eve and Adam chose to be like God, knowing good and evil, just as God chose to know good and evil by splitting into Rishi, Devata, and Chhandas in the beginning. In the beginning, God, too, gave into temptation and ate from the tree of knowledge of good and evil to gain Self-knowledge. Remember, 'God created man in his image.'

"The serpent tempted Eve into making a mistake. But it was a mistake that had to be made. If she had not made that mistake, our world, our history, our evolution would never have occurred. We would not have had the chance to know our Selves. Eve chose something-ness rather than nothingness, just as pure consciousness and God did when It and He and She created the world of duality.

"The serpent did not lie to Eve, though he intentionally misled her. He promised, 'You will not surely die.' In the world of duality, our bodies die but we live on. Remember, in the Gita God promises us we will never die. In chapter two, God says, 'There never was a time when I was not, nor you…Nor will there ever be a time when all of us shall cease to exist.'

"Once our eyes were opened, we were forced to embark upon our circular journey of Self-discovery. Our journey requires us to leave the Garden in order to know Chhandas and Devata as our Self and return to the Garden, our Rishi, to know our Self as the Samhita of Rishi, Devata and Chhandas. It is a journey of diversity followed by unity."

Joseph's hand goes up. "Professor," he says "you keep talking about a mistake. Are you alluding to today's topic, the mistake of the intellect? Was eating the forbidden fruit the original pragya aparadh, the mistake of the intellect?"

"Good point, Joseph. You're ahead of me. The forbidden fruit opened their eyes and they saw they were naked, but seeing their nakedness is a mistake of the intellect. Their intellects mistakenly identified their bodies, their minds, their feelings, as their self with a little 's'. In reality, all of it, all of Chhandas and all of the process of perception, Devata, are different aspects of their Self with a big 'S'.

"Let's apply this concept of pragya aparadh to something more concrete and practical. The word 'disease' comes from the Latin prefix *dis* meaning, in this context, 'without,' and the Old French word *aise* meaning 'comfort, pleasure, or opportunity,' from which we also get the modern English word 'ease.' In the Garden of Eden, there was no dis-ease. In expelling us, God decreed that women would give birth in pain and that men would toil in a world of thorns and thistles to feed themselves and their families. God also told us in Genesis 2:17, 'But of the tree of the knowledge of good and evil you shall not eat, for in the day that you eat of it you shall surely die.' So, our mistake not only caused dis-ease, but also aging and eventual death of our bodies.

"But diseases can have cures. Finding ourselves in dis-ease motivates us to understand our diseases and how to remedy them. Ayurveda, which means 'science of life,' is a part of the Vedas that deals with preventing and curing dis-ease. Meditation, asanas, pranayama, proper action, and proper diet are all part of Ayurveda. According to Ayurveda, pragya aparadh is the cause of all disease, and, accordingly, correcting pragya aparadh can prevent or alleviate many diseases."

Death is a disease Sarah and I will attempt to circumvent. Vedic scriptures say that if pragya aparadh is corrected at the most fundamental level, the physical death of the body can be held at bay until its occupant is ready to go forward.[38] There are rumors of yogis achieving that.

---

[38] Bhagavad-Gita Chapter 7 by Maharishi Mahesh Yogi, 2009, Maharishi Foundation International, Commentary on Verse 29, page 46. "But the Lord says, 'Those who seek deliverance from old age and death'; this indicates the possibility

"Due to pragya aparadh the intellect lost its connection to, and identification with, the Self, or pure consciousness. This was the original mistake. In my mind, it is the original sin, so to speak. Instead of knowing and identifying with our real Self, we began identifying ourselves as just bodies and minds, which are part of Chhandas. When the intellect corrects its mistake and reconnects with its Self, thereby taking nourishment from the *tree of life* within pure consciousness, the healing process begins."

I glance out the window. The rain has picked up dramatically. A moment later, it's hailing. I haven't seen hail in years. I have to speak louder to overcome the roar from outside, but that doesn't overcome my students' interest in the hail. I've lost their attention.

"Let's take a look, shall we?" I say with a wave. The students follow me to the window. It's a deluge. The streets are being hammered, cleansed of the summer's sharpness. The class's momentum has been washed away, and with it, my enthusiasm for today's lecture. This class and I have no future together. It's the last time I'll give this lecture to this class. Without an anchor, I am adrift.

As the hail peters out and the rain dies down, I call the class back to order. "Back to business," I say, trying to sound upbeat. "Now would be a good time for a question. Who's got one?"

Joseph raises his hand. "Professor, in my study of the Kabbalah I was taught that at the end of days, history will complete itself and all mankind will reenter the Garden of

---

of cessation of the process of change for the physical aspect, at least in individual life if not in the whole of creation. The basis of the technique given by the Lord in this verse is 'having taken refuge in Me'. This is a teaching of great significance. It contains a secret world of simple techniques to effect cessation of the aging process and death on the physical level of life."

Eden. In your metaphor, Eden is pure consciousness. You said it is Devata that keeps us from entering pure consciousness. Does that mean Devata is Vedic philosophy's description of the Cherubim with the flaming sword that God charged with stopping us from reentering Eden and eating from the tree of life?"

"Once again, a very good correlation, Joseph. It does seem to fit. Just so everyone knows what we are discussing, I'll read you what Joseph is referring to from the Old Testament." I pick up my trusty Bible.

> "'Then the Lord God said, "Behold, the man has now become like one of Us, knowing good and evil. And now, lest he put out his hand and take also of the tree of life, and eat, and live forever" therefore the Lord God sent him out of the Garden of Eden to till the ground from which he was taken. So He drove out the man; and He placed cherubim at the east of the Garden of Eden, and a flaming sword which turned every way, to guard the way to the tree of life.'[39]

"I think the Bible and Vedic philosophy describe the same thing in different ways and from different perspectives." Normally, I would launch into an extemporaneous mini-lecture concerning the cherubim, the flaming sword, eating from the tree of life, living forever, and how they are related to Devata, but I don't have the focus right now. I'm preoccupied with a more pressing issue: how Sarah and I can get to the tree of life and eat from it. I think that's the key to being able to sneak

[39] Genesis 3: 22-24

past death. There are Vedic philosophers who say that the Bible's reference to 'eating from the tree of life' is an allusion to the same type of techniques Maharishi points to in his discussion of "having taken refuge in Me." When I get to the Raj over Thanksgiving, I'll ask my friend Paul about it. He's interested in such things and should have some practical suggestions as to how Sarah and I could gain access to that "secret world of simple techniques." As my mind wanders, I continue giving my pragya aparadh lecture to my students.

When I get home that evening, Sarah has a lot to tell me. We sit on the couch and she pours me a glass of mint-infused lemonade from an Italian ceramic pitcher that faced a dim future at her store. Off she goes, recounting her whirlwind of a day. She signed three Southern California artists to exclusive contracts. All are struggling to sell their work, but each has a special gift. She's convinced that with proper showcasing their art will sell, and with proper nurturing their work will get even better.

She's rented a nearby storage facility where she can house inventory. Because she plans to add a small markup, she expects a high volume of sales. The store's back room is small and not big enough for the full inventory she thinks she'll need.

She hopes to open the new store the Friday before Thanksgiving. We have a lot to do to make that happen. This weekend will be the beginning of her fire sale. We'll sell everything in Goodness that we can, increasing the discount every few days until it's clear that what's left won't sell. Then we'll donate what hasn't sold and close the store for remodeling. She's already hired a contractor who is having architectural plans made based on her drawings. I'm exhausted just thinking about it all.

"You've been very busy. Is your busy-ness affecting your consciousness?" I ask.

"My consciousness is just fine, thank you. The Sarah part of me is busy, working hard, doing things quickly. That never happened before. She's never been able to focus like that. I'm watching Sarah—but I'm uninvolved and unaffected. I feel like the real me is in silent, constant, boundless bliss. With each passing day, I'm able to integrate the two parts more easily. I'm having great fun."

"Textbook Cosmic Consciousness. Ah, I remember it well. Thank God you cured me of my despair, so I can enjoy your good fortune with you."

"I'm also learning how to be with people without freaking them out, though I've had a few bizarre encounters," she says.

"Pray tell."

"I'll tell you one. One of the artists I signed this morning, a tall, thirtyish Hispanic gentleman, became obsessed with the idea that he had to paint my portrait." She exaggerates her hand and head movements, as she does whenever she tells a story she likes. "Me as a mature Mother Mary who just had sex for the first time."

"Men, all they think about is sex, and we won't even get into that Freudian, Oedipal stuff about mothers," I interject, unable to stop myself. She brushes my remark aside.

"After we met this morning, he kept calling and texting, begging me to come back and pose for him. He offered me his art for free if I would be his model."

"Did he want you to pose nude?"

"We never got that far. I drove back to his studio, looked him in the eyes, and told him in no uncertain terms that I would not pose for him, that he could not paint my portrait, and that I would pay him fairly for his work. I don't think he'll bother me again."

Jealousy rises. I don't want my wife ogled by tall, swarthy, artistic types. Her enlightenment has made her so attractive that I'm not surprised she's being hit on, even at her age. My next thought is that she can more than take care of herself, especially now. *Put it to rest, Abe.*

"Hear any feedback about your course being cancelled?"

I reply: "Silence—I haven't heard such silence since I was enlightened—and it sounds quite suspicious." I exaggerate a twitching of the eyebrows.

Sarah rolls her eyes. "Oh," she says, "one of the new employees I hired is your student. He really needed the job. His name is Tom Griffin."

That's a kick in the gut. She's enlightened. Shouldn't she have sensed he's bad news?

"You hired Tom? You should've asked me first. I wouldn't have given him a good recommendation—quite the contrary. I've heard that he loves to show off how much money he has. I don't think he needs your job."

"I didn't mean financially. I know I should have asked first, but I just found myself wanting to hire him. I had this weird gut feeling it would somehow be a good thing for him and for us—that he would end up helping us in a number of ways. Let's meditate. It's getting late and I'm hungry." Sarah seems unaffected by my concerns.

"Sarah, did you ask Tom about his background?"

"A little. I should have asked more. I know he has problems."

"It's more than that. He is a troubled child. Did you know he was arrested for shoplifting in high school? Is that someone you want to work in your store?"

"I've heard you say, 'He who is without sin, let him cast the first stone.' We all have our problems. Tom just needs nurturing to allow him to move forward and grow up."

I put down my stone.

Thursday morning—I've just finished my lecture on Ayurveda and Ayurvedic medicine. As the students file out, I sit in my classroom chair, reflecting on the lecture. They seemed to enjoy it, especially learning about their body types and tendencies. The students were impressed that the Vedas have a whole section on health, and not just physical or mental health but structural and communal notions of health—Sthapatya Veda architecture, for example. We talked about how architecture can affect an individual and how Vedic philosophy holds that luck and good fortune are not just karmic phenomena but are related to the spatial orientation, design, and quality of one's home and community.

After class, I walk up to my office and do some tedious work. It falls on me each year to revise, edit, and update descriptions of all philosophy courses offered at Pomona based on input from the professors. I hate it. Trying to reach each professor via phone, text, or email to discuss their course descriptions is time consuming. Often, they don't get back to me and then complain that the description wasn't what they wanted. I do as much as I have patience for.

I'm going home. I want to talk to Sarah about Tom. He's a needy child who will suck up her time. I want to make sure she has time to help me.

When I open the door, I hear Sarah laughing, and another male voice that I recognize but don't immediately place. I find Tom sitting at our round table eating freshly baked cookies with a glass of milk nearby. He's sitting where I usually sit. The chair looks tiny. My stomach churns.

Tom gulps down a bite.

"Dr. Levy, I hope you don't mind." He seems nervous, like he was just caught with his hand in the cookie jar. His mood is buoyant, though. "Your wife needed help bringing some stuff home from her store."

I'm about to thank him and show him the door when Sarah comes to his rescue.

"Tom, of course it's OK you're here. I appreciate your help."

Cornered, I have no recourse but to agree. "You're always welcome here, Tom. I'm *so glad* you're here." Both look shocked at what they know to be sarcasm. I'm not doing well.

"Don't worry, sir. I was just about to leave." Tom scoots his chair back an inch. He now looks small and vulnerable. To keep peace in our house—*shalom bayit*—I need to fix this, quick. I sit next to him.

"Have some more cookies. They look delicious." I grab the biggest one, take a bite, and smile at him as I chew. "I read your paper."

Tom watches me carefully. I chew slowly. Maybe Sarah won't be too cross with me after all.

"You read my paper?" he says.

I swallow and say, "Yes." I take another bite, savoring Sarah's cookie.

"Should we not talk about it?" Tom asks.

Everyone waits as I chew and swallow.

"I liked it. Honey, could I have a glass of milk, please?"

"Sure." Sarah turns toward the refrigerator.

"You clearly put some good thought and effort into it. Congratulations."

As Sarah turns, Tom blurts out, "Thanks! I was hoping you'd like it."

Sarah returns with a glass of milk for me and a smile for Tom. The mood in the room has lost its edge.

"Professor, I'm so relieved. It may not seem like it because of my outbursts and stuff, but I really am enjoying your class. It's so cool, the two of you...I even recommended it to a good friend who plans to take it next year."

Sarah and I look at each other. I have to say it. "Word hasn't gotten around yet, but there won't *be* a next year."

Tom's eyes get big. "What happened? You're not retiring, are you?"

"No," I say. "I love teaching. I'm not retiring anytime soon."

"Tom, don't worry," Sarah says soothingly. Tom's eyes shrink; he settles back in his chair.

"The administration decided to cancel the class," I say, as the air hisses out of me.

"You've got to be kidding!" Tom says loudly. "We love your class. We've loved it for...how many years have you taught that class? That's how long we've loved it. It must be some kinda mistake."

I look at Tom's right hand, which rests on\ the table with the tips of his fingers curled and tensed.

"Thanks," I say. "I think it's a mistake." I don't trust him around Sarah. He'll turn on her, just as he has on me, once he decides she's not the savior he's looking for.

"My dad told me that the college often does really stupid things. This has got to be a prime example. They can't do that to you and Mrs. Levy!" Both his hands are now on the table, nails scraping the surface. He's escalating. I don't have patience for him right now. I want to be alone with Sarah, not tiptoeing around this child.

"Tom," I say too sharply. "Don't worry about it. I'll take care of it."

He looks at me, a question on his face. Then it breaks. "Can you take care of it, really?"

Seeing we are about to go down an unpleasant path, I change our direction. "How are your other classes?" I say, looking for an opening to move him out of here.

He holds his tongue, and then, more calmly, says, "They're OK. Sorta boring."

Sarah chimes in. "You're getting your degree in philosophy? Do you have any plans after graduation?"

"Zilch, nada," he says, looking her in the eyes. He sighs. "Mrs. Levy, I just thought of it." He hesitates, having forgotten what he was going to say. "Oh, your new gallery is going to be amazing." He's still looking at her. "Would you...need... someone full time after graduation?"

No way. Not gonna happen. "Mrs. Levy and I will discuss her store's employment needs and get back to you."

"Oh, OK...I see. I gotta go." He takes one last, longing look, and says, "Thanks for the cookies, Mrs. Levy." He bows his head, bidding her adieu. "Professor, I appreciate you not being too mad at me and letting me hang around. Thanks again." He pushes his chair all the way back and gets up. We walk him to the door.

When he's safely out of earshot, I say, "We need to talk."

We return to the table. Sarah starts. "Part of Tom's heart is shriveled. He needs a safe place to grow up."

"Your gallery is a business, not a nursery."

"It can be both. He's worked with me for only a few days, but already his heart is starting to soften and expand."

"I see. That's interesting." My heart softens from Sarah's goodness. I can't stay cross with her for long. "I don't know if he's told you, but one of my other students told me Tom loves to talk about how he was raised by his rich, dominating father. The story is that his father entered into a legal contract with a surrogate mother for the purpose of having his child. The mother agreed not to contact Tom in exchange for a significant monthly payment for the rest of her life. If she ever sees or contacts Tom, the payments stop. Tom's never met his mother and doesn't know who she is."

"Yeah, he told me that during our interview. He also told me that his father gives him more money than he knows what to do with."

She scoots her chair closer to mine, twitching her eyebrows, mimicking my attempts at comic behavior. Hers are much funnier. "Tom mentioned that you snooped around and uncovered his secret program. He's so proud that you were interested enough to investigate. You didn't tell me you were moonlighting as a detective."

"Just tryin' to get to the truth, ma'am," I say in my best southern twang. "I did hear he was up to something. I was only interested to make sure no one got hurt. I don't know what his program is other than it makes him important to his senior class."

"Tom thought you knew all about it. He bragged about how great it's been for his class. It's a free tutoring program where seniors can make online requests for help from other senior class members. Tom adapted an existing app for the program. The tutors submit their hours every other week through the app and are paid, in cash, quite generously. Tom gets envelopes of cash delivered from his accountant to pay them. He says over sixty percent of the senior class has taken advantage of his program. He's let them know that if he fails a course, his father will stop giving him money, thereby ending the program. He's trying to buy the love and attention he never had."

"I've never heard of anything quite like that happening on a college campus before. It explains a lot." I think for a moment. "I have no problem with such a program, and I'm not going to let the college's administration know about it. I'm already on their naughty list. I don't want to get tangled up with Tom, his asshole father, or the administration." I reach for another cookie, but I'm stopped dead in my tracks by Sarah's glance.

"You're not getting it," she says. "Can you imagine how deep his hurt is and how wounded and insecure he must be for him to need a program like that?"

"A pretty deep wound, I guess. It's sad. What's for dinner?"

"Cookies," she says, shaking her head. "Or we can go out. Your choice."

Before going out to eat, with Sarah in the bathroom, I sneak another cookie. I realize that both Sarah and I have had a premonition that Tom would help us—God help us.

I enjoy teaching my Friday classes. Not enlightened enjoyment, but good enough. Sarah works most of the weekend at her store. She tells me that Tom, eager as a puppy, was there with her the whole weekend. She doesn't need my help, so I get a fair amount of writing done. Monday is uneventful. Tuesday, I teach my Self class. The lecture is on Dharma and Desire.

Afterword, walking up to my office, I think about how unusual it is that I still haven't heard anything from my colleagues about my class being canceled. In all my years here at Pomona, such juicy gossip has never stayed private so long.

In my office, long before my office hours, there's a sharp rap on my door. I look up. It's Tom. He walks in without asking.

He picks up some folders from the chair next to my desk and pretends to dust the seat off. "I'll close the door, if you don't mind," he says. Not waiting for my reply, he closes the door.

"How can I help you?" I say.

"You, and especially your wife, have already helped me a great deal. I have, therefore, returned the favor."

"You've piqued my curiosity. How have we helped you, and how did you return the favor?"

"Your words are for the head, Dr. Levy. They sorta helped, but they didn't really change much. But your wife—she really changed things for me. I've never met anyone like her before."

"I agree. My wife is a special woman."

"So, to return the favor, I came up with a plan and it worked."

"It's not necessary, Tom."

"I needed to do it. Do you remember taking Intro to Calculus your sophomore year with my father?"

I think back, beginning to vaguely remember. "Sort of." I did take Calculus first semester my sophomore year.

"When I started your Vedic class, I was talking to my dad about you. He told me about an incident during your final exam. He thought he was giving me fatherly advice about how the 'real' world works. Of course, I'm his son, so I figured out how to use that to our advantage."

"What incident are you referring to?" Something is there, in a fog.

"He said he sat next to you during the final, on purpose. There was an important tricky problem at the back of the test. He didn't know the answer. Near the end of the period, he saw you get excited and start answering the problem. He looked at your answer and realized it was correct. He wrote out a similar answer. You noticed him cheating, but you didn't turn him in."

The haze clears and a long-forgotten memory—or, more accurately, suppressed—emerges. I can picture his father with his thinning, platinum-blond hair, cramped into the desk behind me and to my left. The tricky problem accounted for ten percent of the grade, and toward the end of the test, the answer just came to me. I must have uttered something under my breath and flipped to the end. As I finished, I noticed Ben looking at my paper, having scooted his desk closer to mine when the proctor was on the other side of the room. Our eyes met, and I glanced at his exam with his nearly finished answer. My first reaction was indignation, and I pointed at the proctor and motioned that I was about to raise my hand. Ben was a first-semester freshman. He looked me sternly in the eyes, as if to say it would be my word against his, and that this would end badly for both of us. I backed down. I could tell that Ben was dangerous.

"What did you mean when you said you used that information to our advantage?" I ask.

"I figured out that I could get your class back."

"Tom, I don't want you or your father meddling in my affairs."

"Too late, it's done. I joked that he needed to force the administration to give you your class back or I'd embarrass him at some dinner party or something by telling a few of his special friends about him cheating on a final. He prides himself on how well he did in college—you know, top of his class and all that. I think he sorta liked being blackmailed by his son. Weird, huh? In the end, it turned out to be simple."

This whole thing is weird. "How was it simple?"

"All my dad needed to do was call Brittany's father. He knows him from Sacramento political connections. He applied some pressure and that was that. You have your class back."

I'm pissed. "Please tell your father to stay out of my affairs from now on, and the same goes for you. I am not interested in assistance from either of you."

Tom hesitates, bewildered by my admonishment. He says in a sweet voice, "I'm sorry your light went out. It was so cool having an enlightened teacher, and it made your course seem real. It should come on again, right?"

"This is not my office hours. I have work to do." I shuffle papers around.

Realizing I'm through, Tom stands. "I'll let my father know that you appreciate his help," he says, sensing this might irk me. He's right. He walks out without saying goodbye or looking back.

The next morning, I find an email from the academic dean.

Dear Abraham,

It was good to see you again. I am sorry our most recent meeting was not under better circumstances. After further discussion and review, we have reconsidered the complaint against your class, The Insider's Guide to Our Self. The president of Pomona College, the head of alumni relations, and I have concluded that your course is an asset to the college. It is the college's intention that the course be available to our students each fall semester for as long as you wish to teach it.

Sincerely,

Megan Schneider
Academic Dean, Pomona College

"Mastering others is strength.
Mastering yourself is true power."

Lao Tzu

Chapter Ten

The fire sale at Goodness goes well. By Monday, we've sold ninety percent of our inventory and most of the fixtures, shelving, and props we won't need for the gallery. The next day, Tuesday, October 11, we close the store, cover the windows in white paper, and have a commercial artist write on them:

Coming Soon!
Goodness Art Gallery
"A Home Is Art"

Our contractor gets our building permit without any problems. She starts work on Wednesday, and, unexpectedly, continues to work each day until the job is done.

Tom helps us utilize an iPhone app so that as each numbered piece of art is sold, it automatically notifies employees to replace it with a specific piece from storage. This way the presentation and grouping of the art will always be up to Sarah's standards, and no wall space will stay empty for long. Tom is especially helpful and proactive during this hectic time. He's a much better employee than a student, especially with Sarah as his boss.

Sarah enlists many of her friends, who then enlist their friends, to spread the word about Goodness's affordable art, handpicked by a "style trendsetter." One of them convinces the Claremont newspaper to run an article about Sarah and how Goodness plans to cultivate the artists it represents, helping them get in touch with the source of their art through meditation. Along with the article, there's an amazing picture of Sarah in front of her gallery, looking like the kindergarten teacher we all wished we had. As we get closer to opening day, a few professors, staff, and students tell me they've heard about the gallery and wish us luck. I think Sarah is all the luck I can handle.

While all of this is going on, I complete plans for my trip to Fairfield. Sarah, Amos, and I will drive to LAX early Tuesday morning, November 22. Sarah and Amos will fly to New York to spend Thanksgiving with the girls, and I'll go to Iowa for Panchakarma treatments, Vedic Vibration therapy, and twice-daily meditations in the golden domes where the group program is done. I feel bad about not spending the holiday with my family. Even worse, when I talk to Rose on Thursday, she puts Becky on the phone to say "Zeide, we will miss you *so much* for Thanksgiving. Please come!" It's nearly enough to make me reconsider.

On opening day, a week before Black Friday, Sarah gets to Goodness early to finish the preparations. During the three-day opening, there will be unlimited pink lemonade, three varieties of crustless English sandwich squares, and bite-sized, freshly-baked oatmeal-raisin cookies. The sales staff will wear starched white aprons with the Goodness logo and "A Home Is Art" in golden script. The aprons look great. Sarah has hired three temporary staff for opening weekend and has all the part-time staff working extra shifts. She's more than ready.

Sarah texts me forty minutes before opening that there are eleven or twelve people waiting outside, among them a reporter from *Los Angeles Magazine* wanting to get in early and take pictures. Apparently, Tom contacted the magazine and sold them on the story of an art gallery meant to nurture and support promising artists. Her next text says she let the reporter in.

Sarah continues to update me as the morning progresses. At ten she opens the doors. The lemonade, sandwiches, and cookies are a hit right from the beginning. During the first hour, we sell only two pieces, which the staff replaces with similar pieces within fifteen minutes. The second hour, we sell five pieces, and by lunchtime, the locusts have arrived. Sarah texts, "Come now if you can. We need you to work." Soon, I'm wearing an apron and walking around with a credit-card reader plugged into my phone. I swipe cards, email receipts, and record addresses for shipping. I barely have time to eat my fill of sandwich squares for lunch, but I do find time to pilfer the warm cookies before they're put out. By five I'm exhausted, full of cookies, and ready to go home, even though we're not scheduled to close for another two hours. A few moments later, Sarah stops me. "Let's go home, meditate, and celebrate Shabbat. The staff can take it from here." She doesn't have to convince me.

As we walk up the steps to our house, I notice that the creak in the third step is gone. Maybe the rain did it. "I'm dying to meditate," I say. "I'm tired."

"Me too. It's been a long day." She doesn't appear at all tired. After we meditate, I feel rejuvenated and ready for some real food. Professors can live on cookies for only so long. Sarah gets the candles ready and calls me to stand with her. She lights the two wicks, closes her eyes, and recites the blessing. When she closes her eyes, I find myself closing mine, too, thanking Hashem for allowing me to see my beloved in such an exalted state.

Sarah stir-fries vegetables and tofu in a wok. When the food is ready, I say the blessing over the wine and challah, as usual, and then I decide to do something I haven't done in years. I find the *Eshet Chayil* in my prayer book, which more traditionally religious husbands sing to their wives in Hebrew every Friday night before dinner.

"I don't know if you know, but *Eshet Chayil* was written by King Solomon and concludes the book of Proverbs," I tell her. She nods, accepting my information. I begin, partly reading and partly singing the English translation, "A wife of noble character who can find? She is worth far more than rubies. Her husband has full confidence in her and lacks nothing of value. She brings him good, not harm, all the days of her life…" As I croak out the words, Sarah stands close behind me, puts her arms around my waist, and gently kisses my neck, which feels so good I almost forget to sing.

After dinner, when we've cleaned up, Sarah says, "Can we see how much we sold?"

I find my laptop and connect to the store's QuickBooks Point-of-Sale program. We sold $38,411 worth of art today— unbelievable! Sarah reaches for the computer.

"Let me see."

The program allows us to sort what sold by artist, price range, salesperson, and even by which wall it hung on. It shows total pieces sold and how much was sold during each hour. She reviews it for eight or nine minutes, and then says, "Tom sold the most." It appears I'm going to be stuck dealing with him for a while. I have a feeling this isn't all of it.

Saturday is an amazing day. I'm not planning on working in the store. Sarah says she has enough staff and won't need me, but she's wrong, possibly for the first time since her enlightenment. People drive in from Los Angeles. People drive in from Big Bear and San Bernardino. People even drive in from Rancho Cucamonga. And they come to buy.

By 11:30, Sarah texts me, "Come QUICK! Make sure yr phone is charged! Bring external phone batteries, we r low." She also texts some of the students who said they couldn't work, asking them if they can spare an hour or two. I drop everything, rummage around the house for the batteries, and rush to the store. It's packed with people talking loud and laughing louder. I can barely hear the classical music playing in the background. I put on an apron and start to sell. By the end of the day, we've sold over $47,000 worth of art.

That night, even though I'm relaxed and sleepy after doing our night techniques together, I have a hard time falling asleep. I keep thinking about my last trip to Fairfield. I'd told the Ayurvedic doctor during my intake consultation that I was doing quite well and felt very good. He took my pulse, grinned, and said, "You can feel *a lot* better." On the plane leaving Fairfield, I knew how right he was.

I sleep in Sunday morning and wake up foggy. It's much nicer to sleep deeply and get up early feeling refreshed. We spend the day tying up loose ends, a process which continues through the workday on Monday. It's a lot of work to disengage from our day-to-day lives.

That evening, as we pack for our different Thanksgiving trips, Sarah tells me not to worry. The store will be fine, even if Black Friday is crazy. She has enough merchandise, the staff is well trained, and Tom has stepped into the role of assistant manager. To my surprise, I feel confident that Tom will take good care of the store while we are away. Sarah's magic mothering is working well.

Early Tuesday morning, we pick up Amos at his condo in Westwood and head for LAX. As we're driving and talking, Amos stays silent, letting the conversation swirl around him. That's unusual for him. After a few minutes, he asks, "Mom, is there something I don't know? Something's very different. Something special has happened to you, hasn't it?"

Sarah reaches around and touches his knee. "Honey, everything is good. Your father and I have been meditating more lately. Are you doing your meditations?"

"You and Dad are always cool, but now you are so crystal cool that you're, like, sucking up my worries. I feel like I did when I was a kid and we walked on the beach in Hawaii when the sun was setting and you were holding my hand. Something's different."

Sarah sighs, rubs Amos's knee again, and turns to him. "Let's see what happens. Things come and things go. We can talk about it after we're with the girls."

"Is that why Dad is going to Iowa to get all meditated up? Did you beat him at his own game?"

I am amazed by Amos's insight and bluntness. "As usual, you've hit a home run. Mom is beating me fairly and squarely for now, but the game isn't over. We still have a few innings left."

"You can do it. We're rooting for you, Dad."

I pull up to the United terminal. When Sarah and Amos's bags are on the curb, Amos and I hug before I turn to Sarah. She buries her head in my neck and whispers, "I'll miss you deeply, my love. You can do it. We're all rooting for you." We both get teary-eyed but hold back for Amos's sake, though I'm not sure why. I don't like being without Sarah. I'm lonely and disoriented.

My flight leaves forty-five minutes after theirs. When I get to the terminal, I try to work on my novel, but I can't concentrate and end up listening to classical music on my phone. The music is relaxing, but I board the plane feeling tense. I have no fear of flying; in fact, I savor the break from the past and present that flying represents. Getting off of a plane, arriving somewhere, makes me focus on the immediate future, dynamic and full of potential.

I arrive in Dallas with barely enough time to change terminals and make my connecting flight. Luckily, the transition is smooth. On the smaller plane to Cedar Rapids, I start to feel better. I sit in my window seat, happy to be by myself. I meditate all the way to Iowa.

In Cedar Rapids, the car rental agent tries to convince me to upgrade my reserved compact to a luxury car. Normally, such salesmanship falls on deaf ears, but today I'm feeling affluent. I walk out of the airport into the cold, biting wind and drizzle of an Iowa November looking for my Cadillac.

The Cadillac drives much better than my old plug-in Prius. After more than an hour of luxurious worry over the possibility of a speeding ticket, I pull into the Raj's entrance. The trees that line the long driveway are much bigger than they were when I was here four years ago. Their branches are bare, the ground strewn with leaves. I, too, am looking to shed all but my essentials.

My friend Paul meets me for dinner at the Raj. The dining room is considered one of the best restaurants in Fairfield. Paul looks spry and content. He may have lost a few pounds, which didn't need to come off. He's shaving his head of whatever few hairs still struggle there.

"Abe, you old goat, I missed you."

"Paul, how the nirvana are ya? How's Leslie? And the girls?"

"We're all well." We take our seats at a table in the back. The restaurant is half full, but we choose a quiet table away from everyone, looking forward to a leisurely dinner of conversation and catching up. Paul and I became good friends when we were finishing our doctorates. He taught philosophy at the University of Michigan for many years. About nine years ago I was surprised to get an email from him saying that he had learned TM, loved it, and was taking a job teaching philosophy at MIU. I think I must have been proselytizing even back when I met him in graduate school, though he says he found TM on his own.

"Leslie is still teaching first grade. She loves the little ones. She would have had more kids if I'd let her."

"I know what you mean. I would have had more if Sarah was willing."

Paul shakes his head, incredulous. "You've always been parental, especially to your friends. Do you ever think of your students as if they're your children?"

For effect, I hesitate. "*Aren't* they?"

He laughs.

"How are your daughters doing?" I ask.

"They're all quite well. The oldest two, Doreen and Mary, are married with children, and both live in Chicago now. Lydia, the third, got engaged two weeks ago to a guy in her residency program in Iowa City. They're both doing primary care internal medicine. Christy, my little one, is finishing her BS in computer science here at MIU. She may make more money than any of us. But tell me about Sarah and your kids."

I fill Paul in on the essentials. I feel comfortable and connected as I sit with him. He's a good, smart man. The love and respect that we have for each other is deep and warming. There are few people who see the world like I do. My old friend is one of them. Once we're caught up, I ask Paul for his thoughts about why I'm here.

"I feel funny telling you about this because Sarah and I have exerted a fair amount of effort trying to hide it. But on September 13th of this year, I reached what I thought was Cosmic Consciousness. Obviously, it was an extraordinary event. Fifteen days later, I woke up no longer enlightened. The evening before my fall, Sarah attained CC, and she's still going strong. I'm here to do Panchakarma, meditate in the domes, and get Vedic Vibration for pragya aparadh. I'm hoping and praying to make some progress back toward enlightenment."

Paul leans forward. "I'm sorry for your loss. The fact that you were able to make the transition once bodes well for the future. God willing, it should happen again, to the both of us."

"Thanks, Paul. Just hearing you say that makes me feel better."

Paul puts his hand on mine. "I'm thrilled for Sarah. That's wonderful news. She must make a lovely saint. Your plan is a good one. It should help settle you down." He withdraws his hand after a subtle squeeze. "I'm not sure if you've been keeping up with events here in Fairfield over the last few months? Things are getting exciting."

"I'm updated once a month by those glossy mass emails, but other than that, I don't get many specifics."

"I'll give you an insider's update. Stop me if this is old news to you. In late July and August, we had a large influx of pandits from India. The influx was made possible by Fairfield investors who made a lot of money investing in a company with a novel, ecological way to make high-purity aluminum—LED lights and lithium batteries need it. Also, two of the prosperous software companies in town have grown dramatically due to the success of their product lines. With the growth of the community in general, the new hires, and the new pandits, we've finally surpassed our calculated, phase-transition number of 2,200 for morning meditation program—and the evening program has even higher numbers.

"It's been about three months since we reached that goal, and we've been rewarded. Preliminary data suggests that the ongoing drop in our national crime rate has accelerated and the economy here and nationwide is booming. Most importantly, there are increasing numbers of Sidhas like you and Sarah who report reaching CC. There are many level-headed people who believe we're finally seeing the first rays of the dawning of the age of enlightenment. Pretty bizarre, huh?"

"Indeed. I'm ready for a new day. There's a lot of suffering out there."

Paul and I talk for hours. He suggests I meet a MIU professor who has studied for years with a very old guru in the Himalayas. The professor researches and practices ancient techniques to stop the aging of the physical body. Paul says the professor may also have some insight into how two enlightened souls could transition together from this world to the next. After asking me about my plan, Paul says he's going to bring up the concept with Leslie. That makes me happy.

A little after ten, they kick us out so they can turn off the lights. After we say our good-byes, I walk upstairs to my room. It looks like an average hotel room, but I'll have a beautiful view of the small lake and the swans behind the Raj in the morning. It's an hour later in New York, but I call anyway.

Everyone is asleep except Sarah. We speak briefly, and she doesn't feel so far away.

The next morning, my appointment with the Ayurvedic physician and the Indian Ayurvedic expert is scheduled for 9:30. I was hoping to do group meditation in the dome before breakfast, but I oversleep, blaming the two-hour time difference. Instead, I do asanas and pranayama in my room, sitting on my bed to meditate.

After a light breakfast downstairs, I check in at the doctor's office in the southeast corner of the building. The receptionist is the same German lady who was here when I last came. Stout, blonde, and precise, she could do this job forever and never complain.

"Herr Levy, welcome back. It has been four years and three months since your last visit. You are overdue." Her thick accent hasn't softened in four years. "Follow me."

I walk quickly to keep up with her. She seats me in an exam room. "Take your shoes off and stand on the scale." She scribbles on her clipboard.

"Four more pounds; the doctor will address that," she says ominously. She wraps a blood pressure cuff around my left bicep. "108 over 64, *that* is better. Now we take the pulse." She grabs my right wrist and looks at her watch. "Pulse is 56," she says with approval. "Come with me," and we're off to the races again.

She turns a corner and I almost bump into her. "Wait here. I will get you when the doctor is ready." Six minutes later, she reappears. "Herr Doctor will see you now." I follow her.

"Abe, good to see you again," Dr. Baum says, giving me a firm handshake, bowing just a touch, and looking me square in the eyes. He's also German but his accent has faded. "This is Dr. Reddy." Dr. Reddy is pudgy and dressed in a thick, embroidered jacket with a Nehru collar, sporting a Gandhi cap. He places his palms together, fingers touching his forehead. I do the same. "Dr. Reddy will confer with me about your pulse, and we will decide what Panchakarma therapies you will need. Please be seated." He motions to a large, overstuffed chair.

"As you know, in Ayurveda we treat imbalances we find in the pulse during our diagnosis. If there are specific issues you want addressed, we can discuss those afterward." He moves his wheeled chair closer to me and reaches for my right wrist. He places his middle three fingers on my radial artery and closes his eyes. His fingers move up and down as he concentrates. After half a minute, he releases his grip and pushes his chair back. Dr. Reddy sits on the edge of his chair, reaches over, and takes my pulse in a similar manner. It seems he is done rather quickly, but then he hesitates and starts again with greater concentration.

"Dr. Baum, what did you feel?" Dr. Reddy asks with a thick, almost unintelligible, singsong accent.

"The professor's pulse is good; strong and clear. His Pitta is moderately out of balance, as is his Sadhaka Pitta. He's had a recent disappointment, and there's some sadness. His ama is one plus, but the Panchakarma should be able to alleviate that. His ojas is four plus; very good ojas. I recommend Shirodhara for the first two days to settle his mind and relieve his sadness, then two days of Neem-infused milk massages to settle his Pitta, and a Nasya treatment for his last day to help with his chronically congested sinuses."

"This is a very good plan, Dr. Baum. Did you notice anything deeper in the pulse? I pointed this out to you last month," Dr. Reddy says.

Dr. Baum reflects, thinks about rechecking my pulse, decides not to. "What did I miss?" he asks Dr. Reddy.

"Professor Abe almost had the Cosmic Consciousness. Deep in the pulse there is Sama, evenness. It is there, deep, but not in the present. Take the pulse again and feel deep for the Sama."

Dr. Baum wheels his chair over again. "May I?" I offer my right wrist. He takes the pulse, concentrating, brow furrowed, and then a slight smile shows as he lets go. "Yes, deep in the pulse, I can feel the remnant. How long does that stay in the pulse?"

"The body never forgets such Bliss," Dr. Reddy answers. "It can always be found." He turns to me and says, "You are looking for the enlightenment again. Once tasted, never forgotten, eh?" he says with a knowing nod. "This is a good place to start. Are there other problems you have?"

"No, nothing that re-enlightenment won't fix. Thank you."

We all stand, bow to one another—hands together, fingers to foreheads—and my consultation is over. The body may never forget, and neither will I. I'm hopeful but tired from my travels. My body and I are looking forward to our massage.

After lunch, I go for a walk alone, declining an offer from a group planning to walk to the pandits' campus. I've got some thinking to do. I stroll past a whole village of symmetrically built Sthapatya Veda homes, each with its distinctive cupola in the center of its roof. The homes are staggered and aligned so that the front doorway will bask in the first rays of the morning sun. Every tenth or so driveway leads to a larger and grander Sthapatya Veda home, each owned by a prosperous meditator, no doubt.

I would love to have a Sthapatya Veda home built in Claremont specifically for Sarah and me. I'm desperate for every bit of help. Sarah will have to sell a lot of art and profit from franchising her idea to make that a reality, but the Psalm does say that the meek and enlightened will enjoy prosperity.

When it's time to head back for my afternoon Panchakarma treatment, I drop my clothes in my room and change into the oversized, white, terrycloth robe they provide for the treatments. After a short wait in the treatment room, two technicians come in, one burly with a thick mustache, the other small and wiry. They oil me up with musty, herbal, warm-to-hot sesame seed oil and begin a forty-minute synchronized abhyanga massage that has me relaxed and asleep in no time. I wake only when told to turn over or onto my side, as the massage continues. Afterward, they begin the Shirodhara treatment, my favorite, which is a thin, continuous stream of warm oil on my forehead. This lasts for half an hour and sends me into a netherworld of non-sleep, non-meditative expansion unique to Shirodhara. As I drift in and out of some other comfy state of consciousness, I conclude that Shirodhara does to my mind what a reboot does to a computer.

By the time I shower and return to my room , I barely have time to dress before the group meditation in the men's dome. The drive takes eight minutes past rolling cornfields, scattered Sthapatya Veda homes, and occasional farmhouses. I arrive at the peak of the influx. Over two thousand people are walking, bicycling, or driving to their respective domes, trying to get in before the doors close at 5:45 pm. It's a funny sight, especially in Iowa, where everything is slow and spread out.

I find a place in the visitor's section, settle in, and start pranayama. I didn't arrive early enough to do asanas. I'm sitting on a twin foam mattress covered in a white fitted sheet. The sea of mattresses surrounding me is peppered with backjacks—small, canvas-covered, inverted T-shaped seats with the vertical section tilted back for comfort. Hundreds of Sidhas filter in and find their back-jacks. Most of the men are getting ready to or have already started meditating. I close my eyes.

*Mantra, mantra, mantra, maaaa...*My mind is active. It feels like a solitary buzzing point in a large empty space. *Mantra, mantra, mantraaa...*falling in all directions; no up, no down...suspended. Silence outside diffusing in, mind settles... *The silence around me is my friend. My friends are the silence. Mantra, maaantraaa...*expanding out, melting into group consciousness...at one with the female Sidhas in the women's dome nearby...*I am with my comrades. We are together. Mantra, maaa...*shimmering fog embracing both domes...myriad twinkling lights, one unified mind...negativity being drawn in, love flowing out...I can feel us, as one, sopping up the stress from the minds of our fellow countrymen. Each one is dear. Each one is my brother and my sister and my child. We are all connected at our deepest soul, and from there we share our peace. *Mantra, mantra, mmm...*

A bell rings and the first part of the group meditation is over. Now the hopping begins. Men in full lotus launch themselves forward. I open my eyes to watch, always hopeful, but there's no levitation; just muscle-propelled bouncing. People shake and quiver. Some yelp as the jolt to hop hits them. I watch for a while, see no miracles, close my eyes, and go back to my own practice of the samyama for levitation. A few times I feel very light, like I could float off the foam. A few times I'm zapped by a jolt and hop uncontrollably across the mat in full lotus when my knees aren't hurting. Many minutes of sweet practice go by. I begin to feel sleepy and lie down, but I'm too excited to sleep. I'm part of an army of peacemakers. I'm proud to be part of something so good.

After dinner, I return to my room and do some writing. I could go to the spa's evening Ayurvedic lecture series, but I have a lot of work I want to do. The lecturer is Professor Greene, who has a PhD in psychology from Duke and teaches at the university here. He's discussing his research into ama and ojas tonight. I read his most recent research on that subject with some interest when it was published about six months ago in the *American Journal of Physiology*.

Ojas is a fascinating concept. When digestion happens fully and correctly, the body produces ojas, the most refined product of digestion, instead of ama, which tends to gum up the physiology. Ojas connects pure consciousness to the body and mind, allowing the organizing power and intelligence of pure consciousness to enliven and heal. It is an important part of what prepares and refines the nervous system so that en-lightenment can take root.

Some schools of Ayurveda believe that once a person reaches Cosmic Consciousness, her enlightened physiology can convert ojas into soma. Soma is thought to continue the process ojas began by further refining the ethereal and cor-poreal bodies as well as the enlightened mind, so that God Consciousness and Unity Consciousness can blossom.

I work until just after nine when I decide to call Sarah and the family before they go to bed.

"Abe, my love." Her voice is intimate, as if she's whispering in my ear. "How's Fairfield treating you?"

"Very well," I say, wanting to hear her voice, not mine.

"Have you seen Paul and Leslie and any of their girls?"

"I saw Paul but not Leslie—maybe in a day or two. How are our girls and Amos? How are you?"

"We had a delightful day. The weather is quite nice for this time of year. We saw a fascinating photography exhibit at the Whitney. Even Amos liked it. How's your dome hopping?"

"The atmosphere in the domes is powerful. As soon as I shut my eyes, I was swept away."

"Sounds like fun. Becky needs to go to bed but has been too excited with all of us here. She wants to talk with her zeide. Here's Becky, then *Becky* is going to *bed*." Sarah fades as she hands off the phone.

Becky comes on the line. "Hi, Zeide. It's lots of fun with Bubbe and Uncle Amos and Auntie. I miss you, come soon! My birthday is coming soon. I meditated with Mommy and Bubbe today. It tickled me inside my head and I giggled and giggled. I love you."

"Sleep well, Beck-a-lah. I love you to the moon and more."

I hear Becky say distantly, "Here, Mommy."

"Hi, Dad." Rose picks up the phone. "We're having an amazing time with Mom. She told us what happened to you and to her—mind-boggling. You've been telling us about this since we were kids, but the reality is *so* much better. How are you doing?"

"Quite well. I miss not being there with you all, though. This was the only time I could do Panchakarma for a while. Fairfield is too cold in the winter."

"We understand, Dad. We know how much it means to you."

"How are your classes going? Are you doing any writing?"

"I'm enjoying teaching tremendously, and I'm working with the chairperson of Pomona's English department on how she wants my classes structured when I get there. What's it like living with the new Mom?"

"Inspiring. It makes me want to redouble my efforts, so I can get back up there with her."

"I know what you mean. She's the Mom I always hoped for but on steroids. She's so much fun, has too much energy, and can part the Red Sea at will like Moses. And her anxiety is gone—unbelievable! I'm sorry I never got to see you when you were enlightened. I need to go put Becky to bed. It won't be easy with all this excitement going on. Love ya. Bye!"

The phone switches hands.

"We're missing you, Daddy," says Rachel's sharp voice. "I'm still trying to get my mind around Mom's change. She really is out of this world. It's just, well…unbelievable. I wish you were here to join the celebration. How's Iowa?"

"It's great. I felt like I needed a good, thorough cleaning. The Panchakarma is doing just that. I'm sorry I'm not there with you."

"It's OK. I'll see you soon. I'm planning on coming home for winter break," she says.

We chat for a few more minutes, and then she's ready for Amos to take his turn. When we're done, Amos hands the phone to Sarah, and we talk aimlessly, unable to hang up. As the conversation winds down, she says quietly, "Are you going to meet with the professor you told me about, the one who's studying how enlightened souls could transition together?"

"We spoke on the phone today. I'm taking him to lunch tomorrow."

"That's great," she says. She goes silent for a few moments. "It feels like things are beginning to happen quickly, in a good way."

"Life and death are one thread, the same line viewed from different sides."

Lao Tzu

Chapter Eleven

"Hi, sweetie, I'm outside at the curb with my luggage," I say into my phone, resenting the fumes from the sea of cars. I just had my body cleaned.

"Abe, so good to hear your voice," says Sarah. "I'll be there in a few minutes."

Two minutes later, I spot our blue Prius at a stoplight one terminal up. As Sarah approaches, the double- and triple-parked cars around me finish their pickups in unison and drive away. She pulls up right in front of me. Rose was right. It must be nice to have nature at your beck and call.

Sarah steps out of the car, and we exchange a quick kiss and hug. The traffic cop eyeing us won't allow for any more lingering.

"Do you want me to drive?" I say.

"I'm happy to—it's late. I meditated with Amos in his condo before I had to leave. I'm feeling refreshed. Sunday evening traffic should be light. We'll be home soon."

"Sounds good. How was your flight?"

"Quite nice." She gets into the driver's seat. "I watched two movies and Amos did the same. Our visit with the girls was wonderful. Amos got along well with his sisters, played a ton with Becky, and bonded with Isaac. I couldn't have asked for anything more."

"We have it all, you and I."

"There's one thing we're missing, but I'm on it. Behind every great man is a better woman." She makes a face.

"I agree. With you in the driver's seat, I have no worries."

"Any news on the enlightenment front? Did you make some progress in Fairfield?"

"I definitely feel purified. That Panchakarma is powerful, and the Vedic Vibe treatment was uplifting. Meditating with such a large group helped me get deeper than I've been since the good old days, eight weeks ago. I think I'm much more prepared for re-enlightenment than I was before Iowa. Now it's up to my karma. I gotta be good to get good, I guess."

"Still full of those alliterative aphorisms, huh? Get full of your Self and we'll be making some progress. How'd the lunch meeting with the professor go?"

"Surprisingly well. He's been studying and meditating with a renowned, ancient saint in the Himalayas every summer for years. It's rare that such a special guru will allow a student to be part-time. Mukesh agreed to have a video conference with us during his Christmas break."

"Strong work," she says. "I knew you could do it."

"How'd the store do over Thanksgiving weekend? I didn't get around to checking."

"Tuesday and Wednesday were fair—about $29,000 each day. Black Friday was good—about $45,000—but yesterday was our best day yet. We took in a little over $56,000 and could have sold more if our inventory wasn't running low. Today wasn't so good; not enough good art to sell. Tom drove around for hours last night and early this morning in a rented van picking up art. It wasn't easy getting the artists to open their studios. Tom even reviewed all the pieces and put them in the inventory app so everyone will know where to place the art before we open on Monday. We have a lot of new pieces to hang. The other employees said Tom really took charge while we were gone. I know you have issues with him in your class, but he's doing a fine job in my store."

"Being a student and being in the workplace are very different. I'm glad you have such a dedicated employee. And I'm glad your store is doing so well. It's going to be nice having some extra money."

"Extra money? According to my calculations, I'm sorry to tell you, the art gallery will not make us much more than we made before. We should end up with a little more than we'll lose without you teaching summer school."

"Oh? We're selling a ton of art. If we sell a lot, shouldn't we make some decent money?"

"My intention is that the gallery will be a vehicle to support artists whose work uplifts us. We'll make a profit and we'll be able to pay off our debt over time, but in the end, I think we'll make forty to fifty percent more than we did with the gift store. Do the math and let me know if you agree."

"I thought you said that the new gallery and franchising the idea would eventually make us enough to build a Sthapatya Veda home in Claremont?"

"I never said that. I do think that the gallery will make us financially comfortable enough for you to skip teaching summer school. We should be able to afford to rent a nice, small Sthapatya Veda home in Fairfield each summer."

"Rent a...?" I feel foolish.

When we get home, I put my suitcase in our bedroom, but I don't unpack as I usually do. I get out my legal pad, open my iPhone's calculator, and pour over Goodness's finances on

QuickBooks. According to my calculations, we're paying the artists too much and charging too little for their art, but we're selling a lot. Had I known this, I might have invested in that biotech company Austin told me about. Aaron made a lot of money.

Monday goes smoothly, considering I was on vacation Tuesday and Wednesday in addition to the holiday days off. I'm refreshed from my deep cleanse and Vedic Vibe. Since coming home, my meditations have regained a clarity and stillness I had only experienced the week before my short excursion into enlightenment. A few times I am, again, the shimmering, endless mirror between silent pure consciousness and activity—very promising.

During Tuesday's Self class, Tom is on especially good behavior. He asks thought-provoking questions in an appropriate manner that clearly shows he's thinking about the readings. Toward the end of the hour, he asks a particularly keen question that turns into a lively discussion—I love it when that happens.

After class is done, everyone files out except Chris and Margaret.

"Dr. Levy," Margaret says when everyone has left, "a bunch of us seniors have been talking about what's happened to Tom. It's bizarre how working with your wife has changed him."

"He's working hard at his schoolwork and everything," Chris chimes in.

"Tom told you he's working for my wife?"

"He's telling everyone about it," Margaret says. "We wanted to let you know he's also telling his friends that your wife is magically healing him because she's enlightened. Is she really enlightened?"

I didn't see that coming. I need to fix this.

"Thanks for the information. I'll speak to my wife about it. Did either of you have a question or comment for me or is Tom the reason you stayed?" Both shrug.

"You know," I say, "I've found it fascinating how important Tom's tutoring program is to your senior class. It would be a shame if the administration found out about it. Could both of you make sure that Tom knows that I need him to stop spreading rumors about my wife?"

They look at each other, and then to me. Both nod.

"OK then. I appreciate your help." They stand up and leave together.

Late that night, Sarah comes home from her store. She texted me that she'd be late. I meet her in the foyer with a deep, long kiss. I've been waiting for her.

"Got something in mind?" she asks.

"You know me, always thinking."

"You're a philosopher. I thought you guys thought about loftier things."

"No, not really. Behind our curtains, the same animal lurks. What's up with the long hours at Goodness?"

"I was just about to tell you before you attacked me," she says. "Tom sprung it on me two days ago. I wasn't sure if anything would come of it, so I didn't mention it. Tom had his dad call an organization that incubates not-for-profit startups. The organization is funded by the trusts of some of the wealthiest families in the United States. I met with them for hours this evening after the store closed—much longer than I expected. At the end of our meeting they told me they want to officially observe and investigate the store's operations and business model. They might help me make the store an official not-for-profit organization and take it to other cities."

"That was fast. Is your idea for Goodness that good, or has Tom pushed it that hard?"

"I think it's mainly Tom. Changing subjects, I'm going to let him go tomorrow."

"What? Fire him? He just became your boy wonder, and now he's your rainmaker too. What'd he do?"

"He hasn't done anything wrong. He's just too attached to me. He's stuck because he thinks he needs me to be his mother and his guru. If I let him go, he will let go of me. If I push him out of the nest, he'll realize he can fly on his own."

"Mother bird," I say as I reach for and find her left hand, cupping it in both of mine, "he's become such a good employee. Can't you just talk to him about the problem? Your store, short-term and long-term, needs Tom. Maybe you should wait a few weeks and let him solidify your store's position with the not-for-profit organization."

"The store will be fine. Tom's heart is better. It's time," she says.

"I prefer you'd wait, but it's your store and he's your employee." I free her hand. "Also, he's telling his friends you're enlightened. Please ask him to stop."

"I know. I'll mention it to him."

Living with the enlightened is fascinating. She cares deeply for Tom but is unperturbed by the idea of letting him go. She intuitively knows what is best for him and has no remorse, even though it will upset him greatly and may even precipitate a tantrum. Properly guiding a child often isn't pretty or comfortable. It can be mistaken for being cold.

After a pleasant weekend spent with both Sarah and my growing novel, it's Monday morning again. I'm back to work. I teach my Monday classes. Tuesday morning, when I step out of our home, there's a note thumbtacked at eye-level into one of our painted shingles. On it is written, 'Abe.' I pull the note off and throw the thumbtack into our bushes, mad that Tom had the gall to put a hole in my shingle. I open it. It's neatly typed.

> Abe,
> As you know, your wife had the balls to fire me. I know it wasn't your decision. You would have kept me on because I was good for her store.
> Sir, I have concluded that you are a fraud. Not only are you a fraud, you have bullied Sarah into internalizing your crazy ideas. You were never enlightened, and she isn't either. You used her insecurities against her. You convinced her she was enlightened because you were desperate for that.
> You are deluding yourself because you hate this cruel world. I understand that. You try to escape it with your big ideas. You preach to your innocent students, convincing us you are right as a way to hypnotize yourself. That's wrong and cruel! To give false hope to innocent students to further your nefarious, twisted scheme is a horrible thing. We are desperate to learn what is true, not what you hope is true!

The administration did the right thing in cancelling your class. I should never have helped you get it back and will strive to get that decision reversed.

And don't get your hopes up. I'm not coming to class today, but I'll be back on Thursday. I won't allow you to fail me. Do not forget: Griffins do not fail.

Sincerely,
Tom

I tuck the note into my shirt pocket, planning to file it in Tom's folder in my office. He did threaten to have my class cancelled, again. I might need the note as some type of evidence.

Tom's not right, but he does have a point. To the outside world, many would say Sarah and I appear to have been brainwashed by a mind-bending cult. A psychiatrist probably would say that Sarah and I underwent a form of conversion disorder where we only believed we were enlightened. The psychiatrist would point out that subjective experiences are notoriously unreliable and often conform to our deepest desires. Jesus was right when he said: "Except ye see signs and wonders, ye will not believe." For the world to undergo a phase-transition to a higher state, it will require more than the reporting of subjective, enlightened experiences. We will need the shared, objective experiences of signs and wonders.

I walk into my Tuesday Self class not remembering how I got there or if I visited my office. I check. Tom's note is not in my shirt pocket.

I find the students huddled around someone's new MacBook, watching a video. I go over utterly unnoticed to see what they're watching, almost having to elbow my way in. I'm still not acknowledged. I'm just part of the pack focused on the screen.

A reporter presents a video clip of three smiling, middle-aged Indian-looking men in full lotus who are apparently meditating. The clip shifts to a different group of three men. Surrounded by researchers, they sit on mats, contort their legs into full-lotus, close their eyes, and a few seconds later, one slowly floats up until he is about four feet in the air. Then the other two begin to rise, almost at the same time. One only goes up two feet, the other rises nine inches higher. All three are airborne, eyes closed, big smiles—big Blissful smiles. The camera pans to show the laboratory and cuts to a sign outside: California Institute of Technology.

Chris, finally noticing me, says with more excitement than he can contain, "*Professor*, have you *seen* this?"

"I'm seeing it for the first time now." I get a shiver up my spine and start to expand out. I pull myself back by thinking of my father with the shovel. No time for cosmic distractions. I want all parts of me to be here for this.

The video shifts to a reporter in a newsroom with the caption, "Breaking News: Meditators Levitate."

"Today, scientists at MIT and Cal Tech have issued simultaneous press releases detailing the results of their investigations into the claim made by the leader of the Rishi Patanjali Ashram in the Himalayas that long-term meditators using advanced forms of meditation are able to levitate. The spiritual leader of the ashram has issued a statement pointing out that their meditation techniques that lead to levitation are based on the ancient text, *The Yoga Sutras of Patanjali*. Researchers at MIT and Cal Tech say that after applying exhaustive experimental controls, they have concluded that the six men they have independently studied are able to levitate. We are glad to have Dr. Thaddeus Marconi, professor of physics at MIT and head of the team that investigated the levitation claim at MIT, joining us tonight from Cambridge. Professor?"

The screen splits and Professor Marconi appears on the left with headphones on. "I'm here." The professor is thin, wearing a lab coat and a grave expression.

"Professor, your team concluded that these men are actually levitating. But doesn't levitation defy the laws of physics?"

Professor Marconi says, "The laws of physics cannot be broken. The laws of physics adjust to and conform to the results of proven, replicated scientific inquiry. It appears from our investigations that human levitation has occurred and can be considered a fact. We all, therefore, need to go back and rethink what we know about gravitational theory to account for this."

"That will be very cool," Han says loudly.

Chris closes the browser and the computer, and without saying a word, the students filter back to their seats. Tom's not here. As soon as everyone is seated, Chris raises his hand.

"Yes, Chris." I'm quite shaken.

"Does this change everything? Does this prove that what you've been teaching in this class is the Truth?"

I bite my lower lip. "Does human levitation during meditation change everything? Well, I think much of what Western science and Western academic knowledge has concluded to this point will have to be adjusted based on this fact. We'll need a theory that explains how humankind can accomplish this, and the best theory, in my mind, is the obvious one. I think we have to say that Vedic philosophy and Patanjali have been vindicated. Yes, I think this will change almost everything, and the change will be for the better—much better.

"I'm sorry. I need a five-minute break," I say. I have to call Sarah. I need to talk to Sarah. I pick up my phone and walk out of the room, down to the end of the hall to a window that overlooks the central mall. Students play Frisbee and lounge on the grass. I dial, hear two rings, and Sarah answers.

"Abe."

"Honey, have you watched the news?"

"I got a text from Shoshana. It's on all the channels."

"Isn't it amazing?" I gush. "After all these years of meditating and hoping and praying, it happens just like that. This will be the beginning of the end of human suffering."

"It is wonderful. I'm thrilled for all of us. Abe, I've had an epiphany. Seeing those men levitate means there must be a way we can stay together forever. If our merciful Father built into our universe a way for us to fly, He must have also built a way to fly off together. The thought of being separated from you is more than I can bear. We need to focus all of our energies on accomplishing that goal. I want you to retire at the end of this year so we can move to Fairfield. My mom will be devastated, but she'll survive. What we've saved in Pomona's retirement plan, plus the income from my store and our social security, will be enough. I'll rehire Tom. He'll run the store and take our concept to other cities. Without me there, he'll be an excellent, dedicated manager who will grow our business."

"Retire? I don't want to retire. I love teaching. I've never seriously considered it. Give me a moment." Thoughts race through my mind. I *am* a professor. I love my life here. But when I was almost enlightened, I knew I was so much more than that. I can't think small anymore. I have to go for the highest first: "seek first the kingdom of God and his righteousness, and all these things will be added to you." Times have changed. Sarah is right.

"All right," I say. "It is a good plan. If that's what it will take for us to be together forever, I'll do it. I can't—I won't—lose you."

"I feel better hearing you say it. We'll be fine. Go back to your class."

"I'm coming home now. The class will be fine without me."

"Please, finish what you started."

"OK. You're right. I love you, honey." I end the call and look out at the world through the window. It looks the same, but it's not.

I walk back to my class. Tanisha, who is sitting close to Obinna, raises her hand high. I smile and nod at her…and Obinna.

"Dr. Levy, we're all too excited about what's happened. Would it be OK if we do your scheduled lecture another time and instead discuss levitation and what it means for us all?"

"Absolutely. I think the best course of action is to start with questions. We're all used to having questions asked and answered here. Does anyone have a question?" Hands shoot up.

"Margaret," I say.

"Dr. Levy, do you think the levitators, and even meditators, are at risk from religious zealots?" she asks.

I want to be truthful but not fan their fears. "Change is scary. People fear what they don't understand. Some will see levitation as a form of witchcraft; they'll say those men made a pact with the devil. There will be danger. Zealots, their anger spurred by the forces they fear, will do what they can to stop change from happening. In the end, goodness will prevail. According to Vedic philosophy, that's the plan."

Chris raises his hand again.

"Yes, Chris."

"You discussed earlier that if a lot of meditators meditate together in one place it sends out good vibes that can move us all in a more positive direction. Is that going to happen?"

I take a deep breath and sigh it out. "I sure hope so. It could happen now." I'm thinking about Sarah and my novel. I want to go home. Now that levitation is a reality, I need to quickly finish my novel. If I can get it published, it will help the public understand, not fear, levitation. But by the time it's published, it may be too late. I answer a few more questions, antsy to get out of here.

When the class is finally over, I walk home to Sarah. As I trudge across the green lawn of the central mall, I'm unable to hold back tears. This is the same walk I've taken for years. It hasn't changed, but it will come to an end. I expand outward. I watch as Abe arrives home and hugs Sarah tightly. They decide to go for a jog before meditating together. Abe will be fine. Time will lose its grip on him again. He will be of service conveying important information.

From my expanded perspective I can see our horizon. It's about to rain on the ocean. Each raindrop is returning to its Self.

About the Author

Alan J. Steinberg, MD is board-certified in Internal Medicine and practices with the Cedars-Sinai Medical Group in Beverly Hills, California. He grew up in Las Vegas, Nevada, where he learned Transcendental Meditation in 1975. His undergraduate degree in philosophy is from the Claremont Colleges in Claremont, California. Dr. Steinberg attended the University of Nevada School of Medicine, receiving an MD degree in 1984. His first book was a non-fiction consumer's guide, *The Insider's Guide to HMOs*. It was well received and helped sway the direction health care was heading in the late 1990s.

Dr. Steinberg lives with his wife of over thirty-five years in Los Angeles, California. They are the proud parents of three young adults.